To

BLOWBACK

No turning back

now...

To Janice,

No turning back now...

Mary ♡

BLOWBACK

International Bestselling Author
MONICA JAMES

BLOWBACK
(The Monsters Within Duet, Book Two)

Cover Design: Perfect Pear Creative Covers
Cover Model: Andrew England
Photographer: James Rupapara
Editing: Editing 4 Indies
Formatting: emtippettsbookdesigns.com

Follow me on:
authormonicajames.com

OTHER BOOKS BY
MONICA JAMES

AUTHOR'S NOTE

CONTENT WARNING: ***BLOWBACK*** is a DARK
ROMANCE containing mature themes that might make
some readers uncomfortable. It includes strong violence,
possible triggers, and some dark and disturbing scenes.
This is the point of no return because now, it's time you forgo
what's left of your soul…

CHAPTER ONE

Bull

Blood.

It's what courses through our veins. It doesn't matter what color we are, what god we believe in, or what language we speak; it's the common denominator throughout the world.

It also feels fucking fantastic when it coats your knuckles because you've just busted your enemy's nose.

The crowd erupts into bedlam when the fucker I just knocked out cold collapses to the floor with a thud. Blood smears his face and smothers my knuckles—see, I told you, we're one and the same. Except the one asshole who is the exception to that rule.

He's the reason I'm here. He's the reason for all of it.

Not interested in congratulatory high fives, I push my way through the masses, eager to get the fuck out of this shithole that served as my fighting ring for the night. I nod to Dudley and Vincent, the two minions Stevie hired to help me out, on my way to the bathroom, silently ordering them to collect our winnings from the bookies and deliver them to Stevie.

They don't dare skim off the top because they would pay with their lives.

Once the silent memo is noted, I continue my march until a pretty redhead blocks my path. I look at her, wordlessly demanding if she has a point, to make it fast.

Leaning in close, she cups her mouth and whispers in my ear, "My apartment isn't far from here."

She doesn't need to clarify what exactly will happen at her apartment, but she could promise me all the booze and pussy in the world, and it wouldn't be enough. There is only one person who can quench my thirst, this feral hunger inside, and she hates my fucking guts.

So, without mincing my words, I gently push her aside. "Thanks for the offer, darlin', but I got someplace to be."

I don't stick around to wait for her response because honestly, I don't care. It's the reason I was stupid enough *to* care that I'm in this fucking situation in the first place. Shouldering open the bathroom door, I gesture for the two businessmen snorting lines off the sink to pack up their shit and bounce.

It doesn't matter that I was the one who sold them the blow. Our transaction is over, which means they are nothing but yesterday's news. They take the hint and quickly leave me alone.

Walking over to the barely standing lockers, I shove them aside and reach for my bag hidden behind them. This place used to be a car manufacturing plant, but now it's used for anything illegal. The cops don't bother patrolling because a dozen other buildings just like it are on the same block.

Taking off my skeleton face shield, I turn the faucet to cold and wash away the blood from my nose and busted lip. He got in a lucky shot. Wetting my hair, which has grown quite long on top, I slick the longer strands back to emphasize the shorter sides.

Stripping off my long-sleeved shirt and shorts, I step into my ripped jeans and a short-sleeved shirt. Once my socks are on and the laces on my motorcycle boots are tied, I reach for the silver chain from a secret pocket inside my bag.

The St. Christopher medallion catches the light as I slip it on. Placing it under my shirt, I ignore how this keepsake is associated with an asshole by the same name. However, he sure as shit is no saint.

Putting on a hoodie, I grab my shit and am out the door. I'm working tonight at The Pink Oyster, and if I don't haul ass, I'll be late—again. But this past month, that's all I've been, thanks to selling my soul to the devil. Or in my case, devils.

Slipping the hood over my head, I make my way through the few stragglers, desperate to get the fuck out of here.

Beyond punishing weather means marching outside through thick snow as I search for my truck. I made a deal with Lotus to let me keep it in exchange for working extra without pay. It wasn't her idea; it was mine. She's come to learn I don't like owing anyone anything, so she agreed.

Jumping into the truck, I don't bother with the heat, because no matter how warm it is, I can't shake this constant chill inside me. I know what it is. I try not to think about it, but it's hard not to when I'm confronted with it every fucking day.

I pull into the dead of night when my cell chimes, hinting the Antichrist is calling.

"Fuck you," I answer, gritting my teeth when loud laughter sounds over the speaker.

"Now, is that any way to talk to your boss?"

"You're not my boss, asshole. You're a dead man walking," I correct, clenching the steering wheel.

Jaws ignores me. "I was calling to remind you about our meeting tomorrow."

"How could I forget?" I mock.

"Just making sure. How's my club looking? Is that bitch Lotus ready to get into a partnership with Stevie yet?"

"For the tenth fucking time, no. Are you hard of hearing?"

Silence.

"This is most disappointing. We can discuss it at our meeting."

Our weekly meeting is the one and only time I see Jaws, and it takes all my willpower not to stab him in the throat. But he always comes armed with ten guards flanking him because he doesn't trust me.

Regardless of the fact we've agreed to play civil, he knows all it'll take is for him to look at me the wrong way, and I will gladly end him. But I can't.

Can't is a word I don't usually believe in, but lately, it's been a fucking weight around my neck. I *can't* kill the motherfucker who killed my brother because if I do, the only person who ever believed in me and took a chance on me will pay.

I *can't* see her because if I do, again, she will suffer the consequences.

I *can't* split town, cutting my losses, because if I do, Damian's murderers will walk free. I can't let that happen.

So, as you can see, I can't do jack shit until I can come up with a better plan. I'm a prisoner once again. Although I'm no longer behind bars, I may as well be.

I'm playing both sides, so in layman's terms, I'm a fucking snitch. Even though I "work" for Stevie, everything I learn gets relayed back to Jaws. He is using my intel to strengthen his empire, and only when his throne is high enough will he strike.

Until then, I am stuck being both their bitches.

When I hear a familiar voice in the background, my chill begins to thaw. I can't make out what she's saying, but when her light laughter fills my truck, I remind myself of the last time I saw her—the time when I threatened to kill her if she stood in my way.

So, it doesn't matter what she's saying because she's not saying it to me, nor will she ever say anything to me again. I made sure of it.

Jaws muffles the phone, but the asshole ensures I can still hear him. "Mexican sounds good. I'll make a reservation once I—"

Done being a pawn, I hang up, not interested in speaking to him unless I have to. He didn't call to remind me about tomorrow. He called to rub my face in the fact he has something I want but will never have. He gets to play happy family while I sit on the outskirts, biding my time.

But by doing so, I've ensured Tiger's safety and happiness, and she is worth the sacrifice. Clutching the medallion around my neck, I silently apologize to Damian for choosing her over him because essentially, that's what I've done.

I could have already ended Jaws, not caring what that does to his sister, but I wouldn't have been able to live with myself. I can kill a thousand men without feeling a thing, but the thought of any harm coming to her…because of me— again, I can't do that to her.

She is my weakness, and now, I must pay for it.

There are a lot of things I must pay for.

Just as I do every week, I park two blocks away and keep to the shadows. I'm not here for a social visit. In and out, just as I've been for the past month. It's late, so everyone is locked inside, safe and sound, and away from a monster like me.

Reaching into my back pocket, I pull out an envelope stuffed full of hundred-dollar bills. After doing a quick sweep and seeing that the coast is clear, I continue my casual walk past a house. The lights are off.

Pulling the sides of my hood even farther over my downturned face, I quickly slide the envelope into the mailbox and continue my relaxed stroll. Only when I turn the corner do I quicken my pace and do a lap around the block, before taking the side streets back to my truck.

I jump in without delay, and the moment the engine roars to life, I slip back into the night. Peering into the rearview mirror, I see that the coast is clear.

Breathing steadily, I focus on the road and not on the money I just dumped into the mailbox of the family I destroyed. The Da Silvas have no idea I killed their father and husband. I stabbed him straight through the heart without an ounce of regret.

Seeing his lifeless body gave me a small sense of peace for a split second, before that peace was shattered when Tiger stumbled across what I'd done. The fear in her eyes instantly ruined my high. She ran from me. For the first time, she was actually genuinely scared, and she had every right to be. I was covered in another man's blood.

Once she left, I quickly wrapped Kong's body in the tarp I packed, then stuffed him into a drum. After wheeling his ass into the tailgate of my truck, I drove down to the Detroit River and dumped his weighted ass into it. But not before I took off his wedding ring, Rolex, and gold chain, and removed the wallet from his jacket pocket.

None of this went as planned, however. I had intended to torture him a little more, but I lost control. And then everything went to shit when Tiger appeared. I left the club a literal crime scene because even though I took care of the body, I left behind his blood. I was so panicked to get to Tiger that nothing else mattered. I didn't care if someone found what I'd done; seeing Tiger and explaining what happened was more important than covering my tracks.

But it didn't make a difference.

When I found out who she was, what I had done to her, and what I had to do, it changed everything.

I went back to the club and bleached it clean. I thought I would feel a sliver of relief that one of my brother's killers was gone, but I didn't. All I could think about was what I did to Tiger. Any celebration over killing Kong was suddenly put aside because I killed Hero, the only man Tiger ever loved.

When she confided in me about her past, about how her life could have turned out differently, I realized I was the reason her life was the way it was. Lachlan was going to propose to her. Her happily ever after had been within reach.

But the day I shot him was the day I shot her dreams to hell. I'm responsible for every tear she's shed.

So that was part of the reason I agreed to Jaws's terms. Staying away from her is the best thing I can do because yes, it'll keep her safe. But it will also save her the heartache of having…feelings for her brother's killer because my endgame hasn't changed.

Both Jaws and Scrooge are on borrowed time. Jaws thinks he has the upper hand, but being complacent and cocky means he'll eventually slip up and let his guard down. And I'll be there with my sawed-off shotgun when he does.

Over the past month, I've been getting close to Stevie, but he's paranoid. He has every right to be, especially since Kong "left" due to Jaws gunning for them all. I used that excuse as a ploy to get close to Stevie. He's seen me fight and knows I can protect him, but there is a wolf among the sheep, waiting to strike.

I still have no idea what their beef is. Jaws made it clear they had history, but I just don't know what that means—yet.

We're making progress, but he's still apprehensive to spill

all the details. It'll take time, and I realize that, but time means I will have to continue this charade, when all I want to do is see people die.

Kong's death stitched together a small part of me, but it was at the expense of his family. I've stripped someone else of their father and lover. No matter what a corrupt asshole he was, he was still theirs.

So, this is what sparked the late-night visits to where he once lived.

The night of his death, I left his belongings and a note for his family in the mailbox. The note simply said he was gone and never coming back. For some reason, I needed to see them retrieve his belongings, and when they did, when I witnessed the genuine tears in his wife's eyes, I knew I would be indebted to them for the rest of my life. Just as I am to Tiger.

The money I leave for them is a small token to say I'm not sorry I killed him, but rather, I'm sorry you loved the wrong man. It's all technicalities, but I do this not because I'm a good person, but because it's the right thing to do.

I may live for violence and bloodshed, but only to those who deserve it.

Parking my truck in the lot, I scope out my surroundings, before opening the door. It's quiet once again, which is no surprise. Since Tiger left, the clients did too, and Lotus is weeks away from going bust. I thought Stevie would swoop in while she's vulnerable, but he has yet to strike.

No security stands at the door, which means Lotus had to let Pop go, my only backup guy. The club now only has one person standing watch over this place—me. And when I enter, I can see why she let him go.

Apart from two deadbeats throwing quarters on the stage, the place is a fucking ghost town.

Lotus is behind the bar, polishing glasses, while staring at the vacant club. When she sees me, she discreetly wipes away her tears. "Hi, Bull," she says with a small smile.

"Hey. Sorry I'm late."

"It's fine. It's not like I needed the muscle. The place is dead."

My eyes flick over to the stage. Someone was literally dead there weeks ago. A warm and fuzzy feeling overcomes me, but it's gone a second later.

"I think it's time to cut my losses and call the bank. I can't make this month's payment."

She can't do that. If she does, then Jaws will see it as a failure on my behalf, and the deal will be off. The things he'd do to Tiger, or more specifically, to her son…

Fuck this to hell.

"Let me help," I offer. I've made good bank fighting, and I don't need all of it.

"I can't let you do that, Bull. But thank you." I respect Lotus's pride—I would be the same way—but Jaws has made it clear he wants this club, and if I don't deliver, then Tiger pays.

Before I have a chance to insist, a creep walks up to the bar. I leave Lotus to serve him his beer and make my way through the club. Tawny is sweeping the dressing room floor when I enter. Her face has healed, but the fear behind her eyes lingers.

I have no doubt Jaws was behind her attack because at the time, I didn't understand what the message was. But now I do. He's been watching me the entire time because he's been watching Tiger. When he saw how close we were getting, he wanted to make it clear I knew someone was onto me.

A classic case of wrong place, wrong time—again.

He saw my comings and goings with her, with Kong, with everyone. He was always two steps ahead, which explains how he was able to blackmail me this way. I almost fell into his lap. Irony or fate? I have yet to decide.

"Hi," Tawny says, barely looking at me. I can't blame her, though, because she was disposable to me. She played her part in my story, and when I didn't need her any longer, I discarded her like she was nothing. And, for her efforts, she got beaten within an inch of her life.

"No Whales?" I ask, seeing as she's in here sweeping the floors and not in the VIP rooms.

She shakes her head. "Only Rocks."

I don't like to chat on most days, so making small talk is as painful as it sounds. Deciding to leave Tawny alone, I walk down the hallway, checking in each of the VIP rooms. They're empty.

I close the door to the room where Tiger gave me my first lap, or rather, air dance, and ignore the reason I chose this room to call Stevie.

"Hey. I got it," Stevie says, being ambiguous about tonight's winnings because he's paranoid as fuck.

"Good," I reply, cutting to the chase and speaking his language. "What's going on with Oysters?"

"You know what happened the last time I ate shellfish. I got sick. I'm definitely out."

I was afraid of this.

On the plus side, I'm sure Lotus would sell this place to Jaws for a steal, but goddammit, how can I let her do that? I thought I had time to come up with a plan if Stevie was going to invest, but now he's not going to because he realizes the place will go bust soon. No matter how much money he invests, it won't change the fact the club is a ghost town now that Tiger is gone.

How can he use this place for money laundering if it's not making any money?

And not only that, but I'm sure Jaws also has something to do with his decision.

He's running scared, which gives me an idea.

"These oysters are full of pearls. We just need to find the right ones," I state, hoping he reads between the lines.

If I can get this place up and running again, I'm hoping it'll lure him back in.

I decide to go with my gut and hope it doesn't backfire. "I got a job finding the pearls." Yes, I've just told him I work here now, but this will make him think I'm doing an inside job. And I am. Just not in the way he thinks I am.

"Well, in that case, find me the pearls, and I might change my mind about Oysters." He hangs up, and I let out a sigh, thankful it worked.

Now, all I need to find are dancers with killer hustle. For this place to survive, we need money and women. I have one, and now it's time to find the other.

After filling Lotus in on my plan, she called Pop, who was thankful he got his job back—for now.

Seeing as the place was dead, Lotus agreed it was a good time for me to scope out the surrounding clubs and put feelers out. If I could recruit half a dozen new dancers with a cult following, or dancers who had something unique about them, it would help put The Pink Oyster back on the radar.

Tiger was the star attraction, so I need to find another. This entire situation is because of her, and she isn't even aware of the role she's played. She's too busy playing happy family with her son-of-a-bitch brother. I shouldn't be angry with her, but I am.

I wish she could see through his bullshit because if she did, this could all be over. But Jaws is one sly, manipulative asshole who's giving her what she's always wanted—a family. Not to mention she can make amends for the guilt she feels for falling for his best friend.

Shaking my head, I focus on the task at hand and not the mess I've found myself in.

The moment I step inside Doll House, a club located downtown, I'm met with a packed club and blaring music. Doing a quick visual sweep of the place, I see the VIP rooms are down a roped-off corridor. There are two Bird Dogs manning the rope, which has me wondering what exactly goes on back there.

There is only one way to find out.

Making my way to the bar, I notice the tip rail isn't full, which has me guessing the pretty brunette on stage isn't the house favorite. The bartender with a Mohawk nods at me.

"Scotch," I order loudly. When he reaches for the house brand, I lean forward. "Not that one. That one." He turns over his shoulder to see which bottle I'm pointing at.

When he notices I'm gesturing to the most expensive bottle, he smirks.

We've all got hustle. He's going to hustle me for money, thinking I have green to burn, and I'll hustle him into thinking I'm just some chump who wants his cock sucked because this place is notorious for turning a blind eye to those kinds of "extras."

It sickens me how most of the clubs in this city are run, which is my main selling point for The Pink Oyster. None of that shit happens there because neither Lotus nor I would ever allow it. I can't promise them big tips at first, but I can promise they'll be respected and looked after.

The bartender pours me a glass of top-shelf scotch, before placing the crystal tumbler on the bar. I give him a fifty for his efforts. "Who's your best girl?" I ask, going straight in for the kill.

He has no issues sharing, thanks to the hefty tip I just gave him. "Cherry," he replies without thought. "You just missed her dance. That table over there." He points at a round table near the roped-off corridor. "They're waiting for some one-on-one time with her in the VIP rooms."

About eight men sit waiting. This is unheard of in a place full of women where they can literally have their pick. Cherry must be something special, which is why I want her.

"How much to skip the line?" I'm expressionless as I reach for my glass.

He mulls over my question. "At least five hundred. If you want an all-access pass, it's double that."

Scoffing at his revolting reply, I reach into the inner pocket of my leather jacket and toss down a stack of hundreds. There is at least a grand there. I know I need green to make people talk, which is why I keep fighting. It's easy money and allows me to break some bones while doing it.

The bartender pockets the cash and nods to one of the bouncers. He is by my side in seconds, hinting it's my turn. Tossing back my scotch, I gesture for another. The bartender complies.

I follow the bouncer toward the red rope, savoring the grumblings of the assholes who I just cut in front of. They're all little league and wouldn't dare take me on, which reveals Cherry isn't in with anyone of importance. Just desperate perverts who want a pretty girl to get them off.

The bouncer unhooks the rope, then leads me down the mirrored corridor. The dude knocks on the door once, before opening it for me. I step inside coolly. It's lit a deep red, giving a new spin on Cherry's name.

I don't need an invitation. I know the drill and take a seat on the white couch in the middle of the room. Cherry is sprawled across a similar couch in front of me. I can see where she gets her name. She's a pretty redhead in a tight red dress that doesn't leave much to the imagination.

With plump red lips and deep green eyes, she radiates sex. Her pale, slender arm is bent behind her, accentuating her impressive tits. But I'm not here for that. I want to see her dance.

"What do you want?" she purrs, arching her back off the couch and running a hand down the middle of her torso.

I appreciate her hustle because any hot-blooded man would be all up in her business. But I'm not one of them. Let's hope she can move.

"Dance for me," I order lightly.

She licks her lips as she comes to a slow stand. Her red heels add to her height, though she isn't a dainty wallflower. She is fierce and all fire with that red she wears. A slow song plays over the speakers, and Cherry commences an unhurried dance, swaying her body to the beat.

She makes a show caressing herself slowly because she is in kickass shape, but if she's all gimmick, then I will be disappointed. She is able to read my boredom, though, and suddenly changes her pace. She stops with the seduction and instead, lures me in with her skill.

She loses herself to the music and displays her talent when she drops to the floor in the splits. She is limber and clearly loves to dance. She saunters over, pushing me onto my back, so I'm lying on the couch. I allow her to touch me because I'm trying to recruit her, not scare her away.

She lowers herself onto me—her back to my front. I clench the sides of the couch, breathing deeply to calm myself down. She's too close. She begins to roll her body against me, ensuring she's touching every part of me. She's opted for a bed dance, instead of lap, which has me thinking this brings in more cash.

When she rubs her ass over my crotch, I decide now is the time to strike. Leaning up, I whisper into her ear, "You happy here?"

She giggles, continuing her seduction. "Why? You wanna be my White Knight?"

Of course, she'd think I was some perv, wanting to save her. I decide to clarify because her efforts on me are wasted. She could perform cartwheels in the nude, and it still wouldn't make a difference. I can't help but compare this private dance to the only other one I've had before.

Tiger had me so worked up that I couldn't think straight. Now, I just want this done, so I can move on to the next club.

"Maybe. Just not in the way you think. Call if you're interested." Reaching around her hip, I slip Lotus's business card into her hand.

She freezes, reading over it.

"Who are you?"

"Doesn't matter who I am. Just know, if you worked with me, you wouldn't have to rub over some creep's cock to make a buck. Thanks for the dance." She is stunned as I gently coax her off me, so we both can stand.

As she's shyly rearranging her dress, I reach into my pocket and offer her a wad of cash. "You've already paid," she says, her eyes flicking to the bills and then to me.

"This is all yours," I reply, stuffing it into her hand. She'll probably only see a fifth of what I gave the bartender.

"Thank you." She quickly tucks the rolled-up cash into the top of her dress.

"Nice to meet you, Cherry."

She nods, a blush coloring her pale cheeks. "My name is Charlotte."

Nodding, I turn and walk out the door. She doesn't need to know my name.

The bouncers look at me, surprised I'm leaving so soon. I'm happy for them to think I'm a two-pump chump because better they think that than I'm an unsatisfied customer.

As I jump into my truck, ready to hit the next club, my cell chimes. Reaching into my pocket, I see the text is from Lotus.

> For someone who hates everyone, you sure as hell have a way with them. Cherry is coming in tomorrow.

Most would celebrate their victories, but I'm not most. Make no mistake, I'm doing this for my own selfish reasons. I'm doing what I should have done before I lost sight of why I'm here.

But when Cherry's vanilla scent lingers, I can't help but think about other cherries, cherry blossoms that is. So I roll the window down to let the cool air in.

CHAPTER TWO

Bull

We had seven of the ten girls I spoke to last night come in to see Lotus. All seven seemed interested in what she was offering. She made it clear that the terms of the contract were negotiable, and that when the club picked up, she would ensure they were well taken care of.

It was a hard gig to sell, so I stayed on the sidelines and let Lotus work her magic. I didn't think it was necessary for me to be there, but Lotus asked me to come, so I did.

The girls I recruited are the best of the best, and if all agree to work for Lotus, she will see the club turn around fast. I left her to negotiate the contracts—just in case, she said.

I hope this plan works because as I park my truck by the curb, I don't know how much longer I can do this.

Jaws has arranged our meeting location at some seedy bar downtown. He's chosen this public place because the last time we met, it was in an abandoned building, and when one of his monkeys touched me, I had no issues breaking his nose.

Jaws knows I'm a ticking time bomb, so he is being cautious. But if he thinks there is safety in numbers, he's fucking mistaken. Locking my truck, I make my way into the bar. People gather around to play pool while others sit at the bar.

Jaws is seated in a booth alone, but I'm not fooled. These "civilians" are on his payroll. One wrong move, and they'll flank me from every side. I enter the booth, eyeing him something wicked. He smiles. I scowl.

"I like your tie. Very smart," he says as though we're friends.

The tie he speaks of is just a part of the getup I've worn since I killed Kong—trousers or black jeans, shirt, tie, suspenders, and Converse or boots. When I wear a vest to help conceal the gun in the small of my back, I add a silver pocket watch, a reminder that this asshole is just biding his time.

My tie today is royal blue with an anchor print, chosen in honor of Jaws's friend, who is anchored at the bottom of the Detroit River.

"Enough with the chitchat. Get to the point," I snap, pushing the beer in front of me aside. There is no way I'm having a drink with him.

Jaws appears thoroughly amused, and why shouldn't he? He is sitting on top of the food chain while I'm just chum.

"Suit yourself. What's new since we last spoke?"

Cracking my knuckles under the table, I speak quickly, desperate to get this over with. "Stevie is still running scared. He's undecided about The Pink Oyster because it's almost bust."

Jaws drums his manicured fingers on the table. "That is most disappointing. I hope you have a plan to change his mind."

"I do. It's under control. But why don't you just buy it off Lotus? She'd sell." This is something I obviously don't want to happen, but I need to know his motives.

Jaws stops drumming. "Why would I buy it when Stevie will give it to me?"

This is about money and power. It always has been, so his reply makes sense.

"Fair enough." I casually shrug, not wanting to throw Lotus into the deep end. "He meets his supplier on the first of every month at the steel mill along the river. I don't know who it is yet because the first is in three days."

"Good. What else?"

Folding my hands onto the table in front of me, I shake my head. "My turn to ask questions. When can I meet Scrooge?"

His name is Benjamin Solomon, and he just happens to be one of the richest men in Michigan. His money is "aboveboard" because according to Google, he is an investment banker. But his money is dirty. If he's running with Jaws, there is no doubt his wealth comes at the expense of others.

His listed address is a mansion in a gated community. I drove by a couple of times, but the place was patrolled and sealed tight. I've called his high-rise office almost every other day, asking to speak with him, but his secretary laughs and hangs up. Without an appointment, I'm not getting within three feet.

He has no hobbies, which makes it impossible to catch him unaware. If he attends any functions, he has at least three bodyguards. They even follow him to the bathroom. Jaws has no doubt filled him in, making him paranoid.

I've only seen him from a distance, but that distance was enough. He broke my brother's wrist and stole from him, so it's time I returned the favor.

Jaws laughs, reaching for his beer. "I admire your tenacity. Just as I tell you every week, you give me what I want, and I'll give you what you want."

"What I want is for you to be dead," I reply without pause, deadpanning him.

Jaws inhales deeply.

I may be forced to be his snitch, but that doesn't mean I'm going to make it easy for him. I have to "work" with him to get what I want—to see him and Scrooge dead.

"You can try," he mocks. "But the longer you prolong what I want, the longer you'll wait. What about the fighting syndicate?"

Reaching into the breast pocket of my shirt, I slide a folded piece of paper across the table. Jaws reaches for it and reads over the three names listed. "I didn't think so many people were involved."

His stiff upper lip gives me great pleasure.

"Including those three names, that makes eighteen," I

smugly say, in case he needs a reminder.

"I know," he grits out between clenched teeth.

"Having second thoughts?" I settle back against the booth, enjoying his blistering shade of red.

Jaws clearly didn't anticipate this many people being involved with Stevie. Making him disappear will be a little harder now, seeing as he'll be missed. Jaws prefers to work alone, but Stevie's operation is successful because he has people on his side.

He makes them money or gives them drugs, and in return, they turn a blind eye if he needs a location to use to run his syndicate. His payroll doesn't just include criminals; he has a mixed bag in his pocket. He's earned their trust, which is why he's able to move around the way that he does.

Jaws can't just muscle in and expect people to respect and trust him. He may be feared, but he isn't respected. Stevie is. I've seen it. I don't know who Stevie's drug supplier is, but I'm guessing they're fucking hard-core.

"Get me a name. I want to know who his supplier is. That motherfucker is undercutting me, and I'm losing business. I want to know every single place his stuff is being dealt. Street corners. Clubs. Fucking kindergartens.

"When people buy from him, they're stealing from me."

I yawn in response.

"Anything else?"

"Nope." I pop my *p*, purposely forgetting to tell him the name of the guy who supplies Stevie with his arsenal. I need to keep at least one ace up my sleeve.

I'm not stupid. Once Jaws gets everything he needs from

me, he'll kill me. He has no plans to ever give me Scrooge, so I need as much ammo as I can amass. And I will have that once I meet Stevie's supplier in three days' time.

I don't wait around and slide across the leather to exit the booth, but Jaws's hand snaps out and grips my forearm.

Inhaling deeply, I peer down at his fingers. "Your hand. Off," I snarl, my body vibrating for a fight.

"If I find out you're lying, you know what that means, right?" He snickers, his confidence only fueling this out of control inferno.

Three…

"It won't end well…"

Two…

"For my darling sister."

And one…

Without hesitation, I swiftly elbow him in the nose.

He recoils backward, instantly cupping his bleeding face. Every part of me demands I launch across this table and tear him apart. But when I think about the consequences, about what it would mean for Tiger, I begrudgingly leave him to nurse his broken nose.

Three of his men are by his side in an instant, but I was faster. They shouldn't have allowed it to get that far. I shove past them, ignoring their empty threats as I make my way to the exit.

"Asshole! You'll pay for that," Jaws muffles from behind his hand.

In response, I flip him off with my arm raised high in the air as I walk away. When I get outside, I tip my face toward the heavens and smile. I will happily pay the price for my rebellion because, holy shit, that felt good.

My cell chirps in my pocket, interrupting my afterglow. "I need you to take care of something."

It's Stevie.

"Where?"

"I'll text you the address. No matter what, I want this taken care of, all right?"

"Care to be a little more specific?"

"You'll know what to do when you get there. Dudley and Vincent are useless. They're lucky we need the extra manpower at the moment."

Stevie sounds a little more on edge than usual. This can't be good.

"No worries." I hang up, unsure what the hell I'm walking into.

Jumping into my truck, I wait for Stevie to text me the address. When he does, I see that it's not far from here. It's in an abandoned part of town near the river, meaning I could be walking into anything.

With no time to waste, I drive to the location and park my truck a few blocks away. Reaching into the console, I grab my Glock and 9mm and slip them into the shoulder holster. After looking around to ensure I don't have any witnesses, I slip it on.

Once I have my jacket on to conceal my pieces, I get out of the truck and do one last sweep to double-check no one is watching. When the coast is clear, I make my way toward the deserted building. Stepping through a hole in the fence, I walk around the back, never letting down my guard.

I doubt Stevie has discovered I'm playing double agent, but I prepare myself for every outcome there is. The door is half open, so I push it, and it creaks loudly as I step into the darkness. I stop, taking a moment to allow my eyes to adjust to the change in light. I also take in my surroundings.

When I hear a muffled cry and something metal scraping across the floor, I know what I'm here for. I was supposed to be Stevie's muscle, not his fucking hitman.

Walking through the darkness, I can't help but think about how something relatively simple has turned into this. I've found myself in a complicated predicament, all because I met someone who turned my life upside down.

She made me…feel, which is something I never thought would be possible again. No matter how many times I hurt her, she came back twice as strong, showing me what a fierce, determined woman she is. But none of that matters anymore.

Once again, I find my thoughts drifting to her. I don't know if this is normal or not. I mean, this has never happened to me before. I spent my entire mid-teens and twenties obsessing over revenge and bloodshed, so this is foreign to me, whatever it is.

Focusing on what I'm good at—violence—I walk toward the muffled noises. When I turn the corner and come face-to-face with the source, I shake my head, cursing everyone. I just wanted to kill four fucking people. How hard was that?

Impossible, it seems, because tied to a chair in the middle of the derelict building is some kid. The dirty windows allow some light to stream through so I can see him struggling against the cable ties secured around his ankles and wrists.

When he sees me, his terrified eyes widen, and he screams around the gag.

Not having the time or patience to deal with his melodramatics, I charge over and rip out the gag. Before he has a chance to scream, I slap his cheek, startling him. "Don't piss me off," I warn. "I've had a fucking bad day." *Try month.* "What are you doing here?"

He can't be older than seventeen. What could he have done to warrant being tied to a chair, about to come face-to-face with the muzzle of my Glock?

"I-I don't know," he stutters, licking his blood-crusted lips.

"Kid, you lie to me, you die." Reaching inside my jacket, I produce my gun. I'm not playing.

The kid struggles, attempting to back away, but he seems to have forgotten he's tied to a chair. "Okay, fine!" he cries.

Now he wants to talk.

"I only took a little. I didn't think they'd notice."

"Took what?"

When he hesitates, I press the muzzle into his sweaty forehead, giving him some encouragement to continue. "Money!" he screams, his lips quivering.

"If you don't tell me what the fuck that means in the next three seconds, they'll be your last words."

"Those idiots left their door unlocked when they stopped for gas. I only took some." His panic has him missing some details, but he's said enough for me to piece it together.

"You thieving little prick," I snarl, shaking my head. "You

stole money from someone you should not have."

"I gave it back!" he replies, pleading for me to believe him. But even if I did, it's too late for him now.

"What'd you need it for?"

He swallows, averting his eyes. "I was hungry. Needed a place to sleep."

Judging from his ratty jeans, dirty red sweater, and greasy blond hair, it's safe to assume he's a runaway. But this isn't my problem. Stevie sent me here to take care of it—*it* meaning him, this kid, who stole money to eat.

Something comes over me. Something in the shape of… pity.

"Please don't kill me," he begs, lowering his chin.

"Give me a reason I shouldn't?" I question, hating that his begging isn't giving me the satisfaction it should.

"I—"

His pause has me cocking the trigger, reminding myself of the job I have to do. "Hesitation in life will get you killed. Believe me, I know."

"Because it's not my fault they were stupid fucks!" he says in a rushed breath, catching me off guard. "I saw an opportunity, and I took it."

Well, fuck me. This little jerkoff has balls.

"I only got caught 'cause the cashier saw me. Those morons were clueless."

The more this kid talks, the more I like him. "You done this before?"

He nods. "It's amazing how oblivious people are. When you live on the streets, you either adapt or you die. You can suck cock to survive, or you can outsmart everyone. I don't suck anyone's cock," he adds smartly.

No matter how much I like this kid, I can't let him live. If Stevie finds out I let him go, unless…

"How long you been on the streets?"

"Seven months," he replies.

"Why'd you leave home?"

He bitterly laughs. "Home? It was never a home. I would rather sell my ass for a living than go back there."

This is a bad idea. I know it. But when I remove the gun from his forehead, it feels like a small part of me returns.

"You got a name?"

He blinks, surprised he's not lying in a pool of his own blood yet. That makes two of us. "Paul."

"How old are you, Paul?"

"Nineteen." He's lying through his teeth. And when he sees I call bullshit, he quickly backtracks. "Seventeen."

"I have one rule—don't lie to me. We clear?"

He nods quickly. "What happens now?"

Placing my gun back into the holster, I mull over his question because I, too, want to know the answer. "Want a job?"

"Doing what?" he asks suspiciously.

No matter how many times I tell myself this is a bad idea, it doesn't stop the words from slipping free. "I need you to watch someone for me. But you can't let her know you're there."

Paul cocks his head to the side. "Who is she?"

"No one," I reply, annoyed. He's asking so many questions,

but I remind myself he's seventeen.

"You want me to scare her?"

Launching forward, I grip his sweater and yank his face to mine. He flinches, the slack on his arms tight, thanks to the restraints. "No, I want you to do the complete opposite. Your job is to make sure she's okay. If anything happens to her, it's on your head. The head I will fucking detach from your shoulders if she gets hurt."

"What—"

I raise a finger, silencing him. All this talking is giving me a headache. "You want the job or not?"

"What do I get if I say yes?"

"I don't put a bullet in your head," I counter quickly, watching him gulp. "I'll pay you, give you a place to stay, and you don't have to suck any cock. We got a deal?"

He's really in no position to be picky, but mad props to him as he appears to think over my proposition. "Fine, we got a deal."

Letting him go, I reach into my pocket for a bubble gum-flavored lollipop. "Good choice. Oh, and one more thing," I say, unwrapping my sucker. "As far as anyone knows, you're dead. This can't work otherwise."

If Stevie finds out I let him walk, we'll both pay the price with our lives. But this is too good of an opportunity to let slide. I can't watch Tiger, but Paul can. I need a man I can trust. In this case, it's a boy, but I was his age when my life changed forever.

Is that why I decided to show him mercy?

I don't have time for such sentiments.

"No problem," he agrees with a sharp nod.

Popping the lollipop into my mouth, I savor the sweetness because once upon a time, I had the real thing. But now, all I can do is suck on this with the hope it satisfies the craving. But it never does.

"First things first, you need a shower 'cuz you fucking stink. You also need some new clothes. If you prove loyal, I may have some other work for you."

"Oh, yeah?" he asks, his interest piqued. "What work?"

He's a persistent little shit. He also has no fear, which is why when he's not watching Tiger, he'll be watching Scrooge. Watching and learning. "Just be invisible."

He eyes me with interest. I like that he doesn't back down and can hold his own. "I can do that. It's what I've been doing my entire life."

His comment confirms how cruel humanity can be.

"Good," I reply, biting into the lollipop with a crunch. Why suck when you can bite? Flicking the stick across the room, I reach into my pocket and produce my switchblade.

Paul doesn't waver.

"Do what I say, and you won't have to steal to survive."

"Just who are you?" he asks, mouth parted in awe.

"Your fairy fucking godmother."

He snickers as I cut through his restraints.

I can't help but wonder how different my life would have turned out if I'd had someone cutting through my restraints when I was seventeen. But my shackles were invisible, and I never believed in fairy tales.

I still don't.

CHAPTER THREE

Lily

"**W**hatever you want, kid, you order," Christopher says to Jordy, who looks like all his Christmases have come at once.

Our weekly family dinners—although, today is lunch— are something both Jordy and I look forward to. It's nice to be able to share a meal together because we have a lot of dinners to make up for. Jordy tongues his cheek as he scans over the menu. Christopher peers down at him with a smile. I can't believe this is my life.

I never thought I would be breaking bread—or in this case, pizza—with my brother and son. But here I am, sitting in this arcade that serves ninety-nine cent slices of pizza, proving myself wrong.

When Christopher walked back into my world, I didn't know what to think. It felt like a part of me had returned. But there was a lot of catching up to do.

Thinking back to that night, I can't help but consider it bittersweet. It was the day my brother returned, and the day a man who I had feelings for showed me just how deep those feelings ran.

Bull—or as he finally revealed, Cody Bishop—shook everything up beyond repair. He was my boogeyman, the man who took away everything from me. Yes, the decisions I made are mine, but I was forced to make them because the only man I've ever loved was shot and killed by a man who helped me forget about him.

Thinking of Bull's touches, of the way he made me feel alive, turns my stomach because I feel so fucking stupid. I was sleeping with Michael's killer, and I liked it…a lot. But to him, I was merely a plaything because he made it clear that if I got in his way of vengeance, he would have no qualms ensuring I wasn't in his way for long.

"I will kill your brother. And I'll…kill you too if you stand in my way."

Those words hurt me in ways I never thought possible. I acted with anger, but deep down, my soul wept. After everything we experienced together, I thought that I meant something to him. But I didn't. I was just a piece of ass. So shame on me. He never made me any promises. I was the one who believed he could change…for me. That I was someone worth changing for.

But the only man who believed that is dead.

Bull revealed Michael, or rather Lachlan, died with a ring in his hand. My ring. The ring that's supposed to be on my finger. But that never happened. I lost my Lachlan, and Jordy lost the father he never got to know.

Squeezing my upper thighs, I suppress the anger coursing through me because once I got over the shock and cried a thousand tears, that faded and gave way to this pure rage festering within. I haven't spoken to Bull because I meant what I said.

We are so done.

But nonetheless, I can't stop thinking about harming him how he harmed me.

I've wanted to ask Christopher his version of events because every story has two sides, and I need to hear Christopher's. But the time has never been right. However, I know I can't avoid the inevitable. I need to know, so I can… move on.

"Mom, can I have the buffalo wings *and* the mozzarella sticks?" Jordy asks with a grin that looks so much like his father's.

I find myself seeing the resemblance more so now. I don't know if that's because Christopher is back.

Before I have a chance to reply, Christopher steps in. "Of course, you can. You can have whatever you want." He playfully messes up his hair while Jordy beams.

"You're the best, Uncle Chris."

They have connected instantly, which makes me so happy. But this isn't the first time Christopher has undermined me when it comes to Jordy. I love that he's stepped into the role of uncle with ease, but when it comes to making decisions about my son, that is for me to decide and not him.

Just before I have a chance to correct Christopher, Jordy springs up and races over to his friend. Christopher looks on with a smile, appearing intrigued by Jordy's carefree nature. I suppose our childhood was far from being carefree.

When I reach for my water, Christopher's attention lands on me, and he must be able to read my annoyance. "What's the matter?"

Every bone in my body is telling me to drop it, but I can't. There will never be the "right time" to do this, so I decide to take the plunge.

"I really love how quickly you and Jordy have bonded." He nods, hinting for me to go on. "But I don't like when you do that."

"Do what?" he counters, arching a brow.

"What you did there. Undermining me when it comes to Jordy."

Christopher appears taken aback. "I didn't realize I was."

"I know we're still trying to establish our relationship and work out the boundaries, but when it comes to Jordy, I don't want him thinking he can go to you when I say no. That's not how things work. It's just been us for so long and—"

Christopher cuts me off with a wave of his hand. "I get it."

His harsh tone reveals his unhappiness over me speaking up. It appears he doesn't like being undermined either. Deciding to open up about everything, I clear my throat and hope this doesn't turn ugly.

"I wanted to speak to you about something else. About... Lachlan."

I can see him physically freeze up before my eyes. But I continue.

"Did you know about his…about him dy—" But I can't finish. The fact is still so raw.

"Yes," he finally confesses with a sharp nod.

A deflated hiss escapes me. "Did you know about us?"

Christopher folds his hands on the table. "Yes."

I don't know how to feel. Angry. Betrayed. Guilty. All of the above seem to apply.

"I saw the way he looked at you, but you were just a kid. I never thought—" He stops, clenching his jaw. "I never thought you'd do that."

I avert my eyes as my guilt rears its ugly head. He'd known about us the entire time.

"So, I didn't tell you because even though I was hurt you both went behind my back, I was only trying to protect you from an ugly truth. I knew what it would do to you."

"You should have told me," I reply, swallowing past the lump in my throat.

He ponders over my words. "I guess we should have told one another a lot of things."

And he's right.

The inevitable lingers…did he really kill Damian, Bull's brother?

Bull's description of what was done to his brother and him was despicable, and I don't want to believe my brother and my boyfriend could have done such a thing. I need to know the truth.

"What about that night?" There is no need for me to

clarify when I'm speaking of. There is only one night that triggered our lives to change forever. "Did you do it? Did all of you do it? Did you…kill someone?" I lower my voice, but he heard me loud and clear.

I don't regret my question. The time and place aren't ideal, but will they ever be?

"Yes."

I blink once, stunned. I wasn't expecting that response.

"But will you let me explain what really happened? You've heard *his* side," he spits. "Can you now listen to mine?"

I nod, afraid of what I will say if I speak.

"Damian and a group of his jock friends jumped us. We were just there to have a good time. Bull attacked us first because we were arguing over some girl. A cheerleader. It got out of hand, and before I knew it, the guys were on us, out for blood.

"It was self-defense. It was either us or Damian. None of us meant for it to go that far. They were rich high school kids, and they saw us as nothing but white trash. Bull gave as good as he got, and when he picked a fight with the big boys but couldn't follow through, his brother lost control. Bull was the one who started the fight, and we were the ones who finished it.

"We ran because we were scared. We knew we fucked up, but we couldn't go to the police. Our lives would be over if we did." Christopher lowers his eyes. "But that night, it still haunts me to this day. It haunted Lachlan, too."

I need a minute to digest this.

His version of events seems like a completely different

story. Bull insisted the attack was premeditated, and they tortured Damian before they killed him. But Christopher says that's not the case. He states it was self-defense. Bull blames Christopher and his friends because he started a fight he couldn't finish, and his temper resulted in his brother's death.

It was a tragic accident, one that Christopher and Lachlan regretted.

I did notice a change in Lachlan's behavior around that time. He became withdrawn, and that's when we grew close. When he was supposed to be running wild with Christopher, he used to sneak into the trailer and watch movies with me.

At first, I didn't think anything of it; I was a fourteen-year-old girl in love with her older brother's best friend. But he never touched me. He was well aware of my feelings, but he didn't make a move until I turned sixteen.

"Why did you leave, Christopher?" I try my best to keep my emotions under wraps. "You leaving broke me in half."

He hisses as if my words wound him.

With hesitation, he reaches across the table and gently grasps my hand. "I'm sorry. I know what I did was wrong, and I will seek your forgiveness for an eternity, but I was riddled with grief and shame for what I'd done. I took the coward's way out, but also, I couldn't be around you when I knew the truth about Lachlan. I needed time away to heal. The path I was going down was going to end in only one way."

Damian's death changed him. It changed us all.

"I'd looked after you my entire life; it was time I looked after myself. That's why I left Detroit. This town has caused me nothing but pain."

His touch along the back of my hand suddenly feels… wrong, so I subtly remove my hand from his.

As far as excuses go, I can't help but feel a sliver of resentment toward my brother. He *did* take the coward's way out. Instead of facing the consequences of his actions, he ran when I needed him the most.

"I know it's hard for you to understand, but I needed this. I went off the grid, traveling without a destination in mind, soul searching for what my purpose was in life, and I found it when I met a woman—Bianca."

Something comes over Christopher, but I can't pinpoint what it is. It's a mixture of love but also hate. Just what happened between them?

Once he gathers his composure, he continues. "Bianca taught me all there was to know about succeeding. I learned from her and built a name for myself, investing in stocks from all over the world."

I wait for him to continue, but he doesn't. That's all he is comfortable sharing, it seems, but I don't buy it. I can't shake this gut feeling that some of his dealings aren't aboveboard. Christopher shares what he wants to. But it's the things he doesn't want to divulge that I want to hear about, like who busted his nose.

He told me he got into the ring, and it was an accident, but I don't believe him. That mistrust is there because no matter what he says, he's lied to me.

From the sounds of it, he has lived a full, happy life, while I have struggled to survive. I don't tell him this because I don't want to seem resentful, but I am angry that he left me. I understand he needed to leave, but for him to be MIA for so long hurts.

He's been living the high life while I've been stuck here, wondering if I would ever see him again. It's always easier for the person who left to forget because their life is filled with new adventures. But for the ones left behind, we're merely left with memories.

We aren't the same people anymore. Yes, I love him dearly—he's my brother—but there's something that I can't put my finger on that seems...off.

His story is tied together with a big red bow, and usually, those stories are utter bullshit. But I don't want to rock the boat and cause him to disappear again.

His presence has changed Jordy's behavior dramatically. Jordy is smitten with him. And it seems the feeling runs both ways. Christopher has stepped into his uncle role without a hitch. He picks Jordy up from school when I can't and has taken him to a couple of basketball games.

He said he has lots of lost time to make up for. With Jordy and with me.

"I know it's a lot to take in, but I'm back for good. It's just us from now on. No one is going to stand in the way of us being a family again."

I wish my brain would shut off, but it can't. Whenever Christopher says something nice, about wanting to be a family, I can't help but think it's too little, too late.

Where was he when I rushed Jordy to the hospital with a fever of a hundred and five? Or what about when he fell off his bike and needed three stitches under his chin? Where was he when I didn't have enough money to feed my son? And where was he when I decided to start working at The Pink Oyster because I couldn't make ends meet?

The answer to all my questions is the same—he wasn't here.

"Can you forgive me?" he asks, thankfully keeping his hands to himself.

Every part of me screams that it's not that easy. But when Jordy skips over with a grin I haven't seen on his face in a long time, I eventually nod. No matter how much resentment I have toward my brother, I don't want to disappoint my son.

"This is my uncle. He's like a millionaire," Jordy proudly says to Ian, a friend from school. He's a good kid. I've picked him up from class when his mom's running late. She too is a single mom, so I do what I can.

Christopher chuckles, shaking his head. "You're just saying that so I'll give you more money for the arcade."

Jordy replies with a mischievous smirk.

Christopher digs into his pocket for his wallet, but then stops suddenly and looks at me. "I don't know if your mother approves, though, Jordy."

Narrowing my eyes, I suddenly have the urge to slap him for putting me on the spot like this.

When Jordy spins my way, his grin is soon replaced with a frown. "Mom! Uncle Christopher said his money is ours."

"Oh, is that right?"

Christopher raises his hands in mock surrender when I glare at him. This isn't funny. This is exactly what I was talking about. He looks like the knight in shining armor while I'm the boring one who always says no.

"It's okay, kiddo. Listen to your mom." There isn't a hint of sarcasm in his tone, which makes me feel terrible.

This is a common occurrence with Christopher. One minute, we're okay, and the next, we're not. But it seems to be one-sided. I'm the one who has everything I ever wanted, but I can't decide if the grass is greener.

"Mom!" Jordy whines, but I stand firm.

"Jordan, baby, if you want money, you ask me. Not your uncle, okay?"

Christopher sits back in the booth, not saying a word.

"Okay," he says unhappily.

Christopher slaps his hands together, breaking the sudden awkwardness. "Let's order. I'm starved."

Jordy nods, sliding across the booth to sit near Christopher, and Ian slips in after him. It seems no one wants to sit near the boring mom.

A passing waitress takes our order. Jordy rattles off what he wants while Christopher laughs at how his order is fit for a king. Looking across the table, I see a picture-perfect family; it's what I've always wanted. So, no matter the bothersome scratching just below the surface, I decide to stop doubting this.

Christopher is back, and we're going to be a family—I'll make sure of it.

Washing my hands in the bathroom sink, I'm beyond terrified of my exhausted reflection. I don't remember ever looking this tired before, but I have far more important things to worry about.

Looking at my watch, I realize it's time to go. I'll be late for Avery's appointment if we don't get a move on. Tossing the paper towel into the trash, I open the door and bump straight into an unsuspecting man.

"Oh, god, sorry!" I quickly apologize when he reaches out to stop me from falling on my face.

"It's fine." He laughs. "Are you okay?"

"I should be the one asking you that," I reply with a smile.

Before he has a chance to reply, a huge shadow casts over us, and the man quickly removes his hand from my bicep. I don't know what's going on because it's so unheard of. I don't know if my exhausted mind is imagining things.

But when Christopher shoves the poor man into the wall, it seems I'm seeing things clearly. "Get your hands off her!" he yells, gripping my wrist and attempting to place me behind him.

But I shake him off, furious. "Christopher, calm down."

He does the complete opposite. "You touch her again, and I will end you," he threatens the man, who raises his hands. He knows better than to challenge Christopher.

"I'm sorry, man. I didn't mean anything by it. I was just

trying to help your girlfriend."

My stomach turns, and bile rises. "I'm his sister," I clarify, which suddenly makes this situation worse.

"Well, she doesn't need anyone helping her. She has me, and that's all she needs. Get out of here."

The man doesn't need to be told twice and splits, not looking back.

Christopher turns, examining me from head to toe. "Are you all right? He had his hands all over you."

"Hardly," I reply with bite. "What was that? You can't go around threatening to end someone."

"Watch me," he says, gripping my elbow. He starts coaxing me toward the door, but I recoil from his hold.

"I appreciate you going into big brother mode, but I'm not a kid anymore. I can look after myself. I have been doing so for a very long time."

It's a low blow, but I can't help it. He went from naught to a hundred in a second. Christopher has always had a temper, but this is something else. This behavior is erratic and completely irrational.

Reading my seriousness, he takes a deep breath and transforms from beast to man right before my eyes. It's that easy, which troubles me.

"Sorry, you're right. I fucked up. I'm just overprotective. You can't blame me for wanting to protect you."

With a sigh, I run a hand through my hair. People are giving us sideways glances, and I realize we're making a scene.

Jordy bounces over, none the wiser. "Are we going? Uncle Christopher, you promised we'd play ball."

Christopher nods, composing himself, while I wonder what the fuck just happened. Whatever it is, I don't like it. Our reunion isn't what I thought it would be. We have a lot of healing to do.

"Lily, you don't have to wait with me. I'll catch a cab home," Avery says, interrupting me from my thoughts.

Shaking my head, I grip her cold hand in mine. "You will not. I'm staying with you." Avery's comment is the wake-up call I needed to focus on what's important—her, and not what happened today.

She gives me a weak smile in response.

Her trial treatments are taking their toll on her. Even though her doctors say this is normal, she looks worse than when she came in. They pump her full of drugs and then send her home, awaiting her feedback on the side effects.

They document everything and hope when she gets tested in three months' time, her results will show some sort of change. But they aren't hopeful.

Sniffing back my tears, I quickly help her stand when a nurse comes to get her. She is unsteady on her feet but refuses to use a wheelchair. She will march to her deathbed. I gulp at the thought. The nurse takes over for me and helps usher Avery into the consulting rooms.

"She'll be out in an hour or so," she informs me. "I can call you when she's done."

Settling on a plastic chair, I reach for a tattered magazine. "It's okay. I'll wait here."

Avery turns over her shoulder, smiling. Although she doesn't want to put me out, she's glad I'm here. She shuffles along with the nurse, who closes the door behind them. The moment it shuts, I take a deep breath and bury my face in my palms.

I have no right to cry. I'm not the one losing the fight with cancer. I know it. The doctors know it. And Avery knows it. She's dying. These trials may slow it down, but the inevitable looms—Avery is dying.

My heart constricts at the thought because I feel so damn helpless. My big plan of saving her seems so childish now that I know what I'm up against. I thought buying the ballet studio would help somehow, but at this rate, I won't make enough money in time.

Sucking in a deep breath, I stop hiding and face the harsh light of day. Flipping through a magazine from the early 2000s, I try to focus on the interesting fashion and not on how I'm failing in every aspect of my life.

My cell rings, snapping me from my bubble of negativity. It's Christopher. "Hey," I answer, hoping my voice doesn't betray what I was just thinking about.

"Hey, sis. Where are you?"

"I'm at the hospital. Remember, I told you I was taking Avery for her treatment?"

"Oh, yeah, sorry I forgot. Do you want me to start dinner?"

Looking down at my watch, I see that it's later than I thought it was. I don't know how Avery will feel after her treatment. If she's unwell, at least then I can stay with her.

"That would be great. Thanks."

"That's what big brothers and uncles are for," he replies happily while I roll my eyes. He's trying too hard, and it's grating on my nerves. But I soon tamp down my annoyance.

Though what he says next just incites it once again. "What time are you working?"

Yes, that's right, I'm still dancing at Blue Bloods—the club my brother co-owns with Carlos. And yes, I see how fucked up that is.

"Eleven," I answer sharply.

"What do you feel like for dinner?"

Biting the inside of my cheek, I tell myself not to pick a fight with him, no matter how badly I want to.

"Anything is fine. Oh, I better go. The doctors are here." I don't give him a chance to get a word in edgewise before I quickly end the call with shaky fingers.

Inhaling deeply, I exhale with a sigh, but it doesn't make me feel any better. When I signed that contract, it seems I signed it in blood. Even though my brother is co-owner, the contract was made with Carlos, so technically, he has nothing to do with it.

He said he's tried to negotiate with Carlos, offering to give him the money lost if I break the contract, but Carlos won't budge. He doesn't want to damage his business relationship with him, but he's fine with ruining our already strained relationship.

He said he didn't know I was working at Blue Bloods. That it was merely a coincidence. But again, doubt lingers.

I've told him why I agreed to work at Blue Bloods in the first place, hoping he would offer to lend me the money so I could quit, but he hasn't. God knows he has the cash. But the amount I need to buy Avery out is something he said he can't part with.

He knows how much Avery means to me, but it doesn't seem to make a difference.

I know I shouldn't be angry. It's his money. But I thought he'd at least offer me something so I could stop dancing. But night after night, he comes into work, seeing how I bust my ass being eye candy for the nasty pervs; yet, he still doesn't help.

When he watches me dance, I feel…dirty. I've never felt this way before. But dancing for your long-lost brother while in a thong is as fucked up as it sounds.

It's only for a couple of more weeks, I reason. By then, I will have enough money to go to the bank and ask for a loan. I've saved every dollar I've earned, and when I get that loan approved, I *will* be leaving—contract be damned.

My cell rings again, and I sigh in relief when I see it's Kath. "Hey."

"Hey, hun!" Kath has proven to be a true friend, and seeing as I don't have many, or any of them, I am thankful our paths crossed. "Just checking you're all good for tonight?"

I arch a brow. "Of course. Why?"

I can hear the change of background noise as though she's moving into a quieter room. "Word on the street is that someone is recruiting dancers," she says in a hushed tone. She must be at home, not wanting to wake her nine-month-old.

"Who?" I ask, my interest piqued.

"I'm not sure who, but they're calling him the Robin Hood to strippers." She chuckles while my stomach twists. "Apparently, he's a real looker too. India said he could have asked her to sign over the deed to her house, and she would have agreed."

Rubbing my brow, I beg to whatever god is watching over me that it isn't him.

"He's inked from head to toe, but it's his eyes," she reveals as I curse the fucking universe. "Seven girls from different clubs have taken him up on his offer. On the DL, I think they just want to get into his pants. Especially Cherry."

My cheeks heat for many reasons, but at the forefront is the fact that Cherry is not only a brilliant dancer, but she is also beautiful, confident, and can have her pick of any man.

"What club does he work for?" I innocently ask even though I know the answer.

"The Pink Oyster," she replies, none the wiser I'm about to lose my shit. "He's the Bird Dog, and the girls have no issues having him as their personal bouncer. Do you know who he is? Was he there when you danced?"

Something explodes out of me, something that has been festering since that night. "I might be a little late tonight. Can you cover for me?"

"O-kay," Kath says, drawing out the O. "What should I tell Carlos?"

Fucking Carlos.

"Just tell him I have diarrhea. *No one* will question that."

She snorts in laughter. "You got it. Oh, Lily, you're not

about to jump ship, are you, and go back to your old club?"

The prospect pleases me more than I care to admit because at least I was happy there, happy until Bull walked into my life and sucker punched the shit out of me. "Not in the way you think," I ambiguously reply before hanging up the phone.

The idea of seeing him again pisses me off; yet, it also excites me beyond words. A tremor rocks my body, and I realize this is the first time in a month that I have felt... something. And I like it. More than I should.

God save my soul.

"Are you sure you're okay?" I ask Avery for the tenth time while tucking her into bed. "I can call in sick. We can watch *Billy Elliot* on Netflix."

It's our favorite movie.

Avery gives me a weak smile, snuggled deep under her blankets. "We've already watched it twice this week."

"And?" I prompt with a smirk.

Today's treatment really knocked her around. She passed out the moment she sat in my truck. The vomiting started just as I managed to get her into her apartment, and it's only now just stopped.

The nurse handed me a flyer with expected side effects. So far, Avery has experienced nine out of the ten. I feel so helpless, but the nurse said there was nothing I could do. All I can do is watch her and make sure her temperature doesn't spike. It's thankfully remained steady.

She looks so tired, and all she wants to do is sleep. But the thought of leaving her when she looks so sick...I'm afraid this is it this time. I think that after every treatment.

"I'll call work," I insist, reaching for my cell off her side table.

Her cold hand reaches out from under the blanket, gripping my wrist. "You will not. I didn't raise a quitter," she says, catching her breath. Her lungs are riddled with cancer. Sometimes it even hurts her to breathe.

Her comment has me sucking back my tears because it's true. She raised me right when she didn't have to raise me at all. "Okay. As long as you're sure?"

"I'm sure." She gently clasps my hand. "Thank you for everything you've done for me."

Those tears I've tried so hard to keep away threaten to break the surface. "Hey, enough of that talk. You don't need to thank me. That's what family does."

When she nods, her grip on me loosening, I gently tuck her arm back under the blankets.

"I'll check in tomorrow, okay? I have another late shift tonight. Your phone, water...it's all within reach." I feel like an asshole for lying because she doesn't know what I really do at night. But I can't tell her I work in a strip club. I'm not ashamed, but Avery is old-school, and the stigma associated with being a dancer is hard to break.

Not to mention if it ever got out, it would ruin Everland's reputation.

Her eyes flutter closed, and she's wearing a content smile

on her dry lips. "I'm so proud of the woman you've grown into, Lillian. Whatever you do, I know you're doing it to survive."

My mouth parts in surprise.

Her soft breaths indicate she's asleep; I sit on the edge of the bed, shedding silent tears. I don't know if she knows, but her comment has me guessing I'm a lousy liar.

After ensuring she has everything she needs, I lean forward and plant a soft kiss on her cool forehead. She sighs softly. Leaving her to rest, I keep the hallway light on in case she needs to get up in the middle of the night.

After locking her door, I turn and sag against it. My heart breaks every time I leave her because I fear it'll be the last time I see her alive. Someone opens their door down the corridor, which spurs me to wipe my eyes and quickly make my way to the elevator.

When I walk outside, the bitter wind picks up speed, reflecting how I'm feeling inside—cold and restless. My truck is parked close, so I make a quick run for it because it's freezing. I start the engine and crank the heater.

Waiting for it to warm up, I rub my hands in front of me, blowing on them. My mind is racing. The clock on the dash reveals that I have more than enough time to get to work, but I'm not going there. After what Kath revealed today, there is only one place I am pulled toward.

Adjusting the rearview mirror, I notice a black car parked a few car lengths away from me. Squinting, I'm positive someone is sitting in the driver's seat, but I'm not a hundred percent certain. Putting the conspiracy theories aside, however, because the identity of my stalker, Andre, has been revealed, I put the truck into gear and take off into the night.

This heavy feeling in the pit of my stomach won't go away, but I don't know what it is. I just know the thought of going to The Pink Oyster has it lessening. Gripping the steering wheel, I shake my head.

"What is wrong with me?" I mutter under my breath.

I reason with myself that the way we left things was unresolved for me. That's why I can't stop thinking about him. I need to finish this once and for all. If I get the last word, then maybe I can finally move on.

Yes, that must be it.

Lies.

Lies.

Stepping on the gas, I run with the idea before I chicken out and am slapped with the truth.

During the entire drive, I pump myself up by running through every positive affirmation I can think of. That by doing this, I'm taking back control of my life. But when I pull into the parking lot of The Pink Oyster, all those pep talks get shot to shit.

"What am I doing?" I really need to stop talking to myself. But I never claimed to be sane, which is why I reach for Jordy's baseball hat from the floor and tuck my hair into it as I pull it low over my head.

I'm in jeans, Converse, and a pink knitted sweater that shows off a sliver of my midriff. I could be anyone. But for good measure, I hunt through my console for the pair of oversized pink-tinted sunglasses I used as a part of a costume I wore on stage.

They looked ridiculous, which is why they were a onetime deal only. And when I pull down the visor to look at my reflection, I see that nothing's changed. But I will deal with the absurdity because when I open my door, chin downturned and hands in pockets, they give me the confidence to be anyone I want to be.

The parking lot is busy, which makes me happy. I'm glad things are picking up for Lotus. Could it be thanks to Bull playing PR? He doesn't even like people. But people, or more accurately, women like him. What Kath said about Cherry has me gritting my teeth as I walk through the door.

Pop doesn't recognize me. I silently celebrate my victory and am filled with a rush of adrenaline to be someone other than me. I discreetly scan my surroundings, heart in my throat, but when I don't see Bull, my surge of excitement takes a nosedive.

Lotus is behind the bar, and a wave of nostalgia hits me hard. But when my gaze drifts to the stage, another memory slams into me, and that's of Bull covered in another man's blood—the man he just killed by driving a knife straight through his heart.

Instantly, I clutch my chest, feeling a sharp pain in the dead center. It has nothing to do with what I witnessed, however, and everything to do with the realization that my heart hurts because I…miss Bull. Goddamn him. And goddamn me.

Even after everything he's done, I still can't hate him as much as I should.

This place is like a second home to me. I know which table gets the least attention from the dancers. It's also the table shrouded in partial darkness. It's empty, so I make my way toward it, shifting my chair to ensure I am cloaked in the shadows.

Even though I'm in disguise, I'm still paranoid and look around me, ensuring I'm on no one's radar. When I'm in the clear, I lean back in my seat and bite my nails, wondering what my game plan is. I drove here all gung-ho, but now that I'm here, I don't know what to do.

This was a stupid idea.

Tawny finishes her set and shakes her ass as she gets off stage. It appears some things never change. But when "Cherry Pie" by Warrant blasts over the speakers, it seems some things do. And when the backstage curtain parts and out saunters Cherry, I suddenly wish for the monotony because it's here where things are predictable and safe.

The tip rail is packed full, and a spout of jealousy spills from me. Once upon a time, they were lining up to see me. But now, Cherry is the flavor of the month. And I can see why.

This industry is small, and rumors are rife. Cherry is rumored to be one of the best dancers this town has. And her name, she supposedly got because she tastes well, like cherries. And now she and her cherry flavor are here, owning the place.

Lowering the bill of my hat, I watch her closely as she dances with skill. She is definitely trained in contemporary dance, and the way she moves her body is almost hypnotic. Her curled red hair tumbles down her back, appearing to highlight her soft, pale skin.

She turns her back to the crowd, shaking her ass while

peeking over her shoulder. She places a hand over her open mouth, pretending to fake innocence as the men throw their life savings onto the stage.

I roll my eyes. So lame. She is all smoke and mirrors.

I see red, literally, as she's in a red thong and matching crop top. I shouldn't be jealous, and normally, I wouldn't be. But the thought of Bull seeing her shake her ass and oh, Jesus, her breasts, because she just removed her top, infuriates me.

I have zero claim over him. I mean, I hate him, right? But the more she wiggles and writhes, the more I want to choke her with the string of her thong.

I shouldn't have come here. This was a bad…very bad… sweet mother of fuck…

Bad seems the appropriate adjective to use because the epitome of bad just strolled, no, fucking *sauntered* into the room. It's fight or flight—my hammering heart threatens to spill from my chest, my palms begin to sweat, and my mouth goes dry because standing just a few feet away is the Devil himself.

I take a moment, maybe two, to examine him from head to toe because my memory has clearly done a poor job of remembering him. His hair has grown long and is slicked back like he's run his fingers through it to groom it. It's short on the sides, which only seems to emphasize the length on top.

My fingers itch to run my fingers through it and pull— hard.

His scruff is thick but cut with precision, drawing attention to that supple bowed mouth and defined, sharp jawline.

My eyes can't keep up with the visual godliness because his black boots, ripped black jeans, and white shirt rolled up to the elbows, exposing his tattoos, are almost too much. He's once again wearing black suspenders, which just seem to accentuate his bad boy persona.

But it isn't an image. Cody Bishop *is* a bad boy.

His presence is almost suffocating, and I take three much-needed breaths as I slouch down, afraid he will see me. Even though I'm hidden, when I see his astute eyes—a mismatched kiss from Heaven and Hell—scan the crowd, I feel exposed.

Once he's perused the room, his attention lands on the stage, or more specifically, it lands on Cherry. She notices him watching her and commences a sexy swagger toward him. He stands his ground, arms folded, expressionless.

But Cherry sees it as a challenge and winks his way.

I bunch my fists against my thighs, clenching my jaw. The need to hurt her is real.

I watch him watch her and look for any signs that would betray his thoughts. Did he watch me the same way? My skin begins to blister when I recall the last time he watched me dance. It wasn't in the club. It was when I danced for him in the studio. And when I was done, he bound me tightly and made me feel like a meal prepared solely for him.

I don't remember ever feeling so alive, so animated with an energy that made me feel invincible. But that's how I felt with Bull. Even when he tested me, I always felt empowered because he was a puzzle, one I so desperately wanted to solve.

The room breaks out into wolf whistles and hollers as Cherry finishes her set—completely naked. She is standing in front of Bull, arms spread, her back bowed in an offering, one he seems quite happy about if that shit-eating smirk is anything to go by.

I can count on one hand how many times I've seen that smirk, that smirk which is supposed to be only reserved for me.

A wave of anger whips through me, and my leg begins to bounce. I can't sit still. Cherry bends down and gathers her tips, coaxing Bull over with a curl of her finger. Silly girl. Bull doesn't come when called.

But I soon eat my words when he saunters over to her, helping her collect her cash.

Motherfucker!

The monster lay dormant inside me, but she's been awakened. And now, she's out for blood.

I can't stay here. I will do something stupid if I do. I don't know what that something stupid entails, but at the moment, breaking both of Cherry's kneecaps is what I'm leaning toward. Standing slowly, I ensure my hat is down low and stay hidden in the shadows as I make a beeline for the door.

Thankfully, Bull is across the room, so I can get the hell out of here undetected. Not that he'd notice. He's too busy being the perfect lapdog. I snarl at the thought.

Holding my breath the entire way, I gasp in lungsful of air when I make it outside. But I don't stop. I quicken my step and frantically reach for my keys in my pocket. The truck is mere feet away, and I lower my guard—what a fucking amateur move.

I unlock the door, but before I have a chance to open it, I'm tossed up against the truck, dropping my keys. I desperately try to buck the person off me, but when I'm hit with a juniper punch, I don't know whether to be relieved or terrified.

"Now where do you think you're going?" Bull snickers inches from my ear with his hardened chest pressed to my back. All I want to do is sag against him and surrender, but my pride won't let me.

"Home, to wash my eyeballs out with bleach," I sneer, struggling against him. My glasses tumble to the ground. "Get off me."

He tsks in response. Smug asshole. "Don't be jealous."

Scoffing, I spit, "Jealous? Of what? Being jealous would mean that I care, and in case you missed the memo, I don't."

"Then why are you here?" he counters, pressing me harder into the truck when I continue fighting.

"I thought I left something behind, but I was mistaken." It's a double-edged sword, and he knows it. "Now, would you kindly let me go? Or—"

"Or what?" he challenges, placing his palms on either side of my head.

"Or I'll scream."

There is a shift in the air—the calm before the storm.

I open my mouth, ready to make good on my word, but when Bull slams his hand over it, I smile in victory. What a chump. Without hesitation, I bite down on his fingers—hard. He hisses but doesn't let go, which has me resorting to other measures, such as elbowing him in the stomach.

A pained oof escapes him, and he loosens his hold.

Shoving him off me, I frantically fumble with the handle

and eventually get it open. It only smashes back shut when Bull forces it closed.

Spinning around, I come face-to-face with him, ready to slap his cheek. But it's evident I'm not ready for anything at all because when we lock eyes, I suddenly can't breathe. There is so much fury swirling behind those hypnotic eyes.

The static between us awakens every part of me. My heaving chest betrays not only my anger but my excitement as well.

When he cages me against the truck once again, I shove against his chest, but he only pushes me back down. "You shouldn't be here," he warns, inches from my lips.

"Let me leave, and we won't have a problem."

He tongues his cheek, smirking. That smirk is different from the one I saw inside. This smirk is filled with hunger… for me. "Tell me why you're here, and I'll let you go."

"I was taking a walk," I lie, refusing to allow him to intimidate me. "Last time I checked, that wasn't illegal. But I suppose it doesn't make a difference to you. You do what you want, when you want, consequences be damned, right?"

The hardening of his jaw is the only sign betraying his thoughts. "Finally, it's sunk in."

"Oh, it's sunk in all right," I counter, eyeing him something wicked. "Christopher told me what *really* happened"—I pause, needing a moment—"that night."

"What *really* happened then?" he questions with a cynical grin.

"He said you started the fight. Over some girl. Your brother and his friends jumped him and were out for blood.

It got out of hand, and it was either him or—"

"Or what?" he coaxes, the truck whining under the force as he pushes down harder onto it.

"Or Damian," I whisper, suddenly afraid. "It was self-defense."

Bull's gaze eats me alive as he scans over every inch of me. "Fiction can be fun," he finally says, shaking his head.

"Did you? Did you start it?" I ask, licking my trembling lips. I don't know why it matters. I just need to know if Christopher is telling me...the truth. Today has thrown everything off-center.

Bull reads between the lines and senses my suspicion. Christopher is my brother, and for the most part, I believe him, but a small, traitorous part demands I open my eyes and see the full picture.

The way he responded to that poor, defenseless man today isn't normal. Neither is him watching me dance.

Why would Bull do all this if what he told me wasn't true? Vengeance is blind, and maybe he's seeing what he wants to see, but I don't think he is...and that's why I'm here.

"Yes, I started it," he confirms. "There *was* a girl."

A sigh leaves me. "And?"

But he doesn't elaborate. He's holding back. Why?

"And it seems your brother has told you the rest."

The clenching of his jaw says otherwise. Bull isn't contradicting Christopher's story. Does that mean he's telling me the truth?

This is the moment I should rejoice and forget I ever met Bull, but something is off. There is something he isn't telling me. I don't know how I know, but I just do.

"Are you even sorry?"

"Probably not," he replies with a shrug, not even sure what I'm referring to.

Ignoring him, I press, "Are you sorry you killed him?" I'm talking about Lachlan. I know he told me he has no remorse. But now that he knows who Lachlan is, does he feel any guilt for ruining my life?

Lifting one hand off the truck and rubbing his thumb over my quivering lower lip, he calmly replies, "No."

I can break free at any moment, but I've missed his hands on me—so much. "You killed the man I loved," I whisper, holding his gaze, needing him to see the pain his actions have caused. But he doesn't care. He never did.

"And he killed the man I loved," he counters without flinching. "All's fair in love and war."

A tear trickles down my cheek, and I squeeze my eyes shut to keep any more from falling.

A breath hitches in my throat, however, when my baseball cap is tossed to the ground. Then I feel the soft wetness of Bull's tongue caress my cheek, chasing my tear to claim it as his own. He's addicted to my pain, and I'm about to find out just how much.

"Get in the back."

"Excuse me?" I question, my eyes snapping open.

"I said…get…in…the…back." His pause between each word turns my sadness into rage.

"I know the company you've been keeping lately may need you to speak to them like a child, but try it on me, and you won't like the consequences."

"Ooh," he mocks, pretending to tremble in fear.

However, there is no pretending necessary when I swiftly knee him in the balls.

His eyes widen, and he buckles to the side, giving me ample opportunity to shove him aside and open the door. Storytime is over. I was stupid to think there was a different story than what Christopher told me.

I jump into the truck and quickly lock the door. Frantically patting myself down, I groan, remembering I don't have the keys. I dropped them, thanks to being tackled by a brick shithouse.

"No!" I slam my palms against the steering wheel.

There is a light knock on my window.

Groaning, I slowly turn my cheek to look at Bull, who's outside my window with my keys looped around his extended finger. "You really shouldn't have done that," he says, still bent in half as he catches his breath.

His warning is a delicious lick over every inch of my body.

"And what are you going to do about it?" I challenge with an arched brow.

It's the ultimate stare off, like a duel at high noon. Who is going to reach for their gun first?

He lunges for the door, unlocking it with the key, but I slam down the lock before he can open it. He grins, his longer canines glistening under the full moon.

My breaths are labored as I lock eyes with him, reading his every move. He's fast, but I'm faster, thanks to the adrenaline running through my body.

"You won't be getting far without your keys. So if you want them, come and get them." He steps back, holding my keys prisoner in his hand. He makes it clear he's not budging.

He's right. I can't sit in here all night because I'm already late for work by a half an hour. But if I go out there, I don't know what he'll do. But as my pulse reaches an unhealthy pinnacle, I realize…I don't know what *I'll* do.

What I do know is that I'm not a coward. They're my keys, and I want them back.

Calling his bluff, I lift the lock and open the door. I'm expecting Bull to charge me, but he doesn't. He stands feet away, dangling my keys from his finger. With fire and ice burning through me, I walk toward him, never taking my eyes off him as I reach for my keys.

He looks…proud of me. I don't know why. I don't know anything anymore.

Snatching them from him, I tamp down my nerves. "Asshole," I utter, curling my lip in anger.

"Bitch," he counters with a smirk.

Something happens, something I can't control. It's happened from the first moment I met him, but now, now that I know what he tastes like, I want more.

I don't know who lunges for who first, but it's a fight for domination as his warm lips slam over mine. The taste of him instantly has me melting, moaning and giving in to temptation. I thread my fingers through his long hair and yank hard.

He growls into my mouth, allowing me to manhandle him because he isn't gentle. He bites my bottom lip, sucking the sting away. He locks a hand around the back of my neck, angling my face as he dominates my mouth with his.

When his tongue flicks against mine, memories surface of when I felt the same action, but he was between my thighs. His taste, his smell, the feel of his hot, hard chest pressed to mine are almost too much. I shouldn't want this, but I do.

I want him.

He walks me backward, lips still devouring mine as I wrap my arms around his neck. God knows I shouldn't, but I feel safe in his arms. My back thumps against the truck as Bull opens the door. He reaches around my shoulder, unlocking the back.

The moment it's unlocked, he pries open the door and shoves me into the back seat. Our lips are still locked, kissing, biting, sucking, but when Bull coaxes me to lie down, I know kissing won't be enough. He closes the door, sealing us in.

He is on top of me, his palms pressed to my cheeks as he eats me alive. I know this is wrong, but I surrender when he breaks our kiss and trails kisses over my chin and down my throat. I tip my head backward, granting him full access because I want to feel him all over me.

His fingers burn the sliver of flesh exposed above my jeans when they glide back and forth, back and forth. It's tight back here, but I open my legs, begging him to give me what I want, what we both want. I can feel his hard-on pressing into me.

When he unsnaps the button on my jeans, I whimper in relief. As he hovers over me, we lock eyes when he slides his hand into my pants and begins stroking me over my underwear. I'm wet, and he can feel it, but I don't care.

He rubs circles over me, but it's not what I want. "Bull," I cry in a silent plea for him to touch me in the flesh.

He merely chuckles in response.

Frustrated, I coax him to pay attention to my clit by lifting my hips, but he skates around it. "Tell me you hate me," he hoarsely commands, shocking me. But I have no issues delivering on his order.

"I…hate you," I whimper when he increases the tempo of his fingers.

"Tell me what a fucking bastard I am for liking this so much."

"You're a…oh, god," I cry, bowing my back when he pinches my clit. "You're a fucking bastard."

"Good girl." My responses please him, and he rewards me by slipping his fingers into my underwear. He dips two fingers into me, while rubbing this thumb over my aching clit.

"Tell me this is a bad idea, and you want me to stop."

But I can't. I don't want him to stop. So I compromise. "This is a bad idea," I groan, wrapping my fingers around his wrist and encouraging him to finger me harder, deeper.

Rolling my hips, I hear him curse under his breath as I come apart on his hand. "And you want me to stop?" he encourages, punishing me with a relentless speed as he thrusts his fingers in and out of me.

I can't speak. What he's doing to my body…to my heart robs me of anything but this. "Please," I cry, undulating with every stroke he delivers.

"Say it!" he exclaims, pulling out of me.

"No!" I shriek, missing his touch, but also refusing to say

something I don't mean.

"Why not?" He grips my chin with the fingers that were inside me, forcing me to look at him.

"Because I don't want you to!" I scream, realizing what I said a little too late.

Bull blinks, confused by my confession, but so am I.

We're both breathless, not sure of what comes next. My body is aching, and I hate that it aches for him. My lower lip trembles because even though I hate Bull, I hate myself more.

I'm about to push him off me, embarrassed and ashamed, but what he says, it seals our fate forever. "Tell me you want me."

Forgive me, Lachlan.

Slowly rising up on my elbows, I bring my shaky lips to his and whisper, "I want you."

A moan spills from him, and then it's a flurry of hands and a tangle of limbs. I yank down his suspenders, desperate to feel his chest against mine. He almost shreds the shirt in half as he yanks off the buttons. I split it open, groaning when I run my hands over his warm, muscled chest.

When my fingers brush over the silver barbells in both his nipples, he grunts low in his throat. He doesn't give me time to appreciate his new piercings because he's tearing at my sweater, desperate to get it off. Lifting the hem, I tug it over my head, and when my blue silk bra is visible, Bull lifts the cups and bends forward, suckling my breasts.

I arch my back, unable to control my moans. He twirls his tongue around my nipples, before biting them softly. This is different. When we were together in the past, he never touched and played like this. Our sex was hot, but it was a rush for the finish line.

But now, he seems to savor me, and I like it.

As he's sucking and tonguing my breasts and nipples, I reach down and unsnap the button on his jeans. When I lower his zipper and slip my hand into the waistband of his boxers, a stunned gasp escapes me.

He is hot and hard in my hand, but there is something I haven't felt before. Running my finger over the tip of his cock, I feel a metal barbell. It seems his nipples aren't the only things he got pierced.

I don't know what I'm doing, seeing as I've never stroked a pierced cock before, but the moans tumbling from Bull hint I'm doing something right. As I'm stroking his shaft, he yanks down my jeans. I kick them off, and when my legs are free, I spread them, begging him to settle between them.

He pulls down his pants halfway and gently shifts out of my hand. Before I can protest, he lines himself up with my entrance and teases me with the tip of his cock. The sharp sting of the piercing has me biting down on my lip in excitement.

I don't have any protection, and neither does he. This is so irresponsible and wrong, but what's one more sin when I've already committed a hundred others. Wrapping a hand around the back of his neck, I draw us nose to nose and arch my back.

He doesn't need an invitation. He slides into me, inch by glorious inch. My mouth parts at the sharp intrusion because Bull is well-endowed. But the piercing only adds to the feeling of being consumed whole.

When he's buried to the hilt, he stops, allowing me to catch my breath, but it's only a second-long reprieve because when I inhale, he commences moving. He takes my mouth with his, and his tongue thrusts in rhythm with his body.

I can't get enough of him; I bend to his touches, to his strokes, as he sinks into me over and over. His chest presses to mine, and the thrashing of his heart races with mine. I try not to think about how this is the first time of us being united this way. Missionary might be considered boring, but being this way with him, with him over me, in me, dominating my mind and my body is absolutely perfect.

His fingers wrap around my waist, anchoring me to him as he picks up the pace. Our bodies are slick with sweat, and the noises spilling from us just lead me further and further to my doom. I don't remember sex feeling this good, but with Bull, we fit when we shouldn't. We always have.

But I can dwell on my self-hate later because right now, all I can focus on is coming.

Wrapping my leg around his waist, I open myself up to Bull, begging him to go harder, faster, deeper. And he does. He pumps his hips, sinking in so deep, I scream out in pleasure and pain. The line is blurred, but I don't care.

His hair flicks forward, shielding his eyes, so I reach up and brush it off his face. He lets me, which again, I don't fail to see the significance of. Cupping his cheek, I meet him thrust for thrust, savoring the way he handles my body with wicked skill.

He'll leave bruises where he's gripping my waist and fucking me with a punishing tempo. I arch my hips as he begins to rub over my clit with his fingers. He is all over me, and a blistering wave suddenly threatens to drag me under.

"Oh, god," I cry, threading my fingers through his hair, needing something to grasp.

His piercing keeps skimming over me in the most delicious way, and when he pulls out, rubbing it along my inflamed clit, I shudder, my orgasm swimming so close, I can taste it.

"Give me your mouth," he orders, and I rear up, desperate to have his lips on mine.

He kisses and fucks the shit out of me, but beneath the hunger, I can taste what this is—and we're royally fucked. We should hate one another, and we do, just not enough to keep away. After everything we learned about the other, we just want the other more.

My body, my mind, and my heart are lost to him, and I don't know if they'll ever be found.

"You're my favorite flavor…Tiger," he pants against my lips.

His voice, coupled with his words, are too much. Is he trying to tell me that Cherry isn't a flavor he enjoys or has ever enjoyed? And Tiger, how I've longed to hear him call me that.

"What flavor am I?" I gasp, as my body slams into his.

"Every," he replies, licking the seam of my mouth.

"Every what?" I question, unable to speak in full sentences.

"Every flavor," he clarifies, pulling out of me before slamming back in.

The sentiment touches me in ways it shouldn't, and when he pushes his thumb against my aching clit, then takes my nipple into his mouth, it's too much. My orgasm tackles me so hard, I scream, coming like I've never come before.

Bull continues sinking into me, and only when I stop screaming, does he pull out and come on my heaving chest. Then he collapses on top of me, and our labored breaths are an echo of each other's.

I feel so warm, so full, but when I open my eyes and realize what I've done, my high fades, and the feelings of shame and disgust overcome me. I sought Bull out before I went to visit the grave of the father of my child. Christopher told me where Lachlan was buried, but I haven't been able to go. I was waiting for the right time.

Yet here I am, in the arms of the man who killed him.

"Get out," I whisper, pushing him off me. I suddenly can't breathe.

He doesn't protest. He simply gets dressed, opens the door, and leaves me to my tears.

CHAPTER FOUR

Bull

I'm not in a good headspace—all I can taste are her bubblegum kisses and the shame she felt when she kicked me out of her truck. I should have been stronger, but saying no to her is like denying myself the air to breathe.

But tonight, I can't afford any distractions. I'm meeting with Stevie's supplier, bringing me one step closer to ending this freak show once and for all.

"How's the club?" Stevie asks casually, sipping his scotch from the back of the limo we ride in as some random woman is on her knees between his legs.

"Good. It's only been a few days, and we can't keep the creeps away," I reply, scoping out my surroundings through the window. So much has changed since I've been inside. I'm trying to make a mental note of where we are.

Stevie snickers. "Those creeps are our meal ticket. Good job, Tommy. Looks like I'll be paying Lotus a visit after all."

Nodding, I know sooner rather than later that I'm going to have to come up with a plan to ensure Lotus's safety. My thoughts at the moment are to tell Lotus when I go over her books. But for that to happen, Stevie will have to start depositing money into the club account. Once it's in there, it'll be dirty money. But that would mean things would have gotten way too far. I need this to be as smooth as possible, but it's not looking probable.

"It's going to give me great satisfaction to go up against that asshole, Jaws. We can't fail."

His comment snaps me from my thoughts. "What's your beef with him?" I ask nonchalantly, refusing to look at the blonde head bobbing between his splayed thighs.

Stevie and Jaws are about the same age. They also are in competition with everything it seems. What Stevie has, Jaws wants, and vice versa. They're acting like two brothers, fighting over the same...girl.

It can't be that simple, can it? Especially when he is getting his dick sucked by someone who I'm guessing isn't his beloved.

"Let's just say even though I want to put a bullet between his eyes, we seem to share the same taste in everything— power, money, and women."

Bingo.

"But luckily for me, women, or rather a *woman*, saw who the better contender was." The woman pauses, coming up for air, but Stevie pushes her head back down.

That doesn't give me much, but it's a lead. Their feud is all because of a woman? Could it be that Jaws cares for someone other than himself?

That's a question for another time because when the driver parks the limo in some deserted neighborhood, it's evident we've reached our destination.

I leave Stevie to his blowjob, while I quickly suit up and wait by the car. My shoulder holster carries my guns. I also have one secured to my ankle. Before I shot Hero, I never had any use for guns. But now, I don't have a choice. And judging by the holes in the beer bottles I've used for target practice, my aim is still perfect.

I never wanted this life, but it follows, no matter which path I take. It all started the night I met Jaws. Maybe this was my destiny after all? Whatever it is, I need to stay on my A-game because to survive this, I need to outsmart them all.

Jaws has leverage over me, and now, I just may have some over him.

"Now, remember what I told you. Stay in the background. We do the deal, and then we split. No small talk. That's how he rolls," Stevie instructs as he opens the door. Thankfully, his dick is tucked back in his pants.

Suits me just fine.

The woman looks at me sheepishly, wiping her lipstick-smeared lips, before disappearing down the dark street.

Stevie has a black duffel thrown over his shoulder. We walk toward the derelict brick building in front of us. Half the roof is missing, and all the windows are smashed out. As far as shady ass meetup points, this one ticks all the boxes.

I scan my surroundings, ensuring we're still alone. "Round back," Stevie orders, as I hear him strike a match and light a cigar.

There is no fence, so we continue strolling like we belong here and enter through the open door at the back of the building. Some light streams through, hinting whoever we're meeting is already here.

Stevie walks in front of me, casually smoking his cigar. He is clearly comfortable around his contact, which has me guessing that even if I were to give Jaws the name, the contact may not be willing to deal with him, if that's what Jaws is proposing.

This "business" is filled with paranoid psychopaths. Jaws should know that. And when we turn the corner and I see a row of six scary-looking dudes, this just confirms my claim.

Unlike me, they've made no attempts to conceal their weapons, as they wear their holsters on top of their white T-shirts. They're in baggy jeans and white sneakers, but I don't let their plain attire fool me. These guys are hard core and would have no issues killing their grandmother if she stood in their way.

The black Hummer parked behind the line of men has its headlights on, providing the light I need to see a man step from the car and walk toward us. The men part, but they flank him close. He's the boss. He's Stevie's supplier.

"Amigo, nice to see you." The man appears to be in his early forties, dressed in a blue checkered shirt and navy cargos. He looks harmless enough, but looks are deceiving.

The deep scar running from the top of his eyebrow down his cheek proves it.

"You, too, José." They shake hands while I stand behind, watching and learning.

"How are the kids? Did your daughter get the birthday gift I sent her?"

José nods with a smile. "She did. Tiffany for a nine-year-old? You've set the bar high for my wife and me."

They chuckle like old friends catching up and not like ones about to exchange a briefcase full of cash for a briefcase full of bricks.

José's men watch me closely, though we're no threat. We're outnumbered, which is the message Stevie wants to convey. We're here for business, not trouble. But when one of them whispers to their friend as he eyes me, it seems it can't be one or the other.

José is mid-conversation but suddenly stops. The room falls dead quiet. "What's so important you have to interrupt my conversation, Jesús?"

The man in question and his friend lower their eyes guiltily. I can't help but compare their response to a dog being reprimanded by its owner. I suppose it's not any different.

"I asked you a question," José says calmly, but none of us are fooled. Jesús is about to get his ass nailed to the cross.

He clears his throat before replying in Spanish. I stand firm with my arms folded and legs spread. But I know they're speaking about me. Stevie doesn't move an inch. Once Jesús finishes speaking, José glances over Stevie's shoulder, looking at me.

"Where's your other man?"

Kudos to Stevie for sounding so nonchalant when he replies, "He couldn't handle the job. Split with his tail between his legs."

That's not entirely a lie.

"My boy tells me your new muscle is known to them. He's famous," he adds mockingly.

He watches me closely, looking for any flaws in my design. There are none. I'm fucking watertight.

"Are you famous?" José asks me, jutting out his chin.

"That all depends on who you ask," I reply flatly, never breaking eye contact with him.

This is a test. *Do I have the balls to stand up to the head honcho?* Of course, I fucking do.

José deadpans me, weighing up my response. The next few seconds determine the course of everything.

Three.

Two.

One.

His lips twitch before he breaks out into loud, uncontrollable laughter. His minions suddenly join him in nervous laughter, unsure what's going on. Me. I stand solid, not interested in looking like a trained circus monkey.

"You're *Colmillo*, according to Jesús." I have no idea what that means. "Fang," José clarifies, still laughing. "The name is fitting. He says you tear any man apart under that mask you wear."

I don't bother asking why I have a nickname. I have enough. My disinterest seems to charm José. "He fights for you, Stevie?"

Stevie nods while the mystery of my name is solved. Jesús has seen me fight. I've been careful, but evidently, not careful enough.

"Yes, he does. The best damn one I've seen in quite some time. No matter who wants to fight him, he never loses." Which is why I still serve a purpose to Stevie. This isn't a touchy-feely Oprah moment. I'm here because I'm of use to Stevie. And he's of use to me—he just doesn't know how.

José nods, never taking his eyes off me. "What demons you got locked inside of you, amigo, for you to be so angry?"

"Who says I'm angry?" I refute coolly. "Maybe I just like to make people bleed."

I'm not looking for approval, but I get it, nonetheless. "I like him, Stevie. Keep him around. Maybe I will come watch the infamous *Colmillo*?" he mocks, but he makes it clear I'll be seeing him around.

"Mi casa es su casa," Stevie says graciously.

"And this is why we do business. Luis." José snaps his fingers, hinting playtime is over.

Luis walks over to the Hummer and reaches inside. The air is thick because this part of the transaction is when everyone is paranoid and no one is friends. He rolls a large black suitcase toward José.

"The usual," he says, drumming his fingers against the handle of the suitcase. "You need anything else before we meet again, let me know. The holidays always bring out the best in people."

He's sarcastically referring to Thanksgiving and

Christmas, which are soon approaching.

Stevie doesn't drag out the inevitable and walks over to him, passing Luis the duffel full of cash. José passes him the suitcase, and just like that, thousands of lives are ruined. Stevie shakes José's hand, and the deal is done.

Luis is about to toss the duffel into the Hummer, but José stops him. He unzips the bag and digs inside for a stack of bills. Stevie appears surprised, but when he tosses the stack my way, and I catch it, that surprise turns to triumph.

"For you, *Colmillo*." I don't question it. I simply nod and place the stack of hundreds into my pocket.

José twirls his finger, indicating we're done. The men climb into the Hummer, while José watches me with a smile I know all too well—I'm no longer invisible to him. That money wasn't free. One day, he'll come to collect.

Let's hope that day never comes.

I lead the way with Stevie in hot pursuit. The cool air is exactly what I need to get my head around the fact Stevie's supplier seems to be the Mexican drug cartel. It couldn't be some deadbeat white supremacist asshole. No, it had to be the fucking cartel.

This was supposed to be simple, but every corner I turn, I'm confronted with a fucking brick wall. I'm caught in a feud I wanted no part of. I suppose this is my karma for killing Kong.

The driver opens our door as we make our way toward the limo. Stevie enters while I wait by the hood, ensuring we're not being followed. After I verify it's clear, I jump in, watching with interest as Stevie unlocks a compartment under the liquor shelf.

He places the suitcase inside and arranges the shelving back into position. It's that easy. Out of sight, out of mind.

"José likes you," Stevie says, leaning back against the leather seat and casually crossing an ankle over his knee. "He doesn't like anyone."

"Lucky me," I reply, not interested in being anyone's pet.

Stevie reaches for the crystal decanter and pours two glasses of scotch. He passes me one. I accept. "He is someone you want in your corner. Trust me."

"I don't need anyone in my corner," I state, tossing back my drink.

"I can see that," he says with pride, running his finger over the rim of the glass. "If you didn't have to work tonight, I would show you the books. Next time."

He's comfortable enough to bring me into his inner circle. Shame on him.

"The next fight is scheduled in Chicago. You're up against Tiny." His unoriginal name has me guessing he's anything but.

The fighting syndicate has helped me gain Stevie's trust. It has also allowed me to make a lot of cash and fast. The money Lotus pays me is peanuts compared to what I earn fighting.

I could find another place to crash, but Hudson's has become my home. Venus minds her own business. She doesn't question the hours I keep, or when I come back covered in blood.

All of this almost "fell" into my lap. One may say it was fate. But I still don't know what I'm fated for.

"You need me for anything else this week?" I ask, as I

don't like surprises.

"Not at the moment. Dudley and Vincent are bending over backward for me after their fuckup."

Their fuckup was my gain because I gained an ally. The reason I knew Tiger was at The Pink Oyster was because Paul gave me the heads-up. He's proven to be very good at his job. He watches her and tells me of her comings and goings. He also has been keeping an eye on Scrooge.

And for his troubles, I've put him up at Hudson's. He has a roof over his head and doesn't have to worry about doing disgusting things to sick fucks for a hot meal.

But Stevie doesn't know this. He thinks Paul is just another unfortunate fool who crossed him and paid with this life.

"Got time for a drink?" Stevie asks, interrupting my thoughts.

I'd rather drink gasoline and then set myself on fire. "No. I have to feed my cat."

When Stevie breaks into laughter, I think he believes it's code for something.

It's not.

Once Stevie dropped me off at the bogus location that's supposed to be my house, I called Paul to come pick me up. Tiger was at Avery's before heading to Cleveland to teach. He mentioned she appeared occupied because she ran some red lights and stop signs.

When we got to Hudson's, he grabbed something to eat before heading to Blue Bloods. The fact she was still dancing there pissed me off beyond words. Her asshole brother watches her night after night, seeing the way she works her ass off to help better the lives of others.

He has the money to help her out so she doesn't have to dance, but he chooses not to give her any. Surely, she can see something's wrong with that picture. She's stripping at the club her brother owns; the same brother who watches her.

Paul was able to get in with his fake ID, so he's recounted the disgusting details. From the whispers among the dancers, Jaws never showed his face until Tiger started dancing. He is one sick asshole who needs to be put down.

But until that happens, Tiger is trapped. Her guilty conscience won't let her leave. She thinks she owes her brother something for hurting him by sleeping with his best friend. If she only knew the real story, a story that I can't tell her, but I can help her in another way.

José threw two thousand dollars my way like it was nothing but pocket change. And to him, it is. But to Tiger, it's her ticket out of hell. I've given that money to Paul with strict instructions—no lap dances and no touching. When Tiger dances, he's to ensure she gets it all.

She won't accept money from me, but if it's "earned," then she's none the wiser where it came from.

Parking my truck at The Pink Oyster, I notice a flashy car that sticks out like a sore thumb. Keeping my poker face in check, I casually walk through the parking lot. Peering inside, I find it spotless but have no clue who it belongs to. When I enter the club, however, the mystery is solved.

I knew sooner or later she'd come knocking. I was just hoping it would be later.

Franca Brown sits at the bar, watching one of the newest recruits work her magic on stage. She sips a beer, appearing to like what she sees. That changes, however, when I pull up a stool next to her. Lotus is pouring drinks, but the concerned look on her face gives her thoughts away.

"'Of all the gin joints, in all the towns, in all the world, she walks into mine,'" I say, reciting *Casablanca*.

Franca doesn't appreciate my sarcasm.

She turns over her shoulder. "I thought you worked here?"

"I do," I reply, swiveling on the stool and leaning my back against the bar.

"You're late." She makes a point to look down at her watch. "Being tardy will get you fired, and that won't look good on your report."

With a cocky smirk, I shrug. "Lucky for me, you're not my boss." On cue, Lotus leans over my shoulder and passes me a bottle of water. "Thanks, *boss*," I sarcastically quip.

Franca's eyes narrow. It's good to know I get under her skin.

"Have you got anything to tell me?" she shouts, in order to be heard over the music.

Taking a sip of water, I pretend to mull over her question. "I got a new pair of kicks. *And* I finally caught up on *Gossip Girl*. Can you believe Dan was the culprit that whole time?" Placing the bottle between my thighs, I slap my hands to my cheeks, with my mouth open wide, faking shock.

"Stop being such a smart-ass," she snarls, slapping my wrist. I remove my hands, unable to hide my grin. "I know you're caught up in something."

"Prove it," I counter smartly.

"Oh, I intend to. This fighting syndicate is bound to make a mistake, and when they do, I'll be there, waiting."

"Why do you have a hard-on for this?" I ask, genuinely interested.

"Because there is a lot more going on than just fighting." Franca is close because she's a good cop. She clearly has pieces of the puzzle but doesn't know the full picture. Yet.

I respect her, and I think deep down, the feeling is mutual. She's smart, and it won't be long until she figures it out. And when she does, I cannot afford any blowback.

"If you hear anything, you know where to find me. Until then, you can bet your ass I will be paying very close attention to every single thing you do." She leans in close. It's a threat. Who knows, maybe she already has what she needs and is just biding her time.

This just means I need to move things along.

Sunny finishes her set, and I dig into my pocket for a hundred. Placing it into the top pocket of Franca's shirt, I wink while she doesn't waver. "Sunny will be in the VIP rooms. It's on me."

Her cheeks pale before they burn a blistering red. It seems Franca has secrets of her own. But like I care. She could identify as a unicorn, and it wouldn't interest me in the slightest. I have enough issues of my own to deal with.

She digs the bill out of her pocket and slams it onto

the bar, before pushing through the crowd. I wave goodbye to her back. I really shouldn't push her, but I'm done being everyone's snitch.

"I take it that was your PO?" Lotus asks, slipping a real drink over my shoulder.

Accepting the beer, I raise it in thanks. "The one and only."

"What did she want?"

"To make sure I'm being a good boy," I reply, tossing back the Budweiser.

"And are you?"

The suspicion in her voice has me pausing. Is she onto me? However, when I see who just entered the bar, I realize why she'd ask me that.

Finishing my beer, I spin on my stool and give her a strained smile. "Thanks for the beer. Keep the change," I say, leaving the hundred-dollar bill on the bar.

"Bull—"

But I don't stick around for her to tell me what a bad idea this is. I already know because a few feet away stand José, Jesús, and Luis.

With a casual stride, I walk toward them and instantly extend my hand to José. "Nice to see you again." We shake firmly.

"I hope you don't mind us dropping by like this." Even if I did mind, it's not like I have a choice in the matter.

"It's filled with women and booze; how can you stay away?" I quip, refusing to show my curiosity as to why they're here.

"Can we talk someplace a little more…private?"

I gesture with my head for them to follow me.

The crowd parts when they see us coming. They must be able to read the shitstorm brewing. No one is manning the VIP rooms, seeing as that's my job, and having all these fucking visitors drop in to see me means I won't be getting to my job anytime soon.

The door to the room Cherry usually dances in swings open, and out strolls a jock, happier than a pig in shit. Cherry follows, but when she sees me, she pauses, eyes wide, and like the predator that José is, he smells her fear.

"Hello, *hermosa*. Where're you going?" The jock's high soon fades, and he's doing a brisk sprint for the exit.

Without thought, I grip the crease of Cherry's elbow and draw her into my side. I promised to protect her from assholes like José, and I keep my promises.

"She's up on stage next. Go get ready." I shoo her away, not giving her a chance to get a word in edgewise.

She scurries off, even though her set isn't until later.

Standing by the door, I gesture for José and his lapdogs to enter. They do, appearing saddened there isn't any eye candy to feast on. Once I close the door, I stand in front of it, arms folded, waiting for José to shed some light on why he's here.

"You're a man of few words. I like that. So I will cut to the chase. I want you to throw your next fight."

Well, I did not see that coming.

"Why would I do that?" I ask, arching a brow.

"Stevie bets a lot of money on you winning. You lose… that money is mine," José calmly explains. "It's just business. Nothing personal."

He's full of shit.

"It'll be personal for me when Stevie asks why the fuck I dropped the ball," I reply bluntly.

Jesús takes a step forward, but José grips his arm, stopping him. "We're all friends here," he says, indicating no blood is to be spilled—yet. "What do you say?"

He waits for me to answer as if I have a choice. If I don't do this, then things will end badly for me.

"Of course, you won't go without. You'll get a cut of what I make." Suddenly, I'm struck with an idea.

"I'm not interested in money. But I do want something else."

José's lips twitch. Every man has a weakness, and he's about to find out mine.

"There is someone I need access to. You get him alone for me, and I'll do what you want."

"Who is this person?"

Staring him dead in the eyes, I reply, "Benjamin Solomon."

José whistles. "You don't fuck around, amigo." His comment confirms he knows just who Scrooge is. But I suppose he is known to most, seeing as he's a millionaire with an infamous reputation.

"You do this for me, and we've got a deal." The adrenaline courses through me, but I contain my enthusiasm. I realize what this means. By bending to José's request, I will be at his mercy as he'll have leverage. But it's a risk I'm willing to take.

After a pregnant pause, he nods. "I'll see what I can do." That's as good as a yes because he's the Mexican fucking cartel.

"Once it's organized, let me know, and I'll take care of the rest," I say, not needing to spell it out.

"You go up against him, and you'll have an army against you." José seems amused but also curious about my request to get Scrooge alone.

"Only if I get caught."

"*Colmillo* doesn't get caught," Jesús says with a grin. My personal cheerleader knows about the damage I can inflict.

José is impressed as he places his hands into his pockets. "I don't know what you did to get Stevie to trust you so quickly, but if you ever tire of him, you have my number. I could use a man like you on my side."

On cue, Luis offers me a white business card. When I read what's written on the front, I can't stop my sarcastic smirk.

José Velez—used car salesman.

Placing the card into my top pocket, I nod in gratitude.

"It goes without saying, Stevie cannot know of our little arrangement."

"Of course," I reply. Even though I know José will have no issues blackmailing me if I don't cooperate the next time he comes knocking. This isn't a one-time deal. There is no such thing with the cartel.

"I'll be in touch then." José extends his hand, and I shake it, sealing our deal.

With our business transaction complete, I step aside, allowing Luis to open the door. Luis and Jesús exit, but José stops in front of me. "I don't know what happened to you, but the demons inside you, they'll never go away. They're a part of you. Don't try to beat them. They're what distinguishes you from the rest."

With that food for thought, he leaves me alone, and I wonder what the hell I just agreed to. Deeper and deeper, I'm falling down the rabbit hole, but it seems fitting—because we're all mad here.

CHAPTER FIVE

Lily

"I'm sorry, Ms. Hope. I wish I had better news, but your loan has been denied. You simply will not have enough income to make the minimum monthly repayments on what you want to borrow from the bank."

"I have enough money for a down payment," I argue, but Jeffrey Taylor, the asshole bank manager, shakes his head.

"You do, but with no savings history, we cannot lend to you. We don't know where that large sum of cash came from. If you wait a few months and improve your credit—"

I've heard it all before. This is the third bank that has denied my loan.

"I don't have a few months," I sharply state, angrily gathering my paperwork from his desk. "It's not like I want to buy a fucking island!"

Jeffrey pushes his oversized silver glasses up the bridge of his nose. "I'm truly sorry, Ms. Hope."

Yeah, he looks real sorry.

Standing abruptly, I shove the papers into my bag, overcome with feelings of frustration and failure.

"If you reapply in—"

Clenching the papers in my hand, I inhale, praying for strength. "So help me god, if you say in a few months again, I will strangle you with the cord of your phone!"

Jeffrey shuffles in his leather chair, looking over my shoulder to no doubt alert security. But I'm leaving. I'm afraid of what I'll do if I don't.

Yanking open the door, I push aside the pathetic guard and ignore the stares of the customers. They can stare all they want. They mean nothing to me.

Shoving open the glass front door, I trudge through the snow to my truck, almost tearing the driver's door from its hinges. Once I'm inside, I toss my bag to the floor and give in to the overwhelming urge to scream. I slam my palms against the steering wheel, hollering like a crazy person.

I feel remotely better, but when the screams die, I'm faced with the truth. I am screwed.

Deep down, I know buying the ballet studio won't make a difference to Avery's health. She's growing weaker and weaker each day. But when she takes her last breath, I want her to know her studio, her pride and joy won't be forgotten. *She* won't be forgotten. It'll live on even when she won't.

I want to do this for her because I know how much it

means to her. But I can't, thanks to the Jeffrey Taylors of this world.

I've saved a lot of money and fast, thanks to the generous tips of a baby-faced stranger I've dubbed George. Each time he comes in, he throws down at least a couple thousand dollars. There is no way he is twenty-one, but since he has become quite the generous tipper, the bouncers turn a blind eye.

But it doesn't matter. I could have saved triple what I have, and I still wouldn't be an ideal lending candidate. My fingers itch because I know someone who is.

I've tried to avoid doing this, but now, I'm desperate. Reaching for my cell, I dial my brother.

"Hey," he answers happily. "How's your day?"

I didn't tell him where I was going today because I didn't want to have to deal with the fact that my brother is a selfish asshole. But now, I don't have a choice.

"Terrible. My loan got denied." Silence, so I continue. "I have enough money for a down payment, but without a savings history, I may as well have nothing."

"Lillian—"

But I cut him off. "I'll give you what I have, and I promise, I'm good for the rest. The banks won't say no to you. The loan would be in your name, but I'd handle everything. I just need—"

But it doesn't matter what I need because Christopher won't help me.

"I'm sorry, but I can't."

"Why not?" I question, not checking my anger at the door. "Why can't you? You're the one who told Jordy your money is ours, right?"

"It's complicated," he replies, which is code word for I'm a self-centered bastard who doesn't give a damn.

"Uncomplicate it then," I bite back. "I wouldn't ask if I wasn't desperate. Please, Christopher. Avery is dying."

"Buying the studio won't change that," he says gently, but all he does is piss me off further.

"You don't think I know that?" I cry, sniffing back tears of anger. "Avery was there for me when Mom wasn't. This is the least I can do for her. How can you be so heartless?"

"In case you've forgotten, she wasn't the only one who was there for you," he states, appearing wounded by my comment. "Stop being such a spoiled brat."

"Excuse me?" I spit, utterly offended. "How am I being a spoiled brat? I want to give a sick woman, who is the only mother I know, her last dying wish, but I can't because I don't have enough zeroes in my bank account! Maybe if you hadn't run off, leaving me to fend for myself at sixteen years old, I wouldn't have to ask you to help me now!"

This isn't his fault. It's his prerogative to say no. But what he's giving me right now are excuses, and I can't help but compare this selfishness to when he left. This argument has been a long time coming. I haven't told him what his leaving did to me. I thought I was okay with it, but I'm not.

"Well, maybe if you didn't fuck my best friend and weren't stupid enough to fall pregnant, then I wouldn't have left!"

And there it is. The truth. It's been the big, fat elephant in the room that we've both tread lightly around. But now, the gloves are off.

"I didn't just *fuck* him," I spit, refusing to stand by and allow him to refer to what Lachlan and I had so crudely. "I loved him. And he loved me."

Christopher's mocking snicker angers me further. "You believe whatever you have to, to sleep better at night."

"He was going to propose to me!" The moment the words tumble free, I slap a hand over my mouth. But it's too late.

"*What?*"

"Forget I said anything." I try to backtrack, but it's no use. I picked this fight, and now I have to deal with the repercussions.

"How do you know that?"

My silence fills in the blanks. He knows Bull told me. Although he's never asked me what my relationship with Bull is, he knows. He saw us together. He heard him call me Tiger.

"Your track record with men is reflective of our mother," he slurs, hurting me beyond words. "The apple doesn't fall far from the tree it seems."

Hot, angry tears stream down my cheeks. "Go to hell." I end the call, throwing my cell onto the passenger seat and cradling my face in my palms.

Ugly words were exchanged, but they needed to be. It's time we stopped playing happy family because we're not. Christopher now knows I think he's a selfish asshole. While he's made it clear he thinks I'm a whore.

Sniffing back my tears, I realize I can't go to the only person I want to see. The other night with Bull was a mistake. I shouldn't have slept with him, no matter how good it felt. Not just physically, but emotionally as well.

Never in my life have I felt so alone, which is ironic. In my head, I thought Christopher coming back would be the miracle cure, but it hasn't been. All it's done is highlight the damage to our relationship. I don't know if we'll ever be able to go back to what we had.

Running a hand down my face to wipe away my tears, I take a deep breath and start the truck. I'll drop by the deli near Avery's apartment on my way and pick up some chicken soup. Jordy is staying late at school for basketball practice, so I can spend some quality time with Avery.

Putting the truck into drive, I merge onto the highway and make my way to Cleveland. The drive gives me time to think, and as usual, my thoughts drift to Bull.

The other night was different. Our passion has always had a sense of urgency to it, but underneath it, I felt his hunger, and his desire for me ran deeper than just a casual hookup.

The night everything turned to shit, he thanked me for making him feel, which was apparently a big thing for him. Since Damian's death, it seems he has been shut off to the world. But for someone who claims he doesn't feel, that's all he's shown me since we met.

Sighing, I know I will have to face the inevitable sooner or later and visit Lachlan's grave. Before I take Jordy, I want to be able to go there without this heavy feeling pushing down on my chest. I've told him about his father, about what a kind, caring man he was, but I've left out the details of how he passed away.

I don't want Jordy focusing on that one negative aspect when there are a thousand other positive ones to embrace.

Before Bull entered my life, things were relatively simple. But now, everything's a clusterfuck. However, with the chaos has come the truth. I just need to learn how to accept this gigantic curveball that's been hurled my way.

I drive the rest of the way with the radio turned up, hoping to drown out the thoughts that won't go away.

Once I pick up the chicken soup, I park my truck in front of Avery's building. It's snowing, so I put on my hood and make a mad dash for the front door. It's warm inside the elevator, and everything inside me begins to thaw.

It's a nice feeling, seeing as the past few weeks, I've been stuck on cold. I make my way to Avery's apartment with her keys in hand. I'm looking forward to spending some time with her. Unlocking her door, I hear the gentle hum of the TV in her room.

Softly closing the door, I tiptoe down the hallway, not wanting to make any noise in case Avery is asleep. Carrying the chicken soup, I gently push open the door and peek around the doorjamb. Avery's tiny frame is snuggled under the blankets.

Deciding to let her sleep, I creep into her bedroom and turn off the TV. The glass of water I left by her bed yesterday is still there, untouched. Walking toward her bedside table, I reach for the glass, intent on refilling it with some fresh water.

However, when I glance over at her still form, a heaviness settles over me, and I freeze. I watch for the gentle rustle of blankets, in sync with her breathing, but there aren't any, and that's because she isn't breathing.

"Avery?" I whisper, my voice cracking.

Silence.

I know what I'm seeing, but I can't…I won't accept it. How can I?

With hesitant fingers, I slowly peel back the blanket from Avery's form. *She's just sleeping*, I reason with myself, but her gray complexion hints otherwise. The life that animated the only person who loved me unconditionally is gone because she…is gone.

Avery is dead.

The chicken soup I'm holding tumbles to the floor. My shaky hands are unable to hold anything because the room spins around me. Slumping onto her bed, I stare down at the woman who was my mother, my mentor, my friend.

I should have been here. She shouldn't have died alone. My heart breaks at the thought. "I'm s-sorry," I cry, ugly tears streaming down my cheeks. I failed her.

On autopilot, I reach for her phone and dial 911. I speak robotically, disbelieving this voice is my own. When the operator asks if she's breathing, I tell her no, and from the looks of it, she hasn't in quite some time.

The paramedics arrive minutes later, confirming what I knew to be true. They said she died peacefully, but how do they know?

Is there such a thing when death is involved? It's something we tell ourselves to lessen the grief, but I don't think this hole in my chest will ever go away.

The paramedics gently usher me away from Avery when I stand silent, eyes wide. I can feel the color draining from my cheeks, but I can't let her go. I'm not ready. Shrugging them away, I run toward the bed and throw my arms around her cold, stiff form. Sobbing uncontrollably, I beg her to come back to me.

"Don't leave me," I bellow, choking on my tears. "Please don't leave me."

But she's already gone.

"Is there someone I can call for you, sweetie?" asks the paramedic. I know he is just trying to help, but I don't want his help. I just want this nightmare to end.

"No," I whisper, refusing to let Avery go. The only person I have in this world is gone.

Everything I was so certain of is no more. I had direction, but now, I'm so lost. My game plan is now obsolete.

Where do I go from here?

Once they took Avery's body away, they informed me an investigation would take place because she died alone in her house. It was evident she succumbed to the cancer eating away at her, but it was standard protocol.

I have the number of Avery's lawyer, who has her affairs in order, but I will call him tomorrow. I can't deal with that now. I left a message for her brother who lives in Canada, asking for him to call me. They aren't close, so I'm not sure if he'll call me back.

The funeral home told me to take my time, and when I was ready, we could go over the arrangements. These arrangements they speak so flippantly about are a person. Even though she is no longer here, I hate that she's merely a task to them.

I have numerous missed calls from Christopher, but he is the last person I want to speak to at the moment. The blame game is real, and I don't want to get in another fight with him when he expresses his condolences because actions speak a lot louder than words.

Now that Avery is gone, buying the studio is so bittersweet. I wanted to do it for her, for her to see her hard work flourish before she left this earth, but it's too late. She's gone, and I'm left without her and her studio.

I don't know what happens now. With her gone, I assume the bank will liquidate the assets of the studio to pay off her business debts, and anything else will be distributed in accordance to Avery's will. She told me she had her affairs in order, but I was so certain I would have enough money to take over her business that I didn't want to hear the alternative.

It's always easier to live in denial…but I can't anymore.

With two bouquets of white roses in my hands, I trek through the snow with a numb mind and body. After everything that's happened today, you'd think this was the last place I want to be, but strangely enough, being here gives me comfort. And when I stop in front of the marble gravestone, I realize it's because it brings back the feelings of being loved.

My tears have long dried, and I don't think I can shed anymore. Lachlan's grave is simple but beautiful, just like him. The epitaph is short but appropriate.

Much loved son and brother.
Taken away too soon.

It saddens me that father isn't added because I just know he would have been a great dad. I don't know his parents, and it never occurred to me to look them up. A month ago, I thought their son had abandoned Jordy and me, but now, I wonder if maybe I should seek them out. If they would like to meet their grandson.

I think Lachlan would have liked that.

Uncapping the bottle of water I brought, I fill the vase attached to the headstone and carefully unwrap one bouquet of roses. I arrange them, and when they're sitting perfectly, I sigh happily. They look beautiful. I don't know what to say, so I don't say anything at all.

I simply stand by Lachlan's grave, honoring the man I knew and loved, regardless of his past.

When I can no longer feel my toes, I slip the hood farther over my head and say goodbye to Lachlan. I'll be back, and when I return, it'll be with his son.

With the second bouquet in my hand, I walk the large cemetery until I arrive at the last grave in a row just like the others before and after it. I remove the withered red roses from the grave and replace them with the white ones I bought for Damian.

I know how fucked up this is, but when I did a search online and found out Damian was also buried here, it felt almost impolite not to pay my respects. Seeing his birthdate and date of death make the tears I thought were long gone reappear.

"When I was fifteen, four men killed my brother. One of them was your brother, and the other was—"

Bull's words play on repeat, and being here makes his story, his pain all the more real. "I'm sorry," I whisper. "You were so young. You had your whole life ahead of you. But my…brother and my boyfriend stole that from you."

I don't know why I need to apologize. It just feels like the right thing to do.

"Your brother really loves you. I wish you could see the man he is today. He's dark and violent, but underneath that lies a broken and vulnerable soul. I should hate him, but I don't," I confess to the one person who would understand.

"I think I…" I lick my cracked lips. "I think I'm falling in love with him."

And there it is. The ugly truth I've been trying so hard to avoid. What does this say about me? How can I love the man who destroyed my life? How can I love him when he looked me in the eye with no emotion and told me he would kill me if I stood in his way?

"There is so much more to this story, and the people who hold the answers took them to their graves. Did my brother really do what Bull, what Cody said he did?" I mumble aloud, using Bull's real name because that's who he was before he crossed paths with my brother.

After seeing a side of Christopher today I didn't like, I wonder if putting him on a pedestal has clouded what's right in front of me.

"It just doesn't make any sense. Bull wouldn't do all of this if what he's saying isn't true." Coming here, I don't feel guilty confessing my sins because the dead don't judge.

With Bull, everything has been real and raw. But with Christopher, he seems to be playing a role. He waltzes into my life, expecting me to forget the past, but I can't. How can he be okay with me dancing when he knows I'm doing it because I have to and not because I want to?

Carlos has been MIA since Christopher returned, but maybe that's because he played his part and is no longer needed. A sense of dread washes over me, and my stomach turns.

What if Carlos was merely the messenger, and my brother was the mastermind behind it all? Andre said as much when Bull broke his ankles, broke them trying to protect me. Andre said someone else wanted me. Is that someone Christopher?

The earrings I thought were from Carlos; were they really from Christopher? Has he been here the whole time?

But why?

None of this makes any sense.

Having him conveniently appear out of nowhere does seem strange. Not to mention, he didn't appear surprised when he saw Bull and me together. Was he just waiting to strike?

The more I think about this, the more sense it begins to make. Has he been closer than I thought this entire time? If that's true…I don't know who my brother is, and I can't trust a word that comes out of his mouth.

Instead of rage, a sense of peace falls over me when I

look at Damian's headstone. Coming here has given me the answers that were staring me in the face this entire time. Even from the grave, it seems, the benevolence that Bull admired about his brother has shone through.

"If what Bull says is true...then your death will be avenged," I promise Damian, knowing what that means.

And for the first time in a long time, I'm okay with it.

CHAPTER SIX

Bull

"**A**nd then she wiped away her tears and drove home."

The coffee cup in my clenched fist threatens to break under the force, so I slam it onto the dresser with a snarl. "Motherfucker," I curse to no one in particular as I don't discriminate. I hate the world right now.

Paul sips his coffee, knowing better than to console me.

He relayed the events of when he tailed Tiger two days ago, and the more he shared with me, the more I wanted to break something. Venus stands in the doorway, shaking her head. I know what she's going to say.

"You need to call her. She needs a friend right now."

"Thank you for your advice, Venus, but we're not friends."

She scoffs, not believing a word that comes out of my

mouth because she's right. The need to see Tiger leaves me so fucking restless, I begin to pace the room.

I know how much Avery meant to her. Avery was the reason she worked so hard, selling her soul to that club, so her death will destroy Tiger. And all I can do is watch, dick in hand, from the sidelines.

Avery's passing must have left her sentimental because she visited Lachlan's grave. But what I don't understand is why she also visited Damian's. Paul watched her from the shadows and said he saw her lay white roses by his grave.

After everything I've done to her, she still shows compassion to my family. I feel like an even bigger asshole, if that's possible.

"She only leaves her apartment to pick up her kid," Paul says with a shrug. "That tall, scary-looking dude has stopped by a few times, but she hasn't let him in."

Jaws has been circling her, and I would have thought she'd want his support right now, but clearly, I know jack shit.

Clenching my snarled hair, I continue pacing like a caged animal because that's how I feel inside. I want to go to her. Fuck if I'd know what to say, but knowing she's alone, dealing with this, kills me inside.

"Keep watching her," I order Paul. It's all I can think of right now.

"Should I send her flowers?"

I jerk to a stop, arching a brow. "What the fuck for?"

"That's what people do when someone dies, Bull," Venus says, rolling her eyes with a smirk. "It's called being nice."

"No wonder I don't know anything about this rite of

passage. What are you doing here, anyway? Don't you have rooms to clean or some shit?" There is no bite to my comment.

I'm clearly losing my touch because Venus laughs in response.

I have so much going on right now, and all I want to do is jump in my truck and bang on Tiger's door. Clutching my shirt, I tug at the material over my chest because my heart is beating so fast, it's pissing me off.

"I have some shit to deal with today. I'll be back later."

"Do you want me to come with?" Paul asks.

I look at Paul like he's gone mad because he clearly has. "No, I do not want you to come anywhere with me. Your job is to watch Tiger and Scrooge, not me. And why are you in my room? Don't you have your own?"

Venus mutes her chuckles behind her hand while Paul smirks. He pats Fluffball on the head, before finally getting the hint and leaving. Why are these people even here?

Venus looks at me with that know-it-all look in her eyes. She should also take a hint and leave, but she doesn't. "It's okay to like people, Bull. We won't judge you." Her tone as well as her smirk are filled with sarcasm.

I don't bother correcting her because what would be the point?

She gives me a sassy wave, before sauntering away.

Closing the door, I gather my things because if I don't bounce, I'm going to be late. José sent me a text this morning asking me to swing by his work. It seems he actually is a used car salesman, but no doubt that business is just a front.

Just as Stevie intends to use The Pink Oyster.

I am so sick of these shady ass pricks. They lie, cheat, steal, and make others do their dirty work. They're fucking wimps. This isn't how I run. But this wimp is about to bring Christmas early. He said he'd be in touch when he had news about Scrooge, so he better cough up the goods.

After topping off Fluffball's food, I pat him under the chin and close and lock the door. Venus doesn't bother cleaning my room anymore. If I need anything, I just help myself to the supply closet per her instruction.

Jumping into my truck, I commence the thirty-minute trek to José's. He's smart and won't leave a digital footprint. Anything we discuss will be face-to-face. That's how people don't get caught; be invisible.

My thoughts, as usual, drift to Tiger. The other night with her was something else. I know she regretted it, which is why I left when she asked me to. I was prepared to spill it all, consequences be damned, but I can't make that mistake ever again. So much is riding on this. I need to remember that.

"Sometimes…you have to think about how your actions will affect another."

Tiger's life lesson has stuck with me, and in this case, my action of telling her everything will affect her in the worst possible way. No matter how badly I want her, and I do want her, I have to be strong.

When José's lot comes into view, I park my truck by the curb. It's in a shitty neighborhood—the perfect ruse. I'm packing heat under my jacket, but it's a false sense of security. I'm on José's turf now.

I lower my chin and make my way into the lot. The main

building is to the left. Before I even step foot inside, I scope out my surroundings. The back exit is manned by Luis. He nods when he sees me.

"Come in, *amigo*," José says, standing in the doorway of his office. The windows are thick. Bulletproof. Without delay, I follow him and close the door behind me.

José sits behind his large wooden desk, steepling his fingers. I don't want to sit, but he won't give me what I want if I don't concede. The squeaky leather whines under me as I slump into the chair.

Even in this shithole, José looks like a king. He reeks of authority, and when he leans back in his chair, rocking, I know he is throwing down the alpha vibes. He has something I want. He doesn't want me to forget who holds the power.

"Your man was almost impossible to track down." I hold my breath. "But we had a deal."

Exhaling, I nod, indicating I'm listening.

He hunts through his desk drawer and produces a pamphlet. Sliding it across the desk, I lean forward, reaching for it, but what I see has me clenching the paper in my fist. It crinkles under the force.

Staring at me with a smile is the motherfucker who's haunted me for fourteen years. Yes, when I stalked the internet, gathering everything I could on him, I saw his face, his motherfucking face. But what I didn't see is what I see now, and what I see is him, Benjamin Solomon, aka Scrooge, standing behind a podium, delivering what appears to be a speech, and on his right hand is a championship ring with a green diamond.

Damian's ring.

There is a date and a place printed on the front, but everything is blurred—blurred with a murderous rage. "Why are you giving me this?" I can't keep the emotion from my tone, and it feeds a sadist like José.

"You're going to be there, that's why. You lose that fight, and my men will get him alone for you. The rest is up to you."

"This is the best you can do? This is a fucking gala event." I wave the crinkled pamphlet in my hand in case he missed the memo. "With lots of people." Lots of witnesses.

Goddammit.

José shrugs, untroubled. "You want access to one of the most powerful men in the city, you take what you can. You may as well have asked to meet Santa Claus."

He's right. I know how hard Scrooge is to chase down. So if this is the only in I have, I just have to be smart about it. I'm putting my trust in José not to screw me over.

Reading over the pamphlet, I shake my head in disgust. The gala event is to raise money for victims of child abuse, and the guest speaker is none other than the other asshole who ruined my life. Seeing Damian's ring on his finger has me slowly crumpling the paper in my fist, wishing it was Scrooge's throat I was crushing with my hand.

"What did he do to you, *Colmillo*?"

Meeting José's eyes, I reply, "He fucked with the wrong person, and now, he's going to pay. I'll throw the fight, and when I do, we're done. No more favors, we clear?"

José smirks, leaning back in his seat. "I think you'll miss me," he taunts. I'm clearly wasting my breath because the cartel doesn't ask, they take. But I want him to know I'm no one's bitch.

"Don't worry. I can't piss Stevie off too much. He is family after all. I'd rather he wasn't, but that's not my choice to make."

Motherfucker.

He decided to drop this bombshell in order to shock me, but I keep my cool. "Looks like you lucked out then." Standing, I shove the pamphlet into my back pocket, so done with this conversation.

"I'll see you soon," José says happily, and why wouldn't he be pleased? He has everything he wants.

Not interested in prolonging the inevitable, I leave his office, desperate to get the fuck out of here so I can process what just went down. The pamphlet burns a hole in my back pocket. As I exit the building, I welcome the snow as it helps calm the raging bull within.

The moment I jump into my truck, I grip the steering wheel and take three slow, deep breaths. This is what I wanted, to finally get Scrooge alone. The circumstances aren't ideal, but I'll make it work.

Yanking out the pamphlet, it trembles in my hand as I smooth out the creases and stare at the ring on Scrooge's finger. Memories of that night crash into me, and I squeeze my eyes closed, needing to shut them out.

But all I can see is Damian's wrist being bent at a grotesque angle as Scrooge stole his ring.

My cell rings, and without looking at who the caller is, I answer it. I wish I didn't.

"Meet me at Blue Bloods now."

Hearing Jaws's voice and seeing Scrooge's face are like a shot of adrenaline through my body. I reverberate in utter fury.

"I hope you have the information I want."

Having our weekly "catch-up" is the last fucking thing I want to do right now, but it allows me to kickstart my plan of attack. Now that the stakes are higher than ever, there is no way I can let Jaws get a whiff of what I know or what I plan to do.

"Fuck you," is my response before I end the call. He knows I'm coming. It's not like I have a choice. Shoving the pamphlet into the console, I put the truck into drive and make my way to the club.

I need to calm down, but I can't.

"I can't piss Stevie off too much. He is family after all."

No wonder Stevie was buying birthday gifts for José's daughter. He couldn't get in with the cartel unless he had an inside man. Jaws has no idea what he's up against, which is why I intend on keeping the cartel's involvement a secret.

There is no way I can rat on José. His punishment for betrayal would be far worse than what Jaws could ever do to Tiger. I just need to buy some time until the gala. I need José in my corner.

Parking my truck in the almost empty parking lot, I put my game face on. I leave my shoulder holster on because the club is closed, and I don't trust Jaws. The urgency in his tone and the fact Tiger hasn't wanted to see him since Avery's death hints that something is amiss.

I can't take any risks.

This is the first time he's wanted to meet here, which has me guessing he needs the home turf advantage. But for what?

Banging on the back door, I push past some asshole bouncer who opens it with a scowl. I don't wait for any instructions and march into the club. Jaws appears a second later, his usual calm demeanor shot to shit. His black hair is unkept, his eyes bloodshot.

The pinstripe suit he wears is crinkled, and his tie is off-center. Gone is his cocky arrogance. He wants answers, and he wants them now. I follow as he leads the way toward his office. The last time I was in here was when I was with Tiger.

Everything comes back to her.

"I'm not in the mood for your bullshit," Jaws snarls, leaning against his desk, arms and ankles crossed. "Talk."

"Someone got out on the wrong side of the bed this morning," I quip, unable to help myself as I close the door behind me. Seeing him so restless gives me the warm and fuzzies. "But judging from your appearance, I doubt you even went to bed. What's wrong? Your conscience finally caught up to you?"

He inhales through his nose. I am poking the bear, and I intend to poke some more.

"I may be forced to do your dirty work, but that doesn't mean I'm going to roll over and be your lapdog. Ask me nicely and then maybe I'll tell you all about the meeting with Snow White."

I've thought about this and hope to fuck this works. Snow was the asshole who gave me my six-inch scar because he decided he didn't like me. He got out about a year before I did, and I have no doubt he's back doing what he was doing before he got locked up.

I know enough about his operation because he liked to brag about his grade A product. I will lie my way through this and hope like hell Jaws buys it.

"That's the supplier's name?" Jaws asks, eyeing me suspiciously.

"Yup. A neo-Nazi whose specialty is grade A Columbian cocaine. We met at some abandoned warehouse in Chicago. It's a moving operation, so I can't give you an address. But the name is good."

Jaws runs a hand over his stubble. He appears in thought. "Good. What else?"

"There is nothing else. I have a fight in Chicago in a few days. I won't know who's involved until the day of. You know how paranoid Stevie is."

I keep my cool when Jaws fishes his cell from his pocket and sends a text.

"How's the club? How's the new meat?"

"Fine. Things are picking up, so Stevie will come around. He needs somewhere to hide his dirty money after all."

Jaws nods, but something is brewing behind those soulless eyes. "So everything is on track then? There's nothing you want to add?"

Standing my ground, I shake my head. "Other than I can't wait to see you bleeding at my feet, then no. We done?"

"For now," Jaws replies.

I go to turn, but I should have known nothing is this easy.

"Oh, by the way, Avery died. I'm sure my sister has told

you all about her."

I pause, ready to reach for my gun if I need to. "How is this relevant to me?" I ask casually.

Jaws chuckles, but there is nothing amusing about the sound. "I thought you'd want to know, seeing as you were balls deep in her a few nights ago."

The room is silent…before a searing pulse electrocutes me into submission—literally.

I reach for my Glock, but it's too late. A pain burns straight through me, and I buckle to my knees. But regardless of every part of my body contorting and spasming in pain, I attempt to dig into my holster for my gun.

"I don't think so!" Jaws kicks me in the stomach, winding me as I topple to my side. "Not so smart now, are you, asshole?"

Twitching, I attempt to regain control of my muscles, but seeing as Jaws just used a stun gun on me, I am failing miserably. Jaws exploits my vulnerability for his gain.

"This is what happens when you lie to me. I've been nice, but no more." He zaps me once again before I have a chance to argue that nice isn't a word in his vocabulary. "That's for breaking my nose!"

The shockwave to my nervous system is indescribable. I try to fight it, but the electrical pulse twitches throughout me.

"Snow White isn't Stevie's supplier! He's a bottom feeder. Stevie knows better than to deal with someone like him. I know who it is…I just need confirmation so I can kill them… all!"

If he knows, then why does he need me?

It must be the electrical current that just fried my body

because I suddenly put two and two together. José is linked to Stevie because of this infamous woman both men love. The betrayal in Jaws's tone confirms this.

She chose Stevie over Jaws, and because of this, Stevie is now linked to the cartel. This isn't about drugs; it's about revenge.

How the tables have turned.

"I want him to think he's on top when I take it all from him...just how he did to me."

Jaws's comment now makes sense. He is a lover scorned.

When someone else confirms what you already know, it makes it all the more real. Jaws doesn't want to act in haste in case his paranoid mind is making up tales. But the fact he hasn't acted means he's hesitating in fear because perhaps, what he believes is actually true.

He is underdog to Stevie. The notorious, feared Jaws is the runner-up, and he hates it. He has lost something he loves, and I intend to exploit that because I just found his weakness.

Chuckling intermittently as my muscles continue to twitch with the aftershock of being stunned, I taunt, "Hurts, doesn't it?"

"What does?" Jaws spits, dropping to one knee in front of me and yanking me up by the collar of my shirt.

"Losing someone you love." His face twists into rage, which just breathes new life into me. "You don't want to kill Stevie because you don't want to believe the truth. But you need me to prove what you already know."

He flinches, a flicker of emotion fueling me on.

"You don't want *her* to hate you, do you? Because that's

what will happen if she finds out what you intend to do."

"You shut your fucking mouth!" he screams, shaking me.

I do the complete opposite. My body may still be suffering from the aftershocks of being zapped, but my tongue is working just fine. "She chose *him* and not you because you're weak. And pathetic. Grow a pair and either do something about it or get the fuck over it."

Jaws snarls before placing the stun gun to my stomach. But the electrical surge coursing through my body is so worth it. "I'm pathetic?" he mocks, holding me tightly as I convulse around the gun. "My sister is the reason you're about to fry to a crisp. I hope she was worth it. How'd her pussy taste?"

Spittle runs down my chin as I seize uncontrollably. But that doesn't stop me. "Like…bubble…gum," I manage to push out before I collapse in a heap. I know I need to stop. Tiger's safety is at stake if I don't. But I can't.

This "deal" always had an expiration date. I'm no one's snitch. I was stupid to think I could do this. Sooner or later, I knew I'd fold. I'm prepared to tell her everything because I can't stay away from her. And I don't want to.

Besides, Jaws already knows we broke his little rule when I fucked Tiger in the back seat of her truck. But it was so much more than that.

He was just waiting to strike. This was never going to be a fair fight because our agreement was bogus.

"I see everything. You think you can fool me. I know she went to you when she should have been with me!" I don't know how he knows. I wouldn't be surprised if he followed Tiger. It's clear he has an unhealthy obsession with her.

My body screams *MINE!*

Jaws dives on top of me, resorting to good old-fashioned violence as he begins to beat the shit out of me. I can't fight back. My body is nonresponsive, suffering the repercussions of being on the receiving end of a stun gun.

He kicks me in the stomach, the ribs, and finally, the face. My head snaps back with a crack, and with one eye closing over, I witness him spit on me, just as he did my brother. "The deal is off. It's open season."

My heart constricts, knowing what this means. I did all of this to protect Tiger, but I failed. And now, he will ensure she pays.

"Don't you fucking touch he—" But the words are lost to the darkness as Jaws delivers the final blow, which changes everything forever.

Jolting upright, I push the sweaty hair from my brow, frantically scanning my dark, dank surroundings through one eye. The other is swollen shut. I instantly reach under my collar, sighing in relief when I feel Damian's chain still secured around my neck.

It's quiet. All I can hear is the distant passing of cars and my winded exhalations.

Groaning, I clutch my side because everything hurts. I need a minute to catch my breath before I stand because I don't know if my legs will hold me up. But I suppose that's a normal response to being electrocuted and then beaten unconscious.

I know I should have stopped when I was ahead, but I couldn't. Getting under Jaws's skin is a drug, and I've become addicted. But now, the gravity of the situation hits me hard. I need to call Tiger.

Patting myself down, I realize I'm without two guns and one cell. "Motherfucker," I hoarsely curse under my breath.

Inhaling through my nose, I use every ounce of strength I can muster and come to a slow, shaky stand. It feels like I'm on a merry-go-round, but I place my arms out for balance. Having no idea where I am, I commence a slow stagger, listening to any vibrations of life, which will help me find my way out.

When I woke, I was lying in a puddle of water. Peering overhead, I see the moon peeking in through a hole in the damaged roof. I must have been out for hours, which means I could be anywhere.

Breathing past the pain, I persevere, scanning from left to right. It appears I'm in an abandoned building, but the question is where? The sound of scurrying has me pausing and listening. Adjusting to the darkness, I focus and see a change in the lighting up ahead. It's subtle, but it's a sign that either a door or a window is close by.

Clutching my side, I hobble forward, desperate to figure out where the fuck I am. When I get closer to the light, I see a door jarred open slightly. It's all the motivation I need to quicken my steps and shove it open with my shoulder. It's stuck, but after a few tries, it finally budges.

When I barge outside, I can't gulp in fresh air fast enough even though it's fucking cold. The snow and wind are punishing, but with no other choice, I slowly make my way toward the steel fence a few hundred yards away. The faded address painted on the brick building to my left tells me I'm in Flint.

Needing to catch my breath, I stop and take a minute. I don't have time for this, but I won't be any good to Tiger if I pass out again. Light laughter catches on the wind, which kickstarts my stagger toward the road. The voices grow louder, and when I slip through the serrated hole in the fence, I determine they're coming from a building down the road.

The dim streetlights allow me to see that this neighborhood is almost deserted. The voices are probably coming from some illegal dealings, but that doesn't deter me as I break into a winded dash. The numerous cars in front of the building hint this mechanic is probably a front for a chop shop, but I don't care what they are.

I just need to use their phone.

Banging on the steel door, I hear the voices quiet. I doubt they get visitors often. "Open up. I just need to use your phone."

When there is no reply and no movement inside, I add, "I'll give a thousand dollars for your trouble."

Open sesame.

The roller door slides open and out comes a man in greasy blue overalls. When he sees my state, he pauses from reaching into his inner pocket. He doesn't need a gun. I'm barely standing.

"Thanks." I push past him, hobbling inside. I don't care that there are a dozen or so expensive cars parked inside. This is none of my business. I have enough to deal with.

The man offers me his cell.

Dialing quickly, I don't bother with small talk when Paul answers. "Where is she?"

"Where have you been?" he asks, panicked.

Sometimes, I regret not shooting him. He asks so many fucking questions.

When I don't bother answering him, he drops a bombshell that explains his panic. "She's here, man. Venus let her into your room."

Groaning, I lean against the wall for support. "Fucking, Venus," I mutter under my breath. "How long has she been there?"

"A couple of hours. The last I saw, she was making your bed. She won't sit still. Something is definitely up. She hasn't seen me, though."

I'm relieved she's okay, but a) why is she in my room? And b) why is she in my room? I wonder what Jaws told her. He said it was open season. This can't be good.

"Good, make sure it stays that way. Come get me. I'm at—" I look at the man, arching a brow as I put the phone on loud speaker. He rattles off the address. "Got it?" I ask Paul.

"Whose phone are you calling me from? And why are you in Flint?"

"I'll tell you all about my adventures when you get here," I sarcastically bark, flinching because it hurts to speak.

The man clears his throat, reminding me I'm forgetting something.

"Oh, and be a darling and bring a grand with you, okay?" I don't bother waiting for him to reply before I hang up.

Passing the man his cell, I hobble outside, waiting for the cavalry to arrive. Since when do I have a cavalry? Looking down at the tattoos on my knuckles, which spell lone wolf, I shake my head, wondering when my life got so damn social.

CHAPTER SEVEN

Lily

I didn't second-guess my decision when I jumped into my truck and drove here. Nor did I tell myself what a bad idea it was to ask Venus to let me wait in his room. When twenty minutes became thirty, I realized that if I didn't give myself an excuse to be here, I was going to leave.

Which is what led to my cleaning spree.

Bull's room was clean, but once I was done with it, every corner was gleaming.

Venus was sitting in the office reading a magazine, so I decided to sit with her and wait when Bull still hadn't arrived. We spoke about everything and anything, but I couldn't stop looking at my watch every two minutes. I eventually excused myself and went back to Bull's room.

I've tried calling him all afternoon, but his phone was switched off. So without much of a choice, I pulled back the clean sheets and settled into his bed with Fluffball, which is where I've been for the past few hours—waiting.

The TV is merely background noise because I need something to fill in the silence and drown out the heavy staccato of my heart. Jordy asked if he could spend the night at Patrick's, and Erika didn't mind, as she knew I was going through a rough time losing Avery.

Secretly, I was thankful he wanted to spend time with his friend because I didn't want him spending so much time with Christopher.

I haven't spoken to Christopher since our argument. It wasn't even an argument. It was more of the truth finally being revealed. He's come to see me, but I haven't let him in. It feels almost hypocritical for him to come to my home and offer his condolences when he couldn't give a shit about Avery when she was alive.

I don't know why coming here offers me more comfort than seeing my own flesh and blood. Nothing with Bull has ever made sense, though, so I don't expect this to either.

I need Bull to tell me the truth. The whole truth. I want him to look me in the eye and tell me Christopher is lying because it will confirm what I already know. I've known it all along. I didn't want to admit it because I had my chance at having my family back, but if that family is based on lies, then I would rather be alone.

Jordy will hate me, but I can't have Christopher in my life if what Bull says is true. I wonder if I would feel the same way if Lachlan was alive?

Bull is linked to my past, present, and future. He holds the answers, and I want them—now.

However, when the door bursts open and in hobbles a bloody, injured Bull, it seems my list of questions just grew.

"What happened?" I toss off the blankets and sprint over to help Bull into the room. I wrap my arm around his waist and coax him to lean on me for support, much to his dismay.

We stagger toward the bed, where he slumps onto the end, hissing in pain. He looks like hell. His eye is swollen shut, and his face is bruised an angry red and purple. Dried blood is smeared under his nose.

Rushing into the bathroom, I wet a hand towel with warm water. My hands are shaking so badly when I return to the bedroom and see him hunched over, breathing steadily.

"Bull?" I cry, running and dropping to my knees in front of him.

Making sure not to apply too much pressure, I place my palms to his cheeks and slowly reposition his face so I can look at the damage. "Jesus," I hiss, flinching when I see how badly injured he really is. "What happened? Did you fight tonight?"

I doubt this was a fair fight. I've seen Bull in the ring. He doesn't lose. Someone had an advantage over him to be able to beat him this way. Glancing down at his shirt, I see the white material is stained a dark red.

His suspenders are already off, hanging limply by his sides, so I gently lift his shirt where it's untucked on one side and gasp when I see his burned, reddened flesh. "Wh-who did this to you?"

"I…I ran into a door," he pants. Even beaten and bruised, he can't help but be a pain in my ass. "Stop fussing. I'm fine." He shrugs from my grip.

"You are so far from fine," I argue, standing up. "You need to go to the hospital, but I know you won't go, so I won't waste my breath."

He gestures for the towel in my hand. When I give it to him, he limply wipes at his face, doing a poor job of wiping off any of the blood. Unable to watch him make more of a mess, I snatch it from his hand and take over.

I hide my surprise when he allows me to help him. He must be really hurt.

For minutes, we don't speak. Bull simply sits quietly, letting me wipe his face clean. The bruising turns my stomach, and each time he flinches, I know the bruises I can't see are so much worse.

"Are you going to tell me what happened?"

"Why are you here?" he counters instead.

"Can you, for once, answer my questions…please?" I cry, so done with the games.

Bull's chest rises with an inhale, before depressing with a defeated exhale. "I met with the cartel. I'm doing them a favor for a favor in return."

I blink once, stunned. "They did this to you?"

"Not directly. But because I didn't tell someone the truth, they decided to get in a lucky shot by using a stun gun and then beating me when I was down. Fucking pussy," he mocks, shaking his head slowly. "No surprise he needed to fight dirty."

My lower lip trembles. "Who?"

Bull slowly lifts his chin, reading the desperation in my eyes. I need him to stop lying to protect me, because that's what he's doing. I've always known. I just didn't want to face it…until now.

"Why are you here?" he asks me once again.

Wringing the soiled towel in my hands, I confess, "Because I…believe you. I think?"

"Believe what?" he questions, his jaw hardening.

"Everything," I reply in a whisper, hating how this betrayal changes my life. If only I could live in denial and pretend everything is okay. But I can't.

I won't.

I'm expecting to see relief, but I don't. I get the complete opposite. "Did you tell him this?"

"What?" I ask, nervously licking my dry lips. Why does he sound so…panicked?

When he waits for me to answer him, I add, "No, I haven't spoken to him in a few days. Why?"

"Where is your son?"

My heart begins to beat faster and faster. "He's sleeping over at his friend's house. My neighbor."

"Call her." When I hesitate, he presses, "Now."

I don't know what's going on, but the urgency to his tone has me quickly retrieving my cell from my bag and dialing Erika. I watch anxiously as he comes to a slow, unsteady stand and hobbles to the bedside table. When he opens a drawer and produces a gun, I yelp.

"Hi, Lily." Erika's cheerful tone calms me somewhat

because if Jordy were in trouble, she wouldn't be so calm.

"Hi, Erika. Sorry to call, but I was wondering if I could speak with Jordy real quick?"

I lock eyes with Bull, who waits for her reply. But he knows what she's going to say even when I don't.

"Oh, didn't your brother call you? He came by earlier and said you asked him to pick up Jordy. I didn't want to bother you because I know how tough things have been for you lately."

The walls close in on me, and I suddenly can't breathe.

"Hello, Lily? Are you still there?"

But I can't speak. My entire body feels like it's been weighed down with lead. Bull staggers over, taking the phone away from me.

"What did he say? Word for word," he demands, not bothering with small talk. She must ask who he is because he huffs. "Stop wasting my time and answer my question."

He nods, listening closely but giving nothing away. Maybe I'm just reading into things. Maybe it'll be okay. But nothing has been okay for a very long time.

Hugging my middle, I wait for Bull to finish talking before hanging up. "I'm guessing you didn't ask Jaws to pick up Jordy?"

I shake my head.

He wouldn't hurt him, I reason. He is his uncle. But a thought crashes into me, and my legs threaten to give out from under me. But he'd hurt me.

"Call him and ask what he wants." Bull passes me my cell, but I simply stare at it, numb. I know I should be doing something more, but I can't. I think I've gone into shock.

He walks over and cups my cheek, forcing me to look at him. "I know this is a lot, but you've got to be strong, okay? Call him."

Nodding jerkily, I do as he asks. My fingers tremble uncontrollably as I dial. I put it on loud speaker and hold my breath.

"Hello, lil' sis," Christopher sarcastically replies. "You finally decided to call."

His smug response is all the accelerant I need. "Stop with the bullshit. Where is my son?"

"He's spending some quality time with his uncle."

"You had no right to pick him up without my permission. I'm coming over."

My confidence is short-lived, and everything crumbles before my eyes. "You can go there, but I'm not home."

"Excuse me? Where are you?" I ask, heart in my throat.

"I tried, I really tried," he says with an exaggerated sigh. "You've brought this onto yourself."

"Brought what? So help me God, Christopher, if you don't tell me where you are, I'll—"

"You'll what? Go running to your knight in shining armor? He can't save you. He had his chance, but he fucked up, royally. This is all on him. All on you both," he spits, his true colors finally breaking through the façade.

Bull stands quiet, but the clenching of his jaw hints this is just the beginning.

"What do you want?" I cry, not understanding any of this.

"It's too late for that now. I gave you a chance to choose

right, and you chose wrong. When you chose him, you decided how this ended."

"Christopher, please, give me back Jordy. Whatever issues you have with me, take them out on me. He's just a b-boy," I beg, suddenly unable to breathe.

"Exactly. And he needs me to help shape him into a man. You've raised a sissy."

"You can't do this!" I bellow, tugging at my hair so hard, my scalp aches. "I'll c-call the p-police."

"Go for it. But you won't like the consequences if you do because I am above the law. Besides, I'm not holding him against his will. He hates you anyway. He's left alone most days so you can whore around. I'm doing him a favor."

Guilt swarms me because a small part of me hates that he's right. Not the whoring part, but the fact Jordy hates me. He hasn't had it easy growing up alone. I've tried to be there as much as I can, but being a single parent is hard.

"Give me back my son!" I scream, tears scalding my cheeks as they fall.

"I wish I could, but we're going on a vacation. Jordy told me he's never been on a plane before." He doesn't mask his disgust. "He's safe. For now. He's of use to me at the moment, but when the novelty wears off…"

"Oh my god. Don't you hurt him!" I cry, muting my whimpers behind my hand. "You son of a bitch. I'll find you."

His scathing chuckles reveal just how out of my league I truly am. "You can try, but you didn't have any luck finding me before so your chances aren't so good."

Bull interlaces his hands behind his nape, raising his face

to the ceiling. "You've been here this entire time? You've seen what I've gone through; yet, you decided to remain hidden? Until now?"

"It seems you've bet on the wrong horse all your life, Lillian," he cruelly states.

I don't believe this is real. How can I?

"Why?" It's all I can say.

"Because you chose him over me." And the line goes dead, just like my heart.

"No, no, no!" I scream. Shaking the phone, I can't believe this is happening. I quickly redial, but it goes to voicemail.

Without thought, I race to the door, but Bull, even injured, is faster than me. "Get out of my w-way!" I demand, shoving against his chest.

"We'll get him back," he promises, raising his hands in surrender. "Just hear me out."

"I'm done listening! Bull, move!" Hysteria has taken over, and I don't know who is friend or foe anymore.

But he doesn't budge, infuriating me further.

A surge charges through me, and I push at him, thumping my fists against his chest. But no matter how hard I hit him, he doesn't move. "Please," I cry, my guttural tears unable to stop. "I n-need to f-find him. He's a-all I ha-have. Oh m-my g-god."

Air is siphoned from my lungs, and I wheeze, clutching at my chest. I can't breathe. A shattered cry spills from me, and I buckle.

"Tiger, shh, it's all right." Bull advances, wrapping his arms around me. But I don't want his comfort. I don't deserve it. I fight him off, snarling and cursing, but he only holds me tighter.

He presses his chest to mine, breathing slowly and deeply, allowing me to feel his heart beat against mine. "That's it," he whispers, attempting to calm me down as he strokes my back. "Breathe, Lily, breathe."

Eventually, my winded wheezes calm, and I take in air slowly. But my heart, it aches. No matter that my breathing has quieted, I can't stop the thrashing, the breaking of my heart.

"Tell me everything," I utter without feeling. All emotion has washed out of me.

Bull releases me slowly but doesn't move from his post in front of the door.

He sighs, running a hand through his hair. "Your brother has been blackmailing me. I was to be his snitch and relay information on his rival, Stevie Howells. He wants his drugs, his money, his fighting syndicate all because of a woman.

"This has always been about revenge. It just took me a little while to figure it out."

Unable to digest this standing up, I amble over to the bed and slump on the end of it.

"The night you found out who I was, your brother told me he wouldn't hurt you or Jordy if I stayed away from you. He is a...sick animal. Before I..." He pauses before continuing. "I killed Kong, he told me the reason your brother no longer needed him was because he ordered him to kill...Jordy, but he couldn't do it."

My lower lip trembles as I stare into thin air, seeing

nothing but my stupidity. "Kill my son? Why?"

"Because he is a product of your betrayal, of your love for someone other than him."

My choices have impacted my future in ways I never imagined. My relationship with Lachlan was fated, signed in the Devil's blood.

"I thought if I did what he wanted, you'd be safe. And besides, after everything I've done to you, leaving you alone was the right thing to do."

His regret is clear, but his chivalry cost me my son.

"You should have told me," I say, shaking my head.

"I know, but until I could come up with a better plan, it was the only thing that made sense. So many other people are involved. Lotus, for one. Stevie wants to use The Pink Oyster for his money laundering scam. I can't let him do that to her.

"Jaws wants the club. He wants to own this fucking city. All because Stevie has the woman he wants."

"Bianca," I whisper, remembering Christopher mentioning her to me.

"Who?" Bull asks, revealing this is one detail he's been kept in the dark about.

"He didn't say much. Just that she taught him everything he knew. I could tell there were feelings involved. That's all I know."

"Bianca must be the woman Jaws and Stevie are fighting over. From what Stevie revealed, she is with him now and is the reason he has dealings with the cartel. She's our collateral. She's Jaws's Achilles' heel."

Placing my face into my palms, I close my eyes, needing

a minute to process all of this. This is a complicated web I wanted no part of.

Removing my hands, I ask, "My safety wasn't the only motivator, was it?"

His Adam's apple dips as he swallows. "No, it wasn't." I'm thankful he hasn't lied to me, but this vendetta has nothing to do with me. "Your brother needed an inside man for his revenge, and I needed your brother for mine. If I didn't do what he wanted, I would never avenge Damian.

"He promised me a fair fight, but that would never happen. So, I had to agree to his terms until I could come up with another plan. And now I have one."

"What is it?"

Bull hobbles toward me, and when he drops to his knees in front of me, something tugs at my heartstrings. "If I throw my next fight, the cartel gets me time alone with Scrooge. He will know where Jaws is."

He places his hands on my upper thighs, gripping them softly. "I promise you I will get Jordy back. He won't hurt him because he needs him. He is collateral."

"He's just a little boy." My voice cracks, as does my heart.

"I know, Tiger, but don't forget, he's your son. He isn't helpless. He's a fighter, like you. I've seen it."

"Who did I choose over Christopher?" Nothing makes sense anymore.

Bull sighs before squeezing my thighs. "Lachlan, Jordy, and..." He quickly pauses, but he doesn't need to fill in the blanks.

"And you?" I add softly, placing my hand over his. I'm

expecting him to flinch, but he doesn't.

"Yes." A single word holds so much weight over our future. "He thinks he owns you, Tiger. And the fact you aren't groveling at his feet, apologizing for falling for his best friend and having his baby, is the reason he's pissed off."

"No one owns me," I bark with bite.

"And that's the way it should be."

Chasing away my tears, I gently grip his bicep, coaxing him to come sit on the bed. He flinches, but slowly rises and sits down next to me.

"Why did he come back into my life? Why didn't he just stay gone?"

"At first, it was because you started dancing and interfered with his business," he reveals, not masking his disgust. And neither can I. "He stayed away as punishment. He saw how you struggled, but he didn't care. Now he's come back because he sees you as his property.

"He is angry with you, not for sleeping with his best friend, but because you loved someone more than him."

The way Bull talks, it sounds like Christopher has sick feelings for me. But that can't be true. Growing up, I never felt that way, but now, do I? Thinking back to the way he reacted to the man at the arcade, and the way he watches me dance, how feelings of...shame overwhelmed me, I realize that something isn't right.

"Carlos was hired by Christopher, wasn't he?"

"Yes. He came back into your life for another reason, and that's because he's seen us together. He knew he could use you as collateral against me. If we hadn't acted on..." He pauses, searching for the right word. "*This*, then he would have just left you alone. To him, you were a smart business move."

My stomach roils, and I think I'm going to be sick.

"But when he found out who I was, that's when all of this hatched. He saw an opportunity and took it. He said it was poetic justice."

Bull doesn't need to explain. Christopher saw our relationship growing, unbeknownst to us how deeply we were connected. This is kismet at its most fucked up.

"I'm sorry I ever doubted you." It's important for me to get this off my chest. "It was never self-defense, was it?"

Bull shakes his head, clenching and unclenching his fists. "No. I may have 'started' it, but your brother and his friends finished it when they thought it would be fun to hold back a fifteen-year-old and force him to watch them beat and kill his seventeen-year-old brother. Damian didn't have any friends," he spits. "All he had was me. And I couldn't even help him. But now, I can."

"Lachlan held him down?" I need to know everything. My whole life, I had him on a pedestal, just like Christopher. It's time that changed. Bull isn't the bad guy—they are.

"Yes," Bull replies heavily. I know this is hard for him to talk about, but this will be the last time I ask. "He planted his boot into his back, ensuring he stayed down while Scrooge and Jaws had their fun."

A tear trickles down my cheek, and I allow it to fall as it's the last one I will shed for someone I clearly didn't know.

"He should have called the ambulance. There was never a choice to make because he should have done the right thing."

I remember Bull told me Lachlan was the one who could have called, but he didn't, and in turn, that one choice shattered the lives of so many.

"But he didn't, which shows me I didn't know him at all. We all make mistakes, but that isn't a mistake. That's choosing between what's right and what's wrong."

Bull doesn't show any emotion, but I've come to read him well. His shallow breathing and the clenching of his fists present how closely he's trying to keep a lid on his emotions. Because for once in his life, he has someone in his corner.

I need to believe fate brought us together for a reason. And that reason is revenge. "As I see it, we both want the same thing."

He slowly turns his chin to look at me, waiting, unsure what I mean.

"For Jaws to pay. He is the reason for all of this. You didn't start it; he did. And now, we're going to finish it."

"Jaws?" he questions, as it's the first time I've referred to my brother by his nickname. And it was done with intent.

"The Christopher I know is dead to me…and all that's left is Jaws, the asshole who killed your brother and played me. The motherfucker who took my son. So whatever you have planned, count me in. I know we can't go to the cops, and Jaws is good at disappearing. He's been under my nose this entire time, and I didn't even know.

"If he takes Jordy, I'm afraid I'll never see him again."

I wait for him to fight me, to tell me he's a lone wolf just as his tattoo states. And if he does, then I will just do this on my own. I lured Jaws to the shallows, and I can do so again.

But he doesn't.

Even beneath his bruises, I see a smirk tug at his lips. It feeds the monster within. "I hope you have a nice dress."

"Why?" I ask, arching a brow.

"Because we have a gala to attend."

And just like that, two foes become friends...but we always were.

CHAPTER EIGHT

Lily

"She was such a wonderful woman."

"Yes, she was."

"I'm really going to"—*sniff, sniff*—"miss her. I remember when she—"

Blah fucking blah.

But I ensure my poker face is in check as Melanie Arnolds hugs me for the third time in the span of two minutes.

I don't understand what it is about death that makes people want to pretend they were BFFs with the deceased. Melanie barely acknowledged Avery when she was alive, but now, she's behaving as if they were Thelma and Louise, 2.0.

Looking at the sea of faces who attended Avery's funeral leaves me angry, well, angrier. It's been three days since my brother kidnapped my son, and here I am, pretending to give a shit about people reminiscing about what a wonderful woman Avery was.

This would have been far more meaningful if they'd told these things to Avery's face and not just her ceramic urn. But it's too late, just as it's too late for me to tell Jaws what a fucking asshole he is to his face.

Melanie mistakes my tears as ones of sadness. They are filled with nothing but rage.

Wiping them away with the back of my hand, I excuse myself and make my way toward the drinks table. After pouring myself a glass of scotch, I gulp it down, ignoring the way it gurgles in my empty stomach.

No matter how many times I called Jaws, or regardless of the fact I camped outside his house, he remained a ghost. He was ghosting me with my son in tow.

I started to dial 911 so many times but hung up because each and every time, Jaws's warning played over and over in my mind. What consequences does he speak of? Honestly, it could be anything. He has my entire life in his hands.

Pouring another glass of scotch, I throw it back, the burn matching the one behind my eyes as hot, angry tears scald me raw. I was so stupid to believe his story. Jaws played me for a fool, and now Jordy is paying the price for my stupidity.

Avery's lawyer has been in touch. He said Avery's funeral arrangements were all taken care of. She wanted something simple, and she didn't want to make a fuss. It was just like Avery to go out low-key. Once the funeral was done, he said he'd be in touch to discuss her will.

It was the last thing I wanted to do, but if Avery has any last wishes, then I intend to ensure they are fulfilled. But I can deal with that another day because once this sham is over with, I am one step closer to getting back my son.

It's the night of Bull's fight—the fight he's to throw so he can gain access to the man we both want. Bull believes that Scrooge will know of Jaws's whereabouts. They were thick as thieves when I was a kid, so I trust his gut instinct.

It goes without saying that I'm no longer working at Blue Bloods. Carlos kicked up a stink, threatening to sue as I was in breach of my contract, but he was bluffing. I had some collateral of my own because I have no doubt that Blue Bloods is a front for Jaws's dirty money.

I could go to the cops and tell them everything I know, but I can't because I'll never see Jordy again if I do. Jaws was close by this entire time, and I didn't even know. Imagine what he'd do if he wanted to remain hidden forever.

Bull has asked around, but no one wants to talk.

In short, we're on our own.

Going back to teaching ballet is the last thing I want to do, but I have to do something. I can't sleep. I can't eat. All I can think about is Jordy and how I failed him. If I don't teach and keep busy, I'll drive myself insane. And I refuse to do that because I need to be ready for whatever Bull has planned.

He promises we'll get Jordy back, and I believe him. I have to.

Subtly peering at my silver watch, I see that it's time. Not bothering with goodbyes, I tuck Avery under my arm and walk out the door. No one misses me because they're too busy attempting to absolve themselves of whatever guilt they have for not showing Avery the respect she deserved when she was alive.

The moment I step outside, I take my first real breath. I feel like I've been holding it all day. Seeking him out, I see his black truck parked in the distance. He is my beacon, the only thing stopping me from slipping into a depression and never resurfacing again.

My heels dig into the snow as I march toward Bull's truck, so not ready for what tonight holds. Yes, I've seen him fight before, but this is different. So much is riding on other people. If they don't deliver, I don't know what to do.

But I refuse to think that way. This will work. It has to.

When I open the door and see Bull, the heavy weight pressing against my chest begins to ebb away. But I mask my happiness because the only thing I'm focusing on is finding Jordy and not my growing feelings.

His mismatched eyes drop to the urn under my arm, but he doesn't say a word. I get in and quickly buckle up. The drive to Chicago is long, so I don't want to waste any time. The engine roars to life, and we're on our way.

Placing the urn in the middle console, I reach over my shoulder for my backpack in the back seat. I packed a change of clothes because I never want to wear this black dress ever again. Hunting through it, I grab my skinny jeans.

Kicking off my heels, I slip my legs into the jeans and shuffle into them under my dress. Raising my hips, I zip them up. Without thought, I lift the dress over my head and stuff it into the bag. I'm only in a black silk bra as I hunt for my gray slouchy sweater.

I slip it on, aware of Bull's subtle glances, but I'm too tired and broken to give way to any bashfulness. Untucking my hair from the collar, I unsnap one of the hairbands from around my wrist and tie it into a high bun. I decide to wait and put my sneakers and jacket on when we arrive.

Sighing, I apply some honey lip balm but soon realize since the moment I've entered the truck, I haven't been able to sit still. I'm a ball of nerves, but I am also so restless.

"How long till we get there?" I ask, tugging at the seat belt because it's suffocating me. The question is ridiculous. I've been to Chicago before, so I know how long it takes. But if I don't fill the silence with noise, I will resort to thoughts, thoughts of where my son is and if he's safe.

Bull humors me regardless. "A few hours."

His bruising has faded, but he's still injured. And that's to be expected, seeing as he was attacked by a stun gun my brother used on him. He said it'll make throwing the fight all the more believable because he'll just blame the loss on still being hurt. But I know he will have to make it realistic, which means I'll have to witness him spill more blood.

"How was the funeral?"

"It was a nice send-off. I just wish I wasn't so distracted. I wanted Avery to know how much she meant to me." Peering down at the urn, I run two fingers over the top.

"She knew," Bull says with regret.

Of course, he has firsthand experience with losing a loved one, so he knows what I'm feeling right now. The wave of anger threatens to drag me under, but I subconsciously snap the elastic around my wrist. The sharp sting quiets the voices roaring within.

"I know me asking you to stay in the truck is out of the question," he says, and I nod once, glad we're on the same page. "But stay in the shadows, all right? The fewer people who see you, the better. José can't know who you are. You will just be another pawn to add to his growing collection. We got no business with the cartel."

"If Bianca was someone of importance to"—I inhale, needing a moment before I speak his name—"to Jaws, then maybe she'll know of his whereabouts."

"That's exactly the reason you need to stay hidden," he counters, nostrils flared. "If they find out who you are—" His pause reveals the severity of his warning. "Just please, promise me you won't draw any attention to yourself, regardless of what you see."

His cautioning has me turning to look at him. "What am I going to see?"

His attention is riveted to the road, but I can see how my questions are irritating him. Something bad is sure to go down, but he doesn't want me to know. I find out what that is. "To throw the fight, I have to make it believable."

"Meaning?" I encourage, not wanting to go into this blind.

His cheeks bellow as he exhales. "Meaning, things are going to get bloody for me. The fight will only be called when I'm either unconscious or dead."

I gulp.

"I don't know what'll happen, but if there is any trouble, you take the truck and get out of there, okay?"

"I'm not leaving you," I stubbornly argue. But he's clearly not willing to negotiate on this.

"Goddammit, Tiger!" His jaw clenches. "I can't do this if I'm worrying about you. I need to keep a clear head, and if I—"

"Okay, I promise," I quickly interrupt, mentally crossing my fingers as there is no way I'm leaving him behind. He just admitted he'd worry about me, which means he cares.

I still don't know what I am to Bull. Thinking of my confession in the cemetery, about how my feelings for him are growing every day, I wonder if he feels the same way. In light of what's happening, I know it's trivial, but knowing I'm not alone in this gives me hope.

Placing my head back against the headrest, I close my eyes and give in to the silence, allowing myself a moment of reprieve as I'm unsure when I will do so again.

"Tiger."

Groaning, I open my heavy eyes, wondering where I am because I had the most god-awful dream. I dreamed Christopher took Jordy…

My heart suddenly constricts, the sharp pain a reminder that it wasn't a dream. It's my life, which I am currently staggering through.

"We're here." Bull's voice is my only tether. Without it, without him, I would have floated away.

"Okay," I reply, focusing on where here is. We're in the middle of nowhere. The only thing I can see in this winter wonderland is a large run-down church.

The stained-glass windows are still intact, but the weathered exterior has seen better days. Flashy cars are parked in the snowy field. A few people are smoking cigarettes on the front steps, their plumes of smoke filling the starless sky.

"You go in," Bull instructs. "I'll follow a few minutes later. I have to get ready, so I won't see you until I get into the ring."

I nod, knowing he uses the term ring lightly. This is a free-for-all. A blood sport for the rich assholes with too much money on their hands.

There is no protocol for this kind of thing, so I quickly put on my shoes and socks. When I slip on my knitted beanie and reach for the door handle, Bull reaches out and grips my forearm. I peer down at his fingers and then back up to meet his eyes.

"Be careful, Tiger."

"You too," I reply softly, suddenly questioning everything.

Something shifts, something electric, and goose bumps instantly coat my skin. I am suddenly terrified for what the night will bring.

Bull lets me go, but I watch with interest as he reaches under the collar of his shirt and gently slips his fingers under his necklace. He slides it over his head, the silver medallion catching the shine of the full moon.

"Keep it safe for me?" He offers it to me with a slight tremble to his fingers.

I accept, fingering over the medallion with care. I see it's

Saint Christopher.

"It was Damian's," he reveals with soft sentiment. "His good luck charm."

I can't hide my emotion as I put it on and tuck it safely beneath my sweater. I want to say so many things, like how I'm afraid for him, for me, for us. If something were to happen to either of us, what becomes of my son?

Failure isn't an option.

Tipping my chin, I attempt to conceal my tears. Crying isn't going to solve a thing. But with the gentlest of touches, Bull grips my chin and coaxes me to look at him. When we lock eyes, I allow my vulnerability to show. I'm so tired of hiding.

No words are needed as we remain in a wordless embrace. He thumbs over my trembling bottom lip, before wiping away my tear. He is lending me his strength, and right now, I need it more than ever.

"It'll be okay. I promise."

Before I have a chance to reply, he bends forward, and with a whisper of his warm, hesitant lips, he places a kiss on my cheek. The gesture is filled with so much concern and tenderness, I almost forget to breathe. These moments are rare for Bull. He is still coming to terms with being able to show vulnerability or emotion.

We're both learning how to walk before we run because when we do, there will be no stopping us.

He pulls away sluggishly, gliding his nose across my skin and inhaling before leaving me to deal with this enormous weight pressing against me that's robbing me of air. I zip up my jacket, then open the door and step outside. I don't look back as my feet sink into inches of snow because each step takes me closer to getting Jordy back.

Craning my neck, I see the steeple of the church still has a silver cross attached to the top. Maybe an omen of things to come? The white paint has long chipped away, hinting this place hasn't been used for prayer in a very long time. The stained-glass windows reflect colorful patterns across the snow, but the deep reds leave me envisioning what I will soon see spilled inside.

The three men on the front steps stop talking when I approach them. They're dressed in expensive clothes and not masking their judgment on why someone like me is here. But I do as Bull told me—I act like I belong.

With head held high, I push past them and open the heavy wooden door. The lights are bright courtesy of the generator running in the corner of the room. About two hundred people are crammed inside, hollering and cheering as two men circle one another in the middle of the room.

The pews have been removed. The altar is all that remains, draped in a red silk cloth. The sight is unnerving, as it appears they're preparing for an offering. The wooden floor is dirty, littered with debris and cigarette butts.

Bull gave me a wad of cash to use for bets because this isn't a spectator's sport. Everyone is here to win. If I don't lay down some money, they'll sense something is amiss. A man in suit pants and a blue shirt saunters over, notepad in hand. No doubt this is one of Stevie's bookies.

"How much, and who you betting on?" he asks, pushing

his silver glasses up the bridge of his slender nose.

Reaching into my pocket, I give him the rolled-up stack of bills and reply, "Tiny." This is a sure bet, seeing as I know who the winner will be, so I don't feel so bad giving away all this cash.

The man doesn't ask any questions. He simply dumps the money into a small bag and gives me a pink ticket with some scribble on the front. I'm thankful when he doesn't linger.

After finding the darkest corner as Bull instructed, I stay hidden, watching the two men beat the living shit out of one another. Each time their fists or feet connect with the other, the crowd roars in delight while I flinch, my stomach turning.

This world is so foreign to me. Before meeting Bull, my life had structure, but now, here I am, caught up in an illegal fighting syndicate in order to find my missing son. My fingers drift to the elastic around my wrist, and I begin to flick it, the sting calming the roaring demons within.

Subtly peering around the room, I take in the masses. They're a mixed bunch, but overall, they all share one thing— they're here to win. I wonder how someone comes to know about these events. I know it isn't advertised, so are they listed in some illegal newsletter swap?

When my gaze lands on a well-dressed man with a deep scar down his cheek, I take a guess this is José. He is surrounded by three men. Their eyes scan the room, and when I lock gazes with one of them, I quickly avert my eyes.

I need to be more careful.

Feigning interest, I watch as the fighters attack one another, staggering and bleeding all over the floor. The smaller of the two finally puts an end to the fight when he headbutts his opponent out cold. The crowd erupts into cheers, hands raised in celebration as they drag the lifeless man away.

The winner hobbles toward a door left of the altar. I guess that is where Bull is.

The bookie does a last sweep of the crowd, hinting the next fight is about to commence. I bite my thumbnail, anxiously awaiting the next few minutes. A man smoking a cigar saunters through the door the fighter entered, and from Bull's description, I know this is Stevie, the asshole who wants to exploit Lotus's hard work.

Technically, we don't need to play nice with him anymore. He's played his part. But Bull said until we find Jordy, Stevie may be an ally we need—the lesser of two evils. And the same goes for José. We are siding with evil to defeat evil it seems.

A thunderous roar brings my attention back to the middle of the room where a man, or rather a beast, is bouncing on the spot. He is well over six feet and has biceps the size of my head. Instantly, my palms begin to sweat. He is going to kill Bull.

He's topless, his muscled physique glimmering under the lights, showcasing just how much damage he can inflict. If this were a fair fight, then I wouldn't be so worried. But watching this animal attack Bull is going to be hard to stomach.

The air is tense with an electrical pulse, and that only increases tenfold when the crowd begins to chant *Colmillo* over and over again. I know a little Spanish, so I understand what they're saying.

Fang.

And when Bull emerges from the doorway, his fangs flashing brutally on his face shield, I realize they're chanting out to him.

He pushes through the masses, not interested in praise as his eye is on the prize—Tiny. He knows what he has to do; yet, his arrogance knows no bounds as he sports a winner's walk.

Wearing a long-sleeved top that clings to his defined muscles, he has his hands bound with white tape as well as his feet and ankles. He looks like he's ready for war. His tattooed legs are his only distinguishable feature as he has in his blue contact. I now understand why he goes to the trouble to conceal his identity.

In that ring, he isn't Cody Bishop or Bullseye. He is *Colmillo*. He has a part to play. We all do. And when he advances toward Tiny, throwing the first punch, it seems he's eager to get this show on the road.

Tiny's head snaps back before he wipes his bleeding lip with the back of his hand. Bull got in the first punch because he knows Tiny will get in the last and he needs to put on a good show in the meantime. They begin to circle one another, Bull's focus never wavering from the animal in front of him.

Tiny's tattooed back of a demonic Mickey Mouse blocks Bull from my vision, so I stand on tippy toes, needing to keep my eyes on him the whole time. Tiny strikes out, but Bull reads his move and ducks before delivering a sharp punch to his flank.

A pained oof leaves Tiny, who buckles, and Bull takes full advantage when he connects with his jaw.

Bull is fierce, and the crowd explodes into pandemonium

as they push each other, wanting to get closer to the action. Tiny shakes his head, appearing to focus on the wild beast in front of him. Bull's fists are raised in front of his face, ready to strike, and I suddenly wonder if he is having second thoughts about losing.

He definitely doesn't look like loser material when he dodges another of Tiny's punches before kicking down on his knee. Tiny's leg collapses out from under him, and he drops. Bull then delivers a succession of punches to Tiny's face, ribs, and stomach, which has Tiny falling onto his back.

Bull doesn't waste a second and dives on top of him, punching his face over and over.

The chanting of *Colmillo* only gets louder and louder, fueling Bull to punish Tiny brutally. Risking a glance at Stevie, I see he and José are huddled together, watching on intently. Stevie is nothing but confident, smoking his cigar with a smile. José remains untroubled, but surely, he must be thinking what I am—is Bull backing out of their deal?

Maybe he's come up with another plan? I trust him and know how much is at stake if he wins this fight. We don't get to Scrooge, which isn't an option for either of us.

I breathe a sigh of relief, thankful I won't have to witness him being beaten to a pulp, but that breath is taken in vain because when Tiny punches Bull in the stomach and a winded gasp leaves him, I know all of this was for show.

Tiny grips Bull's wet hair, holding him in place before headbutting him. The hollow noise is horrifying, and I bite down on my tongue to stop my scream. Bull comes to a shaky stand, shaking his head, but Tiny is suddenly on his feet, towering over Bull. He punches him in the stomach, right over his wound from the stun gun.

The pained grunt isn't staged, and I feel the walls closing in on me. Tiny begins to beat Bull senseless, who gets in a few punches, but it's evident he's hurt. He is sluggish on his feet, which Tiny takes advantage of. He hits him in the ribs, the stomach, and the face, but Bull won't go down.

"No," I whimper as each punch Bull takes rattles me to my core.

When Tiny's meaty fist connects with Bull's eye, it instantly swells as it still hasn't completely healed from when Jaws attacked him. Yet Bull continues dancing around Tiny with his fists raised.

My stomach roils, threatening to bring up the scotch I had earlier, but I squash down the nausea and keep my cool. Bull told me to stay hidden, but when Tiny punches Bull so hard in the jaw, I hear a crack, I forget his warning and charge forward.

I don't want to be hidden in the shadows. We're in this together. I want it to be my face he sees, not a sea of strangers.

The masses are nothing but animals, hollering and cheering, demanding more bloodshed, but I shove them aside, desperate to get to Bull. I can't stand by and watch him being beaten this way.

"Move!" I scream at the vile men who are shouting for Bull's blood to be spilled. They look down at me, not masking their crude thoughts.

"You lost, baby?" one of them slurs. The smell of whiskey hints he is drunk on more than just bloodlust.

"Fuck you!" I scream, clawing at him to move out of my way, but he does nothing of the sort. He grips my bicep, drawing me against his chest.

"I can arrange that." He chuckles, cupping my ass.

Anger explodes from me. I'm so sick and tired of the misogynistic pigs in this world. Without thinking, I raise my knee, in hopes I connect with his balls, but he stops me when he grabs my upper thigh.

"We've got a pocket rocket, boys," he hollers over his shoulder.

"Let me go," I demand, trying to shake from his hold. But his grip is tight.

He hauls me forward, groping me without apology as I scream. But my cries are muted by the shrieks of others. I suddenly wish I'd listened to Bull. I just wanted to help. I couldn't stand by and watch him sacrifice himself yet again. I wanted to be there for him, a familiar face showing him how much I care.

His worth to me is more than money can ever buy. And I want him to know that.

But I won't be going anywhere thanks to the asshole who won't let me go. He threads his fingers through my hair, yanking my head to the side before licking along my throat. I kick and slap at him, but the violence in the air feeds his depravity.

Regardless of my flailing, he manages to unsnap the top button of my jeans, but that's as far as he gets before he's violently spun around and dropped to the floor, unconscious. My heart is in my throat as I blink rapidly, unsure of what just happened. When I tear my eyes away from his motionless form on the floor, I see what happened is standing inches away.

Bull is seething. His body twitches as pulses of anger and adrenaline course through him. I gasp because he is beaten and bloody, but when I frantically advance, needing to help him, he shakes his head firmly, demanding I stay put.

The hard set of his rigid stance reveals he isn't playing. And when the crowd parts behind him, he gives me my wish. Bull knows what's about to happen, and he accepts his fate with his eyes locked on mine when Tiny grabs his shoulder, spins him around, and knocks Bull out cold. With a thud, he drops at my feet while I cover my mouth with a trembling hand.

I wanted my face to be the one he saw, and it was. But not before he saved me—again.

Two men lay unconscious at my feet.

For the first time since I entered this shitshow, the crowd is silent. But that is soon replaced with a deafening cheer. Men high-five one another while others tear their scraps of paper in half. I don't know what's going on, but I don't care.

More than anything, I want to drop to my knees and help Bull, but when I notice both Stevie and José peering at me with nothing but curiosity, I leave indents on my palms as I curl my fists. I was supposed to be invisible, but now, I'm on their radar.

With bile rising, I raise my pink ticket in the air, faking victory. If I appear victorious, maybe I'll throw them off. Two men appear out of nowhere, picking up a limp Bull by the arms. His chin lolls against his chest.

His long hair flops forward, shrouding his face, but I saw the damage inflicted to his eye. I can only imagine what hides beneath his mask. The men drag him away like he's nothing but trash as the crowd looks on, clearly surprised the favorite lost.

No one comes for the asshole who groped me, and his "friends" have scattered, showing there is no such thing as loyalty in a place such as this.

People soon disappear as the main act is over. I see the bookie sitting in the corner of the room, handing out the winnings. From the short line, I dare say that a lot of punters have gone home empty-handed. I decide to line up as it'll buy me some time to wait for Bull.

I have the spare set of truck keys in my pocket, but I'm not going anywhere. I know I made a promise, but there is no way I'm leaving him here. As I'm waiting in line, I place my hands into my pockets to stop them from shaking. But when I feel someone behind me, I don't have a hope in the world to mask my nerves.

"Seems we both have a thing for the underdogs."

Taking a small breath, I look over my shoulder and see José and his men behind me. I can't help but look at his scar. It looks like someone tried to gouge his eye out with a melon baller.

He waits for me to reply, so I nod with a smile. "Seems so."

I turn back around, desperate to get away from this man. Even though Bianca is linked to them somehow, Bull is right. Getting mixed up with the cartel will only lead to more trouble.

José, however, doesn't seem to get the hint. "We haven't seen you here before. Who told you about the fight?"

Shit.

Anxiously peering overhead, I see about four people in front of me. I can't ignore him, so I turn back around, and reply vaguely, "A friend at work."

"Oh, yeah? Where do you work?"

If anyone else was asking me this, I'd say they were just making conversation. But there is no such thing as casual chitchat with a man like José.

"If I tell you that, I'll have to kill you," I tease, batting my eyelashes. Bull told me not to share any information because if I do, it'll look suspicious. The vaguer the better, as this *is* an illegal fighting syndicate after all.

José's lips twitch. I've dodged a bullet—for now.

"Smart girl. I hope to see you around." It's a promise. He knows I'm lying. No doubt he saw the way Bull came to my aid. Hopefully, he only thinks Bull asked me to bet on Tiny to win him some money.

The line begins moving, and when I'm up next, I quickly give the bookie my ticket, surprised when he hands over an envelope stuffed full of cash. I don't bother looking inside.

With eyes downcast, I walk the long way around, avoiding José and his men. I can feel his gaze follow me out the door and know this isn't the last I've seen of him. It's snowing, but I don't wait for it to stop. I make a mad dash for the truck, keys in hand, afraid someone will come lunging out of the shadows to stop me.

Opening the driver's door, I dive inside, then slam the

lock down. My heart is in my throat as I breathlessly scan my surroundings, but all I see is crisp white snow.

Reaching for my phone, I send Bull a text.

```
I'm waiting in the truck.
```

No matter how long I have to wait, I will. I don't know how long it takes for someone to recover from being unconscious, but from the looks of Bull, I guess it'll be a while.

Sinking low in the seat, I keep my eyes peeled, watching for any signs of danger. I don't see Stevie, so maybe he's with Bull. I'm sure he's not happy with Bull losing tonight. There is so much unknown, and I hate it. I want to help, but I wouldn't even know where to start.

Peering at my phone at what feels like hours later, I see that the last text message I sent to Bull was forty-five minutes ago. Where is he?

Tapping my fingers against the steering wheel, I contemplate sneaking back inside. Only a few cars remain, as most left the moment Bull was knocked out. I haven't seen José leave, but I wouldn't put it past him to have arrived via private jet.

Just as I'm about to unlock the door, a figure comes hobbling out a side door. Although his face is downturned, I know it's Bull. He's alone, so I wait for him to get closer before I open the door and race toward him.

Seeing him fills me with a sense of peace, which is ironic, considering his state, but I feel like I can finally breathe again. His wet hair is slicked back, so I can see the extent of his injuries. He looks far worse than I ever imagined.

"Oh, god. Let me help you." Looping my arm around his waist, I encourage him to lean against me as we stagger toward the truck.

He allows me to help, which confirms he feels as bad as he looks. I just hope José won't double-cross us. Bull trusts him because although they're criminals, their word apparently is solid. Makes no sense to me, but hey, what do I know?

He stops suddenly, inhaling sharply as he sags against me. "Sorry. I just need to catch my breath."

"Don't apologize," I say with sincerity, giving him all the time he needs.

He's good to go a few moments later, and when we get to the truck, I open the door and all but shove him inside. When he's in, I close the door and run to the driver's side. A sense of security falls over me when we're inside.

After Bull is buckled in tight, I start the engine, eager to get away from this church that has been anything but a sanctuary.

The moment I pull onto the road, I exhale, but my heart is far from returning to a normal pace. Glancing back and forth between Bull and the road, I work my lip between my teeth until I taste blood. He looks to be on the cusp of passing out.

"Bull," I caution, gently reaching over and squeezing his thigh. "Stay awake. You've probably got a concussion."

He jerks awake, shaking his head to clear it. "Are you all right?" he pants, flinching as he grips his side.

"I should be the one asking you that," I assert. "What can I do?"

I feel so helpless. We didn't know what the severity of his injuries would be, so I packed a first-aid kit filled with everything just in case. He said he'd be okay to drive back to Detroit, but each time I hit a small pothole, he winces.

He needs to rest. And I don't think I can drive the few hours home without running us into a ditch. All I want to do is touch him, to make sure he's okay, and I can't. When I see a motel up ahead, I take it as a sign.

"Why are you stopping?" he asks, shifting to get comfortable. But he can't sit still.

"Let's stay here overnight. You need to rest. We can leave in the morning after a good night's sleep."

Again, he doesn't argue.

I park the truck and sprint into the twenty-four-hour reception. The man doesn't bat an eye when I ask for a room and pay in cash. This place is your typical seedy motel, so I'm sure he's seen it all.

Our room is the last one toward the back. There are barely any cars parked here. Just a couple of semi-trailers. The place is quiet, so it's perfect. As I grab our bags from the back seat, Bull opens the door and slowly exits. He stubbornly hobbles toward the room, but I catch up to him quickly.

I don't ask for permission before I wind my arm around him, leading him to our room. The hallway lights flicker, which has Bull shielding his eyes. When we get to our room, I maintain my hold on him as I unlock the door with one hand.

Shouldering it open, we commence a slow stagger toward the bed, where I carefully help him onto the foot of the mattress. I don't fail to notice how this is all too familiar now.

Once he's settled, I lock the door and toss our bags onto the floor. "What do you need?" I ask him, unzipping my backpack.

I packed everything I could think of.

"Painkillers," he replies. "And scotch."

He's in luck because I packed both. But the scotch is for me.

Grabbing a bottle of water and the painkillers, I pass them to him. He doesn't argue but looks at the water like it just told him to go fuck himself. After unscrewing the lid, he pops four tablets and drinks down the water in one gulp.

Hunting through my supplies, I reach for the antibiotic ointment and the alcohol swabs. I have Band-Aids, gauze, and ice packs. I even brought a liquid bandage solution. There is no way I'm stitching him up with a needle and thread again.

Deciding to examine the damage first, I sit down beside him, carefully brushing the hair from his brow. His right eye is once again swollen shut. The other is bloodshot. His nose is about twice the size, and his bottom lip is busted open.

"Goddammit," I curse angrily. I am furious it had to come to this.

Ripping open the alcohol swab, I gently dab at his cuts and scrapes. I keep my hands steady, but my fast breathing gives away my nerves. Bull sits still, allowing me to nurse him. Once his face is cleaned, I reach for his left hand and wipe over his knuckles with a new swab.

His palm sits snugly in mine and touching him has my heart rate slowing and my breathing calming. He anchors me in ways I don't understand. But I don't question it. "Where else does it hurt?"

"I'm fine," he stubbornly replies. The painkillers must have kicked in.

"Take off your shirt," I order, ripping open another swab.

He reads my no-nonsense attitude and reaches over his head, tugging his T-shirt off by the collar. He's traded his trademark shirt and suspenders for a gray T-shirt. He dumps the T-shirt on the floor while I swallow down my nausea.

His flesh is red, and bruising lingers under the surface. There are a few scrapes, which I gently dab with the swab, but his injuries are more internal. Dark bruising has formed around his ribs. Dragging my backpack over, I grab the single-use ice pack and squeeze it together, waiting for it to cool.

"Here." I apply it to his ribs gently.

This close to him, his scent is amplified tenfold, and the tension coiling within begins to unravel. I am suddenly so tired. We are one step closer to getting Jordy back. I can do this.

"Thank you," I say, unable to meet his eyes. "I know you did this for your own personal gain also, but—"

Bull doesn't allow me to finish. He grips my chin and tips my face to his. "I made you a promise, and I don't break my promises," he says, thumbing over my tender bottom lip, frowning. "Why are you hurting yourself?"

I don't understand what he means until I remember it's sensitive because I nearly gnawed it off in the car.

Without warning, he lets go of my chin, only to roll up my sleeve and run his finger over the elastic around my wrist. Hissing, I don't even realize it's red and raw until Bull draws my attention to it.

"Why, Tiger?" he repeats, watching me closely.

Yanking it back subconsciously, I instantly chew on my lip. A force of habit I've picked up, just as flicking the elastic around my wrist is, since Jordy was taken from me.

"I don't even realize I'm doing it," I confess. "But the pain, it feels good. It's punishment I deserve."

"Why do you deserve punishment?" he asks, shaking his head slowly.

"Because I failed my son," I hopelessly declare. "I never should have trusted my brother. I should have listened to my gut. If I had—"

"That's the thing about hindsight," Bull cuts in, still brushing over my wrist. "It's fairly fucking useless. Learn from your mistakes."

Tears sting my eyes. "Do you think he's okay?"

"Yes, I do. He's leverage, and Jaws needs that. And as long as he's of use to Jaws, he will be okay. Jaws needs an inside man and that hasn't changed. He still wants revenge on those who hurt him."

"Just like us," I add, realizing our endgames are all driven by revenge.

"His game plan is still the same. He still wants Stevie dead." Bull releases my wrist but never breaks eye contact with me. "But we have an advantage. Jaws doesn't know we have the cartel on our side. We can't tell anyone about our plans.

"Stevie won't care that Jaws is blackmailing us. Or that he has Jordy. We can't tell Lotus about Stevie's plans. She isn't that good of an actress. We need it to be business as usual until we get Jordy back."

Nodding, I realize Bull has been thinking about this, ensuring everything is rock solid.

"Jaws still thinks he has the advantage and can use us. That we will do anything he says. And we will until we get to Scrooge. He's making us wait to show he's in control. But he'll soon reveal what he wants."

"Why can't he get someone else to do this?" I ask, needing to understand every angle there is.

"He needs a man he can trust," Bull reveals, flinching as he moves the ice pack to sit higher up his ribs. "And believe it or not, that man is me. He has something I want—his head and your son. And I have something he wants—inside information which I haven't given him—yet. It is the only pull I have over him.

"This isn't a business where you trust easily. Jaws would have to start again. After Kong, Stevie won't allow just anyone in on his operation, and Jaws knows this."

"This is all because of Bianca?"

Bull nods. "I think so. It also has to do with his empire. He needs to be alpha, but he isn't. Maybe he's hoping Bianca will see who the bigger man is, and she'll come back to him. I don't know. All I know is that he wants Stevie dead. And to take his business while doing so."

Blowing the hair from my cheeks, I say, "Jesus, I know our childhood wasn't the best, but I don't know who this person is."

"Once we get Jordy back and Jaws and Scrooge are no longer"—Bull swallows deeply, gauging my response—"then we'll go to the police. We'll tell Franca everything."

I now understand why the pause. Bull has thought this through.

"We tell her about Stevie and the cartel. If we don't, and they find out what we did, that we lied to them for our own personal gain, they'll kill us. They saw my response to you tonight, so you're already on their radar."

Unable to hide my guilt, I avert my eyes, angry with myself for not holding it together. "You'll get in trouble," I state, shaking my head. We can't go to the police. Franca will want to know how we know all this. If she digs, she will uncover the bodies Bull has left behind.

"I knew how this would end, Tiger," he replies calmly. "As long as those responsible for my brother's death are held accountable, I can deal with whatever punishment I deserve."

But this outcome is bleak; it means my future will be one without Bull in it.

Instinctively, I reach for the elastic around my wrist. But pause when Bull gently places his hand over mine.

"You look tired. Get some sleep. I'm going to shower."

He's right. I am beyond tired. And this isn't up for negotiation as he comes to a slow stand and tosses the ice pack onto the dresser.

"What if you're concussed? I should—"

"Tiger, I'll be all right."

Biting the inside of my cheek, I know we're no longer talking about his injuries. His mind is made up. There is only one way this will end.

I watch as he grabs his bag and makes his way into the

bathroom, closing the door. It's so final. His mind is made up. But if he thinks I'm going to sit back and watch as he throws himself to the wolves, then he's sorely mistaken.

It's time I made some plans of my own.

Bull

I wake to a warmth I've never felt before.

Slowly focusing out of one eye, I realize I must have passed out sometime last night because the sunlight streaming in through the crack in the curtain confirms it's now morning.

Tiger had passed out on top of the bed while I took my shower, so I drew back the blankets and tucked her in. There was only one bed, so I lay next to her, on top of the blanket, and watched her sleep. I've never slept beside someone before. I didn't think I'd be comfortable with that sort of intimacy, but I was clearly mistaken.

Tiger's shallow breathing tickles the back of my neck as her chest is pressed snugly against my back. Her arm is draped across me, holding on tight. The blankets are a tangled mess at the end of the bed as she must have kicked them off in the middle of the night.

Looking at the clock on the bedside table, I see that it's just after six a.m.

I shift, but Tiger groans softly, tightening her hold around me. Her wrist is still red from where flicking the elastic has left her skin raw. Seeing her hurt herself leaves me with this unsettled feeling in the pit of my stomach.

The significance of the elastic isn't lost on me. She wears it to help her anxiety. The pain when she flicks it against her skin is almost a form of punishment for losing Jordy. Pain is something we both understand, but seeing her hurt doesn't give me the feels like it does for others. I want to shoulder her burden and take her pain as my own.

Sighing, I know I'm so screwed. Whatever the fuck this is inside of my chest continues to grow, and I know sooner or later, I will be consumed with it, with *her*. But who am I kidding? I already am.

When I saw that motherfucker touch her last night, I lost sight of anything but her. I knew my actions would draw attention to her, attention Stevie and José wouldn't miss, but I couldn't just stand by and allow her to be hurt. She's been hurt enough.

This is so fucking backward. I am helping find the son of the man I killed. And to do that, I have to work with the men I want to kill. This is happening for a reason; I have to believe that because I have no fucking clue how I've ended up where I am.

It was supposed to be simple, but what I feel for Tiger... it's anything but that.

She nestles in closer with a contented sigh. I give in to temptation and slowly interlock our fingers. I like the way they look entwined.

My body responds in ways it shouldn't, but I can't help it. I never can when Tiger is involved. I'm not only physically aroused, but emotionally as well, and it's a powerful sensation. All I want is to feel her beneath me as I bury myself deep inside.

My injuries aren't too bad, thanks to Tiger's traveling pharmacy, but I shouldn't be thinking about her soft curves and sweet smell because she is grieving for her son. Getting laid is probably the last thing on her mind.

But when she gently rolls her hips into me, I begin to wonder if maybe I'm wrong.

She squeezes my fingers while gliding her nose over my bare back and inhaling with a sigh. She presses her lips to my shoulder before biting softly. The way she rolls her hips against me has my hard-on straining against my boxers, but I lay still.

She lets go of my hand, only to walk her fingers down to my cock. She isn't shy and begins to rub over the front of my boxers. Touching was once my hard limit, but now, if she doesn't touch me, I think I will fucking lose my mind.

She's only in her bra and underwear as she must have removed her jeans and sweater during the night. We're treading dangerous waters because when she slips her hand into my boxers and begins to stroke my shaft, I know this is only going to end one way.

She continues to bite and suck me as she works my dick with her small hand. Wherever she touches, my body responds, and it's not long before I am thrusting into her touch. Without warning, she swiftly removes her hand and rolls me onto my back.

I don't have time to question what she's doing before she climbs on top of me and unhooks her bra. I grip her hips, staring up at her. She is a fucking goddess, and my chain hanging between her perfect tits only cements this. Her body is toned, strong. Her light pink nipples are hard, begging for me to take them into my mouth. But this is Tiger's show.

Her hair is wild around her face, tangled from sleep, and it only makes her sexier. She runs both palms down my chest, transfixed by her hands on me. I can see the way she studies my tattoos and the barbells in my nipples, and the way her brow puckers when she traces over the scar on my side.

I wish I had something nicer to offer her, something that isn't marred with violence and bloodshed.

She chews on her bottom lip when she reaches the top of my boxers. I reach up, flicking her lip out from under her teeth. A bashful smile spreads across her mouth before she slides down my body and gently removes my boxers.

My dick springs up, and a beautiful rose coats her pale skin when she realizes how hard I am because of her. Brushing her hair over one shoulder, she bends forward and takes me into her mouth.

"Holy fuck," I curse with a shudder. It's been so long since I've had a blowjob that I've forgotten how good they feel. But the ones in the past pale in comparison to what Tiger is doing to me right now.

She takes her time as she works my cock carefully. She appears to be fascinated with my piercing as the tip of her tongue pokes out to flick over the curved barbell. All I can do is watch her, spellbound by her beauty. This isn't some porn movie where she sucks me hard and fast. She seems to be familiarizing herself with me, seeing how far she can go, and I like it.

We're testing the waters as it's been a long time for us both.

She finds her rhythm, gripping my upper thighs as she bobs between them. I almost shred the sheet as I bunch the bedding in my fists. When I hit the back of her throat, she gags and pulls away. I think she's had enough, but she takes me back into her mouth, sucking and whimpering around my cock.

Her jerky movements only make this all the more perfect, and when I feel the sting of her teeth rake across my shaft, I grunt in pleasure. Needing to touch her, I brush the hair from her face and collect it in my fist so I can watch her.

Her cheeks hollow as she takes me deep, and I hold back my need to come because it won't be in her mouth when I do. Her tits swing with her movements, and my chain around her neck is a sight I like way too much.

"Baby, come here," I growl, the term of endearment slipping free naturally.

But of course, she doesn't do what she's told.

She pulls back, tonguing over the tip of my cock while stroking my shaft. I arch my head back, unable to look at her because I am so turned on, and I won't be able to hold on. She uses her hands and mouth in unison, not being gentle, and I like it so fucking much.

When she cups my balls, I jerk in surprise, sliding down her throat. "Oh, fuck," I grunt, everything suddenly too much.

Reaching down, I impatiently tug at the waistband of her underwear. She has three fucking seconds to take them off; otherwise, she will be leaving here without them. Thankfully, she complies, quickly letting me go before pulling them down her shapely legs.

Once she's naked, she straddles me, gazing down at me with a look I don't understand. "Bull, I-I…" She nervously licks her lips.

She leaves the sentence unfinished as she grips my cock and guides it toward her pussy. I instantly reach down, wanting to ensure she's ready for me, but I feel how wet she is when she takes me into her sex slowly.

Groaning, I'm her prisoner as she lowers herself onto me leisurely, ensuring we both feel how deep I am. She whimpers when I'm buried to the hilt. Placing her hands against my stomach, she begins to rock slowly, backward and forward, side to side.

"I don't want to hurt you," she whimpers, touching over my bruises with care.

But I don't want gentle. "You won't."

Gripping her wrists, I watch as she lifts her hips, using her core muscles before slamming back down. My cock is snug and deep, but it's not enough. She begins to move, around and around, drawing her pleasure from me as she moans and tosses her head back.

She rides me hard, pleasure contorting her body, rippling as she gulps in air. She is so fucking beautiful.

Unable to help myself, I cup her tits, rolling her nipples with my thumbs. Her whimpers are music to my depraved soul. As she continues to rock against me, I feel myself slowly spiraling out of control. I usually have a grip on my emotions, but with Tiger, I have no control.

We fit perfectly, her body crafted for mine and mine for hers. I don't understand it, but each time I'm with her this way, a clarity takes over, purging the darkness that eats away at me. Sometimes, it's easy to get caught up in the notion that a happily ever after may be in the cards for me.

But reality soon hits. How could we not have anything but regrets between us? The memories of who I am will never allow her to escape the past. And I won't do that to her. She deserves her prince. Not a villain.

Gripping her hips, I encourage her to use me and milk her pleasure until she's well spent. Her skin is red-hot, slick with sweat as she rides me wildly. "I—"

"You what, Tiger?" I desperately want to know what she wants to say.

Looping my fingers around her nape, I draw her toward my lips, needing to fucking own that mouth. I kiss the fuck out of her, driving my hips upward and fucking her senseless as she takes what I give.

"I, this…" She fumbles over her words. "You."

I am utterly consumed by her, not giving her a moment of rest as I continue to sink into her and encourage her to slam onto me. I hit her deep, and we both moan at the sensation.

She kisses me gently, not wanting to hurt me, but she couldn't. My injuries are overshadowed by her.

She tosses her head back, her long hair spilling over her shoulders and down her bowed back. "Everything," she pants, her body tensing. "You are…"

She doesn't need to finish. I can fill in the blanks; yet, I don't know how to respond. This beauty has allowed me to pollute her with my filth, and here she is, declaring words I don't deserve. But I want them regardless.

I want her because I feel the fucking same. She is everything, too.

She shudders, coming violently around me with a pleasured cry. I pump my hips, suddenly filled with a need to make her come again and again. The moment her cries cease, I grip her waist, coaxing her to climb up my body.

I instantly miss her warmth, but I won't be without it for too long.

She has no idea what I want until I drag her up and position her over my face. She doesn't have time to object when I slam her pussy over my mouth. Rearing up, I lick her entrance, tasting her sweet arousal on my lips.

"Bull, no," she pants, trying to get away. "You're hurt."

I reply by spreading her pussy with two fingers and biting her sensitive clit.

She doesn't stand a chance because she wants this as much as I do. As she rocks over my face, I reach down and grab my cock and begin to pump. I want to come inside her, but I can't. Going bareback has spoiled me, and I want it all.

My hand attached to her waist coaxes her to ride me hard. She grips the headboard, bowing back, giving me what I want. With me, I want her wild and free because that's how I feel when I'm with her.

Driving my tongue deep within her, she rocks back and forth, crying and shuddering around me. I am going to come. But not before her.

Her pleas feed me, and I can't help myself; I stop stroking my cock, only to slap her ass. She rockets upward, a surprised moan spilling free, but she likes it. She arches backward in a silent request for more. I slap her again, harder, groaning against her pussy as she tenses her muscles.

"More," she shamelessly asks, curving her back.

She gets off on pain, she always has, and I like to deliver it. This combination will only lead to a fiery mess.

Slapping her one more time, I crane my neck and suck over her ripe clit before driving my tongue into her. Her body tightens, and I know she's going to come again.

Gripping my cock, I begin to work it hard, and just when she uses her core muscles to raise herself off me before rubbing herself over my lips, a heat spreads upward before it explodes out of me. The moment I come, Tiger sits over my face and comes against my mouth.

She twists and moans, her body convulsing while I let out a string of filthy curses.

I'm breathless by the time I'm done. I've never come so hard before.

Once she stops writhing, she lifts herself off me before shyly lying beside me. Tremors still rock her body, and I like that they're there 'cuz of what I did to her. We're lying face-to-face, breathless, without words.

Reaching for the sheet, I cover us both with it.

She reaches across and gently touches my bottom lip. "I hurt you. I'm sorry."

Tonguing over my lip, I taste the sharp metallic sting of blood. I didn't even realize I was bleeding because all I could taste was her sweetness. "Don't be."

She is bashful, even after everything we just did, and averts her eyes. It seems we're both processing what this is because each touch sends me closer to the point of no return. And her admission…holy fuck. I am so done for.

The moment we get Jordy back, I will finish this once and for all, ensuring her safety. I honestly have no clue what my future holds, but as long as Tiger is safe, then I will deal.

"We should get back," I say. "Lotus already wonders where I am these days."

She nods, but I can see something is weighing on her mind. "Do you think Lotus will let me come back? Now that I'm not working at Blue Bloods, I need a job."

The thought of seedy assholes looking at her godly body has me clenching my teeth, but I have no right to act this way. It's her body, and she can do what she pleases with it.

"This way, I can"—she clears her throat—"be near you in case something happens."

My chest fills with something warm and fuzzy, and for the first time, I don't want to kick its ass. "I think she'd be happy to have you back. And you're right, staying close is wise."

"I'm probably yesterday's news, what with Cherry and—"

But I won't let her speak such lies. "Tiger," I utter, placing a finger over her lips. "You will always be a headline."

Her cheeks redden, and she smiles. "Thank you. So do I have to pretend not to like you?" When she realizes what she just asked, her entire face turns red.

Tiger has been nothing but honest about her feelings for me. I don't understand it. I never will. She likes me, and I like her, but it'll be safer if no one knows about whatever the fuck this is between us.

"Yes," I reply, not wanting to make a big deal about her comment and embarrass her further. "Just because we can't see the enemy doesn't mean they're not lurking. Being linked to me will only get you hurt. I have no doubt Jaws has someone watching us."

"If he already knows about us, then why do I have to pretend?"

"We don't want to poke the bear," I state. "Until we hear from Jaws, it's a guessing game. He took Jordy because he knew about the night in the parking lot."

She swallows, appearing guilty that she gave in. But fighting this between us has been impossible from the get-go.

"We don't want to piss him off anymore. Men like him thrive on power and control, so we make him believe he has both."

"Okay," she agrees. I hate to see that the fire behind her eyes has simmered. She misses Jordy, and without him, she must feel like a part of her is missing. "What happens if I see Stevie or José?"

"You act like you don't know them. Let me handle them."

"Bull, this is so dangerous. We are gambling with everyone. I know we can't go to the police, but we are trusting criminals. How can we be so sure they'll stick to their word?"

She's right. There is no guarantee they won't double-cross me. But what choice do we have? I can't outsmart Stevie or José. They've probably got half the city on their payroll. But this is personal, a war between foes who need a middleman—me.

"Don't forget, Tiger…I am, too."

Her mouth parts, but she doesn't say a word.

Thumbing over her bottom lip, I kick off the sheet and reach for my boxers. Slipping them on, I commence dressing, hinting it's time to leave.

Tiger wraps the sheet around her as she stands and reaches for her bag. "I'll just freshen up." She makes her way into the bathroom, shutting the door softly behind her.

No matter what she feels for me, I need her to remember who I am and what I did.

Once I dropped Tiger off at home, I went to the motel to feed Fluffball and get ready for work. I told Paul the latest and that he needs to keep an even closer eye on her. If Stevie or José come into work and see her dancing, they'll realize she is someone of importance to me. It's too much of a coincidence, and they saw my response to her.

This meeting with Scrooge can't come soon enough.

Cracking my neck from side to side, I focus on Lotus's books and not on Tiger, who will be coming in soon. No surprise, Lotus jumped at the chance to have Tiger back. At this rate, she'll be back on top in a few short months.

Her books are looking good, which will make Stevie happy. There is something I have been debating, and as sick as it makes me, I've decided to allow Stevie to use The Pink Oyster to entrap him. I need proof he's doing something illegal, like money laundering. It won't be for long, as I plan on telling Franca everything the moment Jaws is dead.

The new cell I was forced to get rings, and when I see the caller is unknown, I prepare for anything. I don't bother saying hello when I take the call.

"You delivered, amigo. And I am a man of my word." José keeps it short, sweet, and ambiguous. "Look out for peaches. You'll know what it means." And the line goes dead.

Sighing, I toss the cell onto the desk and run a hand through my hair. This is about the gala, and the only insight I have is fucking peaches. Lotus enters, stopping in the doorway when she reads the pissed-off look on my face.

"Something wrong with the books?" she asks, worried.

"No, they're looking good. This place is already picking up."

Her chest deflates as she exhales. "Oh, thank god. You had me worried. With Lily back, it'll only get better."

She closes the door and walks over to the filing cabinet. She opens the top drawer and reveals a bottle of vodka and two glasses. "Yes, I have a secret stash, but this is a celebratory drink for once."

She pours me a glass and offers it to me. I accept, wondering what we're celebrating. When I find out what it is, I contemplate reaching for the bottle. "Remember the customer I was telling you about? The one who wanted to use the club?"

How can I forget?

I nod, sipping my drink as I lean back in my chair.

"Well, he called me last night and offered to help me out financially." Lotus then goes on to detail Stevie's grand plan of "helping" her out. And she's fallen for it—hook, line, and sinker.

"What do you think?"

I think this is a bad fucking idea, and she needs to open her eyes. No one does anything for free. But she trusts him, and why shouldn't she? She doesn't know what a lying asshole he truly is. He's only shown her the side of him he wants her to see.

Throwing back my drink, I coolly place the glass onto the desk. "I think you should go for it."

I never thought I'd ever feel guilt again. But this heavy feeling in the pit of my stomach is just that.

Stevie must have called Lotus last night after I lost my fight. I don't know what he's playing at because he was tight-lipped when I finally came to. I explained that the injuries got the better of me, and I wasn't in my best form. I lost him a lot of money, so naturally, he was pissed.

And now he goes and does this.

Has he realized something is amiss?

Whatever the reason, I need to be careful and so does

Tiger. If this happens, he will see her working here.

"He said he'd be a silent partner. The place is a clever investment for him. He's a godsend, Bull."

I attempt to keep my poker face in check because Lotus has fallen so hard for Stevie's bullshit, and there is no way she would believe the truth even if I told her. We believe what we want to, and she believes Stevie will be her savior, the one to pull her from this debt.

"That's great news. When does it all happen?"

She pours us another round and raises her glass in salute. "As soon as next week. I just need to talk to the bank, but he's eager."

I'm sure he is.

Finishing my drink, I flip open the book in front of me. "I better finish this then."

Even though I'm pleased to see Lotus's smile, I know the truth, and I'm a bastard for not telling her. But all in good time. I won't let her get into trouble.

As I reach for the calculator, Lotus leaves me to the shitshow. When the door closes, I exhale deeply and slam my fist onto the desk. This is not fucking good. And when the door opens seconds later and in rushes a teary-eyed Tiger, it appears the bad luck seems to follow.

"What happened?" I jump up and round the desk, holding her biceps.

I notice she has something in her hand, and when she extends it to me, I curse. "Motherfucker." It's a postcard from Mexico.

Turning it over, I read the childlike handwriting, now understanding Tiger's pain.

Hi Mom,
I'm having so much fun with Uncle Chris!
Thanks for letting me go on vacation. See you soon.
Love,
Jordy xx

Handing it back to her, I give in to instinct and pull her into my arms. She clings on tight, holding back her tears as she nestles into me. "He's in Mexico," she cries. "Fucking Mexico! We'll never get him back."

"Don't think that. We will." I embrace her tightly, wishing I could do more than just fucking hug her. But until Jaws calls us to make his demands, we're at his mercy. This postcard is just another power play, ensuring we know who's in control.

"I've never wished harm upon anyone before…but I want him dead," she utters against my chest. "He deserves to die for everything he's done. What sort of person does that make me to wish my own brother dead?"

Her trembles have me squeezing her tighter, feeling fucking helpless. "You may be related to him by blood, but he's not your family. Family doesn't betray one another that way."

She stiffens before gently untangling herself from my arms. Just when I'm about to kick myself for saying the wrong thing, she places her hands on my cheeks gently. "You're right. Look at what you've done for your family."

I open my mouth, stunned, but that turns to pure lust when she stands on her tippy toes and slants her lips over mine. I don't hesitate and draw her into me, pressing us chest to chest. This kiss is unhurried, but it's filled with longing.

I like it.

Threading my fingers through her hair, I angle her head to devour her like she deserves. It's hard to believe I was with her this morning because it feels like years, not mere hours ago, but with Tiger, time has no meaning. I could spend every minute with her, and it still wouldn't be enough.

She loops her hands behind my nape, moaning into my mouth as I tighten my hold on her hair. I kiss her slowly, treading uncharted waters once again. I've experienced so many new…feelings with Tiger, and it's still so overwhelming.

But being unguarded with her this way, the fears begin to fade.

Even though this feels fucking fantastic, I need to end it before I throw everything off Lotus's desk and bend Tiger over it.

"Are you going to be okay to dance tonight?" I ask against her warm lips.

She slowly opens her eyes as I stroke the apple of her rosy cheek. "I have to be," she replies, leaning into my touch. "I won't disappoint Lotus again. And I need the money. I haven't spoken to Avery's lawyer yet, but I still want to buy the studio. Letting it go feels wrong."

"I understand. I could—" I inhale, before throwing good sense to the wind. "I could give you some money. I've made good bank fighting and working—"

She doesn't let me finish.

Instead, she presses her finger to my lips.

"Thank you. You don't realize how much that means to

me. But I want to try to do it myself if I can."

Nodding, I admire her independence all the more.

"I better get ready. It's a race to get into the change room now. So I guess I have to go back to pretending to hate you now?" She traces her finger along my bottom lip, following the movement with her eyes.

"It shouldn't be too hard. You hated me once before. I can always make you hate me again," I promise, smirking when I wrap my fingers around her wrist.

A small whimper leaves her when I tighten my hold. But she fucking owns me when she leans in close and states, "I never hated you. I should have, but I never did."

And that's the reason we're here, about to tear one another apart.

Standing on her tiptoes again, she presses her lips against mine, and I surrender, wanting her more than anything I've ever wanted before. She kisses me unhurriedly with confidence and control, and I like it. Cupping her ass, I coax her to use those long legs and wrap them around me.

She does.

Our kisses grow frantic as she tugs at my hair, moaning. If I don't feel the slickness of her flesh this second, I will fucking lose my shit. Walking her toward the door, I lock it before throwing her up against it. She's wearing a skirt, allowing me easy access as I thrust my hand inside her underwear.

She is always so ready for me, which has me wanting to beat my chest like a fucking caveman.

"Oh, Bull," she whimpers, breaking our kiss to gulp in mouthfuls of air.

I sink two fingers into her, stretching her wide, and begin working her body without mercy. She pumps her hips, shuddering when I flick over her clit with my thumb. When her long-sleeved sweater drops off one shoulder, I use it to my advantage and yank it down, exposing her perky tits.

Her nipples are hard, waiting for me to take them into my mouth. And I do. With fingers still working her wildly, I lean forward and tongue over her nipple before sucking. Tiger mewls, turning to hot lava in my hand and mouth.

The need to be all over her, in her, almost robs me of air, but I decide to leave her with a reminder that although we're playing nice, that doesn't mean I've gone soft. Quite the opposite. Just when I feel her squeeze her muscles, chasing a release, I slide my fingers out of her and let her go.

She whimpers, sagging forward with eyes wide. "Wh- what are you doing?" she pants, licking her lips as the heels of her boots touch the floor.

"Just reminding you why you should hate me," I counter, stepping back and slipping the fingers that were inside her pussy into my mouth.

She gasps—aroused, annoyed, and so fucking angry— and I can't help but smile. I love seeing her riled up.

Her taste brings me to my knees—literally—because before she can curse me out, I drop in front of her, lift her skirt, and bite over her clit through her underwear.

She almost keels over, gripping my shoulders to stop her fall. But she continues using me as her anchor when I grip her silk underwear into my fist and tear them in half. Her gasp turns to a moan as I lower my mouth onto her pussy and lick her in one long, smooth motion.

"Oh, god," she cries, her fingernails digging into my skin.

I use her moans as my fuel and begin eating her out like the hungry, depraved man that I am. I bury myself between her thighs and own that pussy because it's fucking mine. Tiger props one foot on the small sofa beside her while I swap my position and sit down so my face is aligned with utter perfection.

Angling my head, I begin to lick her while watching her come undone before my eyes. Her lips are parted as she watches me, and when I twirl my tongue deep, she writhes and begins to circle her clit with her fingers. I'm eating her out while she is playing with herself, and if this isn't the best fucking thing I've ever seen in my life, then I don't know what is.

Her sweater sits off one shoulder, exposing her nakedness, only adding to the building pressure in my balls. I need to fucking come, and I want to do so all over her milky skin. Her taste is beyond potent, and I rub my face from side to side, needing to taste her, smell her, all night.

"Bull, I'm going to c-come." Her fingers work her clit frantically while I continue fucking her with my mouth and tongue.

"Then come, baby."

A scorching heat burns my tongue before Tiger is coming violently. I grip her upper thighs to hold her in place as I draw out every last tremor from her. When she's done thrashing around and pulling out my hair, she slumps forward with a sated cry.

I suckle her pussy one last time before pulling away and rubbing her scent across my lips. She smells fucking delicious.

Standing, I press my lips to hers softly. The aftershocks still rock her body.

"If that was supposed to make me hate you, then I hate you…so fucking much," she teases, arranging her sweater to cover herself up. Such a damn shame.

Her lips twitch when she sees her shredded underwear discarded on the floor. "Looks like I'll just have to go without."

A possessive groan escapes me at the thought of her bare pussy on show tonight, but no one can touch or see but me.

She peers down at my raging hard-on, biting her lip, which doesn't help one bit. "I want you…so bad," she whispers, appearing embarrassed by her admission. "I can't stop wanting you."

Gripping her wrist, I draw her to me and confess, "I can't stop either."

She sighs, understanding how screwed we truly are.

"I'll see you out there." She plants a quick peck on my lips before unlocking the door and leaving.

When I'm alone, I exhale long and hard. I don't have time to deal with my hard-on because Lotus is waiting for me out front. However, with Tiger's taste still lingering on my tongue, having blue balls is so worth it.

The tip rail is full as assholes throw their life savings at

Cherry. She has become quite popular and has settled into Lotus's star attraction with ease. But she is nothing compared to Tiger. Now that she's back, Lotus will have two VIPs, and the place will thrive. Which is why Stevie has decided to strike. Well, I like to think that's part of the reason.

The other, I still haven't figured out.

Every time I think I get my shit sorted; I'm thrown a fucking curveball.

Cherry flashes me a flirty smile as she collects her tips. She hasn't hidden her interest in me, but I've given her nothing. I only played nice with her when I knew Tiger had snuck in that one time to rile her up, but usually, I barely look at her.

Tonight, she seems to have something to prove, like a dog lifting his leg and marking its territory, and when the lights dim and the hollers of men become deafening, I realize why.

"Are you ready?" teases Ricky, the emcee as he hypes up the already manic crowd. "They say good things come to those who wait, and I know you've waited a lonnnng time. But she's back, and holy shit…she is back with a vengeance."

I push past the salivating assholes to get into a better position to scope out the room.

"The one, the only, Tigerlily!"

The patrons explode, and when the intro kicks in for "Crazy Bitch" by Buckcherry, I know Tiger ain't playing. She wants her crown back and intends to win it back ruthlessly. She splits the backstage curtains and saunters onto the stage with a confidence I haven't seen before.

Wearing white hot pants with a matching halter top and gold trim that accents her glowing skin, she doesn't go straight for the pole. Instead, she places a hand against her brow as if examining the crowd. The catcalls blow the roof off the place, but Tiger wants more and raises her hands, indicating she isn't satisfied until they're rabid and foaming at the mouths.

Only when they're wild and out of their seats does she begin to dance as though she's possessed. She knows how to work the crowd and uses that to her advantage when she circles the pole before spinning around and around.

She uses her core strength and scales it with ease. When she's upside down, she does the splits, grinning as the men lose their shit. I try not to look at her because I have a job to do, but goddamn, when she slowly slithers down the pole, I surrender.

She is a goddess, owning every single asshole in this place, but when her eyes land on me, I realize she is interested in owning only one person.

She dismounts and loses herself to the music, combining her love for ballet and dance. She is barefoot, which shows off her technique, not that these shady assholes care. They just want to see her tits and ass. But not on my watch.

She continues eye-fucking me, licking her bottom lip with a smirk. My cock instantly stirs, wanting to rip out the eyes of every fucker for daring to look at her, but she doesn't hide who has her attention. She is dancing for me, and I like it.

When the lyric sounds about being crazy but liking the way they fuck, I take that as a personal compliment because she winks my way.

As I bunch my fists, it takes all my dwindling willpower not to toss her over my shoulder and show her how fucking crazy I can be. A fucker is out of his seat, reaching for her, but I don't give him the chance. I'm there within seconds, shoving him back into his chair.

All I can smell is cherry blossoms, and with Tiger's taste still on my lips, I peer up at her, yielding. She's fucking won, and I intend to reward her by fucking her senseless.

She reads my thoughts and smirks before ending her set in the splits. The room is shadowed in darkness before it detonates in bedlam. The lights come back on as Tiger stands and begins collecting her piles of cash.

Men have thrown so much money onto the stage, I'd be surprised if she isn't able to buy the studio after tonight. As she's collecting the money, some asshole in a suit whistles at her to get her attention. She isn't a dog and doesn't come when called, so she ignores him, quickly raking up the bills.

He doesn't like being ignored and takes matters into his own hands by leaning across the stage and grabbing her ankle. She turns quickly but doesn't have a chance to get a word in edgewise because I charge over and grab him by the back of the neck.

"Do not touch," I warn, squeezing his neck.

He tries to twist out of my grip, but I apply pressure behind his ear, in the pit between his jaw and neck, and press hard. It's a classic self-defense move and hurts like a bitch. He buckles and tries to grab me. I seize his arm and bend it behind his back.

"Motherfucker, are you deaf? Touch her again, and I will break every bone in your fucking hand."

He raises his free arm in surrender, squirming when I

almost snap his other one in half. I let him go, snarling. He sits back down, red-faced while his friends look the other way, drinking nervously.

Tiger witnessed the entire scene and grins. She clearly likes my crazy when she cups her mouth discreetly, and says, "You're my crazy bitch."

She doesn't know the half of it.

Only when she disappears off the stage do I turn my back and walk toward the bar. Lotus is busy serving thirsty patrons, and the line is so long that Tawny is helping her. I'm about to lend a hand when someone enters through the door and stops me dead in my tracks.

Stevie.

He is smoking his usual cigar, and when he sees me, he blows out a circle of smoke. This isn't a casual visit.

Putting my game face on, I walk over, thankful one of my eyes has swollen over so he can't see the mismatched color. To him, I'm Tommy, working here to help him steal the club from Lotus.

"'Sup, boss," I tease, extending my hand. I'm suddenly thankful Lotus is busy.

"Hey. Thought I'd come by and check out my investment." His hungry eyes scan the packed room, and he whistles. "Looks like your plan worked."

"Looks that way." I play along.

"How're you feeling?"

"Fine," I counter, folding my arms across my chest.

"Good to hear because you're coming to dinner."

"Dinner?" I arch a brow, confused.

"Yes. All we do is work. I hardly know a thing about you." And that's how he usually likes it. But now, things have changed.

"Fine. I'll let you know when I'm free."

Of course, this isn't optional.

"Tomorrow night suit you?"

Inhaling slowly, I nod. "Sure, tomorrow night it is."

When Stevie glances over my shoulder, I already know who he's seen. "Bring your friend."

I don't bother with pretenses. I won't waste either of our time.

He confidently strolls over to the bar and takes a seat like he already owns the place. But I suppose he does.

The jig is up, so I turn around and find Tiger. Our eyes lock from across the room. Her gaze darts toward Stevie before nervously returning to me. All I can do is nod that it'll be okay, but for the first time in my life, I can't guarantee that it will be.

CHAPTER TEN

Bull

"Are you listening to me?"

"No," I reply, patting myself down because I can't find my keys.

Paul chuckles in response. "I said I got you something."

Pausing, I arch a suspicious brow. "I don't want anything."

"Too bad," he replies, jumping up from the bed and digging into his pocket. When he produces a brass bull key chain, I continue looking at him like he's lost his mind. "Here, I got you this."

"Why?"

Paul rolls his eyes, ignoring my social ineptness. "To say thanks for—"

But I cut him off. "You don't need to say thanks for

anything. You're doing me a solid, so—"

It's now his turn to interrupt with a laugh. "Just fucking say thank you and stop making it more awkward."

Seeing as this isn't optional, I accept the key chain and look at the bull. I can see a resemblance. The thing looks fucking pissed off.

"It's supposed to bring good luck," Paul explains with a shrug. "Something about feng shui or some shit."

"Cool," I reply, suddenly feeling uncomfortable. I've never received a "just because" gift before. I don't know how to act, so I offer him my fist.

We fist bump, and I'm thankful Paul doesn't make a fuss.

I go back to hunting for my keys.

The mystery is solved when Paul gestures toward the sofa with his head. "Your keys are there. Lucky you now have a key chain to put them on. See, I'm a fucking lifesaver."

I snicker in response, but he's right. I hate to admit it, but I'm kind of getting used to him being around. Maybe it's because I see a lot of myself in him. I can only hope his life turns out differently than mine did.

Grabbing my keys, I shove them and the key chain into my pocket. I know most people would appear thankful for such a gift and use the key chain, but I am still getting used to all this social shit.

"What's up with you? You're acting crazier than usual," Paul asks, opening a bag of Cheetos.

"I have to drop this off before dinner."

"And?" he prompts.

"And I'm running fucking late," I reply. Being late tonight

isn't an option.

"Let me do it," he offers with a casual shrug. "I know what to do."

"Yes, but I won't be there." Paul has come with me before, but him going on his own? I don't like it.

"Yeah and?" he asks, his mouth stuffed full of Cheetos. "I don't need you to hold my hand. I'll look both ways before I cross the road."

Looking at the clock on the bedside table, I sigh.

"In and out. Got it?" I say to Paul, handing over the envelope of cash for Kong's family.

"Yes. I got it," he sarcastically replies, snatching the envelope from my hand. This kid is such a smart-ass, which is the reason he's still here.

After Stevie showed up at work last night, I can't be too careful. As far as he knows, I took care of his "problem." If he sees Paul, it won't end well for either of us.

"So you've finally gotten over your girl phobia?" he says while I look at him like he's lost his fucking mind because he clearly has.

"I don't have a girl phobia," I reply. "Whatever the fuck that is."

Paul nods, but from the grin on his face, he's clearly just humoring me.

"I don't blame you. There is something special about her."

Pausing from placing my Glock into my holster, I arch a brow while he quickly backtracks.

"I just meant, she looks like a nice person."

"Uh-huh," I counter, enjoying watching him squirm.

"Enough with the touchy-feely crap. Come right back here when you're done."

Paul nods, sliding the envelope into his back pocket. "Are you sure you don't need backup tonight?"

"I'm sure," I reply firmly. He needs to understand how serious I am about this. "Do what you're told, kid."

"Yes, Dad." He mock salutes.

His comment has me curling my lip. God help any poor kid if I was their dad.

Once I have everything I need, I reach for my jacket. Dinner is at Stevie's house. He has home turf advantage, but I hope I get a chance to meet the infamous Bianca.

"Okay, I'll catch you later."

Paul nods, slumping back onto my bed like he owns the place. *I only tolerate him because he's good company for Fluffball*, I reason. But deep down, I know the kid is growing on me.

He switches the TV on and waves goodbye.

As I walk to my truck, I dig into my pocket for my keys. Once inside, I pull out the key chain 'cause the bull is digging into my ass. I toss it into the middle console and head over to Tiger's house. I wish she didn't have to come, but I know that if I don't bring her, it'll raise red flags, and Stevie will seek her out on his own. At least this way, I will be with her and can ensure her safety.

When I pull into her street, I see that she's waiting for me in the foyer of her apartment building. She runs out into the snow when I pull up by the curb. "Hey," she says as she jumps into the truck, rubbing her hands together to keep warm.

"You should have waited for me in your apartment," I state, hating how "dad-like" I sound.

Tiger stops rubbing her hands together. "It's fine. Besides, I don't like being in there alone. It reminds me so much of Jordy."

Feeling like a dick for not realizing this, I nod. "Of course. You can always stay with me." The words flow out of my mouth so naturally, I didn't even think to stop them.

She smiles, nervously pulling the seat belt across her chest and buckling herself in. "Thanks. So what is going to happen tonight?"

The change in subject is welcomed.

"I don't know, but whatever it is, I want you to carry this." Reaching over her legs, I open the glove compartment and retrieve a small handgun.

She gasps, recoiling in her seat.

"It's just a precaution," I quickly assure her. "But I'll feel better knowing you're armed." Gently, I place it into her upturned palm. "Do you know how to use it?"

She shakes her head. "No, but teach me."

"This is the safety." I tap my finger over the notch. "Make sure this is on until you need to shoot."

She nods astutely, taking it all in as she turns the gun over in her hand.

"Never place your finger on the trigger until you're ready to shoot."

"What else?" she asks, licking her pink glossy lips.

"If presented with danger, aim and shoot," I instruct, brushing over her pulse.

A sharp inhale escapes her as her eyes dart up to meet mine. "It's that easy?" she asks, her chest rising and falling, betraying her nerves.

"It's that easy," I confirm. "But taking someone's life...it's not always that straightforward."

She quickly casts her eyes downward, knowing I'm referring to Lachlan. Yes, I had no issues shooting him, but the aftermath of my decision has been anything but easy.

Tiger nods as she places the gun inside her small bag.

Putting the truck into gear, I begin the drive toward Stevie's house. It's about a thirty-minute drive, and when I searched for it on the map, I could see it's on a lot of land. The house itself is probably better described as a mansion.

Tiger is quiet, chewing the corner of her mouth as she peers out the window. I can only imagine how nervous she is, but I am too. Not for me, but for her. If she's in danger, I will shoot and ask questions later, but I have to remember that will fuck up my plans of confronting Scrooge next week.

Everything seems to circle back to her.

Sighing, I focus on the road and not on the heavy feeling in the pit of my stomach.

When we arrive at the destination, both Tiger and I peer out the windshield. She whistles. "Holy shit. Being a bad guy sure has its perks. Imagine how many dead bodies pave that mansion," she says with disgust.

And she's right. This house is built on the lives Stevie has stolen.

Pulling up to the steel gates, I open the window and press the button for the intercom. The camera attached in the corner hints they already know I'm here.

"Hello?" a woman says over the speaker a few seconds later.

"Hi, I'm here for Stevie."

"Name?"

"Tommy," I reply while Tiger shifts in her seat. I've told her the ins and outs, but I'm sure this is uncomfortable for her.

The gates slowly open, granting us entry into a place that could have its own personal zip code. I travel the long driveway up toward the front door. The mansion is red brick with a black tiled roof. It has gothic details with modern touches.

Tiger rubs her palms over her long black coat nervously.

When I kill the engine, I look over at her and grip her wrist. "It'll be okay. Remember what I told you?"

She nods quickly.

We rehearsed a speech last night after Stevie eventually left. She had the good sense to remain backstage. He won't buy it, but there is a reason we're here. And when the man of the hour opens the double doors, it seems now is the time to find out what that is.

Tiger takes a deep breath, appearing to need a minute. She is trembling all over but sits tall.

We exit the truck, and although I want more than anything to hold her hand to comfort her, I don't. I can't let Stevie know how much she means to me.

"Welcome," he says as we ascend the marble steps.

Tiger stays by my side.

"Thanks for the invite," I casually reply.

Stevie looks at Tiger, smirking. There is nothing warm about the gesture. "It's so nice to meet a friend of Tommy's. He isn't a big talker. Maybe you can share some secrets with me, eh?"

It's meant to be a joke, but we all know he isn't playing. He saw her the other night at the fight. He knows she's someone of importance.

She nods with a small smile. "I was thinking the same thing." She plays it off. Good girl.

Stevie laughs, but it's strained.

He welcomes us into his home, and the moment I enter, I want to leave this museum. It's probably really nice, but to me, it's so over the top. I wonder if the riches are making up for something else he's lacking. But when a sophisticated woman gracefully descends the marble staircase in front of us, I realize this wealth isn't to impress his guests. It's to impress her.

This is no doubt Bianca.

She is beautiful, with long black hair and piercing green eyes which appear vibrant against her olive skin. I can see why Jaws and Stevie are fighting over her. Her white dress clings to her curves. When Stevie peers up at her, it's no secret he is smitten by her as she is a woman who can bring down an empire.

"It's so nice to finally meet a colleague of Stevie's." I don't notice a wedding ring on her finger, so I'm guessing they're not married, which is the reason Jaws thinks he still has half a shot.

Bianca has both men in the palm of her hands. No

wonder both would do anything to keep her. Unless she is playing both sides. It makes sense.

She knows I'm not a fucking colleague, but I humor her regardless. "The pleasure is all mine. This is Eva." Tiger shuffles her feet.

There is no way in hell I'm giving them Tiger's real name even though they will eventually find out who she really is. Honestly, I can't be too certain they don't already know.

"Nice to meet you." Once Bianca descends the last step, she extends her hand toward me, and I shake it lightly. She then gives Tiger a two-cheek kiss as though they're old friends.

Tiger knows who she is. She knows this woman may be a small reason her brother has transformed into a psychopath. I know it's hard for her to keep her cool, but she cannot, under any circumstances, let on just who she is to Jaws.

She knows the consequences if she does, and she plays her part like a fucking pro. "I love this dress. Is it Versace?"

Bianca arches a dark brow, impressed. "You know your fashion. I think we will get along just fine." She loops her arm through Tiger's, escorting her out of the foyer.

Stevie playfully rolls his eyes. "Women."

I attempt a resemblance of a smile as we follow the women through the house and into one of the many living areas I'm sure this mansion has.

Stevie walks over to the bar, reaching for the decanter. "Scotch?"

I nod, ensuring I stay close enough to Tiger in case I need to spring into action. Bianca leads Tiger over to the couch, chatting happily. Tiger doesn't seem worried, so I pull up a barstool and take a seat.

Stevie passes me the crystal tumbler. The smell of a neat scotch calms the nerves.

"So you're feeling better? You never did tell me who beat the shit out of you."

Sipping my drink, I savor the burn before replying, "I ran into a door." This is code for I ain't telling you jack shit. Just because I'm in his house doesn't mean I'm going to confide in him.

He grins, then lights a cigar. "I must say, I was very surprised you lost your fight. I know you weren't on your A-game, but I know how much you like to win."

"I guess I'm just an overachiever."

"I like you, Tommy." He points his cigar my way. "Kong liked you, too."

The conversation drops to arctic temperatures.

"I always wonder what happened to him. It seems so out of character for him to up and leave like that. I mean, yes, he was a coward, but he was loyal. But I suppose Jaws—"

Bianca suddenly stops talking and clears her throat. "Stevie, no shop talk at home." Her tone may be light, but no one is fooled.

She knows what Stevie does. She knows she gets into bed at night with a drug dealer, a murderer, and an embezzler, among other things. So clearly, Jaws is a touchy subject for her. Could it be trouble in paradise? Or maybe my hunch was right. Maybe she is screwing both.

Stevie doesn't appreciate being reprimanded in his own home, but he doesn't say a word.

"Shall we eat?" Bianca asks, coming to a stand.

Eating is the last thing on anyone's mind, but we humor her, nonetheless.

Everyone is on their best behavior at dinner, but the tension can be cut with the steak knife I'm holding. Stevie seems to be more interested in the red wine while Bianca attempts to play house.

"So you met at the club?" she asks, cutting into her filet mignon.

Tiger nods, reaching for her glass of water. "Yes. The girls and I are happy to have him there."

Stevie leans back in his seat, swirling the wine in his glass. He doesn't know how long I've really worked there.

"Well, Stevie can't stop talking about you, Tommy, so you're one popular boy." Bianca is trying really hard to make conversation with me, but I just want this night to be over.

Pushing back my plate, I reach for my beer and look at Stevie, hinting if he has a point to make it. He thankfully gets the hint.

He takes the bait.

"We will leave you girls to it. We have some business to discuss." Stevie finishes his wine, then stands.

Tiger shifts in her seat but nods discreetly at me. She'll be okay. Insisting she comes with me will only rouse suspicion, and besides, she has a gun, and I know she isn't afraid to use it.

Meeting Bianca's eyes, I recognize the inquiry behind them. She wants to know if we're friend or foe. But is there such a thing in our world?

A part of me is terrified she knows who Tiger is and will somehow use that to get intel on who I am. But I know Tiger would never betray me that way. However, if Bianca gave Tiger what she wants—information on her son—I wonder if her loyalties would shift? I wouldn't blame her if they did.

I leave them discussing the charity Bianca chairs. It's laughable really. I mean, she's set up house with a killer, and here she is, playing Mother Teresa. But it's all for show. These people hide behind the mask of normalcy, fooling others into thinking they're just like them. And when they're accepted, when they've gained the trust and respect is when they strike.

I follow Stevie through the house, barely paying any attention to the rich furnishings. When we walk toward the other side of the property and up the stairs, I know I'm about to learn the real reason I'm here. Stevie must know I'm carrying, but he hasn't said anything—yet.

He opens the door to a den, gesturing for me to enter. The place is furnished simply compared to the rest of the house, and that's because this room isn't for show. It serves a purpose. There are two leather couches, a fireplace, and a large wooden bar. I also notice a door leading out onto a balcony.

"Drink?" Stevie asks, closing the door behind him.

Nodding, I scope out the room.

He busies himself behind the bar while I wait. "You know, I can't find anything on you because the man who would do the research has vanished." He goes straight in for the kill. He can't find anything on me because he doesn't know my real name.

He offers me the glass filled with amber liquid and clicks his glass against mine.

I drink my scotch coolly. "Why are you so interested in me? I do my job, don't I?"

Stevie mulls over my words while tossing back his drink. "I thought so, but after you lost a fight you should have won, I got a little curious."

There is no way he's going to kill me. He would have disarmed me by now. "You know what they say about curiosity," I say, finishing off the scotch. "It killed the cat."

Stevie grins, but he isn't amused. "Well, at least something is dead."

I have no idea what he means until he gestures over my shoulder. I'm hit with a cool rush of wind when the balcony door slides open. I don't bother turning around. I keep my eyes trained on Stevie. This is his show after all.

I hear stifled screams and someone's feet digging into the carpet as they're being dragged along, and when that someone comes into view, I curse the motherfucking universe.

Paul is flanked by Dudley and Vincent. They hold him tight, but that doesn't stop him from flailing, muffling his stifled apologies from behind the gag.

"Unless this little thief rose from the dead, you didn't do your job. You lied to me because you told me it was taken care of," Stevie says, watching me closely.

Still, I say nothing. I need to keep my head calm.

"Dudley and Vincent have been keeping an eye out for

Kong because I thought he'd be back by now. But what they found was most surprising."

Paul's eyes widen as he stares at me, begging I forgive him for getting caught. But I'm the one who should be seeking absolution from him because I've just sentenced him to death.

Dudley digs into Paul's pocket as he squirms, trying to break free. When he retrieves the envelope with the cash, I clench my jaw. I should have done it. I should have made the time and done it myself. But I've been so caught up with protecting Tiger that I forgot others were relying on me to protect them as well.

"So why is this asshole stuffing money into Kong's mailbox? He said someone paid him to do it. Someone he doesn't know, but I don't believe him. Help me understand, Tommy, because I sure as shit don't understand."

Paul struggles, attempting to escape, but he and I are both prisoners.

"I admit, I invited you over for dinner with an ulterior motive. I want to know more about you. I usually don't trust men I just met. But Kong vouched for you. And I've known Kong for a long time. So I know he wouldn't just leave his family unless something happened to him.

"So when I saw the man you were supposed to kill stuffing a large wad of cash into Kong's mailbox, I jumped to conclusions." He inhales before delivering, "I think Kong disappeared because of you."

And there it is, the truth. The reason I'm here.

"First of all, that is a *kid*, not a man." I point at Paul. "And fine, I didn't kill him because I decided to use him as my errand boy."

Stevie narrows his eyes, rubbing over his chin in thought.

"Kong disappeared because, like I told you, he got into some shit with Jaws." This is the only angle I can play as I know he won't ask Jaws if I'm telling him the truth.

"What do you mean?" he asks, the change in his demeanor immediate.

"I don't know the details. All I know is that he asked me to give his family some money to help them while he's gone."

This is my story, and I'm sticking to it.

"I couldn't drop off the money, so I asked the kid to do it. See, he comes in handy."

Paul doesn't look impressed with me, but I'm saving his fucking life.

Stevie pours himself another drink. He doesn't bother asking anyone else if they'd like one. The time for playing gracious host has long passed. "I just don't understand why he wouldn't come to me. He knows Jaws won't cross that line."

He's wrong. Jaws has crossed many lines, like asking me to play double agent.

"You once asked what my beef was with Jaws," he says, rebottling the decanter. "Well, Jaws and I used to be friends. Can you believe it?"

I remain tight-lipped because no, I cannot fucking believe it.

"We both made the streets our home, hustling the corners and selling for the same dealer—Pedro, Bianca's father."

This intricate story has so many layers. Years of revenge to be made up for.

"When we met her, we were no longer friends because we were competing for her affection. Bianca loved the attention. Her little *perritos*. Puppies," he clarifies, which explains so much.

They followed her around, no doubt, while she enjoyed the attention of both. She still does.

"In her own way, she loved us both. But Jaws doesn't like to share, so when she didn't want to choose between us, he wanted to prove who was the better man.

"He got in with her family, wanting to show her father he was worthy of his daughter's love. But that's always been Jaws's problem; he has always thought he was more important than he really is. He organized a big buy for Pedro, but he didn't do his research. They were undercover cops. He got Pedro locked up for life."

I have no idea why we're taking this little trip down memory lane, but I don't interrupt.

"Bianca never forgave him for that even though her relationship with her father was volatile. None of her family did. But Jaws is a leech. He watched and learned and thought if he took over for Pedro, he would earn the respect of the family and win Bianca back. But all that did was piss them off.

"With money comes power, and it seemed Jaws was able to make a name for himself on the streets by bringing down the infamous Pedro. Loyalties were split, and two drug lords were born. There was Jaws's team, and then there was mine. José is Bianca's cousin. But once upon a time, he was Jaws's best friend."

There will be a moral to this story, one that will most

likely end with blood spilled, but this insight is what I need to defeat the enemy.

"José never interfered because Jaws took a bullet for him. He owed him. But things change, and now he is *my* best friend. Jaws doesn't know he is my man. And we like to keep it that way."

He's wrong. Jaws *does* know. And if he thinks he and José are BFFs, he is sorely mistaken. His comment about him wishing Stevie wasn't a part of his family has me believing he wishes Bianca had chosen Jaws instead.

"I don't understand. Why don't you just kill him?" The words burn like poison because no one is ending his life but me.

Stevie throws back his drink, and I can sense his anger. "Because the thing about Bianca is that she still loves the Jaws she once knew. And I cannot hurt anything she loves because it will hurt her. And that's why I'm still alive."

This is un-fucking-believable.

These two lovestruck dickheads have waged a war but have some agreement not to harm the other because of the woman they both love? I suppose infamous wars have started because of a woman. But this is ridiculous.

If José was once Jaws's BFF, then he surely knows Scrooge has ties to him. I don't think he's pieced anything together—yet. But it'll only be a matter of time.

"Kong also used to be Jaws's best friend. Did you know that?"

This doesn't seem like a trick question. His body language reveals he's telling the truth.

"No, I didn't. Seems Jaws used to have a lot of best friends. He should probably get a dog, seeing as he doesn't have the best track record with people."

Stevie smiles. The first real gesture I've seen all night.

"I would like more than anything to end him, but we have come to an agreement. Don't fuck with mine, and I won't fuck with yours."

Jaws missed the memo, seeing as I'm playing double agent.

Stevie sighs, his little tale coming to a close. "So, as you can see, I'm loyal. A man of my word. And I expect my men to be also."

He is far from loyal. I witnessed him getting his dick sucked.

Paul squirms against Dudley and Vincent. He too knows what's headed his way.

"I know you're carrying. So I want you to finish what I ordered you to do. If you can't, then maybe it's time I got to know your pretty little friend better."

Inhaling deeply, I take a moment to compose myself. Tiger was always the backup plan, but I don't play that way.

"No," I finally say, refusing to kill Paul. "He gave back your money. If I should be shooting anyone, it's those fucking morons for letting a kid steal from them."

Dudley grits his teeth together.

"You're right," Stevie says, nodding. "But I don't need another errand boy. I have enough." His insult is slurred my way.

"He's of use to me," I argue, "and that frees up my time to

be more available to you."

Paul is now whimpering around the gag, his skinny legs shaking. I want to assure him that it'll be all right, but I can't show weakness around him. Look where that got me with Tiger.

Stevie ponders deeply, before shrugging. "I suppose you're right. Let him go."

Paul's cries stop while Vincent snarls in protest. But both he and Dudley are walking a thin line with Stevie. I watch as Dudley rips the gag from Paul's mouth. He moves his jaw from side to side while his eyes beg that we get out of here. They push him toward the balcony, but he turns over his shoulder, looking at me for guidance. Always so fucking stubborn.

Stevie isn't going to escort him out the front door. His exit is over the balcony.

"Go," I order him. The drop from the balcony is short. He'll be fine.

"I'm sorry," he says, shaking his head in anger that he got caught.

Now isn't the time for sentiments, but this is fucking breaking me in two. "I said go."

He doesn't need to be told twice and quickly sprints for the balcony door. Just as he opens it and is granted his freedom, it is cruelly taken away with a deafening boom.

Reaching into my holster with lightning speed, I grab my piece and spin around, training the gun on Stevie. But it's too fucking late. In his hand, he grips a piece of his own, the piece that just fired a bullet straight through Paul's back.

Stevie arches a brow, challenging me to shoot him. I grip

the handle, so ready to end this motherfucker, but when I think of Tiger, of Jordy, I know that I can't. Not yet.

With my heart in my throat, I slowly lower my gun, submitting defeat. I failed, I failed Paul because the shot was fatal.

"Go on then," I contest, but he tosses the gun onto the bar. He wasn't carrying at dinner, so he probably picked up the piece when he filled up his glass. "But if you wanted me dead, I'd be dead already."

He smirks, ignoring the fact a kid is bleeding out on his plush carpet. "You're right, I need you alive. We have a great partnership. But let this be a lesson learned—you do what I say, when I say because that"—he juts out his chin toward Paul—"is what happens to people who steal from me and people who lie to me, but you know better, don't you?"

He brought me here to teach me a lesson. This is what will happen to me, to the people I know if I ever disobey him again.

He knows I threw the fight. He doesn't know why, which means he doesn't suspect José. Or maybe he does, but he doesn't want trouble in paradise.

Whatever it is, he's just sealed his fate. I was going to hand him over to the cops once this was done, but Paul's death is on me. And I will make sure Stevie pays for it.

"Clean it up," he orders me, then gestures for Dudley and Vincent to split.

They walk out of the room, their heads held high as they're no longer on Stevie's shit list. They happily sacrificed the life of a boy to please a psychopath.

Stevie doesn't want me to use the door. He expects me to toss Paul from the balcony like nothing but trash. The hatred for him grows to biblical proportions. And he knows it.

"You're angry with me, aren't you? The distant Tommy does have feelings after all," he mocks while I inhale slowly.

I want to drop him where he stands, but I can't. I can't do a fucking thing.

He leaves the room victorious while I'm too afraid to turn around and see the mess I've made. But Paul deserves a hero's farewell. Spinning slowly, I take a moment to process his lifeless body sprawled out on the carpet. One arm is outstretched, his fingers skimming freedom. But that's all he got. A mere fucking taste.

Placing my gun in its holster, I take off my jacket and walk over to Paul with nothing but regret. Standing over his body has memories crashing into me, and I can't breathe. Another life lost because of me.

"I'm sorry, kid," I whisper, feeling something wet sting at my eyes. If I didn't know any better, I'd say they were tears. But I quickly wipe away whatever it is with the back of my hand.

Bending down, I lift his limp body into my arms. A bright red stain has collected on the carpet, enraging and saddening me all in the same breath.

His body is light, warm, but it won't be long before that changes. Sighing, I kick open the balcony door, blinking back the snowflakes which stick to my lashes. Climbing over the balcony, I hold on to Paul tightly and jump down onto the snow.

My shirt does nothing to keep out the cold, but it could be

summer and I'd still feel this bone-deep chill infecting every part of me. I trudge through the deep snow, breathless and totally numb. The only warmth I feel is from where Paul's blood is seeping into my shirt at my chest.

I march toward the truck on autopilot, each step making it harder and harder to deal. When I open the tailgate, I spread out the tarp and gently place Paul down onto it. Peering down at him, I shake my head, feeling nothing but regret.

"I am…so fucking sorry. I failed you."

Paul was something I haven't had in a long time—a friend. I didn't realize that until now. And I repaid that friendship by getting him killed. I shouldn't have underestimated Stevie. I just didn't think he'd kill in his own home.

Once I cover Paul with another tarp, I slam the tailgate shut, wipe my bloody hands on my pants, and trek back toward the house. When I get to the front door, I shove it open, searching from left to right. We're leaving. Now.

Stevie saunters into the foyer, cigar in hand. Tiger trails him, and when she sees the blood on my shirt and my hands, she pushes past him and runs toward me.

"Are you all right?" She frantically touches my chest, but I brush her hands away, angry with the fucking world.

"We're going. Where's your coat?" I should have complimented her on her beautiful blue dress, but I can't. My body is vibrating in utter fury.

A maid appears out of nowhere, carrying Tiger's coat in her hand. Tiger stands dumbfounded, begging for me to explain what's going on, but now isn't the time. Snatching the coat from the poor woman, I spin Tiger around and force her arms into it.

She thankfully snaps into gear and puts it on.

"Bianca has a migraine. She sends her farewells." Stevie is three seconds away from getting his teeth knocked out.

I seize Tiger by the elbow and march her toward the door. However, before I can flee, Stevie coolly says, "Take the backroad to Upper Crest. You can take care of business there."

Snarling, I don't bother replying and yank Tiger out the door and down the front steps.

She can barely keep up, her heels catching in the snow, but if I stop, I will turn around and fucking kill Stevie. "Bull, talk to me!" she pleads, attempting to break free. I only hold on tighter.

All I can focus on is the truck and getting her away from here, a place I never should have brought her.

"Goddammit!" she cries. "Let me go." But I can't. I need to touch her because I am so fucking afraid. "You're hurting me!"

Only when those words leave her trembling lips do I let her go.

She is breathless from being hauled across the snow and also from fear. Her cheeks are pink, her eyes wide. She is looking for answers, but how can I tell her what's been done?

"You want me to talk to you?" I snicker, shaking my head angrily. "Here, let me show you instead!"

Marching toward the truck, I yank back the tarp, flinching when I see Paul's frozen body. Flecks of snow have stuck to his eyelids and under his nose. When Tiger walks over and sees what I've revealed, she gasps, placing a trembling hand over her mouth.

"Oh, oh my god." She looks like she's about to be sick. "I kn-know him," she stutters. "He came into Blue Bloods. He tipped me really well. Why do you—" She stops, realization hitting her. "It wasn't him tipping me, was it? It was you. He what, works for you, and now—"

"And now he's dead?" I offer, gripping the tailgate.

"Why? I don't understand any of this," she whimpers, wrapping her arms around her middle.

"I don't either, Tiger," I confess, dropping my chin.

"Bull—"

When I hear her walking toward me, I jolt back, nostrils flared. "Just don't."

"Don't what?" she asks, wounded by my retreat.

But I can't have her near me, comforting me because all I see is her body lying under that tarp and not Paul's.

"I've never seen you like this. Why are you pushing me away? I thought we were past this."

And we are. That's *why* I'm pushing her away.

She shakes her head and reaches for the door handle. "You know what, fuck this. Take me home. I am so sick of—"

But this time, I'm the one who doesn't let her finish.

Hustling forward, I grip her wrist, drawing her into my chest to stop her from struggling. "I'm scared, all right!" I exclaim hoarsely. "And that's why you haven't seen me like this because I've never been more terrified in all my life. And when I'm scared, I do this. I push people away!"

Plumes of smoke fill the space between us as Tiger gasps. "Scared?"

Nodding, I let her go, defeated. "I'm scared for *you*, Tiger. I'm afraid you'll get hurt. Or worse. All I can see is having to bury your body in a shallow, unmarked grave, and that will… fucking kill me."

My admission spills out of me, unable to stop.

"Paul was my…friend. My first fucking friend. I didn't deserve him, but the stubborn son of a bitch wouldn't leave. But this is what happens to the people I care about. They die. Every time I touch you, you're covered in blood." I mean that literally and metaphorically.

"I hope I don't die," she softly soothes, reaching out to cup my cheek. I need her comfort more than I need air to breathe. "But you're not God, Bull. Only He knows the fate of our future."

"Well, he's a sadistic fucker because what seventeen-year-old kid deserves to be lying dead in the back of a pickup?" I cry, gripping my palm over hers.

She searches my face, surprisingly calm while I'm about to lose my shit. I unfasten two buttons on my shirt, needing air.

"Bull, it's okay." She cautiously moves closer, then wraps her arms around me. I can't remember the last time I've been hugged this way. I don't deserve this comfort, but I accept it because I need it. I need her.

She hugs me tight, allowing me to grieve for a life I never wanted to live.

"I'm sorry," I say against her shoulder. "I'm sorry for everything."

She inhales sharply because does that everything include

killing Lachlan? I honestly don't know anymore.

"So, you care…about me?" she asks softly.

Inhaling her familiar scent, and curving my body around hers, I don't stand a chance to deny her something she shouldn't want but does. "Yes. Too much."

Her body stops trembling, and a peace settles between us. The truth can't set us free because we will never be free until revenge is served, but whatever this is, it finally feels like I can breathe again.

Untangling myself from her arms, I meet her beautiful eyes. I never thought this was possible, but being with her calms the storm within. "Let's go. Paul deserves something better than a fucking shallow grave."

She nods, chewing on her bottom lip.

With a labored sigh, I tuck the tarp around him securely. I will never be able to rid that image from my mind. And I deserve for it to be there.

"Where are you taking him?" Tiger asks, rubbing the cold from her upper arms.

"Away from here. There is no way I will be laying him to rest in a place his killer owns."

Tiger nods.

I open the door for her, and she climbs into the truck, watching me as I close the door and round the hood. So many fucking…feelings are swarming around in my chest, and I think I'm going to be sick. I jump into the driver's side, and just before I start the truck, I open the console.

Paul's gift now highlights what a fucking asshole I truly am.

Without explanation, I loop the keys on the key chain, wishing I could use the luck of this bull to bring back my friend. But I can't.

Turning on the engine, I get the hell outta Dodge.

We're both quiet, the talk radio merely background noise until Tiger closes her eyes, and with a sigh, she whispers, "I care too much as well."

No matter how far I drive, the feelings don't subside.

CHAPTER ELEVEN

Lily

"Sorry I haven't contacted you sooner," says Fred Cole, Avery's lawyer, as he escorts me into his small office.

"That's fine, Mr. Cole. I've been busy." He gestures for me to sit as he rounds his cluttered desk.

He takes a moment to move paperwork aside, searching for Avery's file. I sit on my hands to stop them from shaking. I'm on edge, but I suppose I have been since the moment my son was taken from me.

But tonight, that changes. Well, I hope.

When Fred finally finds Avery's paperwork, he pushes his silver glasses up the bridge of his nose. He reads over the file, his stiff upper lip not really giving much away.

"Okay," he says once he's turned over the page. "Ms.

Everland was very specific in what she wanted. With no children or living relatives, she has left everything to you."

I blink once, needing a moment to process what he's just revealed.

"Her apartment will be used as equity toward what she owes the bank for the ballet studio, but it won't be enough to pay it off completely. She has a small savings, but it seems all the money she had was put into the studio. All her possessions are also yours."

I don't know what to say. I'm the sole heir?

Tears sting my eyes because even in death, Avery has ensured I'm well looked after.

"I will have to finalize everything with the bank, but it was Avery's wishes that the studio be left to you. Are you in a position to buy it?"

I clear my throat. "I just need a little time to get everything together, but yes, I think I will be."

Mr. Cole reaches for his ballpoint pen and writes something down. "Excellent. Once you're ready, we can go over your figures and see what's needed. But I think you'll be able to come out of this either being the new owner of the studio or Avery's apartment."

This sounds like a dream come true, but I can't ignore the stabbing in my chest. This "dream" has come at the expense of Avery passing. Not to mention, this would solve all my problems. I started dancing to better Jordy's life, so making a fresh start in a different state sounds like just the thing we need.

But what I intend to do tonight stirs a moral dilemma.

Do I deserve such happiness when I plan to help Bull take another man's life? I can live a new life but at the expense of another. Nausea rises.

"I understand this is a difficult time. Think about it, and I'll be in touch next week," Mr. Cole says, misreading my silence for shock and not guilt, which is what I feel.

Just when I think he's done, he passes me an envelope. When I see the script writing on the front, tears instantly spring to life.

"It's a letter from Ms. Everland," he discloses, in case I don't recognize Avery's handwriting. "She asked me to give it to you on her passing."

Fingering the corner of the envelope as though it's the most precious thing in the world, I nod quickly, unable to speak.

"Here are her keys"—he slides them across the desk—"in case you wanted to go through her things. But take your time. Let me organize everything, and I'll be in touch as soon as I have any news."

The jeweled ballet slipper key chain was a gift from me. I eye it, nostalgia washing over me. I've been so focused on finding Jordy that my grief has taken a back seat. That doesn't mean I haven't thought about Avery, though. I think about her every single day.

But now, it hits me that she's really gone.

"Thank you, Mr. Cole." Standing, I swipe the key chain from his desk. "You have my number."

Placing the keys and envelope into my bag with shaky fingers, I exit the office and almost slip on the linoleum as I race out the front door. The falling snow caps the landscape beautifully, making it look like I'm lost in a winter wonderland. But I can't appreciate its beauty because all I can think about is the ugliness in my life.

Letting my tears fall, I walk to my truck and dig out my keys. Just as I open the door, my cell rings. Reaching for it, I see the caller is private. My stomach drops, and my fingers tremble as I answer the call.

"Hello, darling sister."

His voice is filled with nothing but triumph, and why shouldn't it be? He's in control.

"Where is Jordy?" I can't keep the desperation at bay. I want to play it cool, but I can't. "I want to speak to him."

"You're in no position to be making demands," he chides, clucking his tongue.

I no longer feel the cold because hearing Jaws's voice sets everything alight.

"What do you want?" Seething, I'm envisioning ways of hurting him and hurting him slowly.

"I want a lot of things," he replies smartly. I listen for any background noise, hoping to get a sense of where he is, but it's quiet.

"Cut the bullshit. You're calling for a reason, so tell me what it is."

"You were always such a demanding little thing. Remember that one time you begged and begged for that Barbie? Which one was it again?" he asks, while I inhale sharply, as this trip down memory lane has me feeling a pang of guilt.

"Barbie and the Rockers," I reply, shivering as the snow

falls around me.

"Ah, that's right. And I got it for you, didn't I?"

"Yes."

"I did everything to make you happy. That Barbie was bought with the money I stole from a little old lady, by the way. But I stole for us to provide you with the best childhood I could," he says, guilt-tripping me further. "And you thank me by fucking my best friend and now, fucking the man who wants me dead."

"Christopher, please," I beg, holding back my sobs. "Just give me back my son. Whatever you want, I will do it. I just need Jordy back."

"*Now* you decide to listen. This all could have been avoided if your boyfriend did what he was told."

"He's not my boyfriend," I counter, which is true. He is so much more.

"So you just fuck random men then?"

A hiss leaves me because it's evident Christopher sees me as nothing but a slut.

"I'm sorry about Lachlan. I know I hurt your feelings."

He is deadly quiet.

"I can't help but feel responsible for this. You're so bitter, angry. You're not the brother I once knew. But you can't help who you fall in love with. You should know that."

I'm playing a very dangerous game, but I need to know what he wants.

And he takes the bait. "What's that supposed to mean?"

"You once told me you met a woman. Bianca. I could tell from your voice that you loved her. What happened?"

"Nothing happened," he spits, anger fueling him. But I know what happened. She didn't love him enough. The fact she is living with Stevie, Christopher's nemesis, confirms this.

It hurts when you love and want someone, and they don't feel the same way in return. In my brother's case, it's turned him into the obsessed psychopath that he is today.

"I don't believe you. But you loving her shows me you're capable of love. You once loved me," I add softly, hoping if he has any heart left, he'll end this here and now.

The emotion unsettles Christopher. "That was a long time ago, Lillian. As I see it, we're on opposing sides now."

"So, tell me what you want," I cry, sick of these games.

"He was supposed to go in there and do one fucking job. But now, I fear he's deeper than I want him to be. They like him. He's made friends with the people who betrayed me. The people who deserve to be dead!" he shouts, wounded.

"And because of this, things have become…complicated. He's become a liability, a thorn in my fucking side."

Christopher is right. He never anticipated Stevie or José liking Bull. Nor did he realize no one tells Bull what to do.

"So, I have another proposition for you."

Gulping, I brace for impact. But nothing can prepare me for this.

"Bring him to me, and I will give you back your son."

"*What?*"

"I will tell you where I am on the proviso you bring me Bull."

I can't speak.

"This was supposed to be simple, but now it's just

becoming bothersome. I have my own arrangements put into play anyway. It's only a matter of time."

"What does that mean?" I ask, finally finding my voice.

"It means if you want something done, you have to do it yourself. I am sick of waiting. But this asshole doesn't get off scot-free. We had an agreement, and he didn't hold up his end of the deal. Therefore, he must pay."

"Who are you?" I spit, shaking my head in disbelief. "You can't treat people this way."

"Why not? It's survival of the fittest, and if you show any signs of weakness, you'll pay with your head."

I don't understand any of this. What happened for things to get this bad?

"Bull won't come. I don't mean that much to him," I reveal, but I begin to question if that's entirely true. And so does my brother.

"You underestimate the power you have over him. Bring me Bull, and I will give you Jordy." And it's that simple.

But nothing in this situation has ever been just that.

"Let me talk to him," I beg.

Christopher sighs heavily, and just when I think he's going to say no, my heart is suddenly whole again.

"Hi, Mom."

"Jordy!" I cry, muting my sobs behind my hand. "Are you okay?"

"Of course, I'm okay. Best vacation ever. Thanks for letting me go."

If only he knew the truth.

"Is Uncle Christopher treating you well?"

"He's the best, Mom! He's taken me scuba diving. And hiking. I'm having so much fun. He told me you couldn't come 'cause you had to work at the studio. I'm sorry I said you were a hooker. Uncle Chris told me where you've really been."

I gulp. So Christopher was the one who fed him such lies.

"Why didn't you tell me Avery was sick? I get it now. I'm sorry for being so ungrateful."

My mouth parts because I am speechless. Jordy has never apologized to me. And why is Christopher painting me as some sort of saint?

"There's no need to be sorry, sweetie. I didn't want to worry you. I miss you so much."

"I miss you, too. I gotta go, okay? I was in the middle of *Call of Duty* and was kicking zombie butt. I love you. Bye, Mom!"

I don't get a chance to say I love him back because he's gone, just like that. He is having the time of his life while I want to curl into a ball and die.

"See? He's safe and having the time of his life. For now," he adds. "Give me what I want, and I will do the same."

"How am I supposed to do this? He'll know," I exclaim, not seeing how this is going to work.

"Again, you underestimate your worth to him. You'll figure it out. So, the question is, who do you love more? I'll call you later, and I expect an answer."

"Christopher! Christopher? No!" I scream into the phone when the line goes dead.

I frantically press redial, but it tells me the service is unavailable, which probably means the phone has already been disconnected.

Anger, fear, and sadness hit me all at once, and I grip the doorframe to hold myself up. The rules have changed, but how can I choose? How can I do what Christopher wants me to do? I cannot sacrifice Bull to save Jordy. But if I don't...

My stomach roils, and I fold forward, suddenly becoming sick. I dry heave, wanting to dispel this sickness within, but I can't. What sort of compromise is this?

"Miss, are you all right?" an elderly gentleman asks, stopping by my truck.

Peering into his wise eyes, I realize if this choice is made, Bull will never get to this man's age because if I have to choose, I will always choose my son.

"I'm fine. Thank you," I say on a rushed breath, standing upright and quickly jumping into my truck.

I can't feel my fingers so it takes me three attempts to get the key into the ignition. Once I do, I put the car into drive and head over to the motel. The gala doesn't start for a few more hours, but I have my dress and everything else I need.

My mind is blank. I feel numb. What is the alternative here? With Scrooge, at least he deserves everything he has coming, but neither Bull nor Jordy are guilty of any crime. But one of them will have to pay to sacrifice the other.

I don't bother wiping away my tears when I pull into the parking lot of the motel. I walk toward Bull's room on autopilot. The door opens before I even have a chance to knock. But that's Bull—always aware, until now.

"Tiger?"

I don't reply. I merely step into his arms, needing his

comfort and his warmth. So when he wraps his arms around me, holding me tight, I realize I am irrevocably in love with him. I always have been.

"What happened?" His scent calms the madness for a split second. It returns far too soon.

"Christopher called me."

His entire body stiffens beneath me as he ushers me inside the room.

Reluctantly, I let him go, but I'm unable to meet his eyes.

"What did he say?"

Toeing over a small hole in the carpet, I shrug helplessly. "He said the rules have changed. He said he has made his own arrangements to take care of Stevie, and it's only a matter of time. But he wants something else."

"And what's that?" Bull knows—he always does—but he wants me to say it. If I do, it'll make all of this real.

"He wants me to trade you…for Jordy." I finally confess and meet his eyes.

He nods with a heavy sigh, weighing what I just revealed. I don't know what I expected to see, but him being this calm isn't it.

"Is that all he said?"

"Pretty much. Jordy is fine," I say with a quiver. "He has no idea what's going on."

"Good," Bull replies firmly.

"So what do we do?" I hate to state the inevitable, but I honestly have no clue what comes next without throwing Bull to the wolves.

"Scrooge is scared, and that's why Jaws called you. He

knows it's only a matter of time."

"But he said if you want something done, you have to do it yourself. That means—"

He cuts me off. "He is just saying he does. If he did, I'd already be dead. And so would Jordy. Scrooge knows tonight is the perfect opportunity for me to strike. They want us to think they're two steps ahead."

I pale at the thought. "But what if he's not? I can't—" But how do I finish that sentence? How do I tell Bull I can't take that risk because my son's life is at stake?

Bull tongues his cheek, understanding my concerns. "What do you want me to do?" he simply asks, but it's not that straightforward.

And the reason is because of what he says next.

"Do you want me to do it? Because if you do...I will."

New tears resurface because this sacrifice is the reason I can't let him go. "You would trade yourself for Jordy?"

"Yes," he replies without hesitation. "Of course, I would."

"But that means Scrooge and Jaws would never pay the price for what they did to Damian."

"I know."

"And you're okay with that?" I ask, my mouth parted in shock. This entire thing was about revenge, but now, it's turned into something else.

Walking over, Bull gently places his hand to my cheek, brushing my tears away with his thumb. "I'm okay as long as you are."

His reply has more tears falling, and I suddenly can't stop.

"He'll k-kill you," I stutter, eyes wide. "He wants you to

pay for not doing what you're told."

"Someone else wants me dead, Tiger. Big deal. He can wait in line. But they're both running scared. I'm getting to them. Good."

"So what do I do?"

He turns poignant, brushing a lock of hair behind my ear. And I see a look I haven't seen before—defeat. "When he calls, you tell him it's a deal."

"*What?*"

I don't have a chance to get a word in edgewise because he shakes his head. "He'll call before the gala to ensure Scrooge's safety. When he does, you tell him to send a car to come get me."

"Bull, no!" I plead, knowing what this means.

"Yes, Tiger. For once in your life, please, do what you're told."

But how can I? I will sentence Bull to death. But if I don't, the same fate is destined for my son.

"I can't make this choice and feel good about it."

Bull brushes his thumb across my trembling lips before reaching into his pocket and sending a quick text. "You're not. This is my choice."

"Maybe you're right. Maybe he's just bluffing," I say optimistically.

"Are you willing to take that risk?" he proposes firmly.

My silence says it all.

"How am I supposed to live with myself?" I whisper, hugging my middle.

Bull doesn't reply. Instead, he walks over to Fluffball and

rubs between his ears. This isn't right. I can't accept this as our fate. But I don't know what else to do.

My cell rings, and I know who it is without looking. I don't bother saying hello when I accept the call.

"Have you made a choice?"

"Yes," I reply, swallowing down my nausea.

"And?" he smugly asks.

"And you motherfucker, you can go to hell! Send a car. Bull will come."

He sighs in victory. "If this is a trick—"

"It isn't," I cut in. "Bull knows what this is. Him for Jordy. If he doesn't do what you want, Jordy will pay."

Bull nods calmly, while my insides wither and die.

"I told you not to underestimate your power. The power of the pussy wins yet again."

I close my eyes, sickened.

"I'll text you the address of where the car will be in an hour." And the line goes dead. Just like my heart.

"I'm sorry," I whisper, keeping my eyes closed. "I don't know how to make this right."

"There is no right. There never was. But I suppose this is poetic justice. I took Lachlan's life, and now I have a chance to save his son's life. It doesn't right the wrongs, but no more innocent people deserve to pay for the sins of the past."

Tears flow down my cheeks, and I don't expect them to stop.

If someone believed in karma, I suppose they could say this is Bull's. But he doesn't deserve this. No matter what he's done.

With my heart in my throat, I open my eyes and run over to him, throwing my arms around his neck. "Please, there's got to be another way."

"I wish there was. It was careless of me to think this would work because nothing has gone according to plan so far. But it'll be okay. I will get Jordy back to you. I promise."

"But at what cost?" I cry, tightening my hold on him as I bury my face in his chest.

He doesn't need to answer. We both know.

"Look after Fluffball for me?"

I sob in response.

"Whatever happens, make sure that asshole Stevie doesn't take the club away from Lotus. Stick to the original plan, okay? As soon as Jordy is safe, you go to the police and tell them everything. I'm sorry this all falls on you now."

"I'm the one who's s-sorry," I whimper. "If you never met me—"

But he doesn't let me finish. "If I never met you...I would have never learned what it feels like to..."

The room falls silent, exposing the ferocious thrashing of my heart.

"To what?" I ask, slowly detangling myself from his embrace.

His chin is lowered, so I gently raise it with the tip of my finger.

He licks his lips. "You once asked me what prison was like."

I nod, remembering the conversation we had in my kitchen.

"Well, I spent my late teens and most of my twenties in there. It was the only adult life I knew. So when I got out, things were so... unfamiliar. But meeting you changed that. You showed me a different side to life, one I never knew.

"You taught me that a lot of badness can be balanced with a little bit of goodness...something I didn't think I had left inside me. I don't understand what this..." He pauses, searching for the right word. "Feeling is inside me, but the thought of never seeing you again? I can't fucking breathe.

"So even though I'm free, I'm still very much a prisoner... to you."

There aren't any words to explain how I'm feeling because like Bull, I too don't understand this feeling inside me. This isn't love—it's more.

The grimmest of circumstances drew us together, and now, they're tearing us apart.

Unable to stand the distance between us, I rise on my tippy toes and crush my mouth to Bull's. His taste is intoxicating, but maybe it's because I know it may be the last time I get lost in it. The kiss isn't gentle. It's frantic, laced with possession and control.

I can't get enough of him and press my body against his. His warmth always melts my cold. He bites the corner of my mouth, growling when I circle my tongue with his. I want him now, always, but time is the enemy. It always has been.

He winds my hair around his fist, tilting my head so he can dominate the kiss in the most delicious of ways. I am lost to him, allowing him to control me because I love it when he loses control. Walking us toward the bed, he tosses me onto the mattress, our lips never missing a beat.

The harder he kisses me, the more desperate I am to hold on tight and never let go. I know what this means, but how do I say goodbye to the man I love? I thought I knew what love was, but I was wrong. We're both experiencing being in love for the first time. And I can't let that go.

"Bull," I whimper from around his lips, snaring his long hair between my fingers. "I can't do this."

I thought I could, but I can't.

I don't know what the alternative is, but I couldn't live with myself if I fed him to the wolves. I want him. With me. Always. There has to be a reason he came into my world…and when he shifts me higher up the bed, placing my arms above my head, I soon find out what that is.

He came into my world to save me…

In one smooth motion, he snares my wrists in his hand as he reaches into the bedside table with the other. Before I can question what he's doing, something tight bites into my skin. I try to move, but I can't, and that's because I'm tied to the headboard.

My eyes snap open as Bull slides off me.

"Let me go!" I exclaim, tugging wildly against the cable tie around my wrists.

"Venus will untie you once I'm gone," he says blankly. He knew what I was thinking, but he wouldn't allow me to change his mind.

"Bull!" I yell, kicking my legs, hoping to somehow launch off the bed, but I'm not going anywhere. "Don't do this. We will think of something else."

He slips something into his pocket, ignoring me.

"Goddammit! Please don't do th-this." When he continues to ignore me, I say the only thing I can to help him understand how he's ripping out my heart. "I…I lov—"

He is by my side in seconds, silencing me with his finger. "Don't say it," he pleads, his eyes a stormy mix of Heaven and Hell. "If you say it now, I won't know if you mean it. If, by some miracle, we make it out alive, then you can tell me. Okay?"

He removes his chain from around his neck and places it around mine.

I open my mouth, ready to protest because I mean it—here, now, and always—but he doesn't let me finish. He seals his mouth over mine and kisses me deliriously slow. It's unhurried, long, and it's filled with love. From us both.

A salty kiss goodbye is how I'll remember Bull because with one last press of his lips to mine, he leaves me a sobbing mess. He's gone to pay the price to bring back my son—his life.

CHAPTER TWELVE

Bull

I was almost fucking there. I almost had it all.

But I should have known it was too good to be true. Life has been a brutal bitch to me so far, so I don't know why I expected this time to be any different.

Being within hours of killing that son of a bitch, Scrooge, fucking stings. But this decision is a no-brainer. There is no way I will risk Jordy's life that way. If he is no longer of use to Jaws, he will kill Jordy. In turn, Tiger would die too, and that is something I will not fucking allow.

So, I have accepted defeat. I failed.

But it seems life isn't done fucking with me just yet.

I'm filling my truck up with gas when a familiar car pulls up beside me. Groaning, I curse the motherfucking universe.

Franca winds down the window with a smile. "We have to stop meeting this way."

I grunt in response, not in the mood for her humor. My tank isn't full, but it'll do. I need to get the fuck out of here before Franca gets wind of what I'm doing.

"Got a minute?" she asks as if it's optional.

"Not really," I reply, slamming the gas tank shut.

"I need a piss sample."

"Now?" I ask, and she raises an eyebrow.

This is all a power play. Just like a dog lifting his leg to mark his domain. However, she's the one in control.

"Or we can always go somewhere. Unless you've got somewhere else to be?"

Extending my hand, she slaps the container into my palm. The gas station is empty, so with eyes locked on her, I unzip my fly. She doesn't look away as I begin pissing into the container. I sure as shit ain't shy. And neither is she.

Once I'm done, I tuck myself back into my pants, screw the lid onto the container, and hand it to her.

She places it into a brown paper bag and smiles. "Where you off to in such a hurry?"

"Church," I counter, opening my door. I already prepaid, so it's time I split.

"You do realize I can force you to talk, right?"

I am running out of patience and time. "What do you want to talk about, Franca? The weather? You got a question, ask me. I don't have time for games."

"Fine. I want to know where the next fight is. I also want to know if you're involved with the cartel."

Keeping my cool, I reach into my pocket and retrieve a stick of bubble gum. Without hurry, I unwrap it and place it into my mouth. "I can't help you, sorry."

She doesn't have anything solid on me. If she did, this conversation would be going a different way.

"Okay, have it your way then."

Blowing a bubble, I pop it loudly. "We done?"

She nods, slipping on her shades. "For now."

I don't wait for her to change her mind and get into my truck. I take off, waiting for her to follow me. She doesn't. But that doesn't mean she won't sometime soon.

This has always been complicated, but with so many game players wanting a piece of the pie, it changes everything.

I drive to the address Jaws sent me to and park my truck. When a black van with tinted windows turns down the derelict street I'm standing on, I know my ride has arrived. Jaws wanted to meet here because it's in the middle of nowhere, setting the stage for what faces me. He wants no witnesses. He wants me to disappear.

The van pulls up by the curb, and the door slides open. A man in a skull mask greets me. If this is supposed to scare me, I'm not impressed.

"Halloween is over, dude," I say, pushing past him and stepping into the back. He doesn't reply and slams the door shut. I take a seat, insulted Jaws only sent three men. But he knows I won't fight.

The driver and passenger are wearing similar masks. Everyone was invited to this party but me, it seems.

Buckling my seat belt, I look at the driver, hinting any

time he wants to step on it would be good. "Safety first."

He seems thrown off by my composure. No doubt they expected me to put up some sort of fight. But honestly, a small part of me welcomes the silence. Slouching back in my seat, I cross my ankles and fold my hands over my stomach. The driver finally gets the hint and takes off into the night.

My thoughts instantly drift to Tiger and how I left her. I told Venus to untie her twenty minutes after I left. She didn't need to ask why. The grave look on my face said it all. Leaving Tiger tied up was the last thing I wanted to do, but I already buried one person in an unmarked grave, I wouldn't do it again.

"You don't look so tough," Skull Boy says, sitting across from me.

I stare straight ahead, refusing to entertain this dickhead.

"I thought you'd be...bigger."

"That's what she said," I counter with an uninterested yawn. I don't know why he feels the need to make conversation. If I'm going to die, I'd like the last few moments of my life to be spent in silence. He thankfully gets the hint and closes his stupid fucking mouth.

I'm not carrying, but that doesn't mean I haven't come prepared. Sometimes, the smallest things pack the biggest punch.

I have no idea where we're going. Jaws was in Mexico apparently, so I'm assuming we have a long journey ahead. I inhale slowly, feeling surprisingly relaxed. That is short-lived, however.

It happens so quickly, and my first response is to laugh.

Skull Boy is sitting smugly one second, and the next, he is propelled through the air like a crash test dummy before slamming into the front seats with a thud. Squealing brakes and the strong smell of gas reveal that we've been hit, and hit hard.

The van comes to a screeching stop with the sound of the horn blaring. Just as I'm about to unsnap the seat belt that just saved my life, the door slides open and I see two men donning face masks that look all too familiar, and that's because they're the same bandanas I wear when I fight.

I don't need an invitation.

Unbuckling my belt, I dive outside and follow the masked men toward their idling van. Once inside, the driver doesn't hesitate and speeds off, leaving the carnage behind. One of the men rips off the mask, and I shake my head, wondering what the hell is going on.

"*Colmillo*," Jesús says with a grin.

"'Sup," I reply with a nod, attempting to conceal my confusion.

"José was curious to why you canceled tonight, so we followed you. Where you going?" I had to text José, informing him something came up and I couldn't attend the gala. But the deal was done. We were square.

I was hoping he'd believe the lie.

"Church," I quip, folding my arms across my chest. It didn't work the first time around. Maybe I'll have better luck the second.

Jesús smirks before reaching over his shoulder and producing a suit bag. "Well, lucky for you I brought a suit then."

It seems José wants me to finish the job because all felons are the same—they may be shady ass motherfuckers, but their word means something. And José doesn't want me backing out in case I come back down the track asking him to pay up.

But I can't, and he can't know the reason that is.

"Tell José we're good. I have somewhere to be."

Jesús shakes his head. "Sorry, but if we don't take you to the gala, then you have to go see José."

Fuck, if Jaws doesn't hear from his men, he will soon figure out something went wrong. And I hate to think of what he'll do to Jordy. He is running out of patience as I can only piss him off so much. And if I don't go to the gala, José will make me bleed until I tell him what's going on.

He was once Jaws's friend. Even though they are no longer acquaintances, there is some understanding between them.

"Turn the van back around," I order as this is the only thing I can do where everyone wins.

Jesús arches a brow, wondering why I would ask that. But when I remain straight-faced, he orders the driver to do what I've asked. He pulls up by the crumpled van that has a flat tire and smoke rising from the hood thanks to the pole it was rammed into.

They hit them from behind and hit them fucking hard. I hope at least one of them is alive. Opening the door, I poke my head into the mangled van, and my hopes of finding anyone alive dwindles as I find the driver wearing the horn as his face and the passenger cut in half by the windshield.

When I hear a groan, I don't hesitate. Stepping inside, I fist Skull Boy's shirt and slam his back up against the van. He's slumped forward and his piss-poor attempt to twist free hints that he is hurt real bad, but as long as his tongue isn't broken, he is of use to me.

"Can you hear me, you worthless piece of shit?" I demand, ripping off his mask.

His chin lolls to his chest, so I grip his hair and yank his head upright. His eyes flicker open, and when he's confronted with the situation in front of him, he realizes he should have been fucking nicer to me.

"What do you want?" he wheezes, licking the blood from his busted lip.

"I want you to call Jaws and tell him everything is A-fucking-okay," I reply. I'm running out of time. Jesús can't know this is happening.

When he hesitates, I reach into my back pocket and produce my switchblade. Shame on him for not frisking me first. In one fluid motion, I press my blade up under his left testicle. A terrified yelp escapes him, which has me pressing in deeper.

"You'll be singing soprano in three fucking seconds if you don't get out your phone."

He raises one hand in surrender, and with the other, he shakily retrieves his cell from his pocket.

I nod, hinting now is the time to make the call. "Put him on speaker."

"Hi," he says into the phone when someone picks up without saying hello. "Just calling to let you know we've got him. We're on our way to the drop-off point."

"Good," Jaws says. It's a knee-jerk reaction for me to force the blade deeper against Skull Boy's nut.

He squeaks and attempts to shift away. But I shake my head, angling the blade higher.

"Once you get to Texas, throw his ass on the plane. Do not let him out of your sight. Got it?"

Texas? Surely, we weren't going on a road trip. Thank fuck the van is now bust.

"Yes, got it," he replies, his wide eyes flicking to mine. "He's not fighting, though."

"Of course, he's not," Jaws confidently states. "I have something he wants. Call me once you get there. I have some calls of my own to make." No guessing to whom.

"Oh, and Baz, if you want to rough him up a little or well, a lot, be my guest. Check in tomorrow."

And the line goes dead.

Skull Boy aka Baz shifts, silently hinting I'm to remove the knife from his balls. But I am fucking raging and need to hurt something.

I have no idea where "there" is, but it makes sense for them to travel by car. Less witnesses and less mess. Flying is quicker, but it's also risky. Even though Jaws knows I come willingly, he won't take his chances.

Removing the knife, I place it back into my pocket while Baz sighs. That relief is short-lived, however, when I grab him around the throat, hinting it's time to move. He doesn't struggle and does as he's told.

I shove him out the door, and Jesús is waiting, eyes wide. He has no idea what's going on but doesn't argue when I hint he's to throw this sorry sack of shit into the van. Once he's secured, I walk to the driver's side and open the door.

I hunt through the lifeless driver's pockets until I find his phone. There is a cell and a 9mm in the console, which I'm guessing belongs to the passenger. I take them too.

Placing the gun at the small of my back, I quickly jog over to the awaiting van and jump inside. Once we're set, the driver takes off once again, leaving the bloodbath behind.

Baz is passed out in the seat, but that's okay. I don't need him until later. I was once his hostage, but now, he is mine. He will check in with Jaws because as I see it, if we don't hint that something is wrong, Jaws will think everything is peachy.

I have every intention of getting on that plane. I just need to make a pit stop first.

I gesture for Jesús to give me the suit because it's time I play monkey.

This monkey suit is the perfect disguise to blend in with the rich and pretentious. When I passed the gold invite to the doorman, he looked at my hand tattoos briefly but then ushered me inside without any problems. Jesús and two other men are invited to this party also. But instead of monkey suits, they've donned a different suit, and that's of the burgundy uniform of the people who work here.

I dare say they're my meal ticket, so all I have to do is wait for the signal—peaches, whatever the fuck that means.

The driver waits with Baz; he was given strict instructions

to break both his kneecaps if he tried to escape.

The gala starts in a few, so I work the venue discreetly, counting the number of exits and verifying how much muscle mans each of them. There is a roped-off area up the carpeted stairs. That's where I need to be.

Breathing in, I remind myself that I've come this far. I can wait.

When the masses are herded into the main ballroom, I wait in line, observing the glitzy venue. It's right on the river, offering romantic and impressive views to most, but to me, all I see is a watery grave at my disposal.

I can barely contain my excitement.

When I finally get to the maître d' and he asks for my name, I give him the one on the invite. "Chuck Bancroft."

I did a quick Google search and discovered he was some low-key banker from LA. José didn't choose someone who would be recognized among the crowd.

The maître d' scrolls through his iPad and when he finds my name, he looks up at me with a furrowed brow. "Where is your plus one?"

"My what?" I bark, ready to give him a plus one black eye if he doesn't let me in.

He clears his throat. "It says you're bringing a Ms. Hayley Cribbs?"

Goddammit.

"She has a migraine," I reply, not hiding my irritation.

"Oh. I will have to let my manager know."

"That she has a migraine?" I sarcastically ask.

He loosens his collar with one finger. "No, that you're

alone. For security reasons, we—"

But his bullshit fades into the background when I am tackled from behind by a scent I associate with coming home.

"Sorry I'm late."

Slowly turning my chin, I see the most beautiful woman standing by my side. Her peacock-colored ballgown draws out the green in her eyes. Twisted into an elegant knot, her hair is fastened with a diamond clip that matches her jewelry.

She once told me she wasn't a princess, but fuck me dead, that's exactly what she is. Graceful, regal, and mine.

"Hi," she says with a small smile when I continue staring at her like a gaping goldfish.

"You're Ms. Cribbs?" the maître d' asks.

"Yes," Tiger replies without missing a beat.

"Excellent," he says, doing something on his device while I can't take my eyes off Tiger.

She has always left me with this heavy weight pressing against my chest, but this is different. I feel like I can breathe again. She is my oxygen, my sustenance to stay alive.

"Someone will lead you to your table."

Tiger nods, reaching for my hand. She presses something into my palm. When I feel the cool metal, a sense of completeness overcomes me. Linking her arm through mine, she gently coaxes me to move toward the door. I get my head back into the game and follow the waiter who escorts us through the large room. I would be impressed with the fancy setting, but it pales in comparison to Tiger on my arm.

We're sitting in the nosebleed seats, but that's what I wanted. To be as far away from the stage as possible. I can't risk Scrooge seeing me. I know Jaws would have called him with the update that I'm currently detained, but surprise, asshole, I'm here, ready to rain on your parade.

We take our seats in silence.

I quickly put my necklace on, the one Tiger slipped into my palm, and tuck it under my shirt. Tiger fiddles with her silverware while I wonder why I'm suddenly so tongue-tied. I've seen her naked and done dark and delicious things to her body, but I suddenly feel giddy, like a teenage boy.

I reach for the bottle of red and fill up her glass.

"You're not drinking?" she asks, breaking the silence.

I shake my head.

She soon understands why that is and reaches for the wine with a trembling hand. "What happened?" she whispers from behind the rim of the glass.

She has every right to ask. Me being here means Jordy is at risk. So leaning in close, I inhale her scent, before revealing, "It's under control. He still thinks the deal is on, and it is. This is just a detour."

She sips her wine, but her wide eyes reveal her fear.

Needing to comfort her, I place my hand on her leg and squeeze lightly. "He's coming home. I promise."

"And what about you?" she asks, suppressing her sniffle.

I don't reply because I don't know where I'll be once this is over. All I know is that it's time for this to be done. The table begins to fill with people, so Tiger and I keep quiet, but I never remove my hand from her thigh.

I wonder how she knew I was here? Was she planning on taking down Scrooge herself?

The crowd is big, suggesting Scrooge has a lot of people fooled. He's conned his way into these people's lives, making them believe he is the good guy when, in reality, he's the big bad. But it ends tonight.

Once everyone is seated, the waiters zip around the room, serving appetizers. Pushing the shrimp in a glass away from me, I instead scour the room, looking for Jesús, but he is nowhere to be found.

The crowd is chatting happily, none the wiser that a murderer is about to scam them into giving away their life savings. I have no doubt Scrooge benefits from this. There is no way he does this out of the goodness of his heart, and that's because he doesn't have one. I wouldn't be surprised if he pocketed the majority of the takings and donated just enough to keep someone from asking questions.

Water is a poor substitute for what I want, but my mouth is dry. As I begin filling my glass, a woman in a tight white dress walks onto the stage and stands behind the lectern. She taps the microphone once, quieting the room with its echo.

"Hi, everyone. I'm Martha York, one of the coordinators of this very important event." Martha then launches into a spiel about child abuse and how prevalent it is in today's world. It takes all my willpower not to scoff and call bullshit because the guest of honor is the biggest child abuser of them all.

She has the crowd eating from the palm of her hand five minutes later when she hollers. "So, please, put your hands together for the brilliant man, who just happens to be my husband, Benjamin Solomon."

The applause is deafening, but all I can hear are the words, "*My husband.*"

Martha York is collateral.

But that can wait because when the blue curtains parts and out strolls a man I made a promise to fourteen years ago, nothing else matters. The huge TV screen mounted above the stage allows me to see him, proving true evil exists.

Memories of that night instantly assault me, and I curl my hands into fists under the table. I remember his laughter, the way he had no conscience when he stole from my brother. Sickened, I turn my cheek, unable to look at his smiling face because I know what ugliness lies beneath the mask.

Tiger places her hand over my fist and squeezes softly. She wants to comfort me, but she can't. The only comfort I'll have is when I'm coated in this motherfucker's blood.

Taking a steady breath, I return my attention to the screen. Scrooge casually grips the lectern, showcasing his pride and joy—Damian's championship ring. Seeing it after so long is surreal. A small part of me wants to believe this isn't his ring. Maybe it's just one like it. But I'm a *realist*, and I'm *really* going to kill this fucker. Tonight.

Scrooge waits for the crowd to quiet before he begins his bullshit speech. "Wow, what an introduction, but can we get another round of applause for the real hero here, and that's my beautiful wife." He is the first to clap, looking at his wife with nothing but love.

The crowd follows suit, totally fooled.

I don't know how long I can sit here. The rage burning inside me has been left to fester, and sooner or later, it'll explode.

Martha blows him a kiss from the side of the stage, gushing over her husband, the murderer.

Once Scrooge is satisfied, he hushes the crowd with his hands, and they quickly obey. "Thank you for being here," he begins, looking into the crowd. "Children are gifts from God, and Martha and I have been blessed three times. Being a father changed my life in ways I never thought possible, and I knew I would do anything to protect my children."

I can't do this.

I take three deep breaths, but nothing helps. I cannot find my Zen because there is no harmony until this asshole takes his last breath.

Tiger is aware of my murderous urges, but she can't offer me any solace. No one can.

As Scrooge continues his speech, I pan over the memories that have never left me.

"Thanks for my ring."

"I like your jacket. I always wanted to be quarterback. But they said I was too small. Not so small now, am I, asshole?"

All I can hear as Scrooge talks are those vile words he spoke to my brother as though he was nothing. I can hear the crack of Damian's wrist and his winded grunts as they kicked and punched him until he was just a bloody heap.

I remember being sick all over myself when the paramedics took my brother away. The rotten smell, the decay of my life crumbling away. I remember it all. Yet, I'm the monster for wanting this asshole dead.

No matter how many breaths I take, it's not enough.

Lowering my chin to my chest, I inhale deeply and close

my eyes. I need one fucking second to…what? When my eyes grow wet, I realize what that something is—I need to grieve for my brother. I've been so hellbent on revenge and now that it literally stands just a few feet away, a monumental sadness overcomes me. It overtakes the rage.

Once I end Scrooge's miserable existence, will that make this emptiness, this heaviness go away? I know it won't bring Damian back, but will it appease the demons inside me? When all of this is finally done with, when Damian's killers are dead, what happens then?

There is no magical potion to make all of this pain, all of this sorrow eating away at me go away, but I thought I would feel victorious once this moment arrived. But I don't. I just feel fucking heartbroken.

That is…until someone who has always held my heart without me even knowing it gently tips my chin up to meet her beautiful green eyes. I am so lost, but when Tiger nods once, then leans in to press her lips to mine, I realize I am no longer alone.

At the motel, I'm pretty sure she was going to tell me she loved me, but I didn't want her to say it. I didn't want the dire situation to influence her decision. But the way she kisses me, and the gentle way she holds my cheek, I don't need to hear it. I can feel it and have felt it so many times before. I was just too stupid to realize what it was.

The only person who ever really loved me is dead. I wasn't worthy of love until now because this incredible, brave woman loves me, and I…I…love her in return.

When she pulls away, she rubs her nose against mine.

Unable to help myself, I wrap her in my arms and hug her tight. I am engulfed with cherry blossoms and love. "You've got this," she whispers, nestling into my neck.

And she's right. I fucking do.

"So, please, dig deep and save a child's life. Every life matters. Thank you."

Every life but his…

And with that send-off, everything comes full circle, and it's time.

The crowd stands, applauding this murdering asshole while he waves like he is Jesus Christ himself. Every time the lights catch the shimmer of green from his ring, I envision the ways I am going to make him pay for what he's done.

He saunters off stage, his wife in tow, while everyone takes a seat and begin taking out their checkbooks. From the loud and lively chatter, it's clear he's totally brainwashed the crowd. The waiters begin to scatter around the room, hands filled with plates.

The main course is about to be served.

Looking over my shoulder, I see that the table behind me has been served beef or chicken, but there's no fucking sign of peaches. Tiger also looks around the room, her straight white teeth tugging at her bottom lip. I notice she's wearing an elastic band around her wrist.

I hate that she feels the need to hurt herself, but I get it. We both get off on pain.

"Excuse me. The filet mignon with green beans." The blonde waitress places a plate down in front of Tiger. "And for you, sir, the stuffed chicken breast with asparagus." She does the same for me while I visually search my plate for peaches.

But nothing is peachy because there are no damn peaches.

Just as I'm about to tell her to give the plate to someone else, her name tag catches my eye.

It reads Peaches.

Holy motherfucking shit.

I was looking for peaches, the food, not Peaches, the person. Kudos to José.

"I might use the restroom before I eat." I come to a casual stand. Tiger peers up and notices the name tag as well.

"Let me show you where it is, sir," Peaches says with a friendly smile. She deserves an Emmy. She looks like the girl next door. No one would question her motives. The occupants at the table are none the wiser that I'm about to slit their hero's throat.

Just as I'm about to leave, Tiger grips my wrist. She can't express what she really wants to say, but she doesn't need to speak. Her worried expression says it all.

Nodding, I place my hand over hers and squeeze softly. "I'll be back soon."

I've never had anyone worry about me before. Well, adult me that is. It's a weird thing to digest.

Pressing a quick kiss to Tiger's forehead, I grab my jacket from the back of the chair and follow Peaches through the crowded room. I don't ask questions. The less I know, the better.

She casually leads me into the main foyer where Jesús is collecting empty champagne glasses from the table. When he sees me, he nods once, gesturing I'm to follow him and

Peaches toward a door in the corner of the room.

I thought we'd go via the stairs, but I don't question it.

When we enter the kitchen, I understand why we're here. Jesús quickly takes off his vest and offers it to me. Peaches reaches for a silver champagne bucket and two glasses. I take off my tie and jacket, and slip on the vest.

Peaches places a white linen napkin over my arm and hands me the champagne glasses. We look the part, and Jesús grins as he looks down at his gold watch.

"Three, two, and one." I have no idea what we're counting down until I hear an array of car alarms sound from outside. A decoy.

"Go, *Colmillo*. You only have about twenty minutes until his wife returns. Little Miss Perfect can't let anything ruin her night. She'll take the guards with her, so he'll be alone. I will knock when it's time."

Tick tock, motherfucker.

Excitement courses through me as I follow Peaches out through another doorway that comes out near the staircase. It's manned by two assholes. They look at our name tags. I now understand why Peaches is with me.

Security is tight and going alone would rouse suspicions. But Peaches is the embodiment of the girl-next-door type. Me, on the other hand? I rouse a lot of suspicions, hence why Peaches is standing by my side, smiling sweetly.

"We're here to bring Mr. Solomon his champagne," she says without a quiver.

One of the men looks at me closely. He is not buying into my new role. Thankfully, the other dude doesn't want to get into trouble with the big boss and removes the rope so we can walk up the stairs. Peaches leads the way while I tail her victoriously. If only they knew they were the first flaw in the design.

Peaches knows the way and confidently walks toward a door. There are no men standing outside it, which surprises me. She takes a deep breath and knocks. "Mr. Solomon, I have your champagne."

When there is no response, I crack my neck from side to side, suddenly tense. What if he's gone?

Peaches knocks again.

The anticipation is unbearable, and just when I think the plan has failed, I hear it. A voice I will soon mute forever.

"Leave it by the door."

Peaches sighs, appearing just as relieved as I am that Scrooge is inside. "I'm sorry, sir. I can't. Health and safety laws prohibit me from leaving anything in the hallway in case of an evacuation."

Scrooge curses before I hear footsteps sweep across the carpet. The moment he's close, Peaches thrusts the bucket into my hands and scampers away. She got me in, and now, it's up to me to do the rest. Inhaling and exhaling, I lower my chin and wait for the door to open.

There is no way I can prepare for this.

When the door opens, I shake hands with the devil inside me. The deal is done.

"Just leave it on the table," Scrooge orders, annoyed as his shiny shoes storm off away from me. I can smell the cigarette smoke.

I don't hesitate. Not this time.

I enter the room, softly closing and locking the door behind me. With my chin still lowered, I quickly scan the room, but it's unmanned. Jesús was right. The decoy worked. Scrooge is alone. He must really love his wife to send his bodyguards away, but he thinks he's safe. He doesn't know the next few breaths will be the last ones he ever takes.

I savor the silence, the silence before the motherfucking storm.

"Are you deaf, boy? I said—"

I don't allow him to finish because each breath he takes is further insult to my brother's memory.

Lifting my chin slowly, I meet his eyes, the eyes that have haunted me for fourteen years. He stops mid turn, anger turning to recognition, and then to…fear, fear that feeds my demons for more.

Scrooge stares at me, wide-eyed, his cigarette hanging from his agape mouth. It seems he can't believe I'm here. Jaws would have assured him things were taken care of, which is why he was careless and sent his guards away.

I had an entire speech planned, but standing here now, all the words escape me because all I want to do is hurt him… and hurt him really, really bad.

It's the ultimate standoff, watching the other for any signs of weakness. He knows who I am. He has information Kong never had. So now, the question is, what is he planning to do with that knowledge?

"You stupid idiot," he mocks, shaking his head while I envision detaching it from his shoulders. "My guards will be here any second, and when they do, you'll regret coming here." He blows a ring of smoke, faking confidence.

He talks big, but too bad for him, I know his secrets.

Tsking, I place the champagne and glasses onto the table. "Wow, what a wonderful story. Too bad it's a load of shit."

I take great pleasure in seeing his eye twitch as he butts out his cigarette in the ashtray.

Getting comfortable as I plan on being here for a while, I take off my jacket. Casually strolling forward, I admire him for not backing away. He stands his ground. Stripping away his cockiness is what I will enjoy the most. That, and slitting his fucking throat.

"I know your three monkey boys are downstairs with your wife." I've struck a nerve, so I decide to continue because seeing him squirm gives me life. "Such a pretty thing, she is. I bet your daughters take after their momma. Am I right?"

The color drains from his face.

During his heartfelt, bullshit speech, he mentioned he had kids, but he never revealed their gender. But I know their ages and their names, all because Paul was the best fucking partner in crime. *God rest his soul.*

"How are the twins? Jenny and Jackie. Such cute names for such cute kids. Can you imagine what someone would pay for such cuteness, such innocence?" I ask calmly. "And your eldest. Wow, you have a little diva on your hands there. I already feel sorry for her future husband."

"Motherfucker!" he seethes, clenching his fists. "What do you want?"

I laugh in response. Is he really asking me this?

"What I want," I reply, walking back to the table and unwrapping the champagne bottle, "I can never, ever have because you and your three motherfucking friends took that away from me." I end the sentence with the popping of the cork.

Pouring us some champagne, I offer him a glass. He eyes it suspiciously but eventually snatches it from my hand.

"Let's make a toast, shall we?" I raise my glass high in the air.

"What are we toasting?" He is playing along, knowing his family's life is on the line if he doesn't.

"To tacos, Gangnam Style, and oh, to your death," I reply, lifting the glass to my lips.

Panic has set in, and Scrooge is seeking out every option for escape. But there are none. This ends now. Kudos to him for thinking it's not.

Just as I finish my drink, Scrooge throws his champagne in my face and scampers for the balcony doors. *Really?* That's his plan? I'm disappointed.

Wiping a hand down my face, I shake my head at his stupidity. In his panic, he gets tangled in the mesh curtains, and this would be fucking hilarious if not for the fact that I want to end this asshole, like yesterday.

Without thought, I reach for the ice bucket and hurl it across the room. When it connects with the back of Scrooge's head and a pained oof leaves him as he drops like a sack of shit, I holler, "Touchdown!"

I stalk across the room, yanking him by the back of his collar.

He turns around, attempting to connect with me, but I use the bottom of the champagne bottle to subdue him when I slam it into his temple. He buckles, though he fights, still attempting to flee. But he's not going anywhere.

"We're going to have a little chat." I don't give him a chance to argue as I shove him into the armchair. He is dazed from all the blows to the head, so he stays seated for now.

"I've been looking for you for a very long time," I reveal, standing in front of his chair. "It was the only thing I lived for. I'm sure Jaws has filled you in, so I won't bore you with the details. But I killed Hero, I killed Kong, and now, I'm going to kill you."

I've stopped looking for answers to why they did what they did because there are none.

He stops groaning and looks up at me. "You are nothing." He spits on my shoe. "If you think threatening me with death is going to scare me, you're wrong. You're still fucking weak. And your brother is still fucking dead."

Tipping my face to the ceiling, I inhale slowly, needing a moment.

By baiting me, he's hoping I'll kill him quickly. He knows how this is going to end. And the coward that he is thinks if he pisses me off, I'll finish him off painlessly. Slowly meeting his eyes, I shake my head. He thought wrong.

"Yes, Damian is dead because of *you*. I wanted answers. I thought that if I understood why you did it, this"—I claw over my heart—"anger would go away. But it hasn't, and that's because knowing there isn't an answer makes things so much worse."

Scrooge waits for me to continue.

"But I think this monster was always inside me, waiting to break free. You killed the wrong brother," I utter. "You killed the one who would have forgiven you. Because me? I don't forgive. And no matter how I kill you, your suffering will never be enough.

"Which is why I want you to know that once I end you, I am going to go downstairs, find your pretty little wife, and defile her in the most delicious of ways."

Scrooge's chest begins to rise and fall quickly as he clenches his fists on top of his thighs.

"And she's going to like it. She's going to beg me for more."

"Don't underestimate my wife," he snarls, blood trickling down his cheek from the wound at his temple.

Nodding, I place my hands into my pants pockets. "And don't underestimate the love of a mother because when I'm done with her, I'm going to drive to your house and end your fucking bloodline."

He pales, a gasp escaping him. "They're just kids. How could you?"

"Funny, that's exactly what Kong said to me before I stabbed him. Too bad your moral compasses weren't in check the night you killed my brother. He was just a kid too. So was I. But that didn't seem to make a difference."

Fear overshadows Scrooge. "I have money. Lots of it. You can have it all."

Curling my lip in disgust, I ask, "What the fuck am I supposed to do with money? Live a normal life? Make someone an honest woman, marry her, and have two point five kids? Is that what I'm supposed to do?"

"I don't care what you do. Just leave me and my family alone!" he cries. "Here, take my watch. It's worth ten thousand dollars." He quickly unfastens his Rolex and tosses it to me. It lands on the floor at my feet, and that's where it'll stay.

Laughing, I shake my head, incredulous of the nerve of this jerk-off. "You're just not getting it, Benjamin. There is only one thing you can offer me... and that's your fucking head. Kneel."

Scrooge blinks quickly, unsure if he heard me correctly. But he did. When I stand unbending, he slowly gets to his knees in front of me.

"Seeing as you've had a lapse in memory, maybe we should reenact the night to help you remember?"

"You already got your vengeance!" he screams, spittle flying free. "You killed Kong and Hero. What more do you want?"

"I really wish you'd stop asking me such stupid questions," I goad. "Do you remember what you said to Damian when he was covered in blood and piss?"

The motherfucker actually appears to contemplate the question as though he's forgotten something so monumental like killing someone.

"Let me remind you." Gripping his hair, I yank his head back at a painful angle. "I always wanted to be quarterback. But they said I was too small. Not so small now, am I, asshole?" I repeat exactly what Scrooge said to Damian. I have memorized every single word.

"You said that to him after you stole his ring. The ring you wear like a fucking trophy."

"You want it back?" he exclaims, attempting to yank it off his finger. "Here, take it."

It won't budge, and that's probably because he's worn it since he stole it from my brother.

I cluck my tongue. "It looks like it's stuck. Here, let me help." And by help, I mean with my switchblade.

When I withdraw the blade from my pocket, Scrooge freezes and realizes it's now or never. With a surge of adrenaline, he leaps to his feet and attempts to tackle me, but these assholes have forgotten I'm no longer a helpless kid.

In my other pocket, I packed some brass knuckles. A gun is too easy for this motherfucker. I intend to inflict as much pain as I can. Looping my fingers through the holes, I wait for him to come at me and give him a small shred of hope that he has a fighting chance.

I soon take that hope away when I swing out and connect with his face. The squelched sound it makes has me hollering in happiness. Scrooge is anything but happy as he sways on his feet, looking for something to hold onto before he falls.

I don't give him a reprieve, however.

I charge forward and hit him again and again, the brass knuckles causing enough damage for his blood to spray across the room and carpet. He collapses to his knees, struggling to breathe. I kick him in the back, and he falls on his stomach, desperate to flee…just how Damian was. And just how he did to Damian, I place my boot into the small of his back, yank his arm backward, and break his fucking wrist with a crack.

He howls, but I can't have him raising any alarms, so I

reach for a plastic apple from the Art Deco piece on the coffee table and shove it into his mouth so deeply, he gags.

Oink, oink, little piggy.

The green diamond catches the light, and a sudden sadness overtakes my rage. Damian was so proud of this ring and to know this vile cunt wore it longer than my brother has me ready to throw down.

Dropping to a squat, I grab his finger and slice through muscle, tissue, and bone until it hangs by a tendon. I yank on it, excitement coursing through me as it snaps free.

Peering down at the finger in my palm, I smile. Damian's ring will finally be on the right finger. I place it in my pocket for safekeeping. "You've worn my brother's ring as a trophy, haven't you, you sick fuck? No wonder you and Jaws are best friends."

Scrooge is anything but smiling as his muffled cries from around the apple hint at his pain. Looking at the clock on the mantel, I see that I'm running out of time.

Yanking back his head by his hair, I press the tip of the blade into the side of his throat, watching his frantic pulse pound wildly against his bloody skin. "Still think I want your money?" I snicker into his ear, removing the apple.

"I'm so-sorry," he splutters, face bloody and bruised. "I will tell you where Jaws is. I will take you to him."

"It's too late for sorry. I know where he is, asshole. If this is your ace in the hole, you lose."

Scrooge thrashes about wildly, the last shred of adrenaline animating him. But he's lost. He lost the moment he killed Damian. "Then what do you want? What do you want!" he screams, bloody spittle dribbling from his mouth.

These rich pricks, they think money is the answer to all their problems, and that's their downfall because they don't understand how something could mean more to me than green. And that's love, an emotion I never thought I was capable of feeling ever again.

But I was wrong.

It's because of my love for Damian, for…Tiger, that I'm here, and no matter what, I protect what I love. "I want you to erase the past fourteen years of my life. I want for my family to be back together. I want to be fucking normal! That's what I want," I declare, pressing the blade into his skin hard enough to draw blood.

"But seeing as you can't give me any of that, I will just have to settle with slitting your throat."

He extends his arms out, surrendering, begging I show him mercy. "Please don't do this. I will get Jaws to bring the kid here. He is going to kill him. You need me."

I need him like a hole in the head, but the fact he knows about Jordy and what Jaws intends to do to him has me hesitating for a split second, which is my bad.

Scrooge takes the opportunity to bring his elbow back and gets in a lucky shot, connecting with my stomach. He scrambles forward, a trail of blood following him as it spurts from where his finger used to be.

I give him a false sense of freedom. I want him to think that maybe, just maybe, he has a chance to break free. He crawls toward his jacket on the back of a chair and reaches into the pocket. Only when he has his cell in his hand, do I strike.

Stalking forward, I grip him by the collar and yank him up. He thrashes wildly, fighting for his life, but he's been living on borrowed time. I punch him in the face, the brass knuckles splitting open his lip.

I continue punching him until he sags forward, limp, but I hold him up, needing to punish him over and over again. When a gurgling noise spills from him, I toss him into the chair. He is still breathing—only just.

His face is a bloody mess. I can see muscle and bone. The sight doesn't give me the satisfaction I thought it would, and that's because my vengeance won't bring back my brother. It'll just chip away whatever humanity I have left.

But this motherfucker needs to pay for what he did. There is no way I can let him live. But him looking so pathetic, so helpless, has a heavy weight settling on my chest. But I push it aside. This was a long time coming.

"You can't do it," he wheezes, peering at me through one eye. "You're still weak. And so was your brother."

He's trying to talk big, but he knows this will only end one way.

"Even as a kid, my brother was more of a man than you are." Reaching for my blade, I walk over to him. "I want your last breath to be taken with the knowledge that I'm going to take away your family…just as you did mine."

Scrooge attempts to escape, but he's trapped. "Fuck you." He spits on me, showing no remorse for what he did. "You don't have the balls. Jaws will kill you all."

Tossing the blade over and over in the air and catching it, I allow this son of a bitch his final words.

"You have no idea what he has planned. You're all disposable, except his pretty little sister. You want to know the real reason he was so upset over Hero and her? Because he was fucking jealous! He didn't want anyone touching what is his."

A growl erupts from my chest. "She belongs to no one." I see her as mine, but she is a fierce, independent woman who can stand on her own.

"That's what you think." He snickers. "Once he gets what he wants, he will kill that kid. It was inevitable. If you want a job done properly, you've got to do it yourself." He is talking about Kong.

Kong couldn't do what Jaws wanted—kill Jordy—which found him on the outs with Jaws.

"And what do you get in all this?" I ask, sickened.

"Jaws has been my best friend since I was eight years old. You don't turn your back on that kind of friendship. We work as a team."

"Your *teamwork* ruins lives."

"People are going to sniff, snort, and inject with or without us. We may as well profit." And there it is. Black and white. Scrooge and Jaws don't care who they extort, exploit, or destroy. This is all about power and greed.

"But it seems Stevie's profit is interfering with yours," I smartly add. "Isn't that why Jaws hasn't killed me yet? I know they have history. I know Jaws was sloppy and didn't do his research, sending Bianca's dad to prison."

"Is that what Stevie told you?" Scrooge clutches his hand, attempting to stop the bleeding. "You shouldn't always believe what you hear."

Could it be their vendetta stems even deeper?

"Stevie set Jaws up," Scrooge reveals, adding yet another layer to this shit pile. "He said the buyers were good. He knew they were cops, but there was only room for one man in Bianca's life."

This tangled web will never unravel.

"Jaws just wants someone to call his own. First Lily screws him, and then Bianca. She is still stringing him along."

"What does that mean?"

"It means what you think it means. She is fucking them both, loving the attention. She's always been a spoiled little bitch. But Jaws is done. He has scores to settle with nothing left to lose."

His comment has me realizing Jaws is a desperate man, a desperate man who has Tiger's son.

Bianca *was* playing them both. I know Stevie wasn't faithful to her either, but these three people deserve one another. Their gluttony and selfishness really know no bounds.

"You are just a small measly pawn. Don't ever forget that."

Laughing sarcastically, I stop tossing the knife and point the blade toward him. "If I'm so small and measly, then why the fuck does Jaws need me? I would be dead if he didn't. You underestimate my worth."

Inhaling deeply, I smirk a deadly grin. "You also underestimate my need to slit your fucking throat."

Done talking, I advance and fist Scrooge's shirt. He tries to fight, but he's spent. He knows he's lost. "I'll say hello to your brother," he slurs, using his last breath to degrade instead of bargaining for his family's life. That's the type of man I'm ridding this world of.

But where he's going, Damian would never be.

"A special place in hell is reserved for assholes like you," I spit, pressing us nose to nose. "I'll see you there soon. Keep it warm for me. In the meantime"—spinning the knife in my hand, I slash it across Scrooge's throat in one fluid motion—"I'll keep your wife warm. This is for Damian, you motherfucker."

A shower of blood coats my neck and face as I stare him in the eye, watching the life drain from him. A look of utter shock overtakes him as it seems he didn't believe I had the balls to end him.

He thought wrong.

He violently convulses, but I hold him up, savoring every moment of watching this fucker perish. His blood is hot and thick, sticking to every inch of me, but I stand unmoving. His breaths are ragged, thanks to the gash across his throat.

After a few short, stilted intakes of air, he stops, and his life slips away. He died looking into his murderer's eyes. When he sags lifelessly, I tip my face toward the ceiling, closing my eyes in ecstasy.

"Three down, one to go," I utter, exhaling in deliverance. If Damian is looking down on me, he would be shaking his head. But I know he turned his back on me long ago. I'm not the same person I once was.

Scrooge topples to the floor with a thud as I let him go. He bleeds out on the carpet while I step over him to retrieve the packet of cigarettes from the coffee table. Lighting one with bloodied fingers, I inhale deeply, the nicotine dancing with my already animated nerves.

I simply stand motionless, looking down at Scrooge's twisted corpse. His bright red blood stains the once pristine white carpet. I'm mesmerized by the image. This man has haunted me for fourteen years and now, he's fucking dead. Dead because of me. And I feel nothing...

Taking a slow drag of my smoke, I ignore the knocking on the door because I'm not ready. He didn't suffer enough. I should have prolonged it and tortured him a little more. But no matter how long he suffered, it would pale in comparison to what Damian endured.

Tilting my head to the side, I understand how fragile life is. One minute, we're here, and the next...we're a rotting pile of blood and bone.

Continuing to leisurely smoke my cigarette, I hope Scrooge will come back to life like a bad horror movie so I can kill him again and again, but no matter how many times I killed him, it would never be enough.

"B-Bull?"

Tiger's distant voice brings me back to the now. I'm covered in the enemy's blood while smoking a cigarette with a smirk. And I don't have the energy to mask my pleasure at the scene in front of me.

Her cherry blossom fragrance erases the strong metallic scent of blood, and I realize the two combined is my favorite smell in the entire world. Both feed the demons within me.

"I got this," Jesús says with keycard in hand. That's how he got in. They've thought this entire thing through.

But I shake my head slowly. This is my kill. I will see it through.

Flicking the cigarette onto Scrooge's corpse, I turn my chin to look at Tiger. I expect to see horror or disgust, but I don't. When I look into her beautiful green eyes, all I see is love; love for the man she loves, and the monster she fears.

"Go outside and wait for me," I order, but she shakes her head. I should have known she wouldn't listen. She wants to see the real me, the one who is covered in blood, and I like it more than I should.

I slip into my jacket before walking over to the doors. I open them and step out onto the balcony. It's secluded, off to the side of the building and away from prying eyes. Stepping back inside, I bend forward, gripping Scrooge by both ankles and drag him across the carpet, leaving a trail of red.

Once he's out on the balcony, I notice a boat tied to a dock. It seems José has thought of everything. Jesús has Scrooge's jacket in hand.

"Take his head and fingers," he suggests, tilting his head to see I already took one. "It'll buy you some time."

No dental records or fingerprints will make it harder to identify him, but I don't plan on him ever being found.

Without replying, I grip Scrooge's ankles and drag him along the balcony toward the stairs. The hollowed sound his head makes as he hits each step is music to my ears. I'm vaguely aware that Tiger has come out onto the balcony, but I can't look at her.

Once I'm at the bottom, I drag Scrooge into the boat. Jesús follows, gesturing to some bricks and industrial duct tape in the corner. Glancing up, I see Tiger standing on the dock with her arms wrapped around her small frame.

Jesús starts the engine, and I contemplate whether I should tell him to go, leaving Tiger behind. And when she looks me dead in the eyes, it's clear she is giving me the option.

The right thing to do would be to give her some money and tell her to catch a cab home, but that line was blurred long ago.

Rubbing my hand against my shirt to wipe off the blood as best I can, I offer it to her. The choice is now hers. She peers at it, working her bottom lip between her teeth. She knows if she does this, she will be an accessory to murder.

I wish I had something better to offer her.

Stepping forward, she hesitantly places her cold hand in mine. I help her into the boat and away from Scrooge's twisted heap. Jesús pulls out his cell and barks to whoever is on the other end to clean up the room.

There is no way they'll get the stain out of the carpet, but they'll know he is missing soon enough, which is why we need to get moving.

Jesús takes off into the night while Tiger takes a seat, watching me with wide eyes. Without delay, I kneel behind Scrooge and push him into a half sitting position. Tiger covers her mouth when his neck flops back, exposing the damage I inflicted with my knife.

I dress him in his jacket, ensuring to take out his wallet, keys, and cell. Reaching for the bricks and duct tape, I drag them over to me and begin placing the bricks in his pockets. I then hold two to his chest and wrap the tape around him, securing them to his body.

When they're fastened, I add two more and then another two. I do the same to his arms and legs until he is weighed down. With a brick in hand, I contemplate smashing out some teeth, but Tiger's tiny whimpers stop me.

Jesús drives for miles, and the farther we go, the more isolated things become. He clearly knows where he is going, so I simply stare into the starless sky, numb to everything.

"I remember him," Tiger says softly, the wind almost drowning out her voice. "He looks different now, though."

"That's because he's dead," I reply emotionless.

Tiger stands and walks over to me. I suddenly don't want her anywhere near me. I am foul—both inside and out—but she doesn't accept my retreat and grips my wrist. "Don't do that."

"Do what?" I question, eyeing her something wicked.

"Don't detach yourself." With a hesitant touch, she tries to touch my face, but I shift away.

"Don't touch me. I'm filthy."

"I don't care," she presses, placing her hands on my sticky cheeks. "None of that matters to me."

I should argue with her, but I don't, and that's because I don't want to. She accepts me for what I am, and for that, I am the luckiest son of a bitch alive.

Jesús stops the boat, killing the engine. We are in the middle of nowhere.

Removing Tiger's hand from my cheek, I draw her fingers to my lips and kiss them. A weak smile is my response.

What I'm about to do will not be pretty, but Tiger won't

cower in fear. Jesús grabs Scrooge's arms while I take hold of his legs. He weighs triple his weight, so there is no way he'll resurface. We commence a slow stagger toward the edge of the boat, his weighted ass leaving us breathless.

We nod, and with a swing, we toss him overboard. He splashes and then drops to a watery grave. I stand by the edge, watching him sink until I can no longer see his body. Even when he is out of sight, I stand unmoving, transfixed by his grave.

He doesn't have a resting place. A headstone to mark who he was. No one will know where he is. He is lost to the murky depths where the motherfucker belongs. Tiger stands by me, giving me space. She too seems mesmerized by what I just did.

"I'll take you back to the motel," Jesús says, restarting the boat.

Shaking my head, I reply, "No, I need to go back to the van. I need that asshole Baz to take me to Jaws."

Tiger shifts beside me, and I realize she has no idea what's going on.

"Get cleaned up first. At least attempt a few hours' sleep," Jesús suggests.

I snicker in response.

"Baz has to check in tomorrow. You've got a few hours to regroup. You need it. I'll take care of Baz."

"I don't have time to regroup," I bark, running a hand through my snarled hair.

"Bull," Tiger reasons. "If we've got a few hours, let's go back to the motel. You can shower and fill me in. You need to sleep."

"What I need is for your brother to be dead already," I counter, cracking my neck. I didn't mean to snap, but sleep is the last thing on my mind.

"I understand, but you're exhausted," she argues. "You won't be any good asleep on your feet. Jordy needs us to be as alert as possible."

Sighing, I hate that she's right. In the state that I'm in, I'm no competition for Jaws. I'm beyond tired.

"And I don't want to be alone tonight," she adds, slipping her fingers through mine. It doesn't bother her that I'm covered in blood. I suppose she's used to it by now.

With my eyes still locked on the water, I eventually nod. A few hours can't do any harm.

CHAPTER THIRTEEN

Lily

I sit at the foot of Bull's bed, biting my nails, waiting for him to finish in the shower. I was surprised he agreed to come back here, but he also knew that with the state he's in, Jaws would make him pay for not being on his A game.

The heaviness in my chest seems to grow with each breath I take. *It's nearly over*, I reason. Bull filled me in on the way back here. Tomorrow, we move one step closer to bringing Jordy back. Baz, the man who works for my brother, is in lockdown with Jesús.

I appreciate their assistance, but I can't help but think this doesn't come with no strings.

We all want something from one another, even me, and when Bull emerges from the shower in nothing but a towel tied low around his tapered waist, I do a poor job at masking those needs.

His wet hair is slicked back as though he's run his fingers through it to sweep it off this face. Droplets of water cling to his inked skin. I envy each one. He sits down beside me, and all I smell is soap and juniper—his unique scent.

I am a bundle of nerves and can't keep my leg from bouncing on the spot. Eventually, Bull places his hand over my knee to stop me.

"It'll be okay. Jaws is none the wiser. He thinks everything is going according to plan." But Bull has misunderstood my nerves. I had to make a choice...and now, I have to live with those consequences.

I simply nod, afraid if I speak, he'll uncover what I've done.

"Do you want me to sleep in another room?" he asks, which has me arching a brow.

"No," I quickly reply, shaking my head. "I don't want that. Why would you ask that?"

He raises his broad shoulders in a sluggish shrug. "Tonight was a lot. I thought you might need space?" he offers, unsure.

But that's the last thing I need.

"I don't want space," I say, slowly straddling his lap. We have come so far. When we first met, he couldn't stand me touching him. And in the morning, sadly, he'll feel the same way once again.

But I'll deal with that tomorrow.

"How'd you know where I was tonight?"

Toying with the hair curling at his nape, I confess, "I didn't know. I just…I needed to go. I know it doesn't make sense, but if you were willing to sacrifice yourself for me, then I wanted to do the same for you. I didn't know what that meant, but I just knew I had to go in case an opportunity arose. Stupid, right?"

And that is the truth.

I didn't know what I was walking into, but when I saw Bull, a wave of relief as well as fear washed over me. Him being at the gala meant something didn't go as planned. But I should have known Bull would never break his promise.

He still has every intention to sacrifice himself for Jordy. Yes, he got his revenge on Scrooge, but that doesn't save him from my brother.

"No, it's not stupid," he says, lifting my chin to look into his eyes. "It's brave. Thank you."

He shouldn't be so quick to thank me when he doesn't know what I intend to do.

"No one has done that for me before," he confesses, and I know how hard it is for him to open up.

The thought twists my stomach, and for a fleeting moment, I just want to forget. I just want to feel.

"I want to forget all of it. Help me forget," I beg, pulling down the straps of my dress and exposing my strapless bra.

Bull hisses, arching backward, but he isn't going anywhere. Lowering my mouth to his, I kiss him softly, savoring the feel, the taste of him because it's become my addiction. His hesitancy soon disappears, and he kisses me back.

But little does he know what this kiss is—it's the kiss of Judas because that's who I am.

With tears heavy in my eyes, I thread my fingers through his long hair, needing to anchor myself to him and never let him go. The towel stirs beneath me, hinting Bull wants me as much as I do him. He slides my dress down so it pools at my waist, and with skillful fingers, he unhooks my bra.

When it falls away, he cups my left breast, kneading it and rolling my pearled nipple with his thumb. Our kisses grow frenzied, both needing to forget. I bite Bull's lip hard. A low rumble spills from him.

"Want it rough, baby?" he says from around my mouth.

Rocking against his hard-on, I whimper and nod.

He lifts me from his lap and throws me onto the bed. I like the savagery and the chase as I scamper toward the headboard, but he grips my ankles and drags me back down. The towel has slipped free, exposing his impressive erection, and my core clenches at the sight.

Bull sits on his ankles at the foot of the bed, watching me closely. I don't know what he is thinking, and the fear excites me. Leaning over my body, he opens the bedside dresser and produces a pair of handcuffs. Not the kinky, pink fluffy kind. These are the real deal. We've apparently upgraded from cable ties.

"Still want to play?" he asks, dangling the cuffs from one finger.

In response, I shimmy out of my dress and toss it onto the carpet. I'm lying on my back in a thong and heels. Bull smirks, an animalistic gesture as he scans down my body with famished eyes.

A startled gasp leaves me when he flips me onto my

stomach and places my arms above my head. The cuffs lock around each wrist with a click as Bull secures them to the headboard. There is barely any slack as I tug at them.

I try to look over my shoulder, but my angle doesn't allow me to turn too far. But I don't need sight. All I need to do is feel.

Bull sluggishly removes my thong without a word. My racing heart is amplified in the silence. I wait for him to do something, but the anticipation is always half the fun.

The mattress dips beside me, allowing me to gauge where Bull is. With two fingers, he unhurriedly caresses them down my spine. "Did you mean it?" he asks hoarsely.

"Mean what?" My skin breaks out into goose bumps. His touch always feels so good.

"When we were in here last…you said—"

His sudden pause alerts me to what he is referring to.

The last time I was tied to his bed, I was going to tell him I loved him because I do. Goddamn, how I do. But he stopped me. He didn't want me to say it in light of our situation at the time. He wanted to make sure I meant it and wasn't only saying it because I feared I would never see him again.

Inhaling and exhaling slowly, I bite my lip, afraid. Where is the big, brave girl now?

Maybe the fear of losing him was the reason I didn't clam up, just as I am now. I have no doubt of my feelings for Bull, but saying them aloud, to him…my heart almost bursts from my chest. What if he tells me he doesn't feel the same way?

"It doesn't matter," he says, breaking the silence.

But it does.

When his fingers come to a stop at the top of my ass, he cups my right cheek in his large hand.

"Bull—" I'm about to tell him that I meant it. I still mean it, but all words tumble in a winded oof when he spanks me.

My body shifts up the bed from the force because he hit me hard. Not that I expected anything less. The blanket beneath me chafes my nipples, and I whimper in pleasure and pain.

"I—" Again, he doesn't allow me to speak when he slaps the other cheek. Harder this time. The sting is felt all the way in my ripe center. I open my legs, needing some kind of relief, but Bull only spanks me harder.

My flesh burns with an invisible handprint I can still feel. "Oh, god," I whimper, shuddering when Bull delivers another smack to my raw ass.

"Enough?" he asks, anger lacing his tone. I wonder why he's mad, but then I realize I didn't answer his question. He must believe my feelings for him were never real.

"No, I will never have enough," I reply. Raising my hips, I dare him to do his best. The comment is a double-edged sword, directed at our situation as well.

I brace for impact, but what I get is something different. My bad for daring him and thinking I could win.

Bull slides two fingers down the pleat of my ass. I try to dodge his advances, but he grips my hip, holding me still. "Has anyone touched you here?"

My cheeks instantly redden.

"I asked you a question," he says, coming to a stop at my puckered entrance.

This is going to be a lot easier if I submit—in every sense of the word. "No," I reply softly.

He hums low.

"That pleases me more than it should," he confesses. I instantly squeeze my muscles when he presses against my tightness.

It doesn't deter Bull, though.

He reaches over my shoulder and places two of his fingers inside my mouth, coaxing me to suck. And I do. I tongue over his fingers, loving the way he tastes and feels. I love everything there is about him. So why can't I tell him that?

Once his fingers are lubricated enough, he removes them from my mouth and places them against my back entrance. "Do you want to see what a depraved animal I really am?"

Instead of cowering and begging him to stop, I nod shakily.

I await a sharp intrusion, but I don't get one. I get amazement instead. "You're fearless, Tiger."

"Hardly," I counter softly.

But Bull perseveres. "You are. You don't back down. Ever. From the first time I met you, I knew you could hold your own. But I never expected you to be…this."

His pause leaves me breathless. "This what?"

He gently removes his fingers before running his hand over my ass cheek. He slaps it again, giving me the pain I need. "This fucking perfect," he confesses, startling me.

"I'm far from perfect," I admit, whimpering at the sting radiating throughout my body.

"Well…you are to me." Before I have a chance to reply, he

places his hands on my hips, encouraging me onto all fours. Even with my hands bound, I'm able to position myself how he wants me.

He comes up behind me, spreads my thighs, and lowers his mouth to my sex.

I tug at the cuffs, shuddering in absolute pleasure. He eats me out slowly, licking, sucking, biting. I rock backward, needing more, wanting more. And more I get.

Bull circles his tongue deep within me, sucking over my clit with just the right pressure. The coarseness of his stubble adds to the heightened sensation, and when he sweeps his tongue upward, circling over my back entrance, I'm certain I will come right then and there.

At first, this feels so taboo, but that soon fades and gives way to this unadulterated pleasure. I didn't know this could feel so good, but when he moves his mouth up and down, and side to side, feasting on my flesh, I am hungry for it all.

He is everywhere, savoring the moment while I cry out in need.

"Like it?" he asks, his hot breath setting me ablaze.

"Yes," I confess, bowing my back and opening myself up further to him.

As he sucks my clit, he sluggishly works the tip of his thumb into my ass. My eyes bulge at the intrusion, but Bull doesn't force his way in. He slowly circles his thumb while paying attention to my needy sex.

"So fucking tight," he says with sensuality. I almost come from his words combined with what he's doing to my body.

He works his thumb in a little deeper, and I feel so full,

so content with having him own and possess me this way. I can't stand it. I need to come. I buck onto his face, desperate for a release, but Bull holds me still, torturing me in the best possible way.

He destroys my body with his mouth, his touch, and I happily surrender. The familiar feeling coils its way upward, and just as I'm about to come, Bull pulls away.

Grunting in frustration, I sag forward, my body crying out in rebellion. Before I can ask what he's doing, he gets off the bed, only to come to rest at my side. "Give me your mouth, baby," he commands, turning my chin toward him.

I do as he asks, and when he slips his cock into my mouth, another hunger hits me. I forget about my pleasure and focus on his because this is fucking hot. He did warn me, and I did ask to see his depravity. So I take him deep and return the favor he just bestowed on me.

With my hands cuffed, I can't move, so I angle my head as best as I can. He gently thrusts his hips forward, hitting the back of my throat. I refuse to gag and take him deeper.

"Holy fuck," he grunts, brushing the hair from my cheeks and fisting it in one hand. He uses my hair as reins, controlling the speed and depth of his strokes, but he never forces me.

Hollowing my cheeks, I suck him hard, loving the way he shudders in my mouth. Being this way with Bull is inexplicable because this is about trust, about mutual gratification, and when I think about when we first met, I realize how far we've truly come.

Bull's generous size makes it impossible for me to take all of him, but tears leak from my eyes as I angle my head to take as much as I can.

"Tiger," he hisses, drawing his hips back, but I only suck him harder.

When I use a little teeth, Bull almost rockets off the bed. "Again," he hoarsely orders.

I do as he asks, incorporating my teeth with my mouth and tongue. Being cuffed while going down on the man I love is kinky and oh, so hot. My needy sex clenches as his pleasure almost makes me come.

His body clenches, and I know he's close. Just as I'm about to take him deeper, he gently grips my chin, coaxing me to let him go. Meeting his eyes, I silently ask why he made me stop. His response has me rubbing my thighs together.

"When I come…it's not going to be in your mouth."

I expect him to take me from behind, but when he reaches into the bedside dresser for the key to the cuffs, I gasp. He unlocks them and trails kisses down my neck and upper back as I sag forward in relief.

"On your back," he commands, shocking me further.

Missionary may sound boring to most, but not to me. This is so intimate, so perfect.

Doing as he asked, I look up at him, suddenly nervous. He lowers his body to mine, then reaches for my arms and places them above my head. With my heart in my throat, I get lost in those mismatched eyes, wanting to remain lost forever.

But I can't. Forever came with a price, one I will pay come morning.

Bull takes my mouth, kissing me with no apology as he sinks inside me. Flesh on flesh is what I need, and I open my legs wider, wanting more. He begins moving gradually, threading his fingers through mine.

Our kisses never end, only intensify as he buries himself deeper. Arching my back, I take him all, but it's still not enough. I will never have my fill of Bull because no matter how much he gives, I'll want more.

Our bodies move in unison because being entwined this way feels like the missing piece has returned. I didn't even realize it was missing until I met Bull. But those moments before I met him feel half-lived. From the moment we met, the world has felt brighter, and flavors have tasted sweeter.

My heart begins to hammer, and it has nothing to do with Bull owning my body like only he knows how. He possesses me, both body and soul, and my fear, the insecurities begin to ebb away. I want him to know that he is loved because I don't think anyone has told him his worth.

I want him to know he means everything to me. He needs to know before it's too late, and that love will turn to hate.

Our lovemaking is unhurried for once, our slick bodies taking and giving in the same breath. He pulls back from our kisses, biting over my chin.

He moves inside me fervently, the low growls slipping past his lips stoking my fire. Hooking my leg around his waist, I open myself up to him, deepening the pleasure for us both. He begins to pick up the pace, sinking in and pulling out, allowing me to feel every hot inch of him.

I will never tire of him, of this feeling of having an unconditional connection to another human. I once said I understood why Bull did what he did to his brother's killers, but I really didn't—until now. If anyone hurt him, did to him what was done to Damian, I too would be hell-bent on revenge.

"Am I hurting you?"

I don't understand why Bull is asking me this until his finger comes away wet with my tears. He slips it into his mouth, savoring my salty sadness.

"No," I reply, shaking my head.

"Then why are you crying?" he asks, continuing to thrust into me.

"Because"—I arch my head backward as he hits me so deep, I gasp—"I...I meant it."

Bull reaches between us and circles over my clit. "Meant what, Tiger? I want to hear it."

He wants to hear me say it, and that's okay because I want to.

His strokes become frenzied, and our lovemaking turns into something more profound, something that seals our fate forever.

"I...I love you," I pant, squeezing my eyes shut as he deliciously brutalizes my body, my mind, my soul. "I am so lost to this feeling, and I never want it to end. I love you... Cody Bishop. No matter what name you go by, I love the man behind each one."

Bull continues to own me, not saying a word, and that's okay. I don't need him to say it back. I lose myself to the rhythm and the liberty of finally being free. When Bull leans down and suckles over my throat, fucking me with intensity and passion, my body seizes, and I give in.

I come so hard; not solely because of what he's doing to my body, but also because beneath his passion, I can feel it... He loves me too.

My orgasm is so fierce, tears spring to the surface. But I don't fight it. This is fucking beautiful.

Bull thrusts once, twice, before pulling back, but I don't let him. Locking my legs around his waist, I grip his cheeks and yank his face down to me. I kiss him fiercely, wanting him to finish inside me.

"Tiger—" He tries to fight me, but I won't let him.

"I want you...all of you."

He groans, and with three quick thrusts of the hips, he growls long and hard, spilling his seed inside me. His body vibrates, and for the first time in his entire life, I think he lets his guard down and just feels.

We're just Lily and Cody—two lost souls who found something beautiful in utter destruction.

With one last shudder, he collapses on top of me, breathing heavily. We're both covered in sweat, our hearts beating in concert with each other. I wrap my arms around his back, pressing us closer, but it'll never be close enough.

He plants lazy kisses down my neck, inhaling my scent with a low hum.

The silence isn't uncomfortable, and I don't regret a single thing.

"Tiger—" he sleepily says, turning onto his side and taking me with him so we're pressed nose to nose. "I don't understand what this is." He takes my hand and places it on his chest over his racing heart. "But I don't want it to stop."

"I don't either," I whisper, running my fingernails over his inked flesh.

His eyes slip shut, and it isn't long until his steady breathing indicates he's asleep.

I watch him sleep for minutes, hours, I don't know. It's cathartic because I've never seen him at peace before. But knowing that peace will soon be shattered kills me. Holding back my tears, I whisper, "Forgive me for what I'm about to do."

Bull has been the…*hero* in this story. And when it comes down to the wire, he'll sacrifice himself for my happiness. It's time I saved him, regardless of the fact he will hate me for it.

But I know he will never forgive me because he's finally given me his heart…only for me to rip it out.

Bull

I wake to utter silence, which hasn't happened in a very long time. I also slept without waking. Again, another first. When I open my eyes, the daylight peeking in through the curtains hints that I slept through the night.

The reason for the quietness sleeps beside me. But when I reach out, I realize I'm alone.

Jolting upright, I rub the sleep from my eyes and search the room. The bathroom door is open so I can see Tiger is definitely not in there. Throwing back the covers, I slip into my boxers and jeans. I don't bother with a shirt or shoes because I'm suddenly overcome with a sense of foreboding.

There is no note, which is not like Tiger. That means something is wrong.

It's fucking freezing out, and I skid along the snow that has collected along the walkway as I sprint to the office. I almost rip the door from its hinges as I open it. What I see turns my blood cold.

"Venus." I run over to her because she's tied to a chair and can't move.

Her chin touches her chest, and blood coats her white shirt, thanks to the note stapled to her chest. Her moans indicate she's alive, but when I gently lift her face, I see she's lucky to still be breathing.

Her head lolls to the side as I remove the gag from around her mouth. "Who did this to you?" I cry, angered someone would inflict this sort of harm on someone who wouldn't hurt a soul.

When she hears my voice, she seems to focus, and her eyes fill with tears. "Bull," she croaks. "She went, went with a man."

She doesn't need to elaborate who. I fucking know.

Looking at the note on her chest, I see an address written in what I'm presuming is Venus's blood. This is Jaws's calling card. He knows what I did, and now, he has Tiger.

"I'll call the cops," I say, but she shakes her head.

"No cops. Police means questions, and I can't do that to you."

I'm beyond moved she's thinking about me when she is the one battered and bleeding. "There is a number behind my desk. Call it."

I sprint behind the counter and call the number written on the pink piece of paper taped to her computer. A man answers, and I quickly give him the rundown. He doesn't ask questions and hangs up after he tells me he'll be here in fifteen.

As gently as I can, I untie Venus, helping her toward the sofa. She collapses onto it with a wheeze. This is my fault. All of it is.

"Go," she orders, clutching her side and gesturing with her head toward the door.

I don't want to leave her, but the thought of Tiger being alone with Jaws has me pecking her on the cheek. "Thank you, Venus. For everything." And I mean it.

She gave me a chance when not many people would have, and honestly, she didn't have to. I'll never forget it.

"I promise, he'll pay for what he's done."

She nods with a weak smile. "Go get 'em, Tiger." Little does she know I intend to do just that.

Running out of the office, I race to my room and throw on a shirt and my boots. I look at my holster, but I can't go armed. It doesn't matter anyway. The rules are simple—trade me for Tiger. Jaws doesn't want to hurt her. He would have killed Jordy already if he did.

This is about being alpha. This is about revenge.

Snatching the truck keys from the dresser, I race out the door and punch the address into my phone's GPS. It's a building about two hours from here. I intend to get there in forty-five minutes. The truck roars to life, and I tear out the parking lot, hell-bent on getting back what's mine.

Thinking back to last night, to what Tiger confessed and how it made me feel…if anything happens to her, I will never forgive myself. Rubbing over my chest, I can't breathe as my heart constricts. Opening the window, the fresh air helps, but my body is a live wire, and I can't stop this…panic that's robbing me of air.

"Please be all right," I say aloud, clenching the wheel and stepping on the gas.

I should have told her how I feel because even though I've never been in love, I've never experienced this sickening feeling in the pit of my stomach either. I can barely breathe when I'm with her. And when we're apart…I would give anything to be close to her.

I want to protect her. I want my fucking happily ever after because if someone like Tiger can love me, then maybe, just maybe, I'm not all bad.

But none of that matters if I don't get to her.

I break every traffic law there is and get to the address in record time. It's some derelict two-story brick building in a seedy neighborhood where no one would look twice if there was a shootout. But that won't happen because I don't have my guns.

Parking the truck, I kill the engine and don't make my arrival a secret as I walk around the back. The door is open, so I enter, not bothering to scope out my surroundings. He knows I'm here. I've just stepped into the lion's den.

It smells like piss and garbage, and I am furious he's brought Tiger here. "Motherfucker, if you're planning on making a grand entrance, hurry the fuck up. It's cold."

I hide behind my wit, terrified I'm too late. But when someone shuffles out from a room in front of me, I see that I'm not. Jaws has Tiger by the arm. She struggles against his grip, but he doesn't let her go. When she sees me, her eyes fill with sadness, and I don't understand why.

I don't make a move, however. This is Jaws's show.

"Nice of you to come," he quips, smirking wide.

"Like I had a choice," I snap, looking at Tiger. "Are you okay?"

She nods quickly.

"Of course, she's okay. I wouldn't hurt my darling sister, would I, Lillian?"

I wait for her to tell him to go to hell, but she doesn't. She lowers her chin, hiding behind her long hair. Something is horribly wrong.

"I never thought when our paths crossed fourteen years ago that you would be such a pain in my ass. But I'll give it to you, kid, you got game. In a different lifetime, I think we would have made a great team."

"I doubt that," I counter, unable to keep my eyes off Tiger. But she continues to evade me.

"I don't. We both want the same thing. Yes, our motives are different, but we're both driven men, intent on revenge."

"Get over it already," I bark. "She doesn't love you. Move on. You're beating a dead horse."

"This has to do with Stevie, the double-crossing asshole!" he shouts, gripping Tiger tighter. I need to watch my tongue. Otherwise, she will pay for my insolence.

"I know what happened. Scrooge told me... right after I took this from his finger." Holding up my finger, I show him the championship ring.

He doesn't seem surprised. He knows the fate of his friend.

"Three down, one to go," he jokes, and why shouldn't he be in good spirits. He knows as long as he has Tiger, he's in charge.

"That's right, asshole. You killed Damian. It was only a matter of time. So, let her go, and we can end this."

Jaws frowns, appearing in thought. When a whimper escapes Tiger, I wonder what the hell is going on. "Let her go?" he questions, eyebrow arched. "I'm not holding her against her will. Am I?"

I wait for my fierce Tiger to emerge, but what I get is my stupidity thrown into my face.

"No," she whispers so softly, I hope I've misheard her. But when Jaws cups his ear, indicating she's to speak up, there's no mistake. "No, I'm here because I…because I called you."

My heart constricts so tightly, a wheeze tumbles from me. She has stolen my breath. She has crushed my fucking heart.

Finally lifting her chin, I realize the reason she couldn't look at me was because she felt guilty. "I'm sorry, Bull," she cries, shaking her head. But I don't want her apologies. "I had to choose. Jordy or you. I'm s-so sorry, but I couldn't let this go on any f-further. He's just a boy. I couldn't take any more risks."

And there it is. The truth.

She couldn't wait for me to see the plan through. I know it wasn't foolproof, but we could have at least tried.

"That's right. She called me, Bull," Jaws says, rubbing salt into my already raw wounds. "She's the one who lured you here, not me. She set you up, and like a chump, you fell for it."

"What?" I gasp, never taking my eyes off a crying Tiger.

But her tears mean nothing to me.

"Tell him," Jaws encourages as he knows it'll hurt all the more coming from her.

"He never kidnapped me," she confesses. "I went willingly, knowing you'd…" She licks the tears from her lips. "You'd think he took me against my will. I knew if you thought that, you would come unarmed."

I stand, speechless, not knowing what to say or think because she's right.

When I saw Venus and the address, I automatically thought Tiger was taken hostage, but I'm the one who's held hostage—hostage to my epic fuckup.

Jaws grins, watching happily as my heart gets ripped in two.

Her lower lip trembles. "I'm so sorry."

"You already said that," I reply, hardhearted. She told me she loved me, promising she meant it, but she didn't mean it. She said it out of guilt because if she really loved me…she would have never, *never* done this.

"I gave you what you want!" she cries at Jaws, ripping from his grip. "Give me back my son." But she is naïve if she thought it would ever be this simple.

"All in good time." He clucks his tongue while she pales. "You've seen that he's perfectly fine. I FaceTimed you the proof."

"What do you want?" she asks, attempting to sound brave.

Jaws taps his chin, faking thought. "I want you to prove your loyalty."

"How?" Her color turns to a sickly green.

"This asshole killed my friends. He also killed your beloved."

She squeezes her eyes shut for a second, shaking her head.

"Now it's time he paid for the lives he took. Scrooge was a good man."

I scoff, folding my arms across my chest. "And now he's a dead man."

Jaws inhales, appearing to center himself. "Thanks to you. An eye for an eye," he mocks before dropping his attention to my finger. "Or I'll settle for a finger."

Tiger gasps, covering her mouth.

Jaws reaches into his pocket and produces a knife. He gives it to Tiger, but she recoils. "Bring me his finger, and I'll tell you where to find Jordy."

"No!" she cries, horrified. "That was never a part of the deal."

"The rules have changed. Now do it." When she hesitates, he reaches into his pocket, retrieving his cell. He isn't bluffing this time, and we both know it.

"Tiger, do it," I order when she meets my eyes, shaking her head quickly.

"No, I can't."

"Yes, you can."

She clenches her jaw, appearing to hold back more tears.

"If you don't, all of this would have been for nothing. You made a choice. Now see it through."

"It's not like that," she argues, but I am done listening. It is exactly like that because she is the reason we're here, and I'll be damned if she doesn't get what she came for.

She hurt me because she had to, and now it's my turn to do the same. "You let him do that to Venus. How could you?"

"I didn't—"

But I cut her off. "All I'm hearing are fucking excuses! Grow a backbone and see your decisions through. You knew what would happen by calling him. So own them."

"I can't hurt you," she confesses with nothing but sadness.

"You already have," I reply, dead inside. "So you can take my finger, you can take my life, but it won't matter because you've broken my fucking heart."

She licks her lips, eyes wide. "Bull, no, it's not—"

But I am done. "Jaws, call your guy then because it seems your sister doesn't have the balls." My words are dripping in venom because I mean them.

The small part of me that felt something is now dead and gone. It will never be resuscitated. I thought I knew what loss was…but this is something else.

Tiger narrows her eyes, angered I would insult her this way. But she started this, so it's time I finished it.

She snatches the knife from Jaws and stalks over to me. I recognize the fire behind her eyes. It's one of the many things I love, *loved* about her.

She stops feet away. "If only you'd listen—"

"I'm done listening," I state. I never thought she'd be the enemy. I never anticipated her to be my grim reaper, but I suppose it's poetic justice. I took from her, and now, it's her turn to take from me.

"Bull—"

"Enough talking!" Jaws snaps, as Tiger closes her eyes and

exhales as if asking for divine intervention to save her. But no one is coming. We're lambs at the slaughter.

Making it simple, I offer her my hand, watching the way the knife trembles in her fingers. She hesitates, biting her lip so hard, I'm certain she'll draw blood. I don't understand why she's so apprehensive.

"This is what we came here for, right?" I question, seizing her wrist and forcing her to place the blade against my finger.

"No!" she screams, tears flowing quickly as she jerks away. Her behavior confuses me. She was happy to feed me to the wolves, but now she can't see it through? She knew what would happen by doing this.

"Okay, enough," Jaws says, disappointed. "Lillian, I suppose you need to learn how to walk before you run."

She breaks free from my hold, dropping the knife and kicking it away. As she goes to turn, Jaws clucks his tongue. "We're not done. You hurt him…or I hurt Jordy. And I will hurt him really bad."

She can't get in air fast enough and begins to tremble all over. "Forgive me," she finally whispers, locking eyes with me. She then slaps my cheek with all her might.

Moving my jaw from side to side, I'm proud of her efforts. But it's not enough.

Jaws comes up behind her, placing a baton in her hand. She peers down at it, expressionless.

"I want to see him bleed, and bleed by your hand. I could do it." He looks at me over her shoulder. "But it'll hurt a lot more coming from you."

And he's right.

She can inflict all the pain she wants on my body. It'll pale in comparison to what she's already done to my heart.

When she hesitates, Jaws grips her hair and angles her head to the side. She whimpers, and the sight, regardless of what she's done, fucking kills me. I know what I have to do.

"Last night, when I said I didn't know what I felt… Well, now I do," I spit. "You're not the person I thought you were. You're a great lay, but there's always been something… missing."

She sniffs, eyes wide. "You're lying."

"No, I'm really not. I didn't tell you I loved you back because I don't. And I realize that now."

Jaws smirks, letting her go.

This is what he wanted. For us to hurt one another. And I will do that if it means I save her from any more pain.

"You're a fucking snitch."

"So are you," she counters, her pain turning to anger.

Good.

"True that. But at least I follow through. You're nothing but a coward. What did you think would happen by coming here? We'd talk it through. I would respect you more if you—"

I don't get to finish my sentence however because I'm suddenly winded when Tiger drives the butt of the baton into my stomach. I snicker, folded in half as I glare up at her.

"Is that the best you can do? Your son is relying on you."

She snarls and hits my torso. Good for her.

Even though I flinch, I know she's holding back. Maybe she needs some encouragement.

"C'mon, I know you like pain. You had no issues with me

using you any way I wanted. And use you I have."

"Fuck you," she spits, slamming the baton into my stomach again. The hit is hard, and I wheeze, gripping my side. She hits me again, this time connecting with my hand.

When it crunches under the impact, she pales as her adrenaline fades. "Oh, my g-god. I didn't m-mean to."

Jaws hollers in the background, enjoying the show.

"I'm sorry," she whispers, sickened. She looks as though she's about to be sick.

But it's too late for that.

"I am too…for ever seeing something in you that clearly isn't there."

"Bull, no," she says, shaking her head as fat tears cascade down her cheeks. Her eyes plead with me to stop this cruelty.

"End it. Now," I order, slowly dropping to my knees in front of her. "I surrender." Little does she know, I've always been her prisoner.

Peering up at her as I cradle my broken hand, I wish she'd just knock me out so I don't have to deal with this suffocating feeling that's wrapping its hands around my throat. Unconscious, I don't have to see her. I don't have to accept all that I've lost.

"Do it!" I scream, daring her to end it because I can't. I don't have the guts to.

"Jordy is waiting for you," Jaws says from behind her, reminding her of what's at stake.

She inhales and exhales as if psyching herself up. She raises the baton, nodding. "It'll be over soon. I promise. I know you tried," she whispers.

"I didn't try hard enough," I reply quickly. Lowering my chin, I accept whatever fate is delivered. The room is filled with an electrical pulse threatening to electrocute us all.

"Drop it."

I don't understand what I'm hearing because it makes no sense. But none of this does.

Lifting my chin, I see Stevie a few feet away, with his gun trained on Jaws. What is he doing here?

Tiger pales but quickly drops the baton to the ground.

Jaws has his hands raised in mock surrender because judging by his shit-eating grin, Stevie being here hasn't come as a surprise.

"I'm here, you asshole. What do you want?" Stevie asks, confirming my suspicions.

"I thought it was time we caught up," he replies smugly.

"I have absolutely nothing to say to you."

"I think you'll change your mind." Jaws's attention drifts to me, and I realize I am so fucking screwed.

Stevie follows his line of sight, looking past Tiger to see me on my knees. At first, he appears not to believe his eyes, but that soon changes. "Tommy?"

Jaws opens his mouth in surprise before he bursts into jovial laughter. "It seems you go by a lot of aliases, kid."

"What's going on?" Stevie snarls, not appreciating being caught by surprise.

Tiger moves beside me, appearing to want to shield me from the shitstorm brewing. I don't bother rising and stay on my knees.

"Let me fill you in," Jaws says with a smile. "You have a

wolf among the chickens…and that wolf is Bull, or as you know him, Tommy."

"What?" Stevie says, looking at me for an explanation. But I got nothing.

"Bull has been working for me this entire time, haven't you?"

Stevie pales while I wonder how the fuck I'm going to get out of this alive.

I don't bother replying. My silence says it all.

"He has killed a lot of men. Some were my friends. One of them was Kong," Jaws reveals calmly. "It was no accident he fell into your lap. He stalked Kong, killed him, and then was sent by me to infiltrate your little operation."

Stevie shakes his head, utterly stunned. "Is this true?"

The jig is up. "Yes."

"What does he have over you?" he asks me, knowing I wouldn't do this unless there was a reason.

"Me," Tiger whispers, unveiling just who she is. "I'm Christopher's sister. Bull did all of this to save me and my son."

Stevie focuses on Tiger, realizing he broke bread with the enemy.

"Yet, here he is, on his knees at the mercy of others," Stevie snaps, unmoved by her admission.

"How do you know him?"

With hands raised, I come to a slow stand. "You're not the only one who has a score to settle with him. Fourteen years ago, he killed my brother. He and his three friends killed my seventeen-year-old brother in cold blood. Kong was one of those men.

"This has always been about retribution. You were just a means to an end," I explain bluntly.

"You killed his brother?" Stevie asks Jaws.

Jaws smiles. "Yes, I killed him, and I've killed a lot more brothers, sisters, mothers, and fathers since then."

Stevie appears wounded by the truth. But I know he is merely angered he allowed me to play him a fool. "You played me?"

Without remorse, I nod. "Yes. We've all played one another, wanting something in return."

Jaws inhales in victory. "I know everything about your dealings. And I intend on taking it all from you when I end your fucking life, you traitorous son of a bitch." Jaws reaches into his pocket and draws out a gun.

Instantly, I push Tiger aside, needing to get her to safety. But it seems the surprises don't stop here.

"Enough!" Bianca says, appearing from behind Stevie.

He spins, panicked. "I told you to wait in the car!"

But someone like Bianca doesn't take orders. "I won't allow you to do this. Christopher, please," she says, turning her soft eyes his way. "Stop this. If you ever cared about me, you'll stop this right now."

Jaws clucks his tongue. "*Cared* about you? You know how much I *care* about you when I was fucking you last week."

Things suddenly get more awkward than they already are. "What the fuck?" Stevie almost gags.

Jaws smirks, victoriously. "It seems we're still her little *perritos*, but at least she didn't neuter me."

"Bianca, is this true?" Stevie asks, paling. I don't know

why he's acting like she committed the ultimate sin. It's not like he's been monogamous.

"Stevie," she coos, attempting to console him. But he steps back, lip curled.

Jaws's plan of destroying every aspect of Stevie's life is coming to fruition. Just how far is he prepared to go?

"You know I've always loved you both," she explains as though he should just accept this bombshell and move on.

"Yes, loved as in past tense. I wasn't aware that love was still current," he spits, shaking his head.

"Darling." Her voice turns seductive, and I can see why she's been able to keep them at war for so long. She is the common denominator they share. They're prisoners to the past. "I love you. But I love him, too."

"Love him?" Stevie scoffs. "He's an animal! Have you forgotten what he did to your father?"

Bianca flinches while Jaws grins.

"She knows the real story. Give it up."

When Bianca doesn't argue, Stevie looks at her as though she's a stranger. "Whatever he told you, it's all lies."

But she shakes her head. "If what he says *is* true, then it's just confirmation that I made the right choice. You proved your love."

At the expense of her father. These people are even more fucked up than I thought.

"If that's true, then how can you be sleeping with *him*?" Stevie spits, disgusted. "If you wanted us both, I'd respect you more if you just told me."

Jaws looks back and forth between the lovers, enjoying

their quarrel.

"I may have forgiven him for what he did, but my family hasn't. I'd be disowned if they knew. Even though you were the one who set him up, Jaws should have done his homework. You're the better suitor. You always have been."

Jaws's pleasure soon disappears.

"You're strong, baby. You're a fucking king. And I'm your queen." She turns on the charm, and like a chump, Stevie falls for it. "It's just sex with him. I love *you*."

I take great pleasure in seeing Jaws break before me.

He thought he'd be in with half a shot, it appears, but Bianca has made it clear he is merely there to scratch her itch when the urge arises.

Her attention drifts to Jaws. "We have co-existed for so long. Why are you doing this now?"

We all seem to want to know the answer to this question. Why hasn't he just let sleeping dogs lie?

Jaws seems touched by her words, and for a split second, I think that maybe he has a heart after all. But he is dead inside. I think he always has been. "Once upon a time, you meant more to me than anything in the world. But now, there is something I want more."

Bianca stands still, unafraid by the gun pointed her way. She is that arrogant. But that will be her downfall. She knows what Jaws did to her father; yet, she doesn't care. Why settle for the love of one when you can be worshipped and adored by many?

But Jaws is done playing her games. He wanted her to choose, but she didn't. So now he has. "And that's to be fucking

king of this town. I need a queen, and sadly…that isn't you."

I see it before it happens, but it's still too late. I dive on top of Tiger before Jaws fires his gun. The room erupts into gunfire while I shield Tiger with my body. Peering up at the bedlam ahead, I see Jaws taking refuge behind a wall while Stevie takes cover behind a shipping container.

"Tiger, we gotta move!" I scream to be heard over the gunshots. I don't wait for her to reply and quickly come up into a low crouch, taking her with me.

I scope out the exits and realize the only way out is back through the way I came. Sadly, that exit is suddenly blocked when Stevie's reinforcements come charging through, guns raised, ready for battle.

Bianca is lying motionless, the front of her cream dress stained red. Even though I knew he was a soulless asshole, I never saw this plot twist coming.

"Motherfucker!" Stevie screams, peering around the container, hoping to get a clear shot. "You fucking killed her! How could you?"

"You didn't think I'd stand by and let her insult me that way, did you? She chose the wrong man, and it's time she paid her dues," Jaws retorts, firing two quick shots. His cold comment reveals what a psychopath he truly is.

The gunfire continues while Tiger and I stay low, hiding behind a wall. "We're going to have to make a run for it," I instruct, tearing a sling out of my shirt so I can strap my broken hand.

"We can't!" she cries. "Jordy."

She's right. If we leave now, she'll never see him again.

After what he just did to Bianca, it's clear he's close to his tipping point.

"Bull, I need to tell you something," she says, the words spilling from her.

But she can tell me later. We need to haul ass right now. Well, she does.

Before she can say another word, I push her behind a shipping container and grab the baton she tossed away. She screams at me but knows better than to follow. My right hand may be broken, but I only need one to beat the shit out of Stevie's men. I keep low, smashing their kneecaps and collecting their guns as they drop them, howling in pain.

I reach Jaws's side in seconds, armed to the teeth. He goes to pull his gun on me, but I smash the handle of my stolen gun against his temple. "Motherfucker, listen. You tell Tiger where Jordy is, and I will help you get out of here. You're outnumbered." I can't believe I'm saying this. "I'll cover you."

He arches a brow—suspicious this is a trick—but he's running out of options. And he knows it. He wasn't counting on Stevie coming with much backup because I never told him he had that many men on his payroll.

"Fucking make the call," I demand, gesturing with my gun toward his pocket to take out his cell.

"Fine." He quickly sends a text and then shows me he's forwarding the message to Tiger. It's an address, the address where she'll find her son.

Something comes over me, and I realize it's genuine happiness. I'm happy Tiger will finally get Jordy back. I guess the saying rings true—when you love someone, their happiness matters more than yours. And I do…I love her so fucking much.

And that's why I have to let her go.

"You did good, brother. I am so proud of the man you've become."

Damian's voice buzzes loud, and a sense of peace falls over me. I have finally become the man I know he would be proud of.

"You ready?" I ask, checking the chambers of the guns to make sure I have enough ammo.

Jaws nods.

"On my count, we run. Then we fucking settle this." I'm not stupid. I know I'm his prisoner. Until Jordy is safe, I am at his mercy.

"One." I cock my gun.

"Two." I scope out the surroundings.

"And three!" I yell when we're as clear as we're going to be.

Jaws and I jump up, guns aimed at the danger around us. We cover one another, firing our weapons at anything that stands in our way. Men duck for cover as neither Jaws nor I miss. I lock eyes with Stevie who cradles Bianca to his chest.

When he sees me aiding Jaws, he promises with a simple look that I will pay for what I've done. I may not have pulled the trigger, but he still holds me accountable for her death. But he'll have to wait in line.

I make my way over to Tiger, who is cowering with her ears covered. Yanking her up, I cover her with my body and drag her toward the exit. I lead the way out the door and toward safety where we make a mad dash for my truck and take cover behind it.

Bullets zip past us, indicating the men left standing are following in hot pursuit. I'm running out of time. "Take the keys and go get your son," I say quickly, placing the keys into her palm. "Here." I give her a gun. "You know how to use it."

She nods shakily.

"Aim for the body or head. It's a kill shot. Don't aim for the leg. It'll only slow them down," I instruct, wishing we had more time.

"No," she begins to contest but soon stops.

"I've sent you a text with the address of where Jordy is," Jaws reveals calmly.

Tiger looks at me, working her lip. "Christopher, please, don't do this."

"It's too late for me, lil' sis. I made my choice. And so did you."

She casts her gaze downward, ashamed.

If this were some Hallmark movie or romance novel, the hero would uncover a way to save him and his girl. But this is real life, and I'm not a hero. I killed him...among others.

Before she has a chance to argue, I press a kiss to her forehead. "I made you a promise, and I never break my promises." And those are my parting words.

I stand, and Jaws follows as we run toward his Jeep. Tiger screams, begging for me to stop, but I can't. If I do, I won't be able to go through with the hardest thing I've ever had to do. Yes, she betrayed me, but I don't blame her. She did what any mother, what any family would do for their kin.

Am I not doing the same thing for mine?

Jaws unlocks the car, and we jump in before he starts the engine and speeds off into the night. Looking over my shoulder, I see the three men fire into the night but miss. I anxiously await the lights of my truck to switch on, hinting Tiger is inside.

When they flick on before the car takes off with haste, I exhale in relief. She's safe.

Turning back around, I don't bother with my seat belt as safety first isn't my motto for this car ride. I cradle my broken hand, numb to any pain. I have no idea where we're headed, but it doesn't matter. The result is the same.

"You really love her, don't you?"

If Jaws is expecting a heart to heart, he's sorely mistaken. I continue staring out the windshield, hoping he stops talking.

"If I gave a shit, I'd play the part of big brother and ask what your intentions are. But I don't care. You're not going to live long enough anyway." But she is his weakness. She's both of ours. If she wasn't, he would have killed Jordy days ago.

"What are you waiting for then? A fucking written invitation?" I snap, so done with hearing his voice.

"There is one more thing I need from you, and then you'll get your wish."

His comment piques my interest. I don't have a chance to ask what he wants, however, because I feel a sharp smack at my temple, and then everything *finally* falls silent.

CHAPTER FIFTEEN

Bull

I wake, but when I feel the sharp sting around my wrists and ankles, I wish for another hour's reprieve. Opening my eyes, I'm surprised I can see and am not blindfolded. I recognize my surroundings.

I'm at Blue Bloods.

Jaws has home turf advantage, and I know this was done on purpose. Didn't I do the same with Kong? A predator feels most comfortable in his own environment. There are no threats here. He can take his time, and when I lay my eyes on him, I know he intends to draw this out for as long as possible.

"Ah, finally, you're awake," he says. He's straddling a chair in front of me, smoking a cigar.

"If I have to listen to you speak for one more minute, I'd

rather you kill me now," I retort, my broken hand throbbing when I tug at the restraints.

Jaws laughs, a deep, throaty cackle. "It's such a shame I have to kill you because I actually like you."

"Well, unlike me, please," I bark, wondering what he's waiting for.

Jaws continues smoking, ignoring my request. "I know José is Stevie's supplier," he reveals. "I just needed you to rehash all the information I didn't know. I have a suspicion he was the one who got you to Scrooge. Only he could pull something like that off."

I don't bother answering.

"Poor Scrooge. I bet he didn't see that coming." If I believed he had a heart, I would actually think he gave two shits. "What did you do to him?"

Deadpanning him, I reply, "I slit his throat before tossing his weighted ass off the side of a boat."

There really is no way to sugarcoat it.

He takes his time inhaling the smoke before blowing a ring in the air. "He was the only one I actually gave a fuck about."

"That's because you're both fucking insane. So what do you want with me?"

Jaws sighs before coming to a slow stand. "You killed all my friends. I need new ones. Stevie knows we're here. It's only a matter of time before he arrives, out for vengeance, and when he does, I will do what I should have done years ago... I'll put a bullet in his head."

This entire thing comes down to one thing—greed with

revenge thrown in for good measure.

"I don't think José will be interested in a long-lost reunion when he finds out what you did to Bianca," I remind him.

But his smirk hints that he's already thought this through.

"Me?" He feigns innocence. "I didn't kill anyone. Stevie pulled the trigger. Riddled with jealousy, he killed his beloved."

I'll give it to him; he's a devious asshole.

"This is the *in* I need to get back with the family. What did you do for José to give you Scrooge?"

"I threw a fight," I reply, not seeing the point in holding back. "José got paid a lot of money. Stevie got left red-faced."

Jaws claps happily. "This just gets better and better. That asshole screwed me over, do you know that?"

"Yes," I say, surprising him. "Scrooge told me all about it…before I severed his vocal cords that is."

Jaws stops clapping, unhappy I keep raining on his parade.

"Why didn't you just kill Stevie back at the warehouse? Why bring him here?"

"Because he will come here, looking for revenge on both you and me. And a man led by his emotions is a weak man." He looks at me pointedly. "I told you, I want to take it all from him. Every minute he's alive, he has to relive the anguish of Bianca bleeding out in his arms."

"I thought you loved her."

"I do," he replies with a wave of his hand. "But where did that get me? Besides, I have another queen now."

Even tied to a chair, I straighten my spine, ready to rip out his tongue. "You leave her alone," I warn, disgusted that he sees Tiger this way. "You got what you wanted."

"I can't believe you'll still defend her after she betrayed you that way. She played you."

Thanks, asshole, for reminding me, not that I could forget. But I don't blame her for what she did.

"No, I didn't actually get what I want," he argues, walking forward. "Once again, I'll have to share her love with a dead man."

I curl my lip, disgusted. "I knew you were a sick bastard, but this is revolting, even by your standards."

He laughs, tipping his face to the ceiling. "Marrying one's kin was encouraged once upon a time. There is nothing wrong with strengthening a superior bloodline."

"Motherfucker, it's called incest, no matter what century you live in."

He tsks me, tilting his head to the side. "We may share the same mother, but our fathers could be any of the random men who visited *Mom's* trailer late at night." I've never heard the word mom sound so dirty before. "So technically, we're only half-siblings."

This is news to me and I'm sure Tiger, as she never mentioned this before.

"That's still called incest, asshole, and rape because there is no way Tiger will become your motherfucking *queen*, you sick creep."

Jaws butts out his cigar on the dance floor. "I suppose you'll never know. My guests should be here any moment now," he says, looking at his Rolex.

Glaring at him, I don't fail to notice his use of the word guests, as in more than one. Seems the reason I'm still alive is about to be revealed.

"You're going to corroborate my story when José gets here. He clearly trusts you. You will tell him Stevie shot Bianca because he found out we were fooling around behind his back, and I had no other choice but to end him."

I shake my head, laughing. "Why the fuck would I help you? Once was more than enough."

"Because if you don't, every person you've grown to love will pay. You think you're dead inside, that a monster lurks within. But tell me you'll be okay with having Lotus, Venus, the girls, your cat. Oh, and of course your parents, your *half-siblings'* deaths on your hands."

Time stands still. *"What?"*

Jaws places a hand over his mouth, faking shock. "Oops, you didn't know? Yes, *you're* now the older brother. To two little rug rats."

"You're lying," I snarl between clenched teeth, but what if he's not? It's not like I can confirm with my parents. I haven't seen them for years. I've been so hell-bent on avenging the death of my brother that I didn't stop to think that life for anyone else has gone on.

I never once thought about seeking out my parents since I've been out. It never mattered, but now, it suddenly does. And I am tied to a fucking chair, once again being blackmailed by this piece of shit.

"I'm not." Jaws's reply is dripping with confidence. "And I have no issues wiping out your entire bloodline."

Inhaling, I tip my face to the heavens, needing a minute.

When I've calmed down, it seems divine intervention

has finally decided to cut me some slack. "Fuck you, you're all talk. You think you own this town, but you're delusional. If you did, you wouldn't resort to blackmailing me. Again. You're nothing."

Jaws's smirk soon fades. He clearly wasn't expecting that response, which is what I wanted as I can't do jack shit tied to a chair.

He takes a moment before storming over and punching me straight in the jaw. Motherfucker can pack a punch, but I laugh in response as hot blood trickles down my chin. "The truth hurts, doesn't it?"

Again, he punches me in the face. And again, I laugh hysterically. The pain, the blood, it's so worth it.

Jaws punches me a couple more times, and I hiss sharply when he breaks my nose. Dropping my chin to my chest, I watch as a waterfall of red stains my shirt and the dance floor.

"Not laughing now, are you?"

"Actually...I am," I whisper on purpose.

"What did you say to me?" Jaws screams, grabbing my hair and jerking my neck back. "I can't hear you."

I deliberately string my words together, infuriating Jaws further because when he lowers his face to my lips so he can hear me, I lunge forward and bite his throat. He howls in surprise, attempting to pull away, but I have him, and I don't plan on letting go until I tear his fucking esophagus out.

I dig my teeth into his flesh, savoring the sharp metallic taste as it spills into my mouth. I don't know if it's my blood or Jaws's, but either way, I bite down harder and take out a chunk of flesh. Spitting it out quickly, I go back for more. But Jaws soon realizes I'm out for more than blood and reaches into his pocket for his gun.

He pistol-whips me once, twice, and a third time, before I let go.

With utter fury, he places the gun to my forehead. I look up at him, smirking. The last thing I'll see is the gaping hole in the side of his neck. Welcoming my fate, I accept my failure, but I also accept my triumph—I learned to love and what a love it was.

"I'm coming home, brother."

Jaws cocks the trigger, and it's deja vu all over again because, as I await my death, it never comes.

"You motherfucker!" There is no mistake. It's Stevie's voice.

Jaws sighs, annoyed he's been interrupted, but when he realizes he's seconds away from claiming what he believes is his rightful place, he grins and removes the gun from my forehead, placing it in the small of his back. The real enemy is here. I'm just someone to pass the time.

Jaws turns to face Stevie, unbothered by the gun trained on him. "Hello, friend. Thanks for coming."

"I'm not your friend!" Stevie exclaims, waving his gun. "I never was."

Jaws takes a moment to absorb what Stevie has just revealed. "This is true because if it were, you wouldn't have set me up that way."

Stevie looks at me briefly. I wonder what he sees. "You were stupid not to do your homework. Don't blame me for your carelessness. But Bianca was innocent in all of this. And now that her blood"—he takes a deep breath—"is on your hands, all bets are off. I will have my vengeance on you both, and then this town will only have one king—me."

Jaws stands tall. "You really think you can handle it? I mean, you choked when it mattered the most. You allowed someone to play you for a fool, and in turn, I have all the information I need."

Stevie glares at me. Jaws is right. He was careless to trust me. "You think I'll just roll over and allow you to take everything away from me?"

A suffocating tension hangs in the air, and that's because Jaws knows he's won. "Yes," he finally replies with nothing but confidence as he craftily reaches for his gun.

Stevie is running on emotion, making him careless once again. I know what's going to happen, and if I don't move, I'll be caught in the crossfire. The moment Jaws draws his gun, I rock my chair backward and connect with the floor.

The room erupts into gunfire, and I use my body to shuffle along the slippery dance floor as best I can. I take cover by the stage, the world tilted as I watch two former friends try to kill each other.

This is a war I wanted no part in, but every war has casualties, and it seems my vengeance has turned me into one. There are no good guys in this story. Just men driven by their own selfish reasons. Me included. But as I watch Jaws and Stevie fight, I find myself rooting for the big bad because there is no way I've come this far to fail.

Jaws will die tonight—just not by Stevie's hand.

With that as my incentive, I forget about the pain and

twist my broken hand, desperate to break free. The cable ties bite into my skin, but as I maneuver back and forth, I'm able to slip free. In his arrogance, Jaws secured me with only one cable tie, which is his bad.

My broken hand is useless, so I use the other to frantically tug at the tie around my ankles. It's done up tight, so there is only one way I'm going to be able to get loose, and that's break the leg of the wooden chair. Just as I'm about to smash it against the side of the stage, someone moves to stand over me.

Peering up, I don't know whether to be relieved or concerned. It's José.

Without thought, he reaches into his back pocket and produces a knife. He cuts through the ties at my ankles. Once I'm free, we both squat behind the stage, watching the scene unfold.

The gunshots ring through the club, but I can hear José loud and clear when he yells, "Who killed her? I know she wasn't faithful, but I want to know...Who fucking killed her?" And this is why he had no qualms betraying Stevie.

He isn't stupid. He clearly knows each and every player in this situation. He has every right not to trust either of them. But why does he trust me?

If I tell him it was Jaws, he will kill him, taking away what is rightfully mine. I can't allow all of this to have been for nothing. Tiger and Jordy are surely safe by now, so it's time I end this once and for all.

"They both did," I reply, which is the truth. Stevie didn't pull the trigger, but if he really loved her, he would have let her go, just as I did with Tiger. "But Jaws is mine. He took something from me…and I want it back."

"What does he have?"

Inhaling deeply, I answer, "My freedom."

I'm expecting José to fight me, but we have always had a mutual respect between us. I don't know why, but he nods, granting me my wish. He digs into his jacket and gives me a Glock. But I shake my head, gesturing for the knife instead.

"What do you get?" I question, not understanding his motives.

He smiles. "Detroit needs a new kingpin, and that will be me."

With Bianca, Stevie, and Jaws gone, there will be no competition and no family loyalty, meaning all the power, all the money will be his. But in this case, better the devil you know.

Once I'm armed, I peer over the stage to see where Jaws and Stevie are. They are hiding behind booths, ready for the other to make a grave mistake. But when Stevie stands, José doesn't hesitate. He aims and shoots him in the chest— like the wound which killed his cousin.

Jaws spins over his shoulder, gun raised, assessing the threat, but when he sees José, a large smile forms.

Stevie gasps for air, his eyes growing wide as he clutches at his bleeding chest. He collapses onto his front with a thud and simply stops breathing. His death is merciful and very anticlimactic. I'm disappointed he didn't suffer more.

"José," Jaws says with a gracious nod. "That bastard deserved it after what he did to Bianca."

This lying sack of shit is convincing, I'll give him that, but

José doesn't care who's to blame. He's ready to take his place on the throne.

"Yes, I know."

Jaws's confidence soon simmers. I assume he told José the basics, but for him to be so certain can only mean one thing.

Coming to a steady stand, I take great pleasure in seeing the surprise flicker to life behind Jaws's dead eyes. He soon composes himself, however.

"*Colmillo* told me Stevie was the one who killed my dear cousin. I always told her you were the better man, but you know she always did what she wanted."

Jaws looks at me for corroboration. He gets nothing in return.

"Yes, she did, which is one of the many things I loved about her." When he looks to be shedding a tear, I clench my fist, so ready to end this asshole's life. "Stevie snapped. Didn't want to share her anymore. But you couldn't tame someone like Bianca. God rest her soul."

José nods while I stand still, watching this motherfucker closely. Knowing these are going to be his last few moments on earth gives me a small sliver of satisfaction, but killing him will never bring back what he stole from me.

"I'll have someone clean this up, and then we can talk," Jaws says to José, implementing his plan even before the woman he supposedly loved is buried. He is truly a sociopath.

José nods, reaching into his pocket to grab his cell. "I've just got to make a call." He exits the club, not clueing Jaws into anything.

Once he's out of earshot, Jaws nods in approval. "Right

choice," he commends, none the wiser. "So, we going to do this?"

"You give me your word no harm comes to my friends and family, to Lily and her son, then yes, let's end this right now."

"You have my word," Jaws says with conviction. If this were anyone else, their word would mean something, but this is Jaws, the animal who kidnapped his own nephew for his own personal gain.

His word means jack shit.

"Call Tiger," I order. I would do it, but I don't want to hear her apologies. What's done is done. She did what she had to, and now, so must I.

Jaws must be able to read my resolve because he digs into his pocket and casually retrieves his cell. He doesn't seem troubled his once best friend lies in a bloody heap just feet away. He dials and puts it on speakerphone.

When I hear her panicked voice, the need to protect her is so overwhelming, I almost lunge for the phone to ask if she's all right. But I stay put.

"Christopher, where's Bull?" she asks on a rushed breath. I'm touched.

Jaws isn't, however, and ignores her question. "Did you get Jordy?"

She exhales. "Yes."

"And he was okay?"

"Yes," she replies with bitterness. "That still doesn't excuse what you did. I want to talk to Bull."

Jaws looks at me, but I shake my head slowly. I got all the

answers I need. "Well, he doesn't want to talk to you. Besides, you did more than enough talking when you decided to betray him."

"You son of a—" Jaws hangs up on her, smirking.

"Satisfied?" he mocks, tucking the cell back in his pocket.

No, I am not fucking satisfied and won't be until he stops breathing, but I nod.

"Good, now any last requests?"

Rocking back on my heels, I nod. "Just one." Jaws waits for me to continue. "I asked you this once before, but I want to know. Why did you do it? I don't accept your flippant response. In this case, shit doesn't just happen. So I want you to tell me different. I want you to tell me there was a reason you killed my brother. That his death wasn't in vain."

Jaws ponders my request. "I've killed a lot of men since then. Their faces, their names, I barely remember, but your brother, I remember like it was yesterday," he reveals with sentiment. "As for a reason…the reason is—"

I hold my breath. Could it be after so many years I get some sort of peace? An explanation that'll satisfy the monster within?

But I should know by now…life doesn't work that way.

"The reason is…why the hell not? Your brother was just like every other asshole who thought they were better than me. And he suffered the same fate. So the answer to your question is I did it because I could. Because people like your brother are weak and taking from them makes me powerful.

"But your brother is one of a kind. They say you always remember your first time, and it's true. Your brother was my first kill," he reveals while I wish Damian was never associated with that title. "I feel a special connection with him. With you. Maybe that's the reason I haven't killed you yet. I can't ignore that fate seems to keep bringing you back into my life. Maybe we both needed one another to grow into the better version of ourselves."

I feel sick to my stomach if he truly believes this.

"So this is on me?" I question, hooking my thumb toward my chest.

Jaws tilts his head to the side, watching me closely. "If you weren't such a little hothead, then maybe things would have turned out differently. But truthfully, I was just waiting for the right moment, and then the universe delivered you into my lap.

"In some ways, I should thank you for allowing me to see my full potential. Killing your brother showed me what I was capable of, of how taking gives you power. I became addicted to that high."

Swallowing down my disgust, I refuse to accept this because if what he's saying is true, then I'm partly to blame for the monster standing in front of me. I shouldn't have let him get to me because if I had just walked away, then Damian would still be alive.

Yes, Jaws was a psychopath in the making. But I hate to think I played a part in nurturing the demons to fruition. I can never undo the past, but I can try to better the future.

"You did all of this just because you could?"

Jaws nods slowly. "This is just an example of wrong place, wrong time. Do you believe in destiny?"

I curl my lip, disgusted he would see our meeting as anything but tragic. He doesn't share the sentiment, though.

"I'm glad it was you."

"Glad?" I spit, shaking my head.

"Yes. Over the years, I've never met a worthy opponent. But you, Bull…I'll never forget you."

I am not touched in the slightest. This asshole doesn't seem to understand the damage he's caused to so many. So, it's time that he does.

"I'll never forget you either," I state, the knife at the small of my back burning me raw. "There is something I want to give you. I don't want it anymore."

"What is it?" he asks, appearing curious.

Raising my hands in surrender, I commence a slow walk toward him. He doesn't flinch, as he believes I'm unarmed. "I never wanted to become this…thing," I settle on. "But I think, just like you, I was always destined to submit to the darkness inside me.

"I always lived in the shadow of my brother, but that night when we first met, that fight was mine. If only Damian stopped being the damn hero, things would have turned out so differently." And I mean it. But in no way is this his fault. Martyrs all die for a cause, and Damian's was being the best damn brother this world ever saw.

Jaws appears to be listening intently.

"I learned a lot that night. I learned that monsters are real. But I also learned that I'm the biggest monster of them all. And I guess I have you to thank for that because when I killed Hero, I knew I'd found my calling in life.

"I live my life in the darkness because no one judges me here for all that I've done. And all that I must do. So what I want to give you is very personal to me. It's something I've carried with me for fourteen fucking years.

"I may never get the answers I sought, but I'm finally okay with that, and that's because fourteen years of suffering, I give to you. It's my gift to you. Take it. It's all yours."

Jaws watches as I reach behind me, believing I am producing a physical gift. But what I have doesn't take on a physical shape. What I have has eaten away at my soul.

The moment I grip the handle of the knife, a sense of peace falls over me. I learned a lot in prison. I learned that hesitation will get you killed. So will underestimating your opponent. Too bad Jaws never learned these lessons because when I strike out and stab him between his vertebrae, he doesn't stand a chance.

The surprise on his face is evident as he collapses to the floor. He tries to move, but he can't, and that's because I've just severed his spinal cord.

Dropping to a squat beside him, I wipe the bloody blade across his shirt. "Do you know there is one particular spot in the spine that I like to call the sweet spot?" I explain, savoring Jaws's labored pants. "And if you're able to stab between the vertebrae, you have to ensure you get it with precision, you can paralyze someone without killing them. So essentially, they're just a head on a stick."

Jaws grunts, still trying to move.

"Which is what you are," I conclude with a sinister smirk. "You're completely paralyzed from the neck down. So stop trying to move. You're embarrassing yourself."

Jaws slams his head against the floor, letting out a scream.

"I could keep you alive for days, weeks even. Nothing would please me more than to see you suffer, seeing you humiliated this way. Shame on you for being careless because this is the end of the line for you."

Seeing Jaws helpless this way is hard to digest. I never thought this day would come. Yes, it's been far from easy, but I'm almost disappointed it's come to an end.

"José," he pants, realizing where I got the knife from.

"Yes. He knows what you did. And he wants to see you pay."

"What are you going to do?" he asks in winded pants.

I pretend to ponder his question. "I think that's fairly obvious," I reply, tracing the side of his face with my knife. "For fourteen years, I've carried this...hatred inside me. I don't want it anymore. I don't know what happens next, but what I do know is that killing you is the start of something new. The possibilities are endless because this entire time, I've been half alive. You've stolen something of mine, and I want it back."

"Whatever you want, take it. Just help me."

"Help you?" I scoff, disgusted by his begging. "You didn't really think you'd win, did you?"

And for once in his life, Jaws experiences defeat. "Lillian will never forgive you if you kill me. I'm the only family she has."

In some ways, I think that may be true. But honestly, I don't think she'll ever forgive me for a lot of things. I don't know what will happen to us. I haven't thought that far ahead.

"I know," I acknowledge without further explanation because there isn't any.

Jaws tries to move away but howls in anger when he realizes this paralysis is a permanent gig.

"You took my freedom, and by killing you...you're giving it back. In return, I'm giving you this person I don't want to be anymore. This person you helped create."

This entire time, I believed killing Kong, Scrooge, and Jaws was for Damian. But now I see that it's for me as well. With death comes new life, and this is my chance to be reborn. Damian doesn't have the same chance, so I will live for us both.

I will always favor the shadows; I was hardwired that way. But the light doesn't scare me anymore. Whoever I see, I'll know that person is no longer a monster—he's merely a man. Suddenly, the future seems a lot brighter.

But there is one final thing I have to do.

"Maybe you're right. Maybe we met for a reason," I consider, flicking my thumb over the sharp tip of the knife. "I will never accept that there was a reason for Damian's death, but his legacy will always live on because by killing you, I've essentially saved millions.

"With Stevie and you gone, the drugs you deal, they're no more. The people you hurt, they're safe. I know there is always someone waiting in the shadows to take over, but better the devil you know."

"You won, kid," Jaws says pathetically. I almost feel sorry for him—almost. "But do you really think you can live with this on your conscience? Each time you see my sister, it'll be a reminder of all that you've done. You might think you're free of me, but I will be with you forever.

"You think you're turning over a new leaf? You're not because with each life you take, you lose a piece of who you are. Believe me, I know."

Shaking my head, I stare him in the eyes. "That's where you're wrong. I never knew who I was…until now. I never really knew my true worth, but now I can see that I'm not a monster. I thought I was. But I'm loyal, strong, and I'm capable of love. And I'm worthy of being loved."

I never understood why Tiger felt the way she does about me, but now I'm beginning to see that the monsters were merely inside my head. It's time I let them go. It's time for me to be free.

"You're going to tell me who your lawyer is. Your banker. Your motherfucking tailor because you're going to leave everything to Tiger. That money is blood money, but as I see it, all those lives lost would have been for nothing if it goes to anyone else."

"All the information is in my phone. Take it." If he believes being cooperative now is going to save him, he is deluded. "Take whatever you want. Just call me an ambulance, and we never have to see each other again."

"It doesn't work that way," I reply, coming to a stand.

"You won!" he screams, spittle coating his chin. "I'm a motherfucking quadriplegic! What more do you want? I may as well be dead."

Tapping my chin with the blade, I pretend to think over

his question. "May as well isn't good enough."

I am done talking.

Gripping the back of his collar, I drag him across the floor toward the wall. I slam his back against it, pressing my boot into his chest to stop him from flopping forward. He is utterly pathetic and demeaning him in this way is payback for what he did to Damian.

"That night, fourteen years ago, you made a decision that kickstarted this. Your parting words to me were, 'This is on you, kid.' And I believed it. But this wasn't my fault. It was yours. I see that now. So this is poetic justice at its best."

Leaning forward, I place the blade across Jaws's throat. The sight of his pulse throbbing frantically has me grinning. He's scared. Good. He'll live his last few moments on this earth afraid and at the mercy of another.

"This is on *you*, asshole. It always has been."

His eyes widen as I press the blade into his flesh. Finally, this ends now.

This is for you, brother.

But it seems we're not done—yet.

"Cody, drop it."

No, motherfucking no.

Closing my eyes for a moment, I curse the universe. I was so fucking close to ending this. But behind me stands Franca Brown—the only person who has the power to stop this.

"I said drop it!" she yells, hinting she's not playing.

I grip the handle, adrenaline coursing through me. Dropping this knife means Jaws lives, and I cannot do that. But if I don't, my ass will be thrown back in jail, and this time, it'll be for life.

Jaws sighs in relief. The action infuriates me. "Please help me! He attacked me. He's mad!"

Seeing him play the victim is as pathetic as it sounds. Franca is smart. She won't buy into it.

"I will tell you everything. Everything," I repeat, my back still turned to her. "But let me end this piece of shit. After that, you can do whatever you want to me."

I try to reason with her. But I know better.

"You know I can't let you do that."

"Fuck!" I scream, tipping my face to the heavens because this has suddenly turned to hell. "How'd you know I was here?"

"We can discuss the details later. Now, I need you to drop that knife."

Her demand has a feral snarl slipping free. "Do you know who this son of a bitch is? If you knew what he did, you would let me end him. I'm doing the world a favor. Trust me."

"I know who he is," she counters, shocking me. "I know everything. I've had a tracking device on his car. That's why I knew you were here."

Time stands still as I slowly turn over my shoulder to look at Franca. She is just feet away; gun raised and pointed my way.

"How?" It's the only thing I need to know.

She licks her lips. "Your girlfriend made a deal."

Even though I've heard her loud and clear, I don't understand what this means. "What deal?"

I can feel Jaws swallow under my knife. It appears he too

has been caught off guard.

"She contacted me with information. I know about the drugs, the fighting ring, the money laundering. I know everything. We made a deal that she'd give up her brother to spare you. But if you kill this asshole, the deal is void."

"*What?*"

Franca nods. "She's been working with me this entire time. She never ratted you out. It was a part of the plan. It just took me a while to get the proper paperwork in order, which is my fault. She was wearing a wire, so I've heard it all. I know what this asshole did."

My brain can't catch up fast enough. But what I do know is that if Tiger has been working with Franca, she never betrayed me. She wanted to tell me something back at the warehouse. I now know what that was. She never snitched on me…she made a *deal* to save me.

This was her middle ground. This was her way to save me *and* Jordy. This was her way so she didn't have to choose. Well, she did choose—she chose *us* over Jaws, and I can't even begin to process how that makes me feel.

My heart, the deadened mass begins to beat strongly once again.

She went to the cops because that was the best way. It wasn't the way I could choose, but she could.

"She was to call Christopher, having him believe she was trading Jordan for you. When he was safe, then we would implement the plan to bring him in. But you know how long the courts take. I had to do this aboveboard; otherwise, it wouldn't stick in court.

"Stevie showing up caught us by surprise, but we know what Christopher did. None of this is on you, Bull."

"If you heard that, then you know what I've done," I reply, wishing it was clear cut.

"Yes, I know. But I can make all of that go away. The information you have can be traded for your freedom. But that only works if he's alive." Franca's gaze swings to Jaws. "I know you want your revenge, but does that mean more to you than your freedom?"

Sighing, I take a minute to absorb all she's revealed.

Tiger was smart. I should have known she was the one to save me. Franca has enough evidence to put Jaws away. Jordy is safe, and as for me, well, Tiger has ensured I don't go back inside. This is the ideal situation where we all win.

So why do I feel cheated? Why do I feel like Jaws has once again gotten away with murder?

"She doesn't want you to live with another death on your hands, Bull. Do the right thing. This can all end now. We do this the right way. No more violence. No more bloodshed. Let the law protect you. It failed you once. I won't let it happen again."

That's one of the many things I love about Tiger. She always sees the good in people. Even though she wants Jaws dead, it'll kill her knowing she played a part in his death. She'd rather he be in jail where he belongs.

But that's the difference between us.

I'd rather he was dead.

"You're a good cop," I say, meaning every single word. "You're a pain in the ass, but you sure as shit are one of the good guys."

"Bull, don't you do it," she warns, finger on the trigger. She knows what this speech means. "Don't throw your life away for this asshole!"

She's right. But that doesn't make a lick of difference. If Jaws lives, I may as well be dead. This way, at least I go down with my freedom finally in hand.

I have mere seconds, and I don't waste a single one. "Tell her, tell her that I love her and that I'm sorry," I say, before turning around and meeting Jaws's wide eyes. He actually believed he was going to live, so killing him will be all the sweeter.

"This is for Damian, you motherfucking asshole. And this is for me."

He opens his mouth, but no words will ever spill from him again because I slash the blade across his neck in one slick motion, slitting his throat. Blood coats my face and body as I watch him bleed out before me, gurgling as he chokes on his blood.

As he did to Damian, I spit on him and snarl, "That's for Venus. And for all the unnamed victims whose lives you destroyed."

Franca's screams are incoherent because all I can focus on is Jaws's twitching, gasping in his last breaths of air before finally, he merely stops. The big bad is finally dead, and my vengeance is now complete. I feel…calmer. But truth be told, I want to resuscitate him, only to kill him once more.

Dropping the knife, I raise my bloody hands in surrender and turn around. Jaws slumps forward with a squelch. Franca's gun is still trained on me. I'm surprised she didn't shoot.

"Why, Bull?" she exclaims, shaking her head angrily. "I gotta call this in. There are bodies everywhere!"

"I know," I reply calmly. "You do what you gotta do. There is a body buried in a shallow grave. His name was Paul Garrison. Make sure he gets a proper burial. Please."

She nods as she regretfully reaches for her cuffs.

I don't move as she walks cautiously toward me. But she has nothing to worry about. I got what I wanted. Just as she snaps a cuff around my wrist, I see a sight which quiets the noise and highlights that only *now* do I have everything I want.

"Bull?"

Franca turns over her shoulder, cursing when she sees Tiger. "I told you to wait in the car. It's not safe."

But Tiger doesn't obey anyone. She holds the world in her palms.

Her attention drifts to Jaws. "Oh, god," she whimpers, placing a trembling hand over her mouth.

I wish I could say sorry, but I can't because I'm not. I happily took away her brother's life, and I would do it again in a heartbeat. She knows what this means. The deal is off. I go to prison for a very long time.

But this is my sacrifice for her. I have nothing to offer her. Now, she can live comfortably and live the life she deserves. Jaws's riches are now hers.

"Make sure Lotus and Venus are okay?" I say, allowing Franca to cuff my hands behind my back. She's careful not to injure my broken one, but I can barely feel pain anymore.

"This club is surely no more, which means Lotus is A game now. Tell her thank you."

Tiger looks to be in shock as tears begin to trickle down her cheeks. Franca begins to read me my rights while I never take my eyes off Tiger—my beautiful, savage Tiger. This has ended the way it was always destined.

"I'm sorry for everything. But for what it's worth…I love—" My words die a wheezed death because the gunshot that rings out deafens me to anything but the smoking gun Tiger holds.

Even though I witnessed it with my own two eyes, I don't believe it. But when Franca tumbles to the floor with a pained cry, there is no denying that Tiger fucking shot her with the gun I gave her.

"Tiger, what the fuck?" I yell, my confusion mixed with rage.

The color drains from her face as she examines what she just did. Franca places a hand over the bullet wound in her leg.

"Tiger!" I scream, jolting her attention my way.

"You s-said to shoot them in the leg to slow them down," she says, her fingers wrapped tightly around the gun. "And I wanted to slow her down."

She looks to be going into shock.

"But why? Why would you do that?" I beseech her to explain what the fuck is going on. And when she does, I don't know whether to fight her or kiss her.

"Because you can't go to jail with your record. You'll be locked up forever. Franca needs someone to take the fall. Let it be me. I'm sorry, Franca." She gives Franca an apologetic smile. "But I can't let you do this."

For once in my goddamned existence, I am utterly speechless.

Franca is tough as balls and pulls herself into a sitting position, hands pressed over her leg to stop the bleeding. She looks back and forth between us, shaking her head. "So, you're going to kill me then?"

Tiger doesn't waver when she replies, "Yes. If you let Bull go to jail, then I will."

Oh my fucking god. My heart, it beats for no one but her.

"How am I supposed to explain this, Bull?" Franca asks as if I hold some magical solution. And I suddenly realize I do.

"You need a witness to bring down Stevie's and Jaws's empires, right?" I know what this means for José. But I won't rat him out. The other players involved, however; I owe them nothing.

She nods.

"Well, I will tell you everything. I did play both sides, remember? It seems being a snitch does have its benefits after all. I know everything from drug distributors to every player involved with the fighting syndicate.

"You call this in, you'll be a fucking legend for years to come. This will be the case that makes your career. Fuck being a PO. You'll be fucking chief of police in six months' time."

We all have a price. I don't care if you're Mother fucking Teresa. And this is Franca's. She's busted her ass, but in this city riddled with crime, unless you break something big, you're just another cop.

"And how am I supposed to explain all the bodies?"

Shrugging, I smile. "The dead don't talk. It's only us who do."

"You want me to convince my superiors that you, what? Were blackmailed into doing what you did?"

I mull over her question and nod. "Yes." Essentially, I was. The gray matter is irrelevant.

"And how am I supposed to explain the almost beheading of that asshole?"

"He kidnapped my son. It was an act of self-defense," Tiger says quickly, shouldering the blame.

"Holy shit," Franca says with a disbelieving laugh.

"I really am sorry for shooting you." Tiger lowers the gun and sheepishly kicks it away.

"So whatcha say, Franca? We got a deal?" There is no way this will work. But when she doesn't tell me to go to hell, I realize this just might stick.

"I can't promise you won't do time…but I'll try my best. You follow my lead and don't open your smart mouth," she orders.

And just like that…a tragedy has turned into a tale of hope and second chances.

Tiger looks at me, appearing just as stunned as I am. I can't believe this actually worked.

She runs over to me and throws her arms around my neck. I'm cuffed, so I allow her to hug me as I nuzzle into her. I am submerged with cherry blossoms and…love.

"I'm sorry," she cries, holding on tighter. "I never ratted you—"

"I know. Franca told me," I interrupt. But she wants to explain.

"I didn't know what to do. I didn't want another death on your hands. Even though Christopher deserves to pay for everything he's done, I couldn't live with myself knowing his death—"

She pauses, licking her lips.

"I brokered a deal with Franca to save your life because you...that's all you've done for me. Saved me, time and time again. I know I went behind your back, but I knew you'd want to be the hero."

I scoff. *A hero?* That's something I'm not.

But Tiger shakes her head. "No matter what you think, you're my hero. You always have been a hero in your own special way."

She continues to amaze me time and time again. "I can't believe you shot Franca."

Tiger buries herself closer, but it'll never be close enough. "I would do anything for you."

"I know. And I you."

She gently pulls away so she can look into my eyes. "I'm sorry for breaking your hand."

"I'm sorry for breaking *you* time and time again," I reply, which has her casting her gaze downward. "I didn't mean what I said to you at the warehouse. I just knew I had to push you away because—"

"It's okay." But it's not. I can sense the doubt lingering beneath the surface.

Rubbing my nose against hers, I coax her to meet my eyes

again. "It's not okay. I hurt you. All I've done is hurt you. I should have pushed you away, but I literally would rather cut off my hands than do that, and I realize the reason for that is because I…"

I suddenly get choked up because I haven't told anyone this since Damian. But telling Tiger this doesn't lessen my feelings for Damian—it strengthens them.

"Is because I…I fucking love you."

Tiger's lips part. I can't read the expression on her face. Have I fucked up?

"Tiger?" I question, suddenly feeling like a chump.

She blinks quickly, fresh tears sticking to her lashes as she shatters my world before piecing it back together again. "I fucking love you, too."

And just like that…I am whole for the first time in fourteen years.

She slams her lips to mine, kissing me slowly because we have forever, and forever has never felt this damn good.

CHAPTER SIXTEEN

Bull

Six Months Later

"**A**nd that's about all of it."

I pluck at the blades of freshly grown grass because winter has made way for summer. The stone in Damian's ring catches the sunlight, and I realize it's the little things I've come to appreciate and that's because I didn't think I'd be alive to witness such trivial things, but I am.

They say everything happens for a reason, and although I will never be okay with Damian dying, I realize some things in this world happen because they just do. It doesn't lessen the pain, nor does it help you accept it, but to honor that person, and their memory, you have to live your life for them.

Each breath I take, I take for my brother because not a moment goes by that I don't think of him. So many years have passed and it's hard to remember him, but for the first time in my life, I see him staring back at me when I look in the mirror.

The night I killed Jaws, something changed—not just physically, but emotionally as well.

I didn't know what would happen, but Franca proved to be an ally I didn't even know I needed. The tale she spun was so convincing, even I believed it. The story was almost true— almost. Jaws killed Bianca in a jealous rage.

He kidnapped Jordy, knowing I would do whatever he wanted because of Tiger.

So far, the truth.

I was forced to snitch, afraid of telling Franca because I didn't want any harm to come to Jordy. During my role as a double agent, I was able to get an inside scoop on the illegal dealings of two major drug lords in Detroit.

Tiger made a deal, knowing I couldn't. Franca knew she couldn't omit that truth because she'd already gotten the paperwork in order. Franca was waiting for everything to be aboveboard before she arrested Jaws, but Jaws got wind of what was going on and fled, taking me with him as a hostage.

This is where we stray toward fiction.

He roughed me up and broke my hand, angered that his plan had failed. Tiger found us. Turns out there is some app where you can find a phone, which is how she uncovered where we were. She begged Jaws to tell her where Jordy was. When he didn't, she snapped.

Stevie was technically the one who killed Jaws. He was out

for revenge, which is true, and when his confrontation with Jaws came to a head, well, Jaws came in second best. Jaws's violent, premeditated death was Stevie's doing. As for Stevie's demise—Franca took the bullet for that.

She came to Blue Bloods just in time. Stevie was about to kill both me and Tiger, furious I betrayed him. She had no other choice but to shoot to kill. But not before he shot her in the leg.

We found Jordy thanks to the information on Jaws's phone.

The corpses of Stevie, Jaws, and Bianca confirmed her story. So did my retelling of everything I knew about the illegal dealings of two drug lords the police have been after for years. They never had enough proof, but now they did.

Did the story stick?

Hell yes, it did.

They didn't care about the discrepancies. Franca just took down two of Detroit's most wanted.

I ended up being what I promised never to be—a fucking snitch. I told the cops everything. Well, my version of course. The dead don't talk, remember?

Kong's family was notified of his death—murdered by Jaws. His remains have never been found. The money they received was from a "friend." Kong put a plan in place for his family if anything were to happen to him.

Scrooge is officially listed as missing. That asshole doesn't deserve a resting place. His wife sure as shit knew who she was married to, so she knows missing means dead. Besides, last I heard, she was doing just fine taking over the matriarchal role of the Da Silva family.

Paul's body was unearthed and laid to rest properly. His death was blamed on Stevie, as I recounted the evening. The DNA match in Stevie's home corroborated my story.

There was one side to the story I left out, and that was José's role. I was a snitch, but I wasn't a fucking snitch. Besides, José is the lesser of two evils. When the cops asked about where the drugs came from, I gave up José's rival.

He is now truly the kingpin of this town. He is unrivaled, which is what he always wanted. And maybe the reason he decided to call me his friend.

With all of this information on hand, Franca brought down an empire. Twenty-two members involved with Stevie's fighting syndicate were arrested, and their involvement uncovered more drugs, more illegal dealings, and more bodies.

Detroit's seedy underbelly was brought to justice on the testimony of me, and because of that, I was given a full pardon of my crimes. The cops weren't happy with the route I took, but it seems just like José, acquitting me of any wrongdoings was the lesser of two evils.

But when I told them why I was involved with Jaws in the first place, all of this began to make sense. Bringing down Jaws didn't just save Detroit, it saved me as well. I achieved what I wanted—Damian's murderer was finally brought to justice because Jaws was officially linked to the crime.

We had the recorded confession from the wire as proof. Yes, the quality was a little poor in some parts, which was thanks to Franca tampering with the evidence, but the cops heard loud and clear that this was about revenge. Jaws killed my brother, which is why I agreed to play both sides.

There were bodies everywhere, which kept the cops busy. If they sensed something was amiss, they didn't care. According to them, the good guys won. And I was happy to run with this story because I was finally, *finally* a free man.

Tiger really did save me in every sense of the word. If she hadn't gone to Franca, I hate to think how this would have ended. Me dead, no doubt. And once upon a time, I would have been okay with that outcome, but when I look into the distance and see my entire world, that's something I no longer want.

Kissing two fingers, I press them to Damian's headstone, then stand and bid my brother farewell. I don't feel guilt when I come here any longer. Maybe one day I'll forgive myself— one day.

I wait for Tiger to approach me because I just fucking love to look at her. Love, a word I never thought I'd use again. But with Tiger, I've experienced so many firsts.

She bought Everland's as a tribute to Avery. She changed it a little and allowed anyone, from all walks of life, to join. The pretentious moms and dads didn't like the change, but Tiger won't allow anyone to make her feel lesser ever again.

It's been an utter success, and she is looking into opening a second studio here in Detroit.

Although she didn't want anything to do with Jaws's money, she knew what I said was warranted. The cops took all of the "legal" dealings, but the illegal stuff was handed over to her by his lawyer. He refused at first, but soon changed his mind when I threatened to expose his role to the cops.

It seems being a snitch does have some perks.

There is a lot of money. Like millions.

Having this at one's disposal can be dangerous, but not to Tiger. She gave to Lotus, to Venus, to Erika, even to Tawny. She gave to anyone who needed it because that's the type of person she is. She knows what it's like to struggle, and although she'll never be in that position again, she'll never forget her roots.

The Pink Oyster is now the hottest gentlemen's club in Detroit. With all the shit that went down at Blue Bloods, Carlos went back to Puerto Rico, not interested in taking the fall for Jaws. Andre got his job back. Lotus is too fucking nice for her own good.

But I guess she takes in all the strays. Didn't she do the same to me?

She doesn't know the full story, but she knows enough. My plan before shit hit the fan was to quit The Pink Oyster as I didn't want Lotus involved in crap. But the truth is, I would miss the place. With the overhaul Lotus was able to afford, the club is double the size.

She said she needed me. But in fact, we need one another.

I'm still a work in progress, but I can finally admit that I can't do this on my own. I tried, and I almost fucked things up beyond repair.

So maybe things really do happen for a reason. A chain reaction of events led me here, and although our past isn't ideal, it's ours, and Tiger, well, she is mine.

The moment I'm hit with cherry blossoms, I smile. I can't help it. Jordy checks me back in line, however, when he scowls. He is slowly coming to terms with the fact I ain't going anywhere. But I like that he busts my balls.

The kid's got game.

"Yo," I say to him.

He replies by placing his earbuds into his ears.

Tiger giggles, which does all sorts of shit it shouldn't. How can it be she gets even more beautiful each time I see her? It could be because she fucking saved me, saved me from myself.

She never gave up on me. Fuck, she should have. But I'm glad she didn't.

"What?" she asks, rubbing her nose. "Do I have something on my face?"

I don't reply. I just look at her because I will never have my fill of her.

"Don't judge me," she says with a grin. "But I ate a bag of Twizzlers on the walk over here."

I never would. She is fucking perfect. And she is mine.

The walk from Hero's resting place to Damian's isn't far, but she could eat a whole fucking cow for all I care. Nothing but the best for her, for her and…my baby.

Let's once again circle around the everything happens for a reason concept. I never in my goddamned existence thought I would want to be a father. The notion was so foreign, I would have laughed if someone told me that I would be.

But here I am, looking at the love of my life who carries our baby.

Stepping forward, I place a kiss on Tiger's nose before cupping her rounded belly. Jordy is disgusted, and I would be too if I wasn't so fucking smitten, by the very PDA and walks off toward the car.

"I never would. You ready?"

She nods, looking at Damian's headstone with a genuine smile. "See you, Damian. Judging by the strong little legs of your nephew, I'd say he'll grow up to be a quarterback just like his uncle."

I know it's not conventional, but this is our story. I like to channel my inner Mufasa and think that maybe this is the circle of life. Don't judge, Tiger has been on a Disney binge since finding out she was pregnant. She said it was the pregnancy hormones, whatever the fuck that means.

I still have so much to learn, and that's okay because for once in my life, I want to experience it all. Which is the reason I've done something I never thought I would.

I called my parents.

When Jaws told me I was now an older brother, something inside me shifted. I'd forgotten other people were affected by Damian's death. At first, it was awkward as all fuck, but the phone calls eventually became longer and less strained, until my mom and dad asked if I wanted to meet them for coffee.

Tiger told me this was them offering an olive branch, so I said yes.

My parents are happily married to other people, but they will always be connected by Damian and by me. I don't have any expectations, but I'm fucking nervous to see them after so long. And meeting my siblings is fucking insane.

So much has changed. But some things are still very much the same.

"Bye, bro. I love you. It's now my turn to be the older brother. Good thing I have the best role model, right?"

Tiger gives me the time I need.

Arranging the flowers one last time, I loop my fingers through Tiger's, and we commence a slow walk toward the car.

She is fucking adorable—yes, I used the word adorable—as she waddles. Our baby boy is big, strong, the doctors say, but with a mother like Tiger, I never expected anything less.

"So, I was thinking about baby names," she reveals.

"As long as he doesn't have a weird ass name like Fidel or Jovian, then I'm good."

Tiger stops walking and turns to me with a smirk. "I don't even think they're real names."

I widen my eyes with a nod. "Oh, trust me, they are. I googled that shit."

She bursts into laughter. "No, I was thinking of something a little more traditional. Something personal." She works her bottom lip, which usually means something is up.

Gently prying it free with my thumb, I arch a brow, waiting for her to speak. And when she does…

"What about…Damian?"

My response is dead silence. I need a minute. Or maybe two.

She takes my silence as a bad thing and quickly backtracks. "Or we cannot. I just thought—"

Pressing my lips to hers, I quickly silence her. She moans into me, leaning her body into mine. The kiss was meant to be chaste, but another thing I learned about pregnancy hormones is that they make women really, really horny.

As much as I'd like to fuck her senseless, this isn't what this kiss is about. Breaking apart, I chuckle as I thumb over Tiger's pouty bottom lip.

"Damian is fucking perfect." The medallion around my neck feels heavy with sentiment.

Tiger's lips lift into a relieved grin. "Perfect."

We make our way to the car in silence because my head and heart are full. I know it's messed up. I took from Hero, and now I'm living the life he could have lived. I know I should feel some sort of remorse, but I don't.

I don't regret my decisions because they brought me to Tiger.

One common theme linked us together, every single one of us, and that's revenge. The faces of revenge varied for every player, but it was the one common denominator that decided our fates. I'm one of the lucky ones as I'm still standing.

My cell chimes in my back pocket, and I suddenly wonder if my parents have cold feet. When I retrieve it, however, I sigh in relief, which is ironic, considering who the caller is.

"*Colmillo*, I haven't caught you at a bad time?"

"Nope, all good. What's up, José?"

"Got half an hour to spare?"

When I meet Tiger's eyes, she shakes her head, but it's noncommittal. She knows José only calls when something is wrong.

"Sure. What's the deal?"

He sighs, hinting I'm going to like what he's about to say. "Some asshole just jumped one of my kids. He was minding his business on his corner like usual. I have his address."

"Enough said," I cut him off. He's already sealed the deal.

"I'll text you the address."

We say our goodbyes while Tiger rolls her eyes.

"I gotta make a pit stop."

We stop a few feet away from the car because even though Jordy has in his earbuds, we don't want him to know what "work" I do on the side.

"This is fucking stupid. And dangerous," she adds, folding her arms around her.

"I know, baby, but some asshole jumped one of José's kids." She knows I'm talking about one of the teenagers he has working for him and not his actual offspring.

"Well, maybe he should be in school and not"—she lowers her voice—"dealing drugs."

She's right. And I love her even more that we have this conversation every time José calls.

"Sometimes school isn't an option for these kids. Look at Paul."

"That doesn't make it right," she argues with a huff.

"I know. So, what do you want me to do? Let the fucker think it's okay to beat up a kid?"

She mulls over my question and sighs. "No. But why you?"

And that's the question I ask myself daily.

I know what you're thinking, and I wish I could say I'd be satisfied living a normal life, but I wouldn't. I've never been "normal" because what the fuck is normal anyway? My life has been far from conventional, and yes, the monsters have subdued, but they still roar, late at night, desperate to stretch their legs.

And I'm okay with that.

I meant it when I said José is the lesser of two evils. If he wasn't dealing, then some other gluttonous asshole would be. I wish this were a world where drugs and violence didn't exist, but we don't live in a Disney fairy tale.

José ensures his drugs are clean and not cut with shit. An addict will find their high anywhere—at least José sells to his clients in moderation. A drug dealer with a conscience? Now that's something new.

I don't condone what he does, but I would be a hypocrite if I thought I was somehow better than him. Didn't I use Paul for my own gain? And look where that got him.

Every job I do is me trying to save someone like Paul. I give them my two cents to do with what they will. But I'm not here to lecture them; I'm here to protect them from the assholes in this world.

Why is this my problem?

Because it seems I actually give two fucks about good and bad. Yes, I do bad things, but I do them to bad people, so surely, that cancels something out, right? José isn't a hero, but neither am I. I can live with that because I've come to finally accept that my darkness is occasionally eclipsed by good.

I've come to realize this by the people I've met in my life. They saw something in me that I didn't, and those people, they're good. So if they can see my worth, then I can, too. My lone wolf tattoo now seems a little obsolete. But it's a reminder of what I will never be again.

Yes, I killed four men without remorse, but the world is a

better fucking place for it. And that's why I help José.

The darkness inside me can only be appeased when I eliminate the pieces of shit in this world—one by fucking one. I won't get them all, but to each kid who feels safer because of me, that makes all the difference.

Even though we have more than enough money, José pays me for each job I do for him. He knows my terms—I act as muscle only when an injustice is involved. I don't hit up people who owe him money, or anyone who looked at him sideways.

I keep the streets clean of filth who would pollute it given half the chance. José once called me Detroit's own Robin Hood. Once being the operative word because he knew not to call me that again when I broke his nose.

Our mutual respect runs both ways; it always has. He allows me to feed my demons, and I ensure he stays on top of the food chain. Are you supposed to like José? No. But you weren't supposed to like me either.

I'm pretty certain Franca knows what I'm up to, but being police captain has kept her busy. Besides, I'm practically doing her job for her.

"Tiger"—I draw her to me—"I'm not one to sit on the sidelines. I can't. I wish this world was perfect for you, for Jordy, and…Damian. But ugliness exists, and the only way to make it less ugly…is to break people's noses."

She laughs, but I know she worries. And I love her for it.

"You're a vigilante with a moral compass," she says, cupping my cheek.

"No. I'm just…Cody Bishop. The man who loves you

more than anything in this entire world."

I'm still grappling with this whole new identity because Bullseye isn't riding shotgun anymore. But maybe like Superman did with Clark Kent, I can be both.

"I love you, too."

And just like that, she's made me the luckiest son of a bitch alive.

Just as I'm about to kiss her, Jordy cracks open the window. "Can you two quit it with the googly eyes? You're making me wanna puke."

Tiger bursts into laughter before a winded gasp leaves her.

Instantly, I launch into protection mode, but she soothes me when she places my hand on her belly. When I feel Damian kick, I gasp, utterly captivated by the feeling. I never thought I could create something so beautiful. However, even though I've taken lives, I've also given life.

And that's the best fucking feeling in the world.

"Come on, your son is hungry," Tiger teases.

"He's always hungry."

I get an elbow in the ribs in response.

Placing a soft kiss on her lips, I don't know what I did to deserve her. But I will do everything to ensure I'm worthy of her love.

Every story has a hero. And it has a villain. But I guess in this story—you got both, wrapped in one.

ACKNOWLEDGEMENTS

My author family: Elle Kennedy, Vi Keeland, Lisa Edward, Christina Lauren, Natasha Madison, L.J. Shen, Kylie Scott, SC Stephens, Penelope Ward, Mia Sheridan—love you!

My ever-supporting parents. You guys are the best. I am who I am because of you. I love you. RIP Papa. Gone but never forgotten. You're in my heart. Always.

My agent, Kimberly Brower from Brower Literary & Management. Thank you for your patience and thank you for being an amazing human being.

My editor, Jenny Sims. What can I say other than I LOVE YOU! Thank you for everything. You go above and beyond for me.

My proofreaders—Lisa Edward—More Than Words Copyediting & Proofreading, Ellie—My Brother's Editor, and Rebecca Barney—Fairest Reviews Editing Services. You girls are amazing!

Sommer Stein, you NAILED this cover! Thank you for being so patient and making the process so fun. I'm sorry for annoying you constantly.

My devil, Andrew England, you're exceptional. P.S. We're

still going out for absinthe.

James Rupapara—your photography is magic. Love, love, love your work.

My publicist—Danielle Sanchez from Wildfire Marketing Solutions. Thank you for all your help. Your messages brighten my day.

A special shout-out to: Bombay Sapphire Gin, K. Bromberg, Tijan, Kat T. Masen, Natasha Preston, Cheri Grand Anderman, Amy Halter, Lauren Rosa, Gemma, Louise, Kimberly Whalen, Christine Estevez, Ryn Hughes, Ben Ellis— Tall Story Designs, Nasha Lama, Natasha Tomic, Heyne, Random House, Kinneret Zmora, Hugo & Cie, Planeta, MxM Bookmark, Art Eternal, Carbaccio, Fischer, Sieben Verlag, Bookouture, Egmont Bulgaria, Brilliance Publishing, Audible, Hope Editions, Buzzfeed, BookBub, PopSugar, Aestas Book Blog, Hugues De Saint Vincent, Paris, New York, Sarah Sentz (you're my fav!) Ria Alexander, Amy Jennings, Rita Roman, Dily—LittleLove_BookAddict, Jennifer Spinninger, Kristin Dwyer, and Nina Bocci.

To the endless blogs that have supported me since day one—You guys rock my world.

My bookstagrammers—This book has allowed me to meet SO many of you. Your creativity astounds me. The effort you go to is just amazing. Thank you for the posts, the teasers, the support, the messages, the love, the EVERYTHING! I see what you do, and I am so, so thankful.

My reader group and review team—sending you all a big kiss.

My beautiful family—Daniel, Mum, Papa, Fran, Matt,

Samantha, Amelia, Gayle, Peter, Luke, Leah, Jimmy, Jack, Shirley, Michael, Rob, Elisa, Evan, Alex, Francesca, and my aunties, uncles, and cousins—I am the luckiest person alive to know each and every one of you. You brighten up my world in ways I honestly cannot express.

Samantha and Amelia— I love you both so very much.

To my family in Holland and Italy, and abroad. Sending you guys much love and kisses.

Papa, Zio Nello, Zio Frank, Zia Rosetta, and Zia Giuseppina—you are in our hearts. Always.

My fur babies— mamma loves you so much! Buckwheat, you are my best buddy. Dacca, I will always protect you from the big bad Bellie. Mitch, refer to Dacca's comment. Jag, you're a wombat in disguise. Bellie, your singing voice is so beautiful. And Ninja, thanks for watching over me.

To anyone I have missed, I'm sorry. It wasn't intentional!

Last but certainly not least, I want to thank YOU! Thank you for welcoming me into your hearts and homes. My readers are the BEST readers in this entire universe! Love you all!

ABOUT THE AUTHOR

Monica James spent her youth devouring the works of Anne Rice, William Shakespeare, and Emily Dickinson.

When she is not writing, Monica is busy running her own business, but she always finds a balance between the two. She enjoys writing honest, heartfelt, and turbulent stories, hoping to leave an imprint on her readers. She draws her inspiration from life.

She is a bestselling author in the U.S.A., Australia, Canada, France, Germany, Israel, and The U.K.

Monica James resides in Melbourne, Australia, with her wonderful family, and menagerie of animals. She is slightly obsessed with cats, chucks, and lip gloss, and secretly wishes she was a ninja on the weekends.

CONNECT WITH MONICA JAMES

Facebook: facebook.com/authormonicajames
Twitter: twitter.com/monicajames81
Goodreads: goodreads.com/MonicaJames
Instagram: instagram.com/authormonicajames
Website: authormonicajames.com
Pinterest: pinterest.com/monicajames81
BookBub: bookbub.com/authors/monica-james
Amazon: amzn.to/2EWZSyS
Join my Reader Group: bit.ly/2nUaRyi

Printed in Australia
AUHW010929270520
328381AU00021B/47